When I first met Raoul, I was a child...

trapped in a game of blind man's bluff with strangers, the children of Sedgemont, who mocked me and were careful to bind the hood tighter and to twirl me faster than they did for their companions. From all sides, I could hear laughter. I felt stifled in that hood, frightened of the darkness. I did not know in what direction the paths ran among the stunted bushes and daisy flowers, and I kept tripping.

Suddenly a hand caught mine to steady me. It was warm and strong, a young man's hand, and the voice which said, "Now little maid, judge who I am," was a young man's voice. Although I made no attempt to guess his name, my captor helped me ease the covering off. I stood looking into eyes I recognized, grey-green, dark-lashed, set in a brown face beneath long gold-silver hair.

"Talisin," my heart cried out, and my longing for my dear drowned brother swept in a wave so strong that even today, I feel its warmth. The day, the game, the darkness, melted into that flash of hope, even as I realized the eyes were not my brother's, and the face, now that I beheld it clear, was one I had never seen before.

"You have not guessed who I am," he cried, and laughed.

I knew only that I did not care who he was, since he was not what I wanted most in this world. In a fit of grief and rage, I bent and bit the hand that held me. He tried to shake me off, but I hung on, feeling my teeth break through the skin.

"Loose me of this she-wolf," he said, with such scorn in his voice even I cringed. "Let her not grace our presence again, lest she feed off us a second time."

ANN
OF CAMBRAY
MARY LIDE

WARNER BOOKS

A WARNER COMMUNICATIONS COMPANY

FOR MY FAMILY AND FRIENDS

CAMBRAY

RAYMOND OF SEDGEMONT
b.1068 d.1145

ROBERT OF SEDGEMONT
d.1131

m.1125

FALK OF CAMBRAY
b.1071 d.1145

EFA OF THE CELTS
d.1136

RAOUL OF SEDGEMONT
b.1114

ANN OF CAMBRAY
b.1136

CALISIN
b.1127 d.1145

ANJOU

HENRY I KING 1100 OF ENGLAND
b.1068? d.1135

ADELA SIOIS m. COUNT OF BLOIS
b.1100?
d.1154

STEPHEN KING 1135 OF ENGLAND

WILLIAM
d.1120 AT SEA

MATILDA THE EMPRESS
m.

GEOFFREY "PLANTAGENET" COUNT OF ANJOU

ELEANOR OF AQUITAINE
divorced wife of King Louis VII of France

HENRY II KING 1154 OF ENGLAND

b.1133

m.1152

CAMBRAY

SEDGEMONT

SCOTIA

IBERNIA

ANGLIA

WALES

LINCOLN

OFFA'S DYKE

SEDGEMONT

GLOUCESTER

CAMBRAY

WALLINGFORD

BRISTOL

LONDON

DOVER

BRITANNIA

NORMANDIA

©1981 FGN

ANN OF CAMBRAY

FOREWORD

URIEN OF WALES, BARD TO THE CELTS, high poet of the old people, record these things. Out of a long silence do I write them, not in my own tongue, but in priestly fashion of the Norman courts, as I learned it ages since so that men who come hereafter should read and remember. It is for the Lady Ann of Cambray that I speak. At her bidding I write, in quiet times, in the long, still days of autumn when the weather here at Cambray lingers on as if in summer. The Lady Ann sits beside me, her tapestry untouched in her lap; the only sounds that disturb us are the cooing of the doves in their cote above the main castle gate and the distant surges of the sea. Old I am as men count years, and she—but she is timeless, to my eyes unchanged as when I first saw her, when I, a child, watched her return to Cambray. Quiet breathes around us, and all the fret and toss of those distant times has sunk to dust, to death. Yet there are moments in the night, or even at the close of day when the sunlight sinks fitful on the floor of the Great Hall of Cambray, that I sense she is tense with listening, waits for the cries of attack across the moors behind us, hears the call to arms and the rasp of steel. Even now, I know she does not think this peace will last and takes each placid lovely day as a gift from God.

"I am a child of war," she told me once, "born in a fateful year when started all those wars that were to plague us nigh on twenty years. Child of war, of woe..." I soothe her then, hold her hand gentle in my own, I who have served her and the lords of Cambray all my days. Yet I cannot deny it is a strange sad story we shall tell, she and I together, of love and hate and treachery. And honor, bright as steel and as deadly. Well then, we must speak of these things. But first I must tell you how these wars, these civil wars that cast their shadows over the whole land, began, for we must endure them to the end, whatever that end may be. Sometimes it seems to me that as time passes, the circle of events grows larger, spreads farther, like ripples from a stone thrown in a mountain lake. In ever-widening arcs do they stretch out beyond our sight, out of the past into a future we cannot guess at. Lord Raoul of Sedgemont told my lady once, in his jesting way that did not hide the import of his words nor his fierce defense of things he held most dear, "Anything that the great do has effect on everyone." I would amend his words. I believe that there is nothing that any of us does that does not have some effect at last, that does not come back upon some distant shore. If we be not there to witness, that does not mean it will not happen or has not already happened somewhere without us.

In truth then, the Lady Ann was born in a fateful year, six months after the death of that great king of England, Henry, first of his name, after whose death began the civil wars to win his crown. She was born at Cambray. It is a small honor, of rough land, rough pasture except for sheep, set along the southwestern sea. There her father, Falk of Cambray, had cleared the land, put peasant folk to till and reap until the yield in crops and herds was sufficient for his needs. A rough tenacious man was this Falk, a landless Norman knight, second son to a small holding in France, having nothing to commend him but his sword and wits. A soldier of fortune, Falk fought when his lord bid him and, in peacetime, followed the tourneys in France to have his living. Come then to middle life he had expected nothing, would have served as knight to his overlord and landless remained all his life at a time when land could be won only by inheritance or marriage. Against all hopes he became a vassal in England of his great overlord and friend, the Earl Raymond of Sedgemont, in return for this gift of land called Cambray.

From his father's holdings in France he brought back horses that he raised up, the famous grays of Cambray, and there he built a castle, of stone in Norman style, not common in his day and stronger by far than any others along the borderlands, for they were mostly made of wood.

An honest man was Falk, they say, honest master, faithful vassal. Hard, not easily swayed, taking little pleasure in women's company. He kept himself and his men ready to put down any dispute and hold the border between the Celts to the west and the Normans to the east—no easy task, and I, a Celt myself, will tell you so. And then one day he came back from his border raids with a wife, a Celt, one of their highborn ladies, so it is said. She bore him a son, and gave him a Celtic name for a Celtic prince, Talisin. And ten years later bore a daughter, Ann. Who was her death.

A lonely man then was Falk, dour and unsmiling. His daughter, Lady Ann, remembered him so through all her childhood years. Little she knew of him and even less of his lady wife. Lady Ann will tell you herself that long it was before she heard men speak of that Celtic princess or heard her story. And longer still before she understood her father's grief. For he turned away from her, his second child, almost as if he blamed her that she was born and lived, so strongly had he loved his Celtic wife, so closely did the Lady Ann resemble her dead mother. But his son, Talisin, was his great joy. Falk kept Talisin by his side, trained him up in the fighting skills he knew, lavished upon him all his hopes and love. And as years passed and Talisin grew to young manhood, he was dearly loved by the Celts both for his lineage and for his own high spirits.

"My brother, Talisin, was the sun of my days, too," said the Lady Ann. "Throughout my growing years, he was my joy. I saw him seldom; but when he came, then came life back to Cambray. For he already rode with my father and his men on their border patrols, and as the wars continued, so they stayed longer away. But when he returned, he was like some Celtic prince of older times, he and his friends, his companions, young men all. They wore golden torcs about their necks, their hair was bound long in Celtic style, and their red cloaks flared across their horses' backs. It was my pleasure to keep watch for them, and he would set me before him on his gray horse and ride with me along the stretch of sand and sea below Cambray. Fast he would ride, the spray showering behind, and I would scream out my delight. But he was Norman-trained by our father, Falk; and he and his young companions followed Falk, who, in turn, obeyed his overlord, the Earl of Sedgemont."

We should have explained before who this earl was, Earl Raymond of Sedgemont in England, Count of Sieux in France, overlord to Falk. But listen now. Earl Raymond was Norman too, having come to England with that great King Henry, first of his name. Although having lands and titles of his own in France, out of friendship to King Henry, he had settled in England. Earl Raymond was a stout-hearted and wise lord. Tall and bent with age, he bestrode his horse as well as any knight, and his bright eyes below dark brows were quick to pick out injustice or treachery. He long had known Henry, fought with him in France, and when chance made Henry king, Earl Raymond came in his retinue to help him subdue his island kingdom. King Henry gave him lands and the title of earl to do him honor and to tie his loyalty to the crown. For that is the feudal bond, lands in return for military service, loyalty for loyalty. It is the feudal law. Cursed be the man who breaks it. The Earl of Sedgemont then held a great tract of land from the king, toward the western marches. In the eastern reaches of his demesne, he raised the keep of Sedgemont, named after a place he knew in France, well built, too, in Norman style upon the site of an older Saxon fort. The rest of his English lands he, in turn as overlord, gave to his loyal followers on the same terms, loyalty to him, lands for military service. So gave he Cambray to Falk. Their duty was simply this: to keep the border along the western marshes at peace. And so Earl

Raymond and Falk and all the earl's vassals did Henry loyal service. For they were of an age, Earl Raymond and his men, knew one another's minds, and judged Henry as a strong and just king. Until disaster came upon the king, as now you shall hear.

Henry was a lusty man, having fathered many bastard sons but only one legitimate prince, who had died before him, drowned at sea. After his son's death, they say King Henry never smiled again. Perhaps so. (You shall hear of another man who, when his son was drowned... but that's to come.) After the death of his son then, King Henry thought to wed again, a younger wife to breed up more heirs. When that plan failed, not willing that the English crown should go a-begging, he summoned up his feudal lords and bade them swear an oath to accept his daughter, Matilda, as queen instead. This daughter, known as empress from her first marriage, had recently rewed a French husband, younger than herself but as ambitious, by whom she had a son, another Henry, who was called Henry of Anjou. Remember his name above all others. Henry of Anjou. You will have cause to know it. Now when Henry the king bade his nobles swear allegiance to his daughter, not once, mark you, but twice, as if he knew in his heart he did the country wrong, there were certain of his nobles who held back, thinking it not fitting that a woman should have the throne. Among these was Earl Raymond. And when Henry in the course of time died, many of these nobles accepted as king instead, Stephen, Count of Blois. Stephen was nephew to the late king, of royal blood then and, as many men avowed, a perfect knight, a godly man well fitted by breeding and temperament to be a just king.

In the year of Christendom 1135, Henry died in France. Stephen hastened to the Channel ports, came to England with the first following wind, and was crowned King of England in London town. Behind him came the Empress Matilda, belatedly calling upon her father's feudal lords to honor their oath to her. This then was how the civil wars began. From being faced with no heir, England was suddenly cursed with two. Which one was better, I leave others to judge. Except this: better either one than both, better anything than civil war.

"So child of war, of woe am I," says the Lady Ann, "child of death, born when King Henry's peace was ended. Thus did my father's grief and country's grief become as one." Yet even then, Sedgemont and Cambray might have avoided the worst of the wars, although the rest of England sank beneath the burden of the fighting as fair land runs to weed when a farmer forgets his duty to the fields. For when King Henry saw fit to order that his feudal lords accept Matilda as queen after him, the Earl of Sedgemont was foremost of these nobles who would not be forsworn. He regarded the oath as ill conceived, the bad judgment of an old unhappy man. Although for love of his old friend he did not take sides against the king, Earl Raymond would not accept a woman as heir, and so a coolness grew between him and the king. Out of fear for his own heir, the earl sent his grandson, Raoul, then a child of six or seven, back to his lands in Sieux in France, the boy's own parents having died of a bloody flux soon after his birth. Safe in Sieux, Lord Raoul was brought up away from the wars in England, but his grandfather, Earl Raymond, like the stout veteran he was, buckled on his harness again when the battles began and rode westward, with Falk of Cambray at his side. Between them, they held the boundary at peace and sided neither with Stephen nor with Matilda, although Matilda, who looked to raise an army from the west, where her half-brother, the Earl of Gloucester, held power, may have seen their neutrality as a threat to her. And I cannot deny, being Celt myself, that the western folk were overjoyed at the start of these wars. While battles raged, they hoped to overrun the border castles, yea, and spill into the eastern Norman parts as well. As things turned out, Sedgemont and Cambray were too strong for them and so kept them in check. So might things have continued,

had not three misfortunes befallen, three blows of fate. We
are come now to the year 1145. Remember that year also. The
civil strife between Stephen and Matilda still raged unchecked,
unsolved. In the early months of that year, the old Earl Raymond of Sedgemont died, full of age and wisdom. Hot upon
his death, his grandson Lord Raoul came back from France to
claim his inheritance, and despite our care, to cast in his lot
with Stephen. And then upon us here at Cambray fell the
darkest hour of all.

At this time will our tale begin. It is the forty-fifth year of
the twelfth century after the birth of Christ. In that year was
the young Lord Raoul confirmed as Lord of Sedgemont but
was not made earl. He was then sixteen. Talisin of Cambray,
had he lived, would have been eighteen. And the man who
was to control us all, that Angevin Henry, son of Matilda,
Henry of Anjou, was twelve. *Ora pro nobis.*

Two last explanations the Lady Ann, womanlike, bids me
append here. One is that she and I are no chroniclers, no
writers of history. We were far removed from the great events
of the times and further still from the great men who began
them. In days of war, news comes slowly, often disjointedly,
and Sedgemont and Cambray lie at the far edges of the kingdom, cut off from the king's court. We can write only what
we know. The second, although I blush to repeat it, is that
she lays her trust in me, that I will not alter what she says,
not changing anything so that foul deeds should seem more
fair than is warranted. Indeed she fain must trust me since she
has neither skill to read or write in our mutual Celtic tongue,
and certainly knows nothing of that priestly one that they say
today even knights can pen like a monk born. And to speak
truth again, she says she has no liking for priests; for gossip
bearing and evil-mindedness, there are none better than
churchmen, none more fitted to know sin, seeing that they
deal in it as other men do business. Indeed, if she were closeted
here with a priest, there would be those, no doubt, who would

1

FTER THE SAD JOURNEY, COMING ACROSS
the drawbridge and under the portcullis of Sedgemont was like coming through a long tunnel, out
of darkness into light. We had been journeying
for more days than I like to recall, through mist and rain that
had kept me penned with Gwendyth, my servant woman, in
the litter. Had it been a normal journey, I might have ridden
in front of one of the men-at-arms who escorted us, or, mounted
on my own pony, gone ahead as I pleased. Now I could tell
we had arrived somewhere at least, by the sudden steadier
clatter of horses' hooves and by the way the men stopped their
chatter and rode still and silently as became their duty. I thrust
my head under the heavy hide curtains that shielded the sides
of the litter, ignoring Gwendyth's tugs and protests. The night
air was damp but the driving rain that had followed us all the
way from the west had stopped; only a faint drizzle fell in the
light of the flaring torches. Men wearing some sort of surcoats
held them; others ran back and forth across the great inner
bailey or courtyard; I saw pages peering and whistling at the
entrance. The castle guards straightened and saluted against
the walls. Then stable serfs sprang to the horses' heads; the
commander of my father's men swung himself stiffly out of the
saddle; the commander of the watch at Sedgemont began to
walk as stiffly and proudly toward him. I realized then that
this was the end of the journey, begun in so much sadness and
haste, out of darkness into light.

The courtyard was large, twice as big, three times, as that
at Cambray. The walls towered above us; I could not see the

battlements, nor guess the size of the keep, whose wide stone steps ran down into the yard. But I took it all in, in gulps, as a child does who has been shut up too long, lurching across half a country. And for all its size, this was something I recognized, girl-child though I was—the heartland of a Norman castle, its working center where its men are garrisoned, its blacksmiths and armorers hammer, where its serfs and peasants and animals bed down together. The acrid smell of the torches, the hiss of resin, the shouts and bustle of armed men, the snorting of horses and the clink of their harness—these were things I knew as well as any boy does. They made me feel at home, and I remember even now how my heart gave a strange surge of expectation and fear. Curious and eager, I leaned out farther, half like to fall out altogether, to watch all that happened: the salute and greeting between the two captains, the slow tread of an elderly gentleman coming down the stairs from the Great Hall, the snapping to attention as he passed (surely that was the earl, I thought, knowing no better), the stir and excitement that our arrival had caused. I might have slipped right out in truth, for all Gwendyth's tuggings, had not a young boy put out his hand to steady me, enabling Gwendyth to pull me back. I glared at them both.

"Beg pardon, my lady." The boy backed in alarm, his clipped speech sounding strange to my ears, which were used to our softer western tongue.

"Hist, hist, my lamb," said Gwendyth, hauling the curtains into place, trying to straighten my disheveled hair, which hung red and lank with heat, and arranging my torn traveling robe. "Forbear now, hush now."

I paid no heed to her grumbles, and would have been out of the litter in a flash had she given me a chance, which she did not. It was light at the end of a long darkness, after confusion and death.

"Let be," I cried to her in our native tongue. "Did you see their armor? Even the guards wear byrnies. And did you see their surcoats and their shields? They have pictures on them, gold and red, was it birds?" I tried to break free again.

"And their horses? They were bigger than ours, but not as good as my father's grays. . . . How big is the castle, think you? Is that the earl himself who comes to greet us?"

"Lady Ann," she said, hushing me, although there was no one there who would have understood our Celtic speech, "we have not come all this way to go tumbling about in the mire with the common soldiers. Look you, how far we have come, cooped up like hens for market" (the only word of complaint she let drop), "and weather to rot men's bones, God save us. You can bide awhile longer in patience, as is becoming. For we are here to seek refuge with your new liege lord and suzerain, Lord Raoul; the old earl being dead, God save his soul. Nor would it be meet for your overlord to come to seek you out, he being a great lord, and you his vassal and ward. That will be his seneschal, or chief officer, that elderly knight upon the stairs. Lord Raoul, being young and unwed, is seldom here at Sedgemont. And you must remember now, Lady Ann, that we must speak as the others do, so all may understand us. And not run behind the men-at-arms and stable boys as permitted by your brother, God rest his soul. And that you are heiress to all the lands of your father in Cambray, and that you hold them in gift and fee of Lord Raoul . . ."

It was not that she was speaking in Norman-French, with less skill than I, for I knew it well enough and spoke it with my father and the upper folk at Cambray, nor was it that she would betray the Celt in us by holding their speech to be of little worth, although I told her that too. It was the words themselves, bleak and uncompromising, that brought the darkness back again. For all its similarities, Sedgemont was not my home. And we were strangers, unwanted here. All around was confusion and death . . . death to brother, father, and all my childhood had known. I turned my back upon the seneschal, Sir Brian; I would not greet his lady wife, who followed to bid us welcome. I would not smile or curtsy to all those staring men. So came I to Sedgemont, and saw it for the first time, and the stable boy, Giles, who would have put his hand out to save me, and Sir Brian and his lady, Mildred. And finally, Lord Raoul himself, whom I disliked the most of all.

I will not count the early days at Sedgemont. They merged as one, into that darkness that followed the leaving of Cambray, the journey there, the horrors before. Sufficient to say it was the autumn of that terrible year. Dark for me, dark for England. Drear weather, poor harvest, rebellion, civil war— everywhere was death. Did it seem a dream or was it as real now as the day his companions brought my brother back, wrapped in his cloak, his arms trailing beneath as if they were too heavy to lift?

"Drowned?" said my father as they met in the courtyard at Cambray. He leaned over the side of his great gray horse and his face turned white under its open helmet. "Talisin, who swims like an otter?" He slid forward from his horse. Color never came back to him again; he was as if a dead man, crushed by grief. Although he sat for two days more with his sword across his knees at Talisin's bier, he never moved or spoke, not even when I was sent to his side to tug and plead with him. So, they say, sat Henry the King when news came of his son's drowning in the wreck of the White Ship. But the king lived on to speak and plan again. Although my father's friends came for the burying, he said no word to them, did not move, and died at the second night with his sword naked in his hand. Nor did he plan for the daughter who still survived, but turned his face to the wall. Did he die of grief, of broken heart and broken hopes, that old soldier, come at last to lands and happiness, only to have them snatched away? Had he guessed something about my brother's death that I was to learn years after? I only know I could not believe that Talisin was dead. He was as skillful as a seal in the rough waters of our coast. At times I used to go with him as he stripped upon the

beach, as careless of me as a puppy underfoot. Clad in the
breech clout he wore beneath his harness, he would run into
the waves, no sport of Normans this, but of the old people,
the sea folk of the first ages. Once I watched him and my
father together. Both their bodies were white except where
wind and sun had tanned them, but my father's was seamed
with old wounds like a gnarled tree. They were of a height,
but my father was thicker, and beside him Talisin looked gan-
gling, not yet grown into his strength. I slid among the sand
dunes, ruining my clothes again, and made my way down to
where they had left their cloaks. There I sat and waited, whilst
behind me the men tended the horses, whistled and laughed
among themselves. Talisin saw me although I crouched low.
He turned to say something to my father, who I thought would
shout at me to begone. But this time he looked and laughed
himself. His indulgence gave me courage. I ran toward Talisin,
gathering up the skirts of my dress to skip over the waves. He
took me by the hand and jumped me over, the green and
brown dress billowed and sank beneath the rush of water like
a piece of weed. I tore it off and let it float away. Naked and
happy, I swam through the breakers, and he bore me on his
back like the dolphins. And when he was done, he wrapped
me in his red woolen cloak and set me on his horse and we
rode back to Cambray together, Gwendyth clucking and fuss-
ing that I would be the death of her. Death. How could the
sea have taken my brother and thrown him lifeless, empty,
upon the shore? Where were his friends that they did not help
him? Why did my father sit with drawn sword in the presence
of his companions? Why would my father not speak to me?

"Look, Father," Talisin had said that day as we rode back,
"she rides as well as she swims. One day there will not be a
horse she cannot straddle. We will never make a Norman lady
out of her."

"The nuns will do it when I bid them," my father said in
his sharp way, but Talisin had laughed again, making things

smooth between us. "She is Celt, my lord, through and through. She is of the old race, with those dark eyes and that long red hair," he said, making my father look at me despite himself. How could he have sat so white and still at the bier and said not a word to me for all my begging? What had I done that he could not endure me? And of those other men who had crowded round afterward, which ones could be trusted, which were friendly, which wished me harm?

So came I then to Sedgemont, to the castle of my liege lord, Raoul, to ask that he should hold my life and lands until I was of age to wed. For although Cambray was my father's, he held it from the lords of Sedgemont; and I could not inherit it until, in due course, they gave me a husband of their choosing to hold it in my name. That, too, I found hard to bear, that I must leave my home and live far away, by the order of a lord I had never met but who could arrange all things to his liking. Had not I been tenacious of life, despite myself, I think I too might have turned my face to the wall then, and let darkness roll me under too deep to find, until Judgment Day bids all rise up again. Yet life there was; whether I would or not, it clung to me. And so time passed; I lived and grew, and events came to pass as you shall hear.

But one more recollection from that time, and let that year be done with. Let it go out of thought, out of mind, if we can keep it there. Yet sometimes, for all our care, those memories come crowding back, as fresh and clear as if they had happened yesterday, as if they have a life of their own, independent of us and our thoughts, as if somewhere God has had them in his keeping and reveals them to us, mirror-changed, what was and is and will be.

No doubt the damp and cold had sickened me; no doubt death had spread his bony fingers to clutch me fast. I lay in the small bed in the anteroom where Gwendyth and I were bade go, and neither stirred nor smiled. I remember Sir Brian's concern, which soon changed to scorn and alarm at my surliness. I remember my father's men in their old-fashioned mail jackets; small and dark and strange they seemed beside these well-fed Norman knights, who looked askance at their old-fashioned ways. Had I been in health, curiosity would not have let me be so indifferent to what was to become of us. As it was, after that first surge of excitement at our arrival, it was indifference and lethargy I felt. And inferiority. I had never been away from Cambray before. Although my father paid me little heed, he and my brother were the sum of my world. At Sedgemont, I was desolate, having no friends, knowing no one, clinging to Gwendyth as she to me, because we had no choice. And although this place was to become my home, I did not fit into its life, as will soon be made clear.

One afternoon, when I was up and about, languid yet restless, Gwendyth decided I should go with the other children to play in the *pleaunce*, or pleasure gardens, which lay outside the main castle wall, built long ago, perhaps by Earl Raymond for his wife and her ladies to remind them of their French castles they had left behind. It was a heavy November day, a day out of season, close and thick as honey, although perhaps the heaviness lay in me, making it difficult to move or breathe. The gardens had been neglected, the grass ran wild, the flower beds sprawled with weeds, but it was a place for the children of the castle to frolic under the care of their nurses, who, in turn, were eyed by the men-at-arms lounging along the walks and at the castle gates. There were not many children even then at Sedgemont, for Sir Brian and his lady had none and Lord Raoul was unwed. What there were, offspring of some of the castle guards, a few younger pages from Lord Raoul's retinue, were older than I, and if truth be told, of lower standing; although they, not I, would have thought of that. We eyed one another warily. Why Gwendyth had brought me there to be with them is beyond understanding. Perhaps she thought it would amuse me, who had little truck with childish things; perhaps, more like, she hoped to make me known and befriended. Poor soul, I never did what she hoped most. These boys and girls, with their clipped speech, were an unfamiliar breed to me. I answered them curtly when they spoke, and no doubt they felt ill used that I should put on airs. I heard their serving women comment on my lack of manners, and when Gwendyth mispronounced a word, they tittered at us both.

"I've no wish to be here, Gwendyth," I told her in our own tongue. "I find no pleasure in these pleasure gardens."

"Nay, my lady, love," she cajoled, "wait, my love, you are but shy. See, they are playing a game now. Go to, join in with them."

It was a silly game, I thought, although children still play it, and had I been alone, I would have held myself too old to take part, for all that the others seemed to enjoy it. They bind your eyes with a hood, then turn you round and round to lose all sense of where you are. You must make your way with halting steps in and out of the bushes along the graveled walks, feeling for the other players as you go. If you catch one, you must say who it is before they unbind your hood. I did not want to take part, and sensing my reluctance, they were careful to bind the hood the tighter and to twirl me the faster, more than they did for their companions. I felt stifled in that hood. The darkness bothered, yes, frightened me. I did not know in what direction the paths ran among the stunted bushes and daisy flowers and I kept tripping over roots and stones. From all sides I could hear laughter, thin and mocking like fingers that point, and beneath the hood, I, who never cried, sensed tears start suddenly. I stumbled from side to side. My new dress, which Gwendyth had taken such pains to copy from theirs, snagged on thorns, and my feet slid in their new high-heeled shoes. If I could, I would have ripped off all and run far away.

Suddenly a hand caught mine to steady me. It was warm and strong, a young man's hand, and the voice that said, "Now, little maid, judge me who I am?" was a young man's voice. I tugged at the hood, its knot cutting into my forehead. "Guess who, guess who," the others cried, but my captor helped me ease off the covering although I made no attempt to name him. I stood looking into eyes I recognized, gray green, dark lashed, set in a brown face beneath long gold-silver hair.

"Talisin," my heart cried out, "Talisin, you have come back," and my longing swept in a wave so strong that even today I feel its warmth. The day, the game, the darkness, melted into that flash of hope, even as I realized the eyes were not the same shape, but slanting, wider set, and the hair was cut long in the French fashion. And the face, now that I beheld it clear, was one I had never seen before.

"You have not guessed who I am," he cried, his voice light with laughter, warm. It was a Norman voice. He stood there in his rich furred cloak and his rich embroidered clothes, his hand still upon my shoulder. The others came crowding round then, and with them the young men and ladies of the castle, laughing at him as he spoke, a man playing at a child's game, and children squealed at the jest of it.

"Come," he repeated with the same hint of laughter, "who am I?"

I only knew that I did not care who he was, since he was not what I wanted most in this world. In a fit of grief and rage, I bent and bit that hand that held me, grief and rage contending against that moment's hope. He started back, trying to shake me off, but like a stoat or weasel, I hung on, feeling my teeth break through his skin, kicking and flailing with those high-heeled shoes Gwendyth was so proud of, hitting at his broad chest with all my might as he swung me off my feet.

They all came running in earnest then, children, ladies, servants, men-at-arms, crying out as we shook and tangled with each other.

"'Tis a wild creature," he said. "God's wounds, loose me of this she-wolf before I crack her skull."

They tore me off, standing aside afterward as if I were indeed some mad thing. He stared at me, blood pouring from his wrist over his embroidered sleeve.

"I thought it a child's game," he said. "Who is she?"

There were many voices quick to give me name, although before not one would have called me by it.

"Lady Ann of Cambray," he said. "I would doubt it."

There was such scorn in his voice that even I cringed. They crowded round him, pointing at the blood although he paid it no heed. I heard someone explaining who I was: "A half-Celt, sir," he said, "whose dam was Celt," as if that explained all. At that insult I would have lashed out again, but they held me back.

"Take her off," he said then to Gwendyth, the gray eyes that had been so merry now cold as slate. "Bear her off wherever you bestow unruly brats. Out of sight. Let her not grace our presence again, lest she think to feed off us a second time."

Red with embarrassment, Gwendyth hauled me away. But I turned once, craning round almost against my will, before we passed from the garden back through the small sally port into the castle. He was standing where I had seen him first, a head taller than the rest, listening to the ninnies jabber at him as if what they said was important. They were a flock of gaily colored birds, I thought, cooing and preening and fluttering about him. And what a fool was he, I told myself, to pay them heed, a popinjay, to preen so among them. That was the first time that I met Lord Raoul, and the last for many years. God forgive me then, but how I did hate him for not being what I had thought; how I did long to rend him as I rent myself.

So, there was darkness and grief, and for all Gwendyth's naggings, I would not show myself abroad to be a butt for their humor. And when I had outgrown my first sense of outrage, Lord Raoul had already gone to join King Stephen at court, and all his guard with him. Sir Brian's wife was left as chatelaine to a half-empty keep, and all the bustle of normal castle life dwindled back to the simple routine of a world of old men and frightened women. Even my small force had gone too, taken by Lord Raoul as part of his feudal levy before I realized it. And we were left alone in Sedgemont, Gwendyth and I.

It was a strong castle. Earl Raymond had chosen well when he took and enlarged the original Saxon keep that stood in a deep valley, surrounded by forests. Isolated, well fortified against attack, it was meant to be a sanctuary, a lord's demesne where he could feel safe. No doubt that is why I was sent there, it being more secure than a border fortress like Cambray. The woods that ringed it were like a wall of green, merging far off into a faint line of distant hills. Long before I ever crossed into those woods, I used to stare at the hills from the castle battlements and wonder what lay beyond, and I never entered beneath those cool, low-hanging trees without a sense of mystery. But the real strength of Sedgemont was in its position upon the edge of a swift-flowing river that fed the valley from its northern end. Built on a great slab of rock that rose abruptly from the meadowland that edged the castle round—another defense too: an enemy force could not creep upon us from the woods without being seen—the great walls and towers surged smoothly up, almost impregnable. We had height, water, a rolling plain before, and miles of wild forest land beyond. No wonder Lord Raoul felt safe to leave it partly staffed, in a woman's hands. A besieging force would have had no easy victory here. And the Lady Mildred's very nervousness was added protection, for she never relaxed watch or ward. True, these were still dangerous times and she was shy and retiring, frightened of her own shadow. In these days of tension and trouble, she saw dangers that did not even exist. But that was just as well. While she and her ladies cowered within the women's bower, the passages, courtyards, and crannies of the castle itself soon revealed their secrets to me, who felt free to roam them as I wished. For I must explain to you who know more settled ways, how different life was then. Had things been normal, I should never have known such liberty. Even at Cambray, I was not so free as I became here. A girl cannot grow up the plaything of a castle, lacking womenfolk, or so my father used to say. Had he lived, no doubt he would have sent me to a convent as he used to threaten. Only Talisin had stood between me and my father's threats before. "Let her bide," he used to say, hiding or pretending to hide me behind him. "My lord, she is still young. She will grow to woman's ways." And he would smile, half to himself, beginning then to know women overwell and, like all young men, sure of himself with them. In my father's court at Cambray, Talisin would have protected me. And had these been normal years, Sedgemont too would have had its share of young folk, pages of good family, come to learn their role at a lord's table, squires to ride and fight on his behalf, young gentlewomen training to catch rich husbands... but squires and pages had all gone with Lord Raoul, or else their fathers kept them at home. In troublesome times, people held their families together under one roof, as indeed my father had kept Talisin; many a man has been ruined by ransom of his son captured in another man's quarrel. And the young ladies who might have come to wait upon a lady of Sedgemont, had there been one, did not seek out the chatelaine. Lady Mildred, as I said, had no children of her own; there soon were no children left at Sedgemont at all, not that I missed them, those giggling silly brats. And I think Lady Mildred preferred to forget that I was there, being content with the older, staid servant women whom she had known since her youth. Since nothing would have persuaded me to turn to her for help, Gwendyth and I were left to fend for ourselves. Gwendyth had put the thought into my mind when she had said it was not meet for us to go running to the lords and ladies of Sedgemont. And Lord Raoul's words too rankled deep. If I was not fit to grace his presence, then I would never seek it out. I swore I would not enter his Hall without his express apology and invitation, nor look for advice from those who served him. And since even at this young age I had a mind of my own, as stubborn as steel, I would not give way, for all Gwendyth's coaxing.

But then came a time when, for pride—and God save the mark, but I was proud, Ann of Cambray, of my small lands and keep, although I could not hold them and they were far off—there came a time I say, when pride would not let me mix with the other ladies of Sedgemont. Cambray's lands lay to the west, and although they were not large, they were rich. Not in farmland as here, but in sheep and horses and cattle. The moneys and goods from those lands were to follow me here to Sedgemont to provide a retinue of men and women to serve me. When we had first arrived, I had paid scant attention how we were bestowed or how Sir Brian intended to deal with my household. I was young, of course, but I knew the men who came with me from Cambray as friends. When malaise or grief or sickness finally left, already some things had changed without my knowledge or consent. I have explained how Lord Raoul had taken my small guard with him; well, it was his right, he being our overlord, but I grieved at not having had chance to bid farewell, not even to those older men I had known all my life. I remember some of them to this day, who would have followed my father or my brother to the world's end, who went with Lord Raoul because he ordered it and never came back again to Cambray. But even had they stayed behind with me at Sedgemont, I could not have kept them. For the road to Cambray was long and wearisome at the best of times. Now it was shut off; messengers and supplies came fitfully, if at all. And finally, one day, they came no more. The way was choked, they said; paths overgrown, the forests filled with outlaws or refugees, villages robbed and pillaged by ruthless men. And so, if the sacks of wool did not pass, nor the casks of mead, the hide and meat, then I, proud Ann, had no resources of my own, no moneys with which to pay my household wants, not even the wherewithal to supply my own needs, and must live upon the charity of Lord Raoul in every sense of the word. And that, too, rankled deep.

But by then I was older, able to give some thought to what should be done. For I would not go to Lord Raoul's Hall or to his chatelaine, and although perforce must I live within his keep, I would take as little from him as I could. Therefore, despite Gwendyth's pleading, I sought for ways to make ourselves independent. "For if they hold me at such little worth," I said, "then have I no dealings with them. 'Like a beast' quoth he. Then shall we live, like animals in the forest who do hunt for what they have, since fate has left us here quite alone. One day they shall find out that to be Celt is no mean thing. And if I have not the wealth to buy fine gowns, yet glad I am not like those braying fools who mince and preen to make the men stare at them so. Our priest at Cambray said that fine clothes do not make fine hearts. I had rather dress in rags than be so low as to fawn on him because he is lord here." So I spoke in my pique, casting scorn on them all. And gradually I slid into a pattern of living, which, although free, was certainly not fitting, as you shall hear.

You would not recognize the way we lived. I scarce recognized it myself. Cut off from the others in the castle, I mean those who by birth and breeding should have been my friends, I wrought a way of life for Gwendyth and me, nevertheless. The size of Sedgemont helped in this. Within its walls there were many places we could go, many things we could do, without bringing attention to ourselves. There was none left to call me by title except Gwendyth. I made my companions now among the serfs and scullions and the men-at-arms. The great courtyard became as familiar to me as the one at Cambray. I grew up at the tail end of the castle world, as free and untrammeled as the wind. Ask me now, who years and events have trapped, how it was when I was a young girl at Sedgemont. I will not tell you of all I remember, for nostalgia, but

I will say that many things I believe and feel come from what I learned then. For those who say I do not think as others do speak more truthfully than they guess. I have known no stouter friends, no more-loving hearts than among the common folk at Sedgemont; and although I professed always to miss Cambray and longed to return there, it is Sedgemont that taught me how to reason for myself, speak the truth as I saw it, and act as I thought right, however convention should bid otherwise. Such common sense rings justly in my ears. I do not say it is always easy to live with and it has cost me dear. But the experiences of those times are witnesses to their integrity. True, we had little enough to eat and were often cold and badly clothed. Those things I could endure. And when rumors came to us, for even the Lady Mildred could not keep out rumor, well then, these wars made little impression upon me, who held them far off and of no import in my life. The young Henry of Anjou was knighted by the Scottish king, his uncle, Robert of Gloucester, died; his mother, the Empress Matilda, went back to France; King Stephen and his son, Eustace, fought against their enemies wherever they could make them stand and fight. Presumably Lord Raoul was engaged in these wars. At least he did not return to Sedgemont; and as long as he was away from us, that was good news. Gwendyth and I kept to ourselves, making virtue of necessity, ate our own food, contrived our own clothes, kept our own counsel. And if you had asked me, I would have said, as would any serf, that what was done in the outside world was none of my concern, provided the great barons of the land kept it far from Sedgemont. And so time passed.

Perhaps I should not say how much those years meant to me. Gwendyth merely suffered them. She was so old I do not recall a time without her, yet she was still round and fat, without a streak of gray in her black hair. She was my father's age, yet she seemed ageless. And she had put the past behind her as if it had never been. She never spoke to me of Cambray;

never, except in moments of great stress, would talk to me in our language, trying always to urge me toward "more cultured" ways, by which she meant the ways of the Norman French. I could never understand why. Now I think that in her great grief she wished to tear all longing and memory away as to pretend it had never been. All I knew then was that she tried to make me into a copy of these Norman ladies, and if giving up her own memories would make this easier for me, she would do that also. She had not counted on my stubbornness. For as I grew older, I began to do many things that she could not approve of. As I have said, even at Cambray I would not have been so free. She disliked my friends, distrusted what we did, saw all her hopes diminished every day. Only her great love for me prevented her from going to the Lady Mildred herself, but I had threatened her if she did, and, God save us, she believed me then. No, they were not happy times for her, but I was young and thoughtless. God forgive me now that I did so little to please her then.

One of the things I took pleasure in was hunting. I was good with a slingshot. Talisin had taught me years ago. How many things there are that I have learned from him; the list is endless. It is a boy's sport; but when we were hungry, even Gwendyth did not grumble too openly that I coursed a hare or found a partridge in the home meadows. It was against the law, of course, the Norman law I mean; but I was careful and the men had too many other worries to be looking out for children. But it was my friendship with Giles that most distressed her. I suppose it was unusual, he being but a groom, a little older than I, a serf at Sedgemont. But from the first day, when he had put out his hand to stop my fall and I had scowled at him, we ever sought each other out. Without Giles, life at Sedgemont might have worn another color. With him, all the rest fitted into place.

When we could we would slip from one of the small side gates (ever since a band of marauders had come down, unexpectedly stealing out of the woods, burning the half-gathered harvest in the fields, the Lady Mildred kept the drawbridge tight so none might leave or enter without her knowledge) and run through the field. The peasants, who lived outside the castle in their own village huts, knew us well enough, but went about their business as we did ours. The castle was there, close at hand, to scuttle to in time of danger. Dressed in simple homespun, my skirts bound up, I seemed, no doubt, a kitchen wench. There was game for all, provided we did not disturb the real preserves, the deer and bigger animals of the forest. That we would never have done, the forest being Lord Raoul's own hunting lands, had not we come to the idea of riding there on horseback. I had always had this wish to go into the forest but had never ventured there at first, it being too far to walk. But once I had reasoned that on horseback we would be safe—no foot soldier willingly tangles with a mounted man, and our chance at profitable game was the much more likely since no one dared go there now—I worked hard to convince Giles of the soundness of my plan. Although no man knew more of horses than he did, he was reluctant to mount one until I showed him how. And when I persuaded him to let me ride the gray horse of Cambray, then were we free to go farther abroad until there was no part of the encircling forest we had not ventured in. The catch we brought back then always justified the risk. The Lady Mildred, for fear of greater misfortunes to come, kept all on half-rations in the Hall, salted fish, tough meats, watered wine. At least, we could bring enough food for our friends, and what Gwendyth and I did not use, we gave freely away. In return, when bad weather shut us in or when we were out of luck, they contrived some way to get food for us.

About the great horse of Cambray. It was one of my father's breed left by some chance at Sedgemont, although all other war horses had gone with Lord Raoul's guard. It was a knight's charger, trained to fight and kill, perhaps left behind because not all men care to ride so conspicuous a beast, preferring more-conventional brown and black. But my father had always ridden gray horses, and my brother too. When I rode it, I felt somehow close to them, of their kind. And then nowhere was too far for us to explore, not even to the edge of those misted hills that hung upon the horizon far away. Yet Giles was always uneasy for me; and truth to tell, it was no mount for a girl, hard to control at a gallop, ready to rear and lash with its hooves. I rode astride, without saddle, but it took both of us to harness it with bit and bridle, and although in time it would come when I whistled, yet I was always careful not to mount alone for fear it should rear if I startled it. Yet once it saved our lives, as you shall hear.

We had been roaming idly through the forest, not hunting, for we had already caught enough, but for pleasure, Giles riding beside on the small pony that suited him better, the two of us chatting without thought of where we were. Carelessly then, we blundered into a clearing that we had not seen before, where a number of men lay sprawled upon the ground, busy at their food. They sprang to their swords; at their shouts, other men came running toward us through the trees. Giles tugged at his short dagger, but he would have been helpless against so many. I backed the gray horse against his, screaming at him to leap behind me. With a great scramble, he heaved himself up, catching hold of my waist with a jerk that almost sent us both flying. There was no time to right ourselves, and the horse itself was startled. Almost without my guidance, it plunged toward the first group of men, bursting through the center of their camp, sending pots and pans flying, scattering the burning embers of the fire underneath. At the first sword prick, it squealed, lashing out with its heels to send the men bowling in a welter of blood. We whirled our slingshots in their faces; they fell back for fear and the gray horse kept the others from drawing close. Then speed got us free, that, and surprise, for they thought to have had us cornered. But I could not have reined it back even had I wished to, and whatever pursuit there was we left soon behind. So the gray horse saved us from our own folly, but both of us had to saw and fight to subdue and finally turn it round. By then, the sun was low. There would be still some hours of light, but here, under the trees, the shadow of evening seemed already come. We moved cautiously, still nervous, still expecting attack long after it would have been possible, still flinching, at least I did, at every rustle in the underbrush. We had lost our supper, tied to Giles's saddle, we had lost his pony, which was worse, and we were not sure even where we were. Our long circuit had taken us away from our usual stretch of wood, yet I do not think we had gone far beyond the boundaries of Lord Raoul's demesne. It says much for the nature of these times that so large a company of armed men could camp at their ease without word spreading to Sedgemont itself.

Finally, when Giles judged we were safe enough, we halted in a clearing in the wood beside a stream. After inspecting the damages—luckily not so many or so deep as to be dangerous, a scratch or two here, a gash that had bled freely—I watered the horse while Giles climbed the highest tree to mark our position. He came sliding down, his hair covered with twigs and leaves, his face shining with exertion. "Not so astray, after all," he said, pleased with himself. "We have headed too far east, but another hour will set us right. We shall be back by nightfall." He came up to where I was standing, my gown looped up still, as I paddled in the stream. At the sound of his voice, the horse lifted its head; water fell in golden drops from its mouth; then it dipped down again and the stream went chuckling by.

"Right well we did," said Giles. Then he too was silent, his head lowered as if he did not want to look at me. I suddenly was aware of many things: of my torn and faded gown, of my bare feet and unkempt hair. I thought, too, of the way his arms had tightened around my waist and his heart had beat

against my shoulder. I looked at him, and it seemed as if I
were watching us from far off, as if I were a spectator there,
of all three, horse, maid, and boy, standing there in the cool
water. There was a clarity about us, a sudden awareness, as if
I saw then what could have been in other places, other times.

Perhaps Giles felt it too. He kneeled suddenly beside me
on the muddy bank, catching at the hem of my dress.

"My life is yours," he said, courtly words coming awkwardly
to him, yet all the more real for that. "I owe you my life."

His head was still bent. I longed to stretch out my hands
to touch him, feel his arms around me to share and prolong
this moment when danger had made us close. Yet I could not.
Shyness perhaps, or fear, made me tongue-tied. He looked up
then, his eyes dark, watching me as they sometimes did without
his knowing. I think he saw part of what I felt, or sensed it
for himself. There were marks I had not seen before upon his
face, weariness and dirt, the face of an older man.

"I am yours to the death, my lady," he said, and I thought
then that the feel of ice, of a cold wind blowing, was because
he too had had a vision and put it resolutely aside. He moved
to stand up, the bank gave way beneath his weight. He slipped
forward, his fingers splayed upon the mud. The air seemed
suddenly loud with noise, the sound of many hooves, the cut
and thrust of swords, and where he lay upon the edge it seemed
a crimson shadow fell.

I screamed, as I had in the clearing, "Giles, Giles," covering
my ears and eyes, until he sat up, sleeving the mud from his
face, scrambling abashedly to his feet.

"My lady," he said again, who never called me anything but
Ann, "what ails you? I did but slip."

He jumped upright, Giles the stable boy, his clear honest
eyes bright, his face a-smile once more, bound to his lot in
life as I was to mine. Had not these strange thoughts come in
between us, had not I thought to have seen his death there
by the stream, I might have fallen with him beside me then.

Well, it would have been no bad thing to have lost a maidenhood to such a man. But something else would have been lost between us, I think, and it was stronger than lust. For he recalled me to myself, and then the horror of that vision I had seen was so deep that I could do no other than remain silent and leave him to guide us home.

We slunk into the gates without notice at last, but it was many days before I would stir abroad again. I was fourteen. I had nothing of my own. All that was mine was dead and gone. The meanest scullion in Lord Raoul's kitchen had more than I, for she knew at least who she was, what hopes or lack of them. I had not even that. My days were passed as in a dream, and my nights were made hideous with cries and red with blood. Giles thought it was for fear of the men in the forest, and gave me his little hunting knife as my own, to keep with me for protection always. I have it still and well it has served me in many ways. But it could not protect me then from what I feared and what I had missed. And so things stood until Lord Raoul came back. . . . It was the beginning of 1152. It was the end of my childhood, the end of an interlude. All things began to move again, and whether I would or not, I was caught up in them.

2

OW COMES A DIFFICULT PART OF MY TALE. But first I must relate how Lord Raoul returned, unexpectedly, after all these years. News of the renegades in the forest must have come to the castle, for Lady Mildred kept double watch and we were penned in, as if under siege. Then, too, the weather worsened as it does at Yuletide, setting people coughing and shivering with agues. Many of us were sick, and hungry too, and Gwendyth had a busy season, for she was famed for her potions and salves and was much in demand among the inhabitants of the castle. But this year her remedies were of little help, not even to her when she fell sick also, and we thought to have a bad while at the spring. People began to talk of the flux which had carried half Sedgemont off before, including the present lord's mother and father, both within a night. But this sickness was not as grave as that, it left us weak but did not kill. Soon the worst we had to endure was the monotony of being shut up within the castle walls until Lady Mildred forgot her fears. I was left alone much at this time, being shy even of seeking Giles out in the stables where he had work aplenty. There was little else for me to do and I took to walking on the battlements, more to listen to the guards talk than for hope of seeing anything of interest. Thus I was among the first to spy Lord Raoul's messengers, posthasting through the mud as if life and death were in their mission, and was at hand when their loud hail summoned the watch to open the gates upon his return. After them, hard on their heels, came the outriders, the red banners fluttering brightly through the drizzle, as I noted sourly, for even pique would not keep me from my vantage point. They were a brave troop when they came, I must admit, and they rode out strongly across the open meadows from the east, cheerfully, horns sounding, hounds baying, returning as if after a long and successful hunting expedition. I could not make out who any of the riders were, for they were full-armed, with helmets on, lances lowered, as befitted a war party in troublesome times; but it seemed to me they were not as numerous as I had thought, and of the men who had come with me from Cambray I could not pick out one. Rumors soon were flying: that they did not intend to stay long; that Lord Raoul had taken advantage of a lull in the fighting to come back to Sedgemont before returning to his lands in France; that he purposed to make up his full complement of force only before the next campaign began. At the time, I paid little attention to this talk. As I have said, the affairs of the great were not my interest, especially not those that concerned Lord Raoul. Remembering the elegant young lordling who had insulted me, I did not suppose he would have taken kindly to soldiering, although, as soon became clear, in this I greatly maligned him. In any case, his arrival set life at Sedgemont all awry, and all our placid, irregular ways ground to a halt. Lady Mildred, jolted out of lethargy, came timidly to greet Lord Raoul, and on seeing her husband, Sir Brian, melted with fine display of sensibility into his arms. At once, the style and flavor of Sedgemont changed. There was a martial clank and clatter about the courtyards; messengers came and went at all hours; the bustle of the castle revived as I remembered it when I had first seen it those years ago. But apart from staring with the rest, all agog over this fine arrival, I kept out of everyone's way. I was not missed, and since it was at this time that Gwendyth herself fell ill, I had plenty of excuse to keep close to the little side room where we had long made our dwelling place. And although I searched among the returning men for news of Cambray, I did not then realize how great our losses had been.

And if for the first time in many years, envoys from the west reached Sedgemont, their business was not with me, and I could glean but little information from them. One man I thought I did remember, a tall dark-faced lord with brows that met above deep eyes, but I could not then recall who he was or what he wanted. He came up with his own guard, as mark of his importance, and was soon closeted with Lord Raoul about some border affair. Since his name is one worth remembering, I set it down now, although then I did not know it—Lord Guy of Maneth, vassal of the dead Earl of Gloucester, one-time companion of my father, as his son, Gilbert, had been friend to Talisin. But whatever they discussed was far from my knowledge or interest, and if I thought it strange to be excluded from what may well have concerned Cambray (and as I have said, there were many rumors abroad), yet I concealed my anger with the thought that in the end it might be better for me to keep myself apart. In that, I think instinct served me right. Although, God knows, I would not have sought attention the way it finally came.

Several days of such confusion and turmoil had already passed. It was on a damp evening that I ventured out from our small chamber. Lord Raoul and his guests were already seated in the Great Hall, and I had come down into the kitchens to fetch food for Gwendyth, for she was still not well enough to move from her bed. Neither Giles nor I had been able to leave the castle, for he was held in stable and yard, seeing to all who rode about Lord Raoul's affairs, and the watch was kept strictly by Lord Raoul's own guard. From Giles that evening I had gleaned some news about the black-browed man, Lord Guy. He was about to leave on the morrow, his suit with Lord Raoul having gone adrift, so it was judged from his bad humor, for he had come himself to see that his horses were ready and had cuffed Giles for some imagined fault. I felt easier that he was leaving so soon, which was strange too, for had it been anyone else, I think I might have found some excuse to question him myself about the western lands. Giles and I had no more time for talk, so I busied myself preparing a trencher of bread and a stoup of broth for Gwendyth. Usually this would have been her task, but as I have explained, she was still far from well; and I had bidden her lie down upon my bed, not that there was much to choose between them, and had covered her with the thick blue mantle that I never wore now because it was embroidered with gold and jewels that looked out of place with my other garments. Poor Gwendyth. She would never have let me wait on her had she been in her right mind. Yet when I had her food prepared, I lingered in the kitchen, for it was warm there and the serfs were relaxed after the first serving in the Hall. Lord Raoul did himself and his friends proud, I thought, or perhaps it was only that we had become used to Lady Mildred's parsimonious ways. I could have had my pick of dozens of dishes or flagons of wine, and the baskets of scraps for the poor were overflowing. Scullions, perspiring in the heat of the open fires, turned the spits of meat and cooks arranged platters of game and fowl. There were even sugared fruits and sweetmeats, delicacies for delicate palates, I scoffed, although it may have been hunger that made me contemptuous. For the first time, a wave of resentment overcame me that I was excluded from these festivities. When my father had had guests, he had let me sit at the High Table and Talisin had given me tidbits from his plate. I had almost forgotten what it would be like to dine in state, the Great Hall filled with the sound of music and laughter. In the body of the Hall, the men-at-arms would lounge along the benches served by the menials, and on the raised dais Lord Raoul and his companions would be drinking and talking, with squire and page at their side to obey every command. When I finally mounted the narrow staircase to our small room, I could hear the sound of that laughter away in the distance and a sense of loneliness, even sadness, made me pause again to listen.

Sometimes I think if I had not paused so often, if I had not

lingered, all would have been different. At other times, I know
if I had gone on, it would have been too late for me too. For
the noise that caught my attention at last had nothing to do
with laughter. It was a familiar noise, yet strange in that place
at that time, the strike of boots and spurs on the stone steps
above me, hurrying, yet cautious. At first I thought nothing
of it; there were always armed men about these days. But there
was something about the way the footsteps sounded softly,
almost stealthily, that set my heart jumping. They came on,
running down faster; I cannot describe what I heard without
the hairs on my head rising up as do a dog's at hint of danger.
I looked round, suddenly anxious not to be seen.

It was a narrow staircase, cut out of the thickness of the
wall at some time, not a main thoroughfare that all men might
use, and as far as I knew it led only to our chamber, where
no one would go. At one of the angles in the wall, a leather
curtain had been hung across an alcove, and as quick upon
the thought, I slid behind it, praying that none would notice
me.

There were two men. I was right that they came in haste,
taking the stairs at a stride, yet running tiptoe. I could not see
their faces, for they wore their riding cloaks with the hoods
drawn, but I took heed of their voices, muffled like stones
dropped into a deep well.

"Art sure?"

"Sure."

"And the other?"

"A servant woman. Off about her business, none the wiser."

"'Twere well to take them both."

"One is enough."

Their voices came hissing back as they ran past me, down
into the part of the castle I had just left, where it would be
impossible to trace them.

I waited until I was sure they were gone, leaning back upon
the stones to steady my trembling. Some dread seemed to have

overcome me, like to that I had felt with Giles in the woods but more urgent, real. Then I was forcing myself up the stairs, rounding the narrow treads as fast as I could, food and soup forgotten. The door of the room where we lodged was tight shut as I had left it. I swallowed hard and jerked it open. Nothing had changed. The small fire under the eaves had died to ash, and the tallow candle was unlit. Gwendyth still slept in the dark under the cloak. I took the candle and held it to the fire, blowing until the flames started. Then, shielding the light with my other hand, I approached the bed. Gwendyth lay as I had bidden her, the cloak pulled over her head against the dark, which, like all Celtic women, she feared. I smiled on seeing her and felt a rush of gratitude for all her years of devotion. And wished, more for her than for myself, that soon we could go back to Cambray. I shook her shoulder to wake her, and felt the dampness spread beneath my hand, saw the stains now upon the cloak, saw the knife hilt stabbed through, all clearly, far off. When I tried to pull her upright, the cloak fell back and the blood gushed forth. She opened her eyes, said something that I could not understand, although I think it was my mother's name in the old tongue. Then nothing again, silence, the shifting of the fire, the guttering of the candle flame.

I do not know how long I held her in my arms, but it was long enough for the blood to congeal and for her to stiffen and grow cold. It was only then I realized that all my holding would not bring her warmth again. I looked about me. But there was still no sign of disturbance, no stool upturned, no plate broken, nothing moved from its place. Like the wind, then, they had crept in, stabbed her as she slept, and left. And I had heard them on the stairs, watched as they passed, listened to what they said.

Sure?

Sure.

And the other?

Under my cloak, asleep in my bed, Gwendyth had been murdered. By whom? Why? In my place. It was that thought that tore like steel. Had I not begged her to lie there, covered her with my rich cloak, loitered on my mission, they would have known her for what she was and left her unharmed. Or would they have waited there for me to return? And she, waiting with them—what would they have had to do to ensure her silence? At these thoughts some rage filled me. I hardly know what I did, it overwhelmed me so. Murder, while I had stood to gossip with my friends; murder, while Lord Raoul and his minions laughed at their feasting. I laid her down gently, pushing the dark hair back from her face, crossing her arms decently upon her breast. The knife I did not touch. Let them find that when they came looking. From a coffer under the bed, I ransacked the things that it held until I reached the bottom, where my father's ceremonial sword lay wrapped in some oiled silk. Not half the size of his fighting sword, it was still too heavy and long, the belt too wide and broad for my waist, yet I strapped it on somehow. Beside it lay a thin gold chaplet that had belonged to my mother. I tore off the head-dress I usually wore these days in Norman style, freed my hair from its plaits so that it fell in a red veil across my back, and set the circle in place. Then, pulling the bloodstained cloak about me, hiding the sword underneath, I went running back down the stairs, scarcely thinking, toward the Great Hall.

The meal was almost over now. As I had imagined before, they were still sitting at the tables, replete, listening to a minstrel singing. The heralds would have barred the way but I pushed past them and the guards, letting them seek for a name to call out afterward. Once inside the door, I did not hesitate but made my way by instinct toward the dais where the High Table stood. As I had thought, they had dined well. Trenchers of bread and broken meats lay on the table and the wine goblets were half-empty. Underneath, the hounds were sniffing among the rushes. Before them was an open place where a man had been singing. Poor fellow, I brushed him aside into silence so his lute wavered and his voice cracked. They all looked up at that. Yes, there was Sir Brian beside his wife, the Lady Mildred, and around them the other lords and knights of Sedgemont with their ladies, dressed in their best. They sat in the carved oaken chairs like statues, and beside them the pages and squires stood as motionless. And all behind me in the Hall, I felt the ripple of interest and surprise run like a gust of air.

"My lords," I said, "I am come to demand justice."

No one moved. Now I could pick out Lord Guy of Maneth sitting to the right of the man in the center chair. Maneth was leaning forward, speaking urgently into his ear.

"Murder there has been," I said. "Even as you sit here, murderers are abroad."

There was a scream at that, quickly stifled, Lady Mildred it was, clutching her husband. Behind me, I felt that ripple of surprise move again, and the hanging tapestries on the walls stirred once. But the man in the center place did not move. He had been peeling some kind of fruit and I watched how his hands closed across it and were suddenly still. Yet his face remained in shadow. I did not know who he was, although Lord Guy, beside him, was shouting now. But I did not understand his words either.

"Is it your will, then," I said, "that death goes unnoticed here? Have there been so many deaths that one more means nothing? Shall I lead you to the room to show you where an old woman lies stabbed? What profit to you? What vengeance shall she have?"

The lords and ladies were talking to one another now, their eyes wide with astonishment or fear. Lord Guy was still shouting; I could see his dark eyes glinting and the flush on his face. But the man in the center said nothing.

I pushed back the cloak and edged my father's sword from its sheath. It was heavier than I had thought, the hilt carved

in some Celtic fashion. Years of neglect had stiffened the
leather casing and the blade caught and jerked as I strove to
drag it forth. I felt the edge slice across my arm, yet I hardly
noticed the pain of it. With both hands I heaved it up; the
lights from the tapers caught and twinkled on the rich gold
carvings. My mother's father had given it to him once as a
pledge of peace, witness of the faith between them. Now I
would raise it as a sign of vengeance for the wrong that had
been done.

"Justice," I cried again, and then louder, in my own tongue,
"Vengeance. Against murder and betrayal. To me, Cambray."

It was the battle cry of my house. Behind me in the Hall,
I heard one faint echo: well then, there was one man at least
to back me. They were all on their feet now, the womenfolk
agape, the lords at the High Table starting. Lord Guy was
repeating my name, "Ann of Cambray. Tis Ann of Cambray
herself."

"Who is with me?" I cried again, not turning although I
could hear the guards pounding up the Hall, and the rasp of
their weapons. "Who stands by me?"

The man in the center chair moved so suddenly that everyone gasped again. In one movement he had leaped from his
place and vaulted across the table, sending goblets and plates
clanging on the stone. Behind him, the chair crashed slowly
to the floor and his guests and courtiers started forward like
puppets tied to a string. He came limping toward me, hand
outstretched.

"There is no need to cry for vengeance, Lady Ann," he said.
"We shall do what is needful."

I stared at him. Would I have known him after all? It was
not the mincing boy I remembered, that conceited fop whom
I had kept to scorn in my thoughts. He seemed larger, taller,
broader. And he wore simple clothes as a soldier wears who
stands not on ceremony. No jewels even, except a heavy gold
chain about his neck. And the hair was different, cut in a fringe

across the front and waved to shoulder length. But the face, the slant-shaped eyes, the cold gray-green stare, I had never forgotten.

We stood side by side, his hand clasped about mine upon the hilt. We might have been fighting with one sword between us, and the blood from my arm ran down his as he raised the sword higher, repeating my cry, "To me, Cambray."

Then I could not move. The cloak fell from my shoulders; my blood mingled with the other stains upon my gown. I heard them all clearly now, panting and pushing. I was some animal whom the hounds circle, smelling the scent of wounded flesh. They were all around, servants, guards, soldiers making a circle. My grasp upon the sword slackened against my will; he caught it before it fell and lowered it so that it rested, point to the ground. I tried to pull the cloak back in place to hide from their prying eyes, but the circle grew smaller.

"You are hurt," he said sharply, "where, how?" his hands rough on my shoulders and along my ribs. I tried to tell him that it was Gwendyth's blood, not mine, her blood he must avenge, but could not. Something tore and jerked in my throat; the circle grew so small that it disappeared, and I within it fell through into darkness beneath. . . .

When I came to myself, how much later I do not know, and where and when it was not at first clear, I lay cocooned in a comfort that I had never known. The room was large, too large to make out all of it in the dimness that surrounded me. The bed was softer than down, spread with silk coverlets and rugs and curtained round with rich material whose design I presently made out in the flickering light of a fire. At first I lay still as if in a swoon, seeing all these things but not aware of them. Then gradually awareness came back, and with it grief and pain. Beyond the curtained bed, I could hear now the sounds of people moving, talking, of furniture shifting as a chair scraped upon the stones, the thud of a man's boots as he strode back and forth.

"Nay, my lord." A voice I did not recognize at first, hushed and unctious, as if used to explaining things to the old and ailing. "Nay, my lord. There is no danger. Great exhaustion, but no fever."

Another voice, impatient, curt: a young man's voice.

"Deep, my lord, not dangerous. The flesh is healthy. Twill heal with a scar, but that is all."

Another question. I strained to hear the reply.

"Her father's, my lord. She bore it into the Hall beneath the cloak. Dragged it more like. It is old and heavy. She could not draw the blade clear."

"So much the better." That was Sir Brian who spoke now. "It was madness to come upon you, so armed. What did she expect to gain?"

I lay within the cocoon of the bed and listened to them talking, almost idly, detached, as if they were speaking of someone else. The only things that were real were the softness of the bed and the ache along my arm. Perhaps I even dozed for a while. But the talk went on.

"Your concern does you credit, my lord. But remember who and what she is. The Celts are never to be trusted. They are as sly and smooth as snakes. Who knows what plan she had in mind, or what use she meant to make of such an exhibition? There are men who can use this to their advantage." Sir Brian's voice was full of scorn, like the one which had sneered at me as a child for my birth. It would sneer at me again.

"I think not," said Lord Raoul. I recognized him now. "I think she acted on impulse, out of shock and fear. I do not think she counted the consequence."

"If Anjou comes to England again, as he purposes, the western borders will be of consequence," Sir Brian said. "The Celts may rise on his behalf as they did for his mother. That might be motive enough for her to win their sympathy."

"Guy of Maneth thought of that also." Lord Raoul's voice was thoughtful. The walking back and forth continued. I even knew his walk now, a slight limp, as if favoring one leg.

"But she has had no converse with anyone, not even with Cambray, let alone the Celts beyond," he went on as thoughtfully as if continuing an argument with himself. "Nor is there any proof the Celts will rise, nor rally to Anjou or to anyone else. And Maneth's power has grown overfast since the Earl of Gloucester's death for me to hold him as detached observer of the borderlands. I do not remember that he played an important part in the last struggles."

"He is a good fighter," fretted Sir Brian, "better on our side than the other.... It might be wiser to have granted his request."

"Well, so be it." Lord Raoul sounded more impatient again. "I refused him. Let it be sufficient that she will live. I thought her cut in twain."

"But there are other wounds, my lord," said the soft, older voice. I knew who spoke now: it was the castle leech. We had ever been on good terms with him and he had always held Gwendyth's skill highly. In truth, she had not had the same confidence in him, but I think she misjudged him, for he spoke kindly of her. And of me, as he now proved. Silence followed his remark.

"God's teeth, what mean you?" Lord Raoul said. "Will you bandy words with me?"

"My lord," said the old man again, "this only. Have you thought what has become of her all these years while you have been away? She has grown from childhood."

"Why should his lordship wonder?" Sir Brian spoke sharply. "He has had cares enough without thought for a half-breed wench. And my lady wife has been here to befriend her."

"Patience, good sir," Lord Raoul said, "let the fellow speak."

"I meant only, lords," he said, "that you have been gone overlong and she has had no one to check or guide her if you did not, as her liege lord and guardian. I speak out of turn, but she and that old woman who was killed lived as poorly as the serfs out in the fields. If she has acted rashly, it was for lack of guidance surely."

"Then why stayed she not with the Lady Mildred and the other women in the bower?" Sir Brian asked. "Why set she up her own household, God save the mark, as if she were a princess of the blood? Why came she not under our protection as she should?"

"I mean no harm, my lord, no harm." The old voice quavered at Sir Brian's anger, yet went on, good, kind, old man. "God forbid that I should speak against you. The Lady Mildred has held this castle well and all within it safe. But look you, my lords, if the Lady Ann and her servant have lived as servants themselves, perhaps you should know of it. For pride perhaps she lived so, not wishing to be beholden to your lordship. I know not. No one will say it was your prime concern. . . ."

Lord Raoul broke in at that. "Judas, I have been battling across a country to keep a king on the throne; I have had little time for what concerns the women in their bower at Sedgemont."

"True, true, my lord," the voice went on soothingly, "but things beyond all men's control have made her no man's care. The Celtic lords may remain firm but they will not be pleased to know their kinswoman is nigh starved of hunger and ill of neglect."

"You speak out of turn, old man," said Raoul. "You tempt me to harsh reply." But his voice was not harsh. "Those are not easy words, to be taken lightly."

"Then see for yourself, my lord," said the leech. "Is this a sleep of exhaustion? Faintness and pallor like this come not from flesh wounds."

A sudden movement gave me warning, time enough to turn my face aside and close my eyes. I could feel the light upon my hair now, and beneath my lashes, sense rather than see how Lord Raoul came close to the bedside. But it was Sir Brian who spoke first.

"God save the mark," he swore, "but how that hair flames red as Hell. And yet, my lord, it is an unusual face. It may be men will make a bid for her and take the burden upon themselves no doubt. They say her mother was the fairest of her race. So may she be if she be true."

His words were blunt enough, not cruel so much as detached. He might have been speaking of Lord Raoul's horse.

"Nay, look," said the leech, "see this then."

He switched aside the bedcovers. I lay exposed to their gaze, naked for a linen shift open to the waist, my arm strapped to my side. Rigid with fear, I dared not move or breathe for fear they would see how conscious I was of their scorn. Where the others stood and how they looked I cannot tell. But I knew that if I opened my eyes I would see first Lord Raoul's cold gray-green stare. At last he reached out and pulled the covers back in place.

"'Tis skin and bone," he said. "God's death, is there never end to woman's folly? Rot me if there has not been more trouble these past hours than all seven years previous. Send then to Guy of Maneth, that my mind will not change. He leaves at dawn and would learn how she does. You marked how he was last evening, first not knowing her, then overeager to claim acquaintance. . . . But he had not seen her since Cambray. . . . And when she wakes, bid the Lady Mildred take her to her charge. We will think on things further. And that, too, you may tell the Lord of Maneth. But I will avouch this, sirs: she has grown taller perhaps, but no different from that hellcat I remember when I left."

His voice ended abruptly. I heard him go limping from the room. When all were gone, I lay upon the down-filled bed and felt my body shiver with shock. It was not so much what they said, their plans and policies and military moves—those made my head ache to think on but I did not at first consider them as closely as I should. It was their disdain, disinterest, that men should think so little of Gwendyth or me as to make her death and my grief of no importance. Except for the kind old leech, not one had spoken of me but as something "worth bidding for," as Sir Brian had so gracefully expressed it. No doubt they did have plans for Cambray, no doubt it was as important as I was not. But no man could have the one without me too. That was the law. As for Lord Raoul, when we had first met he had called me "brat," "she-wolf," and I had not forgotten. But to be labeled thus—"hellcat" was it? "sly as a snake," and worst of all "skin and bone"—these things lay not within the realm of forgiveness. Long would he rue the day he spoke those words. Yet I tell you now, in part he spoke truth, for I was slow in coming to womanhood and was then as slender and unformed as a boy. And he did not know that I heard him. But, for those words, I could have killed him where he stood. So thus between anger and grief, I watched the rest of the night through.

After the death of my brother, I count these the saddest hours I have ever known. For now I truly was alone and must make use of my wits, such as they were, to save me, since there was no one else I dared to trust.

How long I lay thus, I care not to remember. I woke to full consciousness to see the Lady Mildred advancing purposefully across the room, the leech bowing and muttering behind her. God's death, but she could so fill a space with purpose when she wanted, that, small woman that she was, she seemed the largest of us all.

What had been spoken of in the night, what had happened, became now as a dream that I had imagined. Reality was billowing arms, and honeyed words and determination, strong as steel. For a little body, who gave the impression of fragility, she was indomitable. For the first time I realized that the Lord of Sedgemont had not made so poor a choice in having left her to guard his castle in his absence. Now, having been told to take me to her charge, she was determined upon her duty. I was too weak at first to protest and, in some ways, found amusement in watching her. As for the other maids and wait-ing-women, well, one might do worse than echo Lord Raoul's observation about women in their bower. They bored me silly within the day with their chatter and their concern and their sly prying. Yet I found I could not lift a hand or foot without their help. The worst part of that convalescence was having them dance in attendance around me. I was washed and groomed and fed like a lapdog whom they half-feared would bite. And although once it was clear that my wound was mended, I sank from favor, yet grimly Lady Mildred clung to the hope that she would yet make a lady out of me. Well, Gwendyth had hoped so, too. We would see who would win at this second try. One thing at least was true. Under her wing, I need have no fear of any new attempt upon my life. She would not have let a man within the room without first rousing all of Sedgemont about his ears.

When the summons came for me to attend upon Lord Raoul himself, I had not the strength to resist. Yet I had been half-expecting it, like a soldier who knows a battle is coming and keeps one thought always to his defense. The messengers waited at the door in their brilliant reds and golds, while the women braided my hair and hastily cobbled up some dress for me to wear. I heard them tell me how to walk and smile and curtsy, thus and thus, to turn my lord's anger aside, but paid their advice scant heed, too. But before I left I took care to slip the little hunting dagger Giles had given me into my sleeve. Thus armed and ready, I followed meekly while the guards clashed and swaggered through the castle halls.

Lord Raoul's quarters were in a far part of the castle which had been seldom occupied as long as I remembered. Now there were fires blazing in the stone hearths and men-at-arms everywhere in the courtyards and on the stairs. I noted too how even the common men went armed, and the guards kept all their accoutrements about them as if ready to march at short notice. It was unexpected, this martial readiness. And yet, looking about me as we went toward his chambers, I wondered which of these fine fellows was so much Lord Raoul's man that killing of harmless womenfolk was not accounted a sin. Who among them then was so loyal that a bribe would not ease him into betrayal?

Lord Raoul believes himself safe, I thought, with his armed companions about him, but if there are murderers and villains in the pack, let him beware. They will slit his throat one day, too. When he is alone and out of favor, let him look for loyalty. I little knew how close my thoughts came to the truth later, how close and how far. But that lies ahead. Then I knew only that for all my brave thoughts, I was shaking when I came to the large room where he was waiting.

"Lady Ann," he said, "you are welcome."

His voice, when he spoke in courtesy, still had that timbre of laughter, a vibrancy about it that I remembered from my childhood. It was, I thought, the only attractive thing about him.

"I trust you are recovered," he was saying. "You are kind to grace our presence."

Courtly words. No sign of that anger that they had warned me against. I made him no reply, but curtsied as low as I could, to do Gwendyth credit, although it galled me to make him obeisance. And if I had not come, I thought sourly, no doubt you would have had your guards haul me here by the hair if it pleased you. But I said nothing, kept my eyes downcast, hands folded together, as was fitting in a great lord's presence. I had been watching Lady Mildred's maids; I knew humility now well enough to ape it.

"Sit you here, then," he said at last.

"Nay, my liege lord," I simpered, "I had lief stand as it pleases you."

"Well, stand," he said more abruptly. He heaved himself out of his chair and limped toward the open fireplace, leaning against it while he kicked a fresh log into place with the heel of his boot. Two brindled hounds that had been lying close by stretched and padded behind him. In a corner of the room a chest stood open, its contents spilled out carelessly.

But his war gear, coat of mail, shield, and sword belt were neatly laid upon a bench, and his war helmet and great sword lay unsheathed nearby. This was a campaign room of a man who expects to be called to duty momentarily. I had thought Sir Brian would be beside him, but he was alone, save for the guard who stood at the door. That gave me more courage. Presently, when I still said nothing, he gave off playing with the dogs and called for his squire to bring him wine. He took the goblet then, and offered it to me formally.

"By your leave, lady," he said, and bowed to me to drink. Again, it was a courtly gesture that none had made to me before but I held firm to my intent.

"'Tis not fitting, my lord," I said.

He scowled at my words, tossed off the wine himself, poured more, and limped from one side of the room to the other with his halting stride. I watched him beneath my lashes.

"God's teeth," he said at last, broke out with as if he had meant to remain calm, "but will you not even sit or drink in my presence? What ails you?"

"I do not know what your lordship means," I said, smiling to myself.

"God's teeth," he swore again, then, slowly, as if willing himself to manners, "this is a change, is it not, from she who came storming into my Hall, sword in hand, demanding vengeance but days ago."

"I had cause," I said.

"I do not deny that. I have called you to hear it. But this," he waved his hand in my direction, "does not help."

"What does not, my lord?" I asked, echoing his words, as if simple.

He gestured again, a gesture that took in meek face, meek hands, the carefully arranged clothes and hair.

"Have you nothing to say? You intimated much that night. Or perhaps you prefer to forget what you said."

His anger gave me heart. That I had come prepared for.

"Perhaps, my lord," I said, choosing words carefully, "perhaps since then I have learned discretion. Perhaps I have also learned to be afraid."

He swore again at that, a soldier's oath that sat ill with his more formal words.

"What does that mean?"

"Nothing, then, my lord," I said, "as your lordship pleases."

"Devil take it," he cried, "does your fear so prevent you from sitting or drinking in our presence? Or do you think I shall try to poison you with the first mouthful?"

I said nothing.

He said slowly, "This murder hath grieved and startled you, lady, as it must all God-fearing men. I wish only if there be cause or reason perhaps that you know of . . ."

His echo of Sir Brian's words began to anger me in turn. Yet I had sworn not to lose my temper, because then I might say too much.

"Cause, cause," I said, "what cause could there be to kill an old woman who lived as a pauper in my charge. Except, my lord, it has occurred to me, if not to you, that she was killed in my stead. Next time, the murderers will not be so foolish as to make the same mistake. But forgive me, my lord, that I prefer there be no second time. And until I know who are my enemies, it is hard to guard against them."

He drank another stoup of wine, seeming perturbed by what I said. I still watched him beneath my lashes. Good, if I did but goad him further, it would be sweet revenge.

He said at last, "Why speak you of enemies?"

"My lord," my reply came pat, "I have long lived here at Sedgemont as ward and dependent, against my will and liking, God knows. But no hurt came to me until now."

He scowled. "What mean you by that?" he said again, gritted out. I could see the pulse beat in his cheek. Later I came to know it as a sign of mounting rage, held in check by will. But now his anger was plain.

"Nothing, my lord," I said, and slid the last barb neatly into place. "You have heard tales enough of how we lived. I make no complaint. But we lived at peace with all until your lordship's return."

We stared openly at each other then. I suddenly felt moved to say what was in my mind, even if it threw away the advantage I had won.

"Perhaps," I said, "it is your lordship's plans that cause my enemies to rise. Perhaps, although I am of little worth, Cambray is more."

It was a shrewd blow. I saw he had not expected it.

"I have no plans," he said at last, lied, had I not heard him talk of them? "None that could wish you ill."

I was silent still, hands folded. Underneath the stuff of my sleeve, I held the handle of the little dagger. He would not take me off guard again.

"Lady Ann," he was saying, "you do me wrong in this. I do not deny that Cambray is the chiefest fort held by the king's faction along the western border. If I can use it to secure the border for Stephen, it will be to our great advantage. Henry of Anjou will look for help from the west as his mother did before. The death of Gloucester has left a hole in his support there. Cambray may be of more value than you know. And only a fool would let Henry of Anjou take advantage of the lack of a lord of Cambray to call the Celts across the border to his aid."

Henry of Anjou, Henry of Anjou, I thought. They use his name as a shadow to frighten children. Who is this Henry of Anjou?

"And what have I to do with Henry of Anjou?" I said. "I want to go back to Cambray, back to my own lands, that is all."

"I cannot send you back now," he said.

"But they are my lands."

"No, by God, they are not," he shouted suddenly. "God's wounds, but you hold them from me. And you are my ward until I give you leave otherwise."

"Then have a care of them, my lord," I said smoothly, "and

of me. Else your wardship may be found wanting."

"Rot me," he said, "but you try the patience of a saint."

He loomed over me, taller by a head, powerful in his open jerkin and linen shirt, his arms braced against a chair. I would not flinch. Within my sleeve I felt the cool steel of Giles's knife.

"Show not your rage to me, my lord," I said. "I could hold my father's men to my will. You need not fear the Celts either. The Celtic princes swore peace with my father."

"Who had a Celt as wife," he said, still staring at me. His eyes were dark and stern. Strange eyes, I thought them, large and set wide apart like a deer's. I would not show him I was afraid.

"She was my mother, lord," I said. "I am half-Celt, as you have often baited me with. I am kin to those Celtic princes who rule the lands and people across the border. They will keep peace with me."

"You speak proudly," he said. "Who would have guessed your race from your looks and speech? They say your kind have power to change shape to shape at will. From raging harpy to demure nun? You will not sit or eat or drink with me for a childish fret that once I was angered by your tantrums. Yet you dare draw sword against me at my own table. Do you know what doom is decreed for those who come armed into their liege lord's Hall? Death it is, lady, slow and painful, to raise weapons against your lord, and he unarmed."

With a swiftness that unnerved me, he caught hold of my arm and shook it until, with a clatter, the little dagger fell hilt-foremost between us, on the floor at his feet. He bent to pick it up, and still grasping my arm, pulled me toward a small table where he dropped the dagger and stood looking at it and me.

"And you could not even have used it," he said suddenly. "Any child at an army's tail could tell you that you have but one chance to strike and kill, and if you miss . . . If you would sleeve knife, then have the blade at hand, not the hilt, like so. How can you hope to strike with a handle? And hold it firm so that when a man runs upon you, his weight gives you the force your own arm lacks."

He showed me how to hold the knife so that the sharp edge slid point-first into the palm of my hand.

And then he threw it abruptly on the wooden table so that it struck there quivering.

"And by the troth, lady, I do well to show you how to kill me," he cried, half-angry, half-laughing. "Come, can we not forget what has passed between us? When first we met, you were a child and I, forgive me, was not much older than you are now and should have known better than to cross you. And I have a wound that is half-healed and like to lame my leg if I cannot rest it. And I care not to sit if you will not, and I have overthrown the wine so that we cannot drink. Shall we not let bygones be bygones and sheath all weapons for a while? I owe you some amends of neglect and you shall allow me to nurse my present hurts before inflicting new ones."

The smile he gave me was infectious, the hand warm and steady. I let him lead me to a chair by the fire and waited while he shouted for more wine and food. Seated then like that, with his leg propped before him, he did not look so threatening after all, nor so different in some ways from the teasing lad I remembered.

"I am not handy with weapons," I said at last, hesitatingly.

Then he did laugh, the young laugh I also remembered.

"Only with slingshots," he said. "They say you are a great huntsman with stone and sling."

I blushed at that.

"And rider, too. But there may be time for such pleasures without stealing my horse. We can find more-fitting mount than knight's charger."

I made no reply but noted the words *stealing my horse* for future thought. Perhaps he marked my displeasure, too, for when the food had been brought and the wine (all of which

I would have eaten or drunk from hunger had not I remembered how he called me "skin and bone," so sat and nursed pride and determination), he said slowly, as if thinking of ways to please, to recall old times, "I knew your father well."

I was too startled to reply. I had not looked for that.

"He came often to Sedgemont," he said, "before these wars began. He was my grandfather's best friend. He took me on my first hunt. He bore me before him on the saddle of his gray horse."

I felt him looking at me as I sat there, saying nothing.

"He was the best horseman I have ever known. And the gray horses of Cambray were famous even then. And I was my grandfather's only heir, my parents being dead before this. Yet, from among all others, my grandfather chose him to bear me from Sedgemont to our lands in Sieux in southern Normandy." He paused before going on, "So heard I of your brother, Talisin. And of the little sister with red hair. I knew of you long before we met, Lady Ann. Think you not that it is better to be friends as Lord Falk and Earl Raymond were? For my part, I would not have enmity between us."

There was a silence then that lengthened until I broke it.

"It has been long, my lord," I said awkwardly, "that any have spoken to me kindly of Cambray. Even Gwendyth seemed to have forgotten it."

"She who was killed?"

"Yea, my lord."

We were silent again.

"My lord," I said abruptly, "I have had no traffic with the Celts these many years. And they were not Celts who killed Gwendyth. I saw them. They passed me on the stairs."

He leaped to his feet, grimacing with pain, and limped toward me.

"Which stairs? Why spoke you not of it at once?"

"They lead from the kitchen, a small spiral stair almost built over, where no one goes. . . ."

"I remember it," he said; and when I looked at him, surprised,

"Well, I once was a child here, too. What were you doing there?"

I hesitated to answer that.

"Come," he said, "it will be easier if you tell all you know."

"I had gone to the kitchen," I said finally, "for food. Well, that is the way we lived. And we lodged in a small room above. I heard men running and hid."

I gulped, remembering again that stealthy clink, those soft running feet, the hissed whispers.

"I marked them as they passed. They spoke Norman-French as you do, my lord."

"From among my men?" he said. "I think that impossible. How were they dressed? Saw you their faces? Who was at Sedgemont that night?"

He limped back and forth, the hounds padding beside him. "Who would dare?" he said again. "How looked they?"

"Armed," I told him, "with heavy cloaks drawn over their heads. And spurred for riding."

"We feasted in the Great Hall," he said, running over names aloud of guests, messengers, and envoys who had been there. When he came to Guy of Maneth's name, he stopped.

"Guy of Maneth," he repeated then. "But he rode out next morning. He and his men. And they are from the border, speaking as you do." He turned to me. "What do you know of this Lord of Maneth?"

"Little enough, my lord," I said truthfully. "He used to come to Cambray from time to time. He was, I think, a minor lord, vassal to another, not to Sedgemont. His son Gilbert was Talisin's age."

"You do not like him," he said sharply. "Your voice betrays you."

"He has a weasel look, my lord," I said at last, lamely, for I could not then put into words the dislike that seeing him had roused in me—dislike and unease. "His eyes are set too close. . . ."

He laughed at that as if relieved.

"By the rood, lady," he said, "if that is all, I shall not set great store by your likes or dislikes. It is not by a man's looks that he is judged. He seemed in good spirits when we feasted that night. He seemed concerned for you. And he has border men about him."

"Not all," I said. "They say, in the stables, that he gets his men wherever he can find them. And they say," I hesitated again, "that although in public he spoke fair, in private he was angry; that he shouted and raved. . . ."

Lord Raoul's face grew thoughtful.

"A man may lash out at his underlings for many faults," he said at last. "Maneth had no need to plot against Cambray or its heir."

He paused now, as if thinking, seemed to be about to speak again, limped from side to side, then said abruptly, "You spoke truth, Lady Ann. There must be plans made to secure Cambray. If war comes again, the king must be sure of the western marches. And war is coming, of that you may be convinced."

"I thought that now all was peaceful at last," I cried. "Is not Stephen accepted as king?"

He said, "Henry of Anjou is not about to sit peacefully and lose his hope of inheritance." He paced about. "A while ago, you asked what your life had to do with his. Lady Ann, let this be your first lesson in diplomacy. Anything that the great do has some effect on everyone. Henry of Anjou is as yet occupied in France, but he will not bide there long. When he has made himself secure in all the lands that he covets there, then will he turn his attention back to England. He was raised up here as a child. You should remember he knows England well. He will not let his mother's claim go begging."

"I did not know all this, my lord," I began timidly, when he broke in.

"Well, that is the advantage of a safe fortress at least— not even news can get in. By his father's death is he Count of Anjou. By war has he won the duchy of Normandy and the King of France has given him title to it. And if what is rumored comes true, the divorced queen of France, Eleanor of Aquitaine, will wed with him and bring with her all her vast possessions in southern France. Then will Henry of Anjou own more land in France than the French king himself. Then will he have time and money enough to come back to England."

"And do all men fear him so much, my lord?" I asked again, for, in truth, this was the first time I had thought of such things.

"Do not lions breed true?" he answered. "Even as a child, they say his mother brought him to watch condemned men die that he might grow used to blood. He has been bred up for a purpose. They are clever, those Angevins. When they are stronger than the French king, whom they despise, they will not make the same mistake, letting their vassals become too powerful for their control. And they are ruthless. I have seen for myself in France how his father, Geoffrey, has destroyed his own followers when it pleased him. The Angevins are noted for the way they will sack their own vassals' estates if they think it will enhance their power. Henry of Anjou has grown into the man that he promised as a boy. Having France, he will unleash a pack of war hounds when he comes back to England. He has wealth and power enough to buy the scum of Europe as his mercenaries... well, these be unfitting thoughts for maiden ears...."

"Nay, my lord," I protested, "but it strikes me strange that you and he both should be caught up betwixt France and England in your loyalties. Are you not of one place or the other? Could not France content him?"

He shrugged as if he had not thought of that before.

"It is the way," he said at last. "The lords of Sedgemont were counts in Sieux and Auterre long before we came to England. It is to our advantage, too. For I am returned to Sedgemont now to call up my feudal levies here upon the coming of Anjou. Then shall I go to France and wait upon my French knights there and raise money upon my lands for arms."

His easy roll of names and titles frightened me. I had not thought of him as so great a lord. But I persisted still.

"And Cambray?"

He paced about in his halting stride as he said, "I can do little now to free the passage of your revenues until I go there in person to put things in order. But it is a charge I shall take upon myself. More to the point is your safety here. You shall be well treated here at Sedgemont as is your right. Men to guard you, womenfolk to wait upon you . . ."

"I do not want womenfolk about me," I said. "One man to guard would suffice." And I thought suddenly, If he will agree, we can go on as before.

"There is one man, my lord," I said hesitatingly, "a groom of your stables. He would watch me well. His name is Giles. . . ."

Lord Raoul stared at me. "Yes," he said thoughtfully, "I have heard report of him also. But if you wish it . . ."

"Indeed I do."

"Then let him wash off the muck of the stable and dress as squire and attend you, with the Lady Mildred's permission."

"But I had not her in mind," I cried, dismayed. "I did not think to be locked up with her."

He laughed at that.

"I am sure not. But there are some things that she can do that I cannot, and she will certainly hold you safe until I return from France. You are growing, Lady Ann. Cambray will need more than a hoyden to rule it one day."

As my look grew sulky, he said, "Come, come, when I return, we shall go hunting in the forests of Sedgemont. It is overlong since I rode there. I hope you have left me some deer."

He was teasing me again.

"Have you not missed Sedgemont while you have been so long gone, my lord?" I asked him shyly.

But he was staring at the fire now, and his thoughts had gone far away.

"I think of it as you do," he said, "a place to live but not my home. That is best remembered in Normandy. One day, please God, we shall all be free to live in peace and travel on our own lands."

"When there is peace, will you come back to live in Sedgemont?"

He still stared at the flames. His eyes were green now and the silver-gold hair curled with the heat.

"I have had so much of camp and battle," he said, "to tell you truth, I have not thought overmuch what else I should do."

He suddenly turned to me, one of those abrupt movements that I was never prepared for.

"Why did you leap at me when you were a child?" he said. "I did but seek to help you free of your blindfold."

"I thought you were Talisin," I said at last. "I thought for a moment he had come back to me."

"I never met your brother," he said, "to my loss. But I shall always bear the mark of his sister on my arm. Look."

He thrust it out, laughing. I did not notice then the faint white lines on his hand; my eyes were drawn to the vivid scar that ran across his right wrist. He saw what I was looking at.

"Not that, God's death," he said. "That all but cost me my fighting arm, if not my life. Even you could not do that, Lady Ann. But have we leave to hope that your scars of Sedgemont will be less painful?"

"Indeed, my lord," I smiled at him at last, "you may at least hope so."

He stood aside then to let me pass.

"When you smile," he said, "you almost look as I imagined you."

And so he had the last and better word after all.

3

NE THING I DID AFTER LEAVING HIM, knowing that once Lady Mildred was in charge, such escapades would be difficult, I sought out Giles in the stable. The guards let me pass easily enough from Lord Raoul's quarters and I had no difficulty finding Giles. He was grooming a tall, rangy black stallion that started and shied at any sudden noise.

"Wild it is," Giles said good-naturedly, standing on tiptoe to reach its head, "mad tempered, worse than your Cambray gray you're so fond of."

I watched him affectionately. I had wanted to tell Giles of his good fortune myself. For it was good fortune and so I told him, tactfully, for no one likes to know that his menial position is clear to everyone. But from a place where he would be bound for the rest of his life, from which he could never have risen anywhere, a nonfree man, he had, by one stroke, moved to squire's rank, halfway even to that of knight, the highest of all. Even a king has to be a knight first. It was advancement he could never have expected, and how great a difference it would make, he must know better than I. But like many things, what seems done for good often turns out for ill. Although I swear that day none of us thought so far ahead.

Giles was stunned by the news. "It cannot be," he kept saying, collapsing to the straw under the forefeet of the great horse, which, in the contrary way of bad-tempered things, beasts as well as men, took no more notice of him than of a fly, although if I had done the same it would have broken me with its hooves.

"It cannot be, Ann, I'm not sure it's right." He was more agitated than I had ever known him, running over in his mind all the changes—leaving of a way of life, habits, and customs that were not only his own but had been the way of his folk for generations.

"A groomsman is a groomsman," he said despondently, yet at the same time eagerly, as if hoping I could convince him. "I know horses, no one better. But I don't like them much. And as for fighting—I'm good with a dagger. I'd be as clumsy as you with a sword. . . ."

It says much for our friendship that I did not clout him for that unfortunate remark, but instead worked to convince him. It was true he was not a horseman, a rider I mean, but, "Look," I told him, "how you lie sprawled beneath that brute's feet. No one else I know would dare that. The other things you can learn. And, Giles, we'll not be parted. We shall see each other all the time. We can still ride together. And we can talk."

"Ann," he said soberly, "but it will be different. Better for us, I think, if I stay where I am and tend your horses all my life."

He searched for words to explain what I think he foresaw more clearly than I, how great the difference between us would be. As stable boy and hoyden, to use Lord Raoul's word, we had run together, free enough, but as lady and squire there would be an immeasurable gap between us. Perhaps, being older and a man, he sensed it; or perhaps, because he loved me, he resented it. But I knew so little then of love or all its subtleties. I could think only how happy I would be to have him still as a friend, still converse with him sometimes, and I let my happiness convince him.

When we had settled these affairs to our mutual satisfaction, at my request he went to find the one man who had called out in the Great Hall that night, the only one who had answered the Cambray battle cry. I had been curious to know who he was. His name was Dylan, a small dark man, like many from the borderlands; I did not remember him well, yet he had been one of the escort who had ridden with me from Cambray those years ago, one of some dozen of them, and only he had survived to come back.

When he and Giles returned, I squatted down, as in the old days, upon a bale of hay, eager to question him. I took no notice of the surliness with which he greeted me at first. Border people are like that, cautious and leery, not wearing their charm on their sleeves for all to see, like some.

Bit by bit, I drew out from him what I wanted to know, and he warmed to the task as a soldier does when he speaks of old battles. I will not tell you now all he said. Sufficient that he and the other men of Cambray had seen war enough, and those who had died had died like men, for all their ill-fashioned gear and ways. Lord Raoul could have found no fault with them, the men my father had trained. But it saddened and angered me to think how many were gone who had survived all the hard years my father had given them when he had first built Cambray and pushed the Celts back from the surrounding lands. And at Cambray itself, Dylan said, there were few fighting men left, some of them having come with me, others scattered; only a handful of the house guard remained.

"But that, too, will change," he said, "for there is talk of our return there soon. But, look you, Lady Ann, such fighting we have never seen, harder than any in your father Lord Falk's day. There is nothing worse than civil war, friend against friend, brother against brother, so you know not who is friend or foe. Please God, say I, it be ended with this truce." And he took a great pull on the flagon of ale that Giles had thoughtfully given him, as if to drown his memories.

"And Lord Raoul?" I had been longing to ask. "What sort of man is he?"

"A bonny fighter," said Dylan, shattering my hopes of hearing ill of him, "leads well, asks nothing that he won't do himself. Now I remember at the second battle of Lincoln, a slash near took off his right arm. But he learned to fight as well with the left: Two-Handed Raoul, they named him, for that, and because with all the women about him, he had both arms full. . . ."

His laughter, showing blackened teeth, choked off into silence at Giles's reproving nudge. He set down the ale pot and wiped his mouth with the back of his hand.

"Ah, well, but he is young," he said lamely, "and wears wounds as a sign of valor. He got a spear point through the thigh at Worcester a month gone and yet continued with the seige even when he could not walk."

"Does he have no sense then?" I asked, hoping to spot a weakness.

"Nay, plenty," Dylan said, settling down, glad to play the soldier's favorite pastime of gossiping of his generals. "They say he tried to prevent Prince Eustace, the king's son, from running amok three years ago. The prince was all for burning and harrying the south. 'Not so,' said Lord Raoul, 'I've seen the like of that too much in Normandy. We'll have no such Angevin work here.' Spoke out sharply for I heard it myself. They say the king thinks highly of him for all that he is young. He is a good man among men, I know that well enough."

"And Lord Guy of Maneth?"

"Ah, that's another kettle of fish. Such men be hard to gauge," he said, echoing Lord Raoul's own words. "I'd be not overeager to trust him."

"Where gets he all his power?"

The old soldier shrugged. "He was vassal to the Earl of Gloucester. After the earl's death, who kept the underlings in check? He used to claim he was the equal to Lord Falk, your father, having not a quarter of Lord Falk's land or standing, but he was often underfoot at Cambray, thrusting forward with friendship."

"And his men, who follow him?"

Dylan shrugged again, and repeated what Giles and I had already heard. "He brings into his service many oddities, scraped from where he can get them. But his castle of Maneth, north of Cambray, lies along the western border, too. He has border men at his command, sod them. And Norman French when he can scrounge them."

"Then Maneth castle will be of importance to the king if there be another war?"

"Perhaps," Dylan said shrewdly, "for who can trust a man like that, jumped up like an ill-grown weed? Yet I'll swear to this, Lord Raoul is Stephen's man. Blood oath he gave upon a battlefield and he's not one to turn his back upon an oath so sworn. I'd not give a broken arrow for any of the rest. If Henry offers them enough, they'll turn to him, and the king can whistle in the wind. But for all that, Maneth castle will not hold the key to the west. Cambray will. Mark my words, lady, you will be needed at Cambray in the end."

"I?" I said, surprised. "Why?"

"Have you not thought of it? You are the last of your name. If there would be anyone the Celts would heed it would be Ann of Cambray. And we have all been gone too long, my lady."

"I know," I said sadly, for had I not said the same things to Lord Raoul myself to provoke him. And now this dour soldier said as much to me.

"But Lord Raoul holds me as his ward."

"Well, well," he said, his dark eyes quick and assessing, "you have grown much, Lady Ann, from the little wench we left. One day, you will see, you will return to Cambray. Then glad shall I be to your service or your lord husband's."

"It may be so," I said, rising, trying to brush off the straw from my skirts, not liking the implications of his words, although I had time to reflect on them in the months that followed. None of us could have known then by what strange paths that day at last would come.

That was my last chance of liberty. As I had guessed, Lady Mildred kept me close, and although Giles stood armed at the door, I had small chance to speak to him alone, and he must often have been bored, on guard at the women's bower with only their chatter to amuse him. As he had intended, Lord Raoul left abruptly, taking advantage of change in wind and weather to hope for quick passage to France from a southern port. The summer wound on slowly. News came a little more readily now, for most of Lord Raoul's men remained behind at Sedgemont with Sir Brian in charge. People came and went as I presume they had done before the wars began; it seemed a pleasant sort of existence, and even the harvest promised well; the great fields around Sedgemont were heavy with grain. At times, travelers came to spend the night and tell us of doings elsewhere. In this way we heard of the death of the Queen of England. They say she had been greatly loved and the king grieved for her heartily. And these journeyers brought us tales of the marriage, as Raoul had predicted, of the onetime Queen of France, Eleanor of Aquitaine, to Henry of Anjou; it was a scandal of the greatest kind, despite the fact that she brought him so much wealth, as Lord Raoul had said, as to make him the most powerful man in France.

The Lady Mildred told us as much of the story as she saw fit, savoring the scandal, I think, from the safety of her own virtue, how this Eleanor had gone on holy war with the King of France but been so unwifely as to have refused to bed with him, even when, upon their return, the pope himself had placed them both therein and reblessed their marriage. But little good that had done the godless lady, who had slipped from the court at Paris and fled back to her own lands, there to wait the coming of the young Lord of Anjou as her next husband. This tale, if the Lady Mildred had but known it, only served to inflame a hope of mine, growing daily. For perhaps, I thought, I too could find means to escape from Sedgemont, although the lands I fled to were nothing compared with the broad acres of Aquitaine and Provence. But every day the Lady Mildred had some story of good and evil to keep us in our place and make us reflect what would be our fate if we did not learn to behave modestly, bow down meekly, submit to men's will. Like Gwendyth, she was appalled at my choice of pastimes and companions. Unlike Gwendyth, she had the power, she and Sir Brian both, to reform me at her pleasure. I began to realize more than ever that the life of a lady was not what I had in mind at all.

It was several months later when I sat one afternoon in the solar at Sedgemont, the large upper hall above the main one where we feasted. Usually this would have been occupied by the lord of the castle and his family, but Lord Raoul kept bachelor quarters elsewhere. There were more ladies than hitherto, women who had returned with their husbands or fathers, the wives and daughters of Lord Raoul's own knights or of his nearby vassals. I still had scant liking for any of them, a gaggle of geese I thought, pecking and scratching at one another. The days had dragged slowly by, although the Lady Mildred kept us busy from dawn to dusk about women's tasks. But I took unkindly to such work—even now, you have noticed it—well, there are some things that I learned from her that made sense, and high or low, all women see to them: the ordering of the food, the setting of the table, be it only crusts of bread, the seeing to the use of meat and drink so that the first-come stores are taken first, the latest kept in clean bins and casks, safe from vermin—that makes sense. A woman needs such knowledge just as a man must know how to oversee his stalls and byres and put his own tools and weapons in order. Even if there be servants and serfs to do such things, the mistress and master of the house need learn them first so that they know when they are well served. The daily tour of inspection of the crofts and storerooms at Sedgemont was a triumph of efficiency. We followed in the lady's train as she swept from one place to another, attended by Sir Brian, who

kept the keys and opened the doors for her. Models of neatness
were these stores, and wherever she passed, skirt dragging over
the floor without fear of rubbish or dirt, the menials made
great show of effort, sweeping and strewing the halls with
fresh rushes daily, scouring the trestle tables before they were
stacked away until the next meal, cleaning the plate and pewter
and setting it in place.

"Chaos and dirt bring all to confusion," she was fond of
saying. "A castle stocked is that much safer from attack."

But the other chores, those I hated. Mountains of mending,
sewing, the making of new garments for the folk who worked
within the castle walls, from serfs to lords, that kept her most
occupied and gave me most labor. Carding of the wool we
learned, and dyeing it and weaving it, and cutting it, and
sewing it... and finally, for the higher folk, embroidering it.
This last work she reserved for herself and her old women,
that Lord Raoul's clothes should be well adorned, although it
seemed to me I seldom saw him wear finery now. But what
miles of seams she left for us to finish. Even my dresses I
learned to stitch, those I had once worn having grown so tight
that I had either to make new or go indecent. And I had sworn
to take nothing from the coffers of Sedgemont! Yet, to speak
fair, the Lady Mildred was generous to us all, if we but merited
it by hard work, and although the colors and shades she chose
were often more suitable for an older man like Sir Brian, she
labored long to bedeck Lord Raoul and his guard as befitted
their high station. Yes, I know the men at Cambray do not
now complain too loud in my hearing of my deficiencies and
I have trained women to please them. But I take little part in
these sewing rites. Though you must admit that I have learned
from the lady what is due in other things.

Embroidery was the Lady Mildred's joy. She told us often,
at least once a day, how she had been trained at the Norman
court of the Norman dukes in the tradition of the duchess
whose husband had become the first Norman king of England.

The great banner that the duchess and her women had stitched in honor of the Norman victory must be a marvel of the world, to hear her talk of it. And now she sought to make one similar here for the lords of Sedgemont, where for seven years she and her women had sat and sewed it, panel after panel, a saga of Sedgemont history.

This afternoon, I sat with my segment stretched upon a frame, and all the puckered stitches caught awry whilst I daydreamed with my hands upon my lap.

"You tug and fret at it," the Lady Mildred said at last, taking it from me with her small white hands, which could undo the worst of tangles. "You rush at the work not caring for it." And she rapped my knuckles with the points of her small gilt scissors until I was hard put not to stick my fingers in my mouth.

"You must go slowly," she repeated, "small stitches, so that the back is as fair as the front."

I swallowed logical reply. For if this mighty work was to be hung upon a wall, where it hangs today, who would ever see the back? But the part that I was set to stitch, with its red bird cobbled in haste to hide the pinpricks of blood, was never finished.

"See how the colors clash." Another rap upon the fingers. "And the design is out of trim. You have not even matched it with your neighbor." The girl who sat next to me gave me a glance, of sympathy or scorn I could not be sure. I wound my hands into my skirts and bade myself be still. Again a rap.

"You will never learn if you pay no heed. You should have begun such work years ago. You have much to learn if you would control your own household."

There was a giggle at that. The catching of a husband, and the arts to acquire him, was something the Lady Mildred also spoke frequently about, although I sometimes felt she marked me out for the greatest share.

"No man will wed a slovenly wench," she said, "who cannot braid her hair without knots and whose dress is often unlaced." And she flicked her sharp scornful stare about me, where I sat. I might even then have erupted into rage, as I had tried before, only to have Sir Brian reprimand me before them— which was worst of all—had not there been a disturbance at the door. We all turned our heads willingly, for seldom anyone came to the women's quarters, save Sir Brian, and unless there was some guest of special note, we never even dined in the Great Hall. It was one of Lord Raoul's men, wearing his gold and red surcoat thrown over his chain mail in the new fashion. A tall fellow he was, with yellow hair, blushing and grinning sheepishly.

"I bring greetings," he said, "to the Lady Mildred from my lord and news of his return from France."

We all murmured at that, the girl beside me most of all. She was watching the young man with her heart in her eyes.

"And purposes to stay through the autumn months, God willing."

The Lady Mildred rose to accept his greetings, staring down poor Cecile, next to me, into silence. I thought crossly that she should have been married to Lord Raoul himself. He deserved such a shrew as wife. And she knew all the courtesies befitting such high state. No doubt she told Sir Brian so every day. It was a pity that he had no lands of his own where she could perch and crow to her heart's content.

"And to the Lady Ann, Lord Raoul sends special messages."

That was a surprise. No one had sent me greetings before; the Lady Mildred's fingers jammed into my ribs, but she need not have concerned herself. I knew how to respond in proper form and sent a flashing smile with it, to the fellow's distress, for he turned more crimson than before.

"Lord Raoul bids you, that is you ladies all, that is . . ." he floundered the more beneath our smiles, "to the first hunt of the season. Until then, he lodges with his southern vassals. But he bids you prepare. Tomorrow that is, tomorrow prepare. And for a feast that same night."

We smiled at him again and he turned and fled, leaving the bower ahum with excitement. Lady Mildred looked grave. I knew she could not ride herself but would not dare forbid it when Lord Raoul himself had invited us.

Beside me, Cecile, who had looked at me askance before and who had been like to run toward the tall messenger, whispered, "What luck for you, Lady Ann. What shall you wear? Pray that the weather holds. He who brought the news, Geoffrey, is my betrothed. Now he returns, perhaps we shall be wed. What shall you ride? My father will give me one of the horses he took as booty this past year."

I bit my lip in vexation. Her father was one of the castle guards. Her betrothed was returned to Sedgemont. But I had nothing to wear and nothing to ride, although the lack of the one was more troubling than the other.

"She can use the green gown we gave her," the Lady Mildred said, hearing the murmurs, setting her seal of approval in her own way. "And you, Mistress Cecile, should think of other things, less worldly. As for horses, there are plenty, I have no doubt, fit for a woman, in the stables here. So must we all take what God offers us, not puffing ourselves up with sloth and pride."

"Pooh," Cecile whispered, her eyes flashing, "she would have us all on donkeys or mules. If Geoffrey and Lord Raoul are here, you will see a great gathering. That green is not becoming. Wear your best."

"I have no other," I said absentmindedly, for I was already thinking of something else; despite myself, plans had leaped ahead. But I needed Giles's help.

She tutted in sympathy. "I will see what I can lend you," she said. I did not know then that it was an offer of friendship, one of the first I had ever received.

"All the castle guard will be there, and Lord Raoul's men. It will be more excitement than we have known these past weeks. How lucky that you were asked, Lady Ann."

But while the others talked about their luck, even Lady Mildred unable to hold them quiet under such news, I let my thoughts run freely.

When there was a lull, I took advantage of it to draw Giles aside and explain to him what I wanted him to do. His face paled at the thought.

"'Tis not fitting, my lady," he said, "not wise nor safe."

"But you will do it, Giles," I said. "God's wounds, am I to be always cloistered like a child? Leave off your babbling, or I will do it all without you. And I can manage, as well you know. I will not have them mock me that I cannot have even a horse to my name."

"I do not think they mock you, Lady Ann," he said. But his eyes were troubled. He did not like to be laughed at either. Both he and I had had our full share of it these past months as we tried to fit into a new pattern of living. Both of us had had much to learn that went against our old ideas. So I cajoled and wheedled until I knew he would agree. Then was I able to rest happy. For all of us, and especially Giles and I, thrilled at the expectation of a hunt. Yet, I must tell you, when I saw one it did not appeal to me so much as I had thought. For us, hunting had always meant a search for food. There was the point of it. The Normans hunt for pastime, for pleasure, and there is never end to their sport. For that purpose do they set aside these miles of woodland for private use, and all their joy comes from the killing.

The day dawned fair as those autumn days do, the sun as bright as mid-July, a faint breeze to dry the dew, the scent clear. When I came to the great inner courtyard, the hunt was already gathered. Lord Raoul and his guards were mounted, he on that black beast that Giles had tried to groom, many of his chiefest nobles about him. No doubt, he was using this as a way to woo them to his plans, but I thought it too fair a day to be thinking of war and diplomacy. I watched Lord Raoul as his horse moved skittishly at the center of his entourage. It was the first time I had seen him surrounded by his court since the day in the garden when we were children playing together. I noted how even Cecile pushed forward with Geoffrey beside her. I did not care to join them. It was enough that Lord Raoul had remembered his promise and sent me word. Now I would show him what Cambray and I could do.

The horse the Lady Mildred had chosen for me was a pony, so fat and small I daresay it could not have cantered a length. I said not a word as Giles helped me mount, although I could almost have straddled it from the ground. Half-puzzled, half-amused, Giles mounted his own bay that Lord Raoul had given him. He rode better than he had a year ago, but then he had practiced in the meanwhile as I had not. We waited in the shadow of the wall as the rest of the hunt went across the drawbridge toward the forest. A brave sight they made in their finery and plumes, the horses leaping, the peasants shouting as they passed. When they were out of sight, Giles and I urged our own beasts as fast as we could to the meadow close to the river's edge. He had kept his word, too. There grazed my gray horse cropping grass. An old saddle was slung upon its back, and it was already bridled. But when I stood beside it, and measured its height, and thought again how it, too, had been unused to riding these last months, my heart almost quailed. Yet I pulled up my skirts, Cecile's skirts rather, and beckoned Giles to help me up. Finally we got the beast to stand still so that he could swing me high upon its back. I had always ridden bareback before, but this was a knight's saddle, high in the front so that it would take a lance to knock you out of it. I rode astride and Giles helped me pull my skirts down about my knees, his face still mournful with doubt.

"Good cheer," I told him. "If I am in at the kill you shall have the credit."

"And if you fall?"

"No one will blame you, and I requite you here of my death." I laughed at him. "This will be better sport than you or I have

ever known. Go and enjoy it. Tell them the truth if they ask,
that I could not keep up with you on Lady Mildred's pet, so
found one more to my liking. And when you come to Cambray
you shall have a gray horse of your own."

He released the reins. I let the horse plunge forward. At
first I was frightened. I had forgotten how fast it could run,
and it had certainly forgotten me. And I had never let it go
full tilt like this, only once, when it had saved us from the
men in the clearing. But gradually confidence came back, and
it was certainly easier to sit in the saddle than bareback.

The hunt was far ahead now and I could hear the huntsmen's
horns along the distant rides. But I knew the forest better than
most who were riding there, and once I could quiet the horse
enough, I steered it in a circle so that, guessing from wind
and weather, I would come across them which way they must
go to follow the game. For all that was said and done afterward,
that ride was one of the memories of my life. I have said before
that I felt strange kinship when I rode, as if my father and
Cambray and I were one, and I thought of my brother's proph-
ecy that one day I should ride as well as they had ever done.
So that when the hounds drove the quarry to bay, although I
could not see what game we chased, at least I was there abreast
with it, although farther to one side than the others. And
without hesitation, I thrust my horse through the thickets that
separated us from the main hunt, right into the middle of the
milling, yelping pack. They had trapped some animal in the
bushes at the end of a small open space. I recognized the place
as one Giles and I had often passed but avoided, for it backed
into some rocks at one end, thus shutting off escape. I knew
at once what must be done. The cornered animal had gone in
under the rocks and must be driven out for the men to kill
cleanly before the hounds tore it apart. I hauled at the reins,
bringing the gray horse almost to its haunches before it would
stop, shouting the while to the beaters who were on foot nearby
to come and help me. The gray horse reared and shook but I

forced it to my will. A huntsman came running toward us from the main ride, but although I waited for him to come to lift me down, he stopped and would not approach closer. What with the hounds' baying and my horse's plunging, I could not make him hear me, nor could I hear what he said. Finally, in desperation that he would not do my bidding, I knotted my dress together, let go the reins, and threw myself to the ground. It was a long fall but I landed on my feet, without harm. I meant to keep hold of the reins, of course, but at the last moment had feared to pull the horse on me, so that now I had no way to catch it again, and even if I had, I could not have mounted without help, for it went thrashing past me to one side. I called again to the huntsman and walked slowly toward the outcrop of rocks. The man did not move from the shelter of the trees but I heard his shouts more clearly now. "Mount, mount," as if any fool could not see that was impossible even if I had wanted to. So I smiled at him and waved to bring him closer. And then, God help us, I saw why he had not moved and why the horse was plunging so and why the hounds milled and screamed underfoot. It was no deer or hare that we had trapped under the rocks, but a boar, a huge wild boar with tusks already stained red and small evil eyes that darted looks about to find where next to turn.

I stood alone, in full view, my skirts bundled to my knees and the trees a score of yards away. It was suddenly very quiet in the glade there then. The sun beat off the rocks, even the hounds seemed to halt their baying, and the gray horse at last stood calm. The animal under the rocks was still also, tossing its head so I could smell its fetid breath and for a moment know the paralyzing fear of death. Then the hounds bayed again, and the boar shook at them as if tossing gnats and scraped its tusks upon the ground. Behind me came the thud of other hooves, shouts, the sound of running feet. But I could not take my eyes from this thing that moved half in the shadows, gathering its strength to charge. And then, as I waited, suddenly I heard Lord Raoul's voice at my back; his arm, half-round me, was heaving me behind him. In one hand he held a wooden stave with which beaters knock down bracken to flush the game.

"Feel for my knife," he whispered, "slowly. For your life, make no sudden move."

He stood in front of me, his body edging before mine, as we backed toward the trees, facing the boar. And it was coming full into the sunlight now, a great misshapen thing, its head lifted restlessly. But we were moving too. Lord Raoul's dagger lay within my grasp. I pulled it gently, felt it catch, and heard his grunt of exasperation. Then it was free, and I slid it into his left hand.

We had moved back again, but the boar had kept pace, tracking us with its half-closed eyes. Hands about his waist, guiding him backward, I could go faster now. Three steps would bring us into the shelter of the trees. But it was too late. The jerkin on his back was wet with sweat and the ends of his hair curled with it. Our hearts thudded as one.

"My lord," I whispered, "put the stave here against the tree root. I will try to hold it as he runs upon it."

There was no time for more. I felt him nod and tense at the same time. For the boar had come clear out; the hounds closed about it but it thrust them aside in a welter of blood. Now it was upon us, foam flying, tusks spread. I felt Raoul bend, the flimsy stick in his hand thrust upward. My hands were about it, too—we held it loosely so it would run full tilt. Raoul had leaped to one side. The great mouth and hot breath and tusks were on me. The wooden stave sunk deep into its chest so that gouts of blood flared up. The butt of the wood held firm against the tree. Then my hands were torn off. Men rushed to jerk me aside. I saw a long knife flash once, twice. There were other men, dogs snarling, more blood, and the sun full in my eyes.

"A kill, a kill, my lord," they were all shouting. The clearing was suddenly full of horses and people. Under a tree, a great bulk jerked and heaved but could not rise.

"By the rood, lady," Lord Raoul said, pleasantly enough, although his breath came in great gasps and his face was pale. "You held that reed like a huntsman born. I drink to your health."

He was smiling, his face streaked with sweat and dirt, but his eyes were cold, unsmiling.

"God's wounds, wench," he glinted at me, so none could hear. "What fool's trick is this?"

I dropped him a curtsy with trembling limbs that would scarce let me stand.

"My thanks to your lordship," I said. "I did but ride with you as you bade."

"We must hunt these woods more often," he was saying. To me, "Who set you on such a steed? Who bade you ride so far ahead?"

"It was my pleasure, my lord," I said, still aloud.

"Will you seek death before them all?" he said to me. "Keep your voice down. What folly made you take such risks?"

"I did but take what is my own," I said, with a coolness I was far from feeling.

"Your own!" he said, his voice breaking with rage. He moved closer, wiping his sleeve across his face so that words came muffled. "Then for your life, which you hold so cheap, do you mount another horse to ride back with me. I will take that one, with or without your leave."

He lifted up the wine they had given him and faced the others.

"Ride on," he said. "The Lady Ann wearies of the sport. Change me that horse there, ho. Thank God that although she is slow at drawing sword, she can pluck forth dagger in haste."

There was a flurry of laughter, easing the tension as he doubtless intended. One of his men helped me to another horse, the gray was brought round, and Lord Raoul swung himself upon it. I marked how it stood for him as I could never make it. And saw for the first time the gash from his hip to his knee, running red.

He raised one hand in salute, gathered up his reins and mine with the other, and urged us out of the clearing, taking the fastest way back to Sedgemont. Behind us his guard scrambled for their own horses. The rest of the hunt waited behind us, chattering and curious.

"I can ride without help, my lord," I said furiously, the more so that I was not sure I could, for I still trembled so. I was forced to hang on to the saddle, or be bounced out of it. Presently, when the castle came into view and we entered the home meadows, he dropped back to a walk and I could catch my breath. Only then did I venture to say what was most on my mind, although it galled to acknowledge it.

"I have not thanked you, my lord, for my life."

"Thank me not," he snarled. "Save the thanks that I did not give way to my first impulse and let you be run through. Then would I be rid of much trouble."

"You speak unjustly, my lord," I said. "What have I done so amiss? I did but ride my horse. And if you had given me word what game we hunted, I should have kept well out of its way."

"Or look to be thrust through with a thistle," he snarled again. "Or be trampled at a fence or drowned at a ditch. Ill luck favors you, lady. Did you not revile me for being but indifferent keeper of my ward? Did not I set the squire of your own choosing to keep you safe? Where was he to let you run abroad? And all the vassals of Sedgemont there to take note."

I was silent. Giles had said much the same.

"A plaything was the pony of the Lady Mildred's," I said at last. "I merit better than that."

"Yet such you will ride before you hunt with me again," he roared.

We clattered under the portcullis, his men close behind him. The watch sprang to attention as he hurled himself from his saddle, jerking me off as roughly.

"Save your excuses," he said, forcing me to run beside him, his hand hard on my wrist. We passed the Lady Mildred hastening down from the castle walls where she had gone to watch the hunt, but he waved her aside, snarling at his men as he went.

"My lord," I gasped, "you will harm your leg if you walk so fast."

"I have endured worse than that," he said, although he lied, for it was the leg that he had hurt before and that wound must have been scarce healed.

I thought desperately then of ways to curb his temper. Even my father had never been so angry as this.

He crashed into his room, thrusting aside the door with his shoulder. The pages who had been crouched before the fire scrambled to their feet as if fearing he would boot them from his path.

"Who gave you leave?" he said again. "Who helped you?"

"I myself."

"You could neither catch nor saddle such a brute. Who?"

I was silent then, for the first time fearful for Giles.

But he had already remembered him, before I had. We waited without speaking, while the men below found Giles and brought him up, white-faced himself, hands bound together. They thrust him into the room so that the three of us stood apart, Lord Raoul, Giles, and myself, while the pages cowered in a corner.

"Was this the man who helped you?" he asked. I was silent again.

"Did you do the Lady Ann's bidding?" he asked Giles.

I suddenly saw the trap that I had made for him. "It was not his fault," I cried desperately. "He only did what I asked."

"I took you from the stable," Lord Raoul said, ignoring me. "I gave you post as squire. Your duties were not heavy but clear. Think you that you have fulfilled them?"

"It was not his fault," I said again. But both men ignored me.

"Nay, my lord."

Lord Raoul waved him toward his men. "Then take him outside and thrash him," he said coldly. "You deserve worse."

I threw myself toward Giles, not caring now what they thought or who heard. "You may not, you dare not," I cried. "It was my fault, I tell you."

"Lady Ann," said Giles, forced to speak although nothing would have made him plead on his own behalf, "I beg you. I knew the danger. I knew it wrong."

Lord Raoul had turned away, his face set. Once more he gestured, and although I clung tightly, they put me aside, gently enough, and hustled Giles toward the stair. Then did I turn and run at Lord Raoul himself.

"You cannot," I screamed. "It is unfair to an innocent man."

"I do not hold him innocent," he said, "nor does he himself."

"Why not punish me," I cried, "if so great a wrongdoing it is? Punish me, if it please you."

"It would please me well enough," he said. "If you behave like a child, you must be treated like one. But I am not your father to whip you as he ought these years ago."

"I will make a bargain with you," I cried as passionately. "Spare Giles and whip me. See, I am not afraid."

I forced him to look at me, challenge and rage like weapons between us. Even the men watched open-mouthed. Fine tales they would tell this time, but I cared nothing for that. Even as he made signs for them to go, which they did reluctantly, I have no doubt, I shook the sleeves of Cecile's gown from my shoulders so that the bodice hung to the waist. Then with a great breath, I tore the stuff of my shift so that it too came undone and my back and neck were bare.

My hair came untied; I gathered it before, and with head bowed turned my back on him.

I heard him breathing heavily, breath of pain and anger. I

saw, under the cloud of hair, his hands fumble with his sword belt, until it swung free and I heard it snap in his hands. I felt his arm rise, heard the whistle of leather, and braced myself for the blow. The buckle crashed upon the wall behind me.

I spun round and looked at him. He was staring at it and at his hands.

"No, Lady Ann," he said, and his voice was suddenly calm. "I have never yet beat woman, although you have made me come close to it, near enough to have found pleasure in it. Had hurt come to you, God forbid, any kind of death, you cannot know the mischief it would cause. If you care not for your own safety, think of that."

"And Giles," I said, "what of Giles?"

He shrugged.

"I pity the fellow," he said, "on my oath, I pity him. But he did not speak against the sentence. It is already done, easier, I think, than I would have done with you."

"It can't be so," I said, stunned with disbelief. "We made a bargain. . . ."

"Not on my side," he said, suddenly smiling. "God's teeth, I made not one. But he has felt worse, I warrant you. They will not kill him."

His laughter made me lose what little restraint I had left. As I tell it, it seems mad that I should have thought to overthrow him, yet I sprang at him with that intent. Crying, screaming, what words I care not to repeat, I clawed at him, beating at him with all my strength. He tried to fend me off, but his leg buckled and we fell to the ground, he rolling underneath with a grunt of pain, I on top, scratching and tearing while I called him all the names that are vile in Celt and Norman-French. So we rolled on the floor, my legs locked around his, heels drumming in his side, oblivious of dirt and blood, bare flesh to flesh. Then, as abruptly, it was over. He straddled my body, pinning my arms to my sides, kneeling on my hair to keep me still.

"God's wounds, girl," he gasped, but the coldness had gone from his voice; he might almost have been laughing again, "but you fight like a wildcat still. Perhaps it is no matter you are so slow with sword and knife. You would tear a man's heart out. Leave over. I am too lame to go wrestling with a half-naked maid."

His words made me aware of what I must look like, breasts naked, arms naked, clothes rucked around me.

"God's wounds," I swore myself, the words out before I could stop them, "the Lady Mildred will have my blood for this."

He did laugh then, easing himself upon his back.

"If she cannot control you," he said almost to himself, "who am I to try? Such a devil needs a church to whip it forth."

I took the ends of the cloth and tied them into a knot. Poor Cecile would never recognize her dress again, I thought, as I forced my arms back into the sleeves. The rips perhaps I could mend, but the bloodstains would never go away.

"God's wounds," I swore again, "she'll make me rue this."

"Then that will be punishment enough, I think," he said. "See, Lady Ann, how we seem to maul each other when we meet. We shall hack each other apart before we're done. Let us agree to speak no more of this. Giles, your squire, will smart for a while, but less, I wager, than I do. And he still shall be your squire, although I could send him back where he came from. He also will have learned a lesson, I think."

I swallowed my pride at that "also." For it was true, he could have had Giles killed for disobedience.

"And you must deal with the Lady Mildred as best you can. But remember, she has long been chatelaine, since I was a child, and Sir Brian was my grandfather's oldest retainer here at Sedgemont. Do not expect me to protect you against them. However," as I turned to protest, "you are not forbidden our Hall. I expect your presence, nay, will command it. And when we ride out again, you shall stay where I can see you."

He was laughing at me, I knew, yet I could not fault what he had said.

I scrambled to my feet, hair flying but more presentable. "Yes, my liege lord," I said and dropped him a curtsy.

"I have told you before," he said, "mock servility does not please me. Use your wits. I cannot rise unless you give me a hand, for this scratch has stiffened. You will not be so churlish as to refuse."

I stretched out my hand gingerly, not sure what trick he meant, but he merely grasped it and, with the help of a chair, pulled himself upright. I could see the half-healed scar that this new gash cut through.

"My lord," I said, "I have some knowledge of healing. That cut should be seen to. A wild beast is unclean."

"Have you now," he mocked me, seating himself in the chair, stretching his leg carefully. "Hensbane you speak of, no doubt, rubbed in tenderly to make it fester. Or salt perhaps to make it burn."

I refused to rise to his baiting.

"Our people have understanding of herbs and plants. Ask anyone. Gwendyth was well loved because of it. And I have watched her often enough. You should steep soothing herbs that will draw the poisons out and make it easier for you to move, so you do not limp for days, or months, as you did last time."

That was a shrewd remark. I could see him digesting it.

"And you should not move now until the bleeding halts."

He eased himself into the chair, eyeing me curiously. Yet he looked as disreputable as I did, with his torn and bloodied clothes. Any peasant among his huntsmen would have been better dressed.

He said at last, "Well, try then. I yield me to your care, lady. There be salves aplenty in the coffers yonder, although what leeches do with them is beyond my understanding. He who tended your arm must count you the first success in many months."

I stifled a smile. Gwendyth would have said the same, yet

the man had spoken on my behalf and I should speak him well in turn.

"I will say this for you, Lady Ann," Lord Raoul was adding, as I turned to seek the things I needed, "for all that things go awry when you are near, you are a good comrade to have at one's back. I may have saved your life, lady, but you helped at least save mine. Half the women I know would have swooned at the sight; the other half would never have got close enough to see it in the first place. . . ."

His half-compliments and jests unnerved me. I had never known anyone who spoke with such a mixture of mockery and sense. I ignored him, moved to the fire where I set water to boil, took one of his fine shirts—I recognized the Lady Mildred's work before I tore it with my teeth—and set it to soak. There were dried herbs in plenty, although none as fresh as Gwendyth would have used, but I put all I could to steep, and before he could complain, slapped cloth and herbs as hot as could be borne upon the open wound. He gave a cry like a scalded cat.

"Judas," he shouted, "do you think to boil me alive!"

But I forced him back into the chair.

"It will draw what poisons are left," I said primly. "It may hurt now, but it will take the pain out in time. Let it lie until it cools, then get your pages to heat more."

"Of a certainty," he said, "such treatment takes fiendish thought. And now, lady, look to your own repairs. Else scandal will be a-brewing as well."

His gesture to my torn bodice and skirts angered me.

"I can fend for myself," I said waspishly. "And if you would listen to me, there would be no trouble as you term it. Give me leave to go back to Cambray. . . ."

"That so fills your mind," he said, almost curiously. "That is all you want?"

"You went back to France," I said, "to Normandy, to Sieux, which you count as home."

"And found it not to my liking," he said abruptly, his mood

changing. His eyes darkened; he shouted to his pages who still skulked nervously outside.

"We cannot have all we want," he said, dismissing me suddenly. "In good time, as God wills, you may yet see Cambray."

"As God wills, or you," I retorted unwisely. "Take castles, revenues, lands, but let me at least breathe fresh air again, western air, that is."

"When you are angry," he said, "you are like a wet hen, all froth and feathers. Mind your speech, lady."

"And you yours," I snapped back. "You curse as freely as a peddler at a fair, although less skillfully. I see little to choose between your tempers and mine, except that you are older, who should be wiser, and a man, who should speak a lady fair."

"And your liege lord," he added.

"I forget it not, my lord," I said. "Every day, every hour, do I recall it. With every mouthful, every stitch, is your bounty impressed."

"Now, by God," he said, dragging himself up, "you do me wrong at that. You have an evil tongue, Lady Ann. Perhaps this will stop it since nothing else does."

Before I knew what he was about, he had pulled me against him, crushing my arms against my sides as if to break them off. His mouth clamped down on mine to choke off breath. For a moment, I felt his rage flare against my own. Then a new emotion that I did not know took hold instead. His tall frame was hard against my own. And my weak body, instead of fighting back, seemed to fold and bend into place against the lines of his.... I should have struggled, but could not any more than I could have moved that day in the sunlit glade. And where there had been anger was something else I did not then know, but as strong and forceful. He released me violently, thrusting me from him. Did he feel a similar like and dislike? Did he sense in me the conflict of resistance and compliance together? He sprawled back in his chair, shirt torn, leggings stained and bloodied, as oafish as a peasant in the fields. I felt a blush of shame and pleasure stain my cheeks as he watched me. Then I swirled round, almost running into the startled men at the door, and fled away to safety in the women's bower.

4

TRANGELY ENOUGH, THE LADY MILDRED did not scold as much as I had feared. Cecile received back the wreckage of her dress in silence. Perhaps they thought Lord Raoul's anger was enough. Nor did they question me. No doubt there was no need, for rumors of what had happened would have flown far and wide. But there were many things that seemed strange at that time, and gossip was the least of them. My own moods confused me, by turns happy, sad, angry, pleased, I was furious with myself and with him. At best, I thought, he had bested me, making me seem a plaything, of little worth; at worst, he had revealed thoughts and longings that should have been kept hidden.

It was difficult even to say what those feelings were. Remember, I had lived much on my own, not knowing people of my own age or rank. Among the common folk, it is enough to live and exist; they have no time for subtleties. Thoughts came to me slowly. I was still unknowing, not of the facts, but of the ways of the world. But gradually I resolved that since Cambray and I could come together only when some man took me to wife, the obvious solution lay there.

Today, maidens are not so blunt, so practical. And yet I think that not only practicality brought the idea to mind. The season continued warm and mellow, a summer-out-of-time, they call it, when everything seems ripe to overflowing. Even the Lady Mildred's censoring could not dampen our spirits on days like these. We lazed that autumn away, as if there should never be an end to it. Often we would find shade in the forest among the beeches and old oaks, and as we lay or sat under the trees, Giles and the other young men would climb the branches and send nuts falling into our laps. The peasants, off in the meadows, would be tying up the last stooks of corn. The slow curl of smoke would mark where they were preparing the fields. Then Geoffrey or one of the other men would tell us of the courts of love that this Eleanor of Aquitaine, new Countess of Anjou, used to hold among the nobles of her southern court to bind them to her will. I would lie upon my back and watch the leaves float down from a pale blue sky and wonder what the future would hold for me, and whether one day I would have poets sing my praises and young men faint for love of me. What harm was there in such thoughts? Do not all young girls dream sometimes? I had grown up in a sterner world, but there could be no harm in dreaming.

Cecile now, and her yellow-headed Geoffrey, did not she tie him to her will by promises of delight? I think we held our courts of love and lust at Sedgemont in those days, and all hearts turned to thoughts of marriage then.

One afternoon, it was as still and fair as a May day, we had come into the woods as usual, and were sitting in our little groups, talking softly among ourselves while the Lady Mildred tried to bring order to the work she had set that morning. Geoffrey was strumming to himself upon a lute. Some of the other knights had brought their horses to the water's shallows and were letting them drink and stamp to cool themselves after a long ride at the tilting yard.

Cecile said to me, "He watches you, Lord Raoul. Did you know that?"

I looked up surprised. I had not spoken with him since the day of the hunt although at night I dined in the Great Hall as he had ordered. It had seemed, sometimes, when I looked up quickly from my place, that his gaze slid past as if it would not be caught. I cannot say if that pleased or displeased me. He seemed, perhaps *thoughtful* is the word, but I supposed it was his wound that made him morose; and since he went out each day about his affairs, I presumed some worries of his own made him preoccupied. I had not given thought to what they might be. Certainly I did not imagine he was concerned with me.

"He watches you," said Geoffrey, "because I think he must make plans for Cambray soon. Now that he has lost Sieux, Cambray will count the more." At my stare of surprise, "You did not know that Sieux was lost? Well, Geoffrey of Anjou took it for his own in his last campaign before his death. Henry of Anjou is Count of Sieux now. It is a hard loss to Lord Raoul."

"They say he is no longer betrothed," Cecile said; "is that true also?"

Again my surprise must have been obvious. I had not thought Lord Raoul a man betrothed. He had not acted like one.

"I cannot speak to that," Geoffrey said uneasily, that he was spreading unwelcome news. "We went not to see her in France. Well, she was older than he was. Not all her lands and wealth would have made me bed her. I think he had as little liking, by all I have heard. The Lady Mildred had best look to her maidens now."

"Hark how he talks of wealth and lands who has yet to win them by his sword," Cecile said, smiling to herself. "I can reach higher than a landless squire."

Geoffrey seemed so abashed at that that I felt sorry for him, remembering my father's life.

"When I come back to Cambray," I said, "there will be place and lands for all."

They all smiled at that, indulgently, at hearing something that a child dreams on. Once I would have resented their smiles as mockery. Yet all the same, underneath my words I felt discomfort grow. I had not known that misfortune had hit him so close. I had not known that he had plans to be married. Yet both Dylan and Geoffrey had hinted that he treated all women lightly—well, he would not make light of me.

Geoffrey sighed. "If Cambray is to be of use to us," he said, "you must look for a husband, Lady Ann. While Lord Raoul holds you as his ward, we are helpless here."

"Why not indeed," I said to make them laugh. But I thought, Why not, since I have little to gain or lose.

"The soldier Dylan has promised to serve you well. I, Geoffrey, shall be your knight, and you, Cecile, lady-in-waiting."

They laughed again, play-acting their roles. Well, it was long ago, did we ever then expect things to turn out as they have?

"And you, Giles, her squire."

He smiled with the rest, more serious, not jesting as they did. It was after all what we had planned for him long ago. Yet Giles too had changed. I cannot say it was the beating that had caused the change—a stable boy is always in the way of cuffs and blows—but this time had been different. I could not put into words how I became sure of this: he never spoke of it again, who once had had no secrets from me. He had not been so angry as I would have thought, nor yet so uncaring either. And he was changing in other ways, filling out, becoming broader. Each day now he trained with the other squires, learning to use sword and buckler and handle a horse, although he would never be as skilled as those who had begun this work when they were children. But he took these things seriously. Was that the difference, that when the others played at games, he did not? One thing I knew: although more-loyal friend, devoted companion, I would never have, he had found a sense of fitness, duty, that had nothing to do with me. My squire he might be, but not my lover now. And that both saddened and excited me.

That night, I spent longer than usual preparing for the feast. Cecile was kindness itself, lending me another overtunic to hide the deficiencies of the poor-fitting gown beneath, binding my hair with ribbons until I felt like some ox going decked to a country fair. When she had finished, she showed me her handiwork in the small hand mirror she had. Yes, I too had changed, filled out. I had not Cecile's prettiness, my eyes were still too large and dark, my hair was still the same shade, still flared out in wisps and webs and not smoothed to sleekness, my complexion had not her pink and white, but no one, I think, would have called me "skin and bone." That night I wore my mother's chaplet as my sign of rank; that night I sought among the men at Sedgemont for someone to win me back Cambray.

When you are bound to a course, it is a chain that binds you tight. Perhaps I would have been more discreet had not Geoffrey's words made me hasty. I cannot tell how well I practiced all the tricks I had been watching in the ladies' bower. But I had noted that beneath their downturned eyes, they knew how to look as fierce as men; their low-tuned voices rang out clearly when they would. If they said little, it was with intent. If they talked of walking here or riding there, it was to let someone know the time and place. If they smiled at one man, it was to tease his neighbor. If they moved restlessly for lack of air or heat, it was to expose a glimpse of breast or thigh. Well, despite all the Holy Church says contrary, it makes no sense to me that of all the female kind, women alone should not find pleasure in their mates, nor seek them out as do the lowly beasts. Nor can I see, to speak plain, why men should know more pleasure in their beds, except that they expect women will not, who often do not dare express what they feel. Well, I am no laggard. I learned how easy it is to look and smile when you want, and then, when you have forgotten why you must, easier still. That night, I, who was always silent among the rest, a stranger, showed how I laughed and flirted. And at the meal's end, when they spoke of dancing in the lower hall, my voice was raised as high as the rest.

The menials ran to brush back the straw and clear a space before the fire. The dogs crept to the sides and the men waited by the wall benches to watch. Others brought out viols and flutes, and even the Lady Mildred's foot began to tap. And at the High Table, Lord Raoul sat with a face of thunder and drank alone.

Some of the dances I did not know. Others I remembered from childhood days and called for those again and again. I danced with older, heavier men who made an effort to keep themselves light of foot. I danced with Giles, who knew as little as I and complained of dizziness. I danced with Cecile's Geoffrey and smiled at him, for practice, no more. "He dances as he talks," I told her, "trippingly. You must scold him, Cecile, to take more pains."

"It will not be I who scold," she said.

"Who else?"

She jerked her head to where Lady Mildred and Sir Brian stood, to the table where Lord Raoul sat.

"They are too old to care," I said laughingly. But I wanted Lord Raoul to care.

"I think you mean to anger him," Cecile said shrewdly. "Beware. He is not one to bandy nonsense lightly."

I took a hurried look. He still sat alone, drinking heavily but not sottishly as some men do. I vouch there was not one woman there who would not have left all the rest to go with him had he beckoned.

"He will be too far gone in cups to remember anything," I said.

Perhaps I spoke too loudly; perhaps he guessed what I said. The next dance was new from France. I thought it safer to sit at the back and rethread the ribbons in my hair and keep myself out of his black looks. I wanted to anger him, but not too much. I wanted him to notice me, but not too closely.

"So you will not dance to Norman tunes, lady?" His voice coming unexpectedly made me start.

"Why should I, my lord?" I said. "They do not interest me."

He swore under his breath.

"Then learn you shall with me," he said, jerking me to my feet. "Dance you shall when I bid you."

"Your courtesy demands my obedience, my lord," I said angrily, until common sense told me to keep my temper. I made an effort to be pleasant. Was it my fault he took it amiss?

"Your wound will pain you. You should take care."

"You count me a dolt," he said, "or an old man, that I must creep across the floor?"

And in truth, since the wine did make him lurch so that he put out a hand to steady himself, I was forced to hide my smile.

"Why, nay, my lord," I said, looking at him in this new way I had been learning, "but I thought men of war had not the time for such gentle arts."

He swore again at that.

"So you prefer games after all," he said, holding my hand tightly, forcing me to trail after him. "It seems but yesterday you were begging for rescue from them. . . ."

"Ah, my lord," I said with a sweet smile, although I could have kicked him for such mean memory, "but look how much I have changed since then."

We had come to the far side of the room. He suddenly pushed me by the shoulder out the small doorway there that gave onto one of those inner courtyards which was hemmed in by walls all round. Someone long ago had planted a bush at the side, perhaps the same lady who had planned the pleasure gardens without the walls, and in the warm weather its white flowers still shone as if it were full summer. He pulled me before him until I had almost gone head first into the bush and would have been buried in its leaves had he not stopped in time to swing me round, so that we faced each other. I could feel the soft fur that lined his tunic against my cheek, but his face was in the shadows.

"My lord," I said, striving to speak calmly to hide my fear. "Your men will wonder where you are. They will follow. . . ."

"No, they will not," he said, "unless I give them leave. And I have not given them leave. They remember, which you do not, that I am master here."

"No, my lord," I protested. "I too remember it."

"Damn your eyes," he said. "Who taught you to look so?"

"There seems little to please you, my lord," I said. "Speaking or looking I give offense."

He said, "I prefer your jabbering. When you are quiet there is mischief abroad. So now, mistress, what deviltry are you about to have my men tripping on their swords to serve you?"

I smiled to myself at that. "They do me courtesy, my lord," I said, "or perhaps they have learned from you what ways to pleasure women."

"God's teeth, brat," he said, "you take much upon yourself. No woman is worth so much fret. . . ."

"Not even your betrothed, my lord?" I asked sweetly.

"You speak out of turn," he said, sobered. "Out of ignorance."

"Or perhaps she is far away in France. And you forget your troth. . . ."

"No," he shouted, "I do not forget it. But I have no mind to wed."

"I beg your pardon, then," I said, "I thought to have heard you were betrothed in France and wished to give you joy."

"Where got you your news?" he said. "It is outdated, lady. No bride waits for me in Sieux. Or anywhere else, I trust."

"Do not you wish for one?" I said. "Do not you want heirs to your estate?"

"To have heirs, Lady Ann," he said, cold-voiced, in the deliberate way that always made my anger flare, "to have sons, one should have something to leave them. Heirs must inherit, no?"

I started to reply but he broke in, "Your news is not only outdated but ill placed. I have not lost a bride but Sieux itself. I told you the Angevins were free with other people's demesnes. They long have eyed Sieux and now they have it. And my bride, whose lands run close to mine, has quickly found new interests to her father's better liking. I doubt if she thinks overmuch of me, although she would have liked to be Countess of Sieux. So do not grieve for her or me. It was my grandfather's choosing, not mine. Sieux and its adjoining estates of Auterre and Chatille, those you may grieve for. But speak not of marriage to me. I have no wish or thought of it."

The bitterness in his voice gave me pause. I had not thought he would mention it, yet something of the loss he felt struck a cord in me. But I steeled myself. I had not come to pity him, merely to force my own will.

"But I do, my lord," I said.

"Indeed," he said. "I am afire to know more."

I flushed at the sarcasm but went on. "You still have Sedgemont, Lord Raoul. All your English lands. And Cambray."

"And so?"

"If once you thought to be betrothed, to wed to knot up your lands in France, why then I think to do the same. I ask you, as you have wardship over me, to find me a husband of my own."

He stared, and laughed.

"You may find much in me to mock," I said stiffly. "But I think that this is so. My father was your loyal vassal and held those lands of Cambray loyally. I have inherited it but cannot claim it until some man holds it of you. Then I will have a man to hold it in my stead."

"You are overbold, lady," he said. "It is not for you or any maid to make such a demand. Even your father, had he lived, must have waited at my pleasure. That is my right as overlord."

"She who was Queen of France, this Eleanor who now is wife to Henry of Anjou," I said, "did not she leave the King of France and take a new husband of her own choice? And did not she take her lands with her?"

"You do but guess at great affairs," he said, still half-amused. "Do not think to ape your betters."

"If you had not kept me mewed up in Sedgemont," I said hotly, "I could be as capable as any, how to judge these things. You do not explain yourself overclearly, my lord. Perhaps it is because you are not willing to admit women are capable of thought at all. I do not set myself up against the highest. I know my place, far beneath you great lords. But the worth of Cambray I know. You have already told me its importance in a future war. It would be better settled soon."

"And who then," he asked, "have you in mind, Lady Ann of Cambray, that you offer your lands as bait? Which of my men have you selected with your airs and smiles just now? One of Sir Brian's cronies, scarce able to heave himself upon his horse, let alone a bridal bed? Or one of my younger squires, he of the yellow crest, who swoons at your favor? Or your stable lad? I think you are overfond of him. . . ."

"It is easy to make a fool of me," I said. "I have no protection. . . ."

"Protection!" he roared. "You make that claim like a bell to Mass, pat upon the hour. What woman ever could hold her mind straight without twisting all to her own ends? Protection, says she; wed, says she; demand, says she. Then, Madame Know-All, hear this."

He took his hand from my shoulder and struck it against the wall as he spoke.

"One: Cambray is mine to give as I choose. To him who will serve me well, who will hold Cambray as a soldier should, doing military duty along the border. Two: I have your future in mind even to the point of considering marriage for you— if there be man who can have the patience to make you fit to wife. Three: I have your welfare so much in thought that I have already refused one offer when it was made in the spring. Four: Times have changed. I may not be so nice of choice a second request. . . ."

"Who was it then?" I cried. "How dare you, without telling me. Why was I not told?"

He stopped at that. I do not think anyone had spoken to him so.

"Four," he continued slowly. "I am not so free as once I was to bargain with Cambray. My choice may not be to your liking."

"Perhaps not," I cried, as angry as he, "perhaps not. But do not think that all my worth is to be bargained in some war that has naught to do with me. It could be that I shall use you. I have some value of my own, although you scorn it."

"I have no doubt you think so," he said, slowly again. "Use you. I wonder if you know what you say. When you look thus, I could use you very well."

He took another step toward me, although there was nowhere I could go, half-buried as I was in leaves.

"Thus it is, lady, that saucy maids are used."

His hands were round my waist, dragging me out. His kisses were on my face, lips, throat, half-demanding, half-contemptuous. I struggled against him, beating on him. I might as well have hit out at wall or tree, for all I could hold him off.

"And thus also are saucy wives tamed," he said, at my ear. "Think you that before you make so bold demands again."

I told myself I hated and reviled him, that this was what he did to all maids, that his men should have nicknamed him as they did. I could feel my heart beat against him as he held me off the ground and swung me round to avoid my heels. I could feel every hard line of his body, every curve against my own. As he could mine. His grip tightened so I could scarcely breathe. His free hand ran across my breast, along my flanks, searching out the pleasure points. The flowers smelled sweet, sweet was his breath, and all the air flowered round us. I freed myself long enough to cry, "You have no right."

He released me then, with a look I could not understand.

"In this world, Ann," he said, "men have all the rights. . . . So tempt not my castle guard. And remember this: it is a Norman custom that when ward weds, her lord has leave to bed her first. That may be a right I shall claim if you tempt me to."

"You would not dare," I cried with my last ounce of will.

He smiled down at me. "When you are grown to womanhood," he said, "speak to me then of dare. I will not cross you again."

Then he was gone, dropping me like cloak or glove upon the ground. I stood begrimed with leaves and twigs, and in my turn beat at the wall, that in nothing he counted me of value, not even as a woman. And forgot, until it was too late to ask, that he had not told me who it was who had wished to wed me for my lands.

Perhaps he had never meant to tell me even that much. It may have slipped out in speech without his noticing. Or, as was his way, he may have meant to keep his own counsel on the matter and was angered at his carelessness. I do not mean that he was devious. But remember. He had long had to manage his own affairs. He had had charge of Sieux from an early age, and since his grandfather's death had controlled it and Sedgemont. He had survived at Stephen's court. Such men must learn the art of making decisions and keeping quiet when they are made. In this we were mismatched. Scarce had I thought of something, I must blurt it out for all the world to hear. Caution, distrust, if you like, had become second nature to him. And he was proud, arrogant as a Lucifer. All our weaknesses ran on the same paths. We were bound to rage and flare against each other.

But I move ahead. First must I tell you how a second marriage offer was made for me, without my asking, and how Lord Raoul managed that, and how we crossed each other for the third time. For since it was clear to me, at least, that our wishes never would run straight, I had sense to see we would never avoid a battle of will. Except I was young enough then to hope that in the end I might win.

It was not difficult to guess who had made the offer for my lands. I was not vain enough to think my person of importance in this. You will have guessed it, too. For it must have been someone from the west, well placed, ambitious for more power, having something of his own to offer Lord Raoul in return.

Only one such man there was, and he had come to Sedgemont in the spring. My flesh crawled at the thought. And while I lay as in a swoon, I had heard them discuss it; no wonder I had guessed right—like a horse that is to be bought or sold. Then, too, there was the man himself. He was old, widowed with grown children, my father's contemporary although younger than he had been. Yet not so old then that he might not want a new young wife who could bring him added land and power, how had Lord Raoul put it, "knot up" his own estates along the border with Cambray's. And Sir Brian, what had he said, "A good fighter, better on our side than on the other." Perhaps then, if he came wooing again, Cambray would be the prize to win his support. And his support was needed if Henry of Anjou came back to England. I tell you that before I had no care for kings or queens, although I have known them and their courts since. But for the first time then I saw how our lives were bound together, such is the chain of things, from highest to lesser to least. And whether I would or not, my little life would be tied to greater causes, and a kingdom's battle. *Anything that the great do has some effect on everyone.* So had Lord Raoul said. So it proved.

They say among my people, who have such powers, that if you think upon a thing long enough, you can will it to happen. I knew, before Giles came running to tell me, who had arrived in the night and entered Sedgemont gates at early dawn. If I had been Maneth and had heard of Sedgemont's loss in France, I would have galloped all night, too, to catch him disadvantaged and press a suit that was so much to my own interests. But I was calm when Giles described who had come, remembering each horse as other people do faces. He knew how far and fast they had been ridden and which Lord Guy had brought with him.

"But two horses are missing," he said, "two bays that came last time." And he described them and their peculiarities that I might remember them. We looked at each other, thinking. Lord Guy would never risk bringing men I might recognize.

Nor would he come on the same errand again unless he had some hope of success this time. That frightened me. Yet it must be borne, and I could not change my fate either.

I was calm too when they came to bid me attend the lords in the Great Hall. All knew why they had come. I tell you, it was in the air, that even dark-faced older men should think of it. Lady Mildred herself helped deck me for the ritual, exhorting me the while on duty; Cecile, thinking of love, twined garlands as if for her own bethrothal feast. But she could not wish me joy; she was too honest for that. Giles kept close watch at the door with sword drawn. But even he could not keep away what was to be. Yet I could not believe my hopes would end with such a man. And the dread, if that is not too strong a word, that I had felt when he was here before revived.

When I came into the Great Hall, they were all standing around the fire. The false summer had long gone; the rains fell winter-cold and hard. What else is there for men to do on such days, except drink and talk and plan the world? Few of Lord Raoul's men were there; for the most part, they kept to the outer halls. Sir Brian and his friends sat at one end, engaged in a game of chess. They favored long furred robes against the cold, and caps upon their heads. Only Lord Raoul wore more martial gear, leather jerkin, belt with dagger, hose cross-gartered into boots. His squire kept watch at the door, with sword and shield, perhaps to cut me down where I stood if I did not obey.

"This is the lady," Lord Raoul said, taking me by the hand. I did not look at him but felt my arm tremble beneath his touch. He led me forward. I kept my eyes downcast but had already noted Lord Guy of Maneth, heavy cloaked, dark faced, large. It is the hardest thing that I know for women not to show emotion. Else they will take us for heifers offered for sale, mindless as beasts. Yet, for all my poise, I felt a cold wind blow.

"Lord Guy of Maneth," Lord Raoul intoned his rank, lord

of this, holding land of that, vassal to another... how much he held already along that border, how much he had gained in this short while, how well Cambray would round out his possessions.

"And his eldest son, his heir, Gilbert of Maneth."

Here was an unexpected difference. I looked at him more carefully. A tall man also, but heavy, so that Raoul beside him was almost slight. Dark skinned like his father, but soft-looking where the older man was hard. Him I seemed to remember also, and the cold wind blew louder. I heard what was said, but far off. I seemed to stand outside myself and hear the words form like rain.

"Lord Guy of Maneth has come," Lord Raoul was saying, his speech hurried, unlike his own, "to renew his suit, but for his son Gilbert, whom you may remember from long ago."

Gilbert bowed and smiled. I should have remembered that smile. It seemed to grow and fill my mind. So had he smiled when he walked behind Talisin at Cambray.

"I knew your brother, lady," he said. "We were fast friends, Talisin and I."

I recalled what Talisin had said of him: *He clings like a leech.* "And as he loved me best of all would I have you love me."

Steer clear of him, my father had warned. *I would not trust father or son too close.*

I remembered them walking through the castle yard at Cambray, my brother ahead, Gilbert at his heels. And so it seemed to me then that all the stretch of beach and sea opened wide, and I heard the waves thunder on the shore. Gilbert stood with their cloaks about his arm and Talisin ran down into the water as I had watched him a hundred times. He dived into the waves that brought him laughing back upon a rush of foam. And Gilbert took his arms as if to draw him upright, and as the next wave swirled underfoot, thrust his head and held it under, held it under. Then the wave rushed back and Talisin lay like empty weed upon the shore.... And Gilbert of Maneth turned and laughed, his laugh louder than the waves' sound, and the wind blew colder through the Great Hall of Sedgemont.

"Why look you so?" Lord Raoul was saying. "Lady Ann, you are white as death. Why do you not answer?"

The salt spray lay on my cheeks like tears. The great sea rolled far off. So rolls it, they say, to the world's end, mile after mile.

Drowned, my father said. His men wrapped his son in a heavy cloak and brought him to Cambray. My father leaned from his horse and drew his sword as if to cut his heart out of grief.

"Perhaps she dreams of Cambray," said Lord Guy.

"She thinks of it, certainly," said Sir Brian, moving a pawn.

"Then shall she return," Lord Guy of Maneth said.

"I shall bear you back there as wife." Gilbert smiled.

"What ails you?" Raoul said at my side.

How could I tell him I saw two things plain, set one upon the other like two pictures painted on a single frame. I have not spoken of it all these years. Yet I tell you true. Explain it as you will. While I watched Gilbert smile at me in Sedgemont Hall, I saw my brother drowned on Cambray strand. I only know that I believe there is no action, good or bad, that does not at some time come home upon a distant shore. And so to God may all things seem ripples moving endlessly on a lake. Three times in my life have I stepped outside recorded time, for grief and pain, and never wished to know it. Three times. This was the second and the worst. I would not for all the prayers in the world have spoken of what I saw. But I have told and will tell you true.

"The lady needs time to think on such things." Lord Raoul's voice was warm and comforting.

"Let my son give her the kiss of peace, that they be counted betrothed."

"Thus will the affairs of Sedgemont and Maneth be knitted up," Sir Brian echoed.

Beside them, Gilbert bowed again and preened.

And I said, "I will not wed with murderers. They have slain my house."

Then they all shouted at once. What an outcry of noise, spilling down about us. Gilbert of Maneth made the most of all. Sir Brian upset his chess pieces, scattering them upon the reeds. Then was he at Lord Raoul's side whispering advice. Lord Raoul himself was silent, but I guessed what anger that silence held. Nor did Guy of Maneth speak except for one start, as if exclamation was forced from him. But his men hissed as at outrage.

For my own part, I had nothing more to add. I had said it all. I wished it had never been. If gift it is to catch time out of joint, I would not know it. It comes not of my seeking. They say there be those who can cull such things from the air, what has been and will be. I wish them joy of it. It brought me no such joy.

"Last time I was here," Lord Guy said at last, and as he moved, his cloak fell wide as if the fire's heat overwhelmed him, and I saw the glint of steel, "she spoke of a servant killed. Now she speaks of murder of all. She sings to but one tune. Maids were more careful in their talk once. I come not to be trifled with."

"She is mad," Gilbert said, his small eyes starting, "bewitched. I'll have none of her. . . ."

"Or overwrought." His father pressed his arm to silence him. "We should talk again at your leisure, my lords. But time is wasting. No doubt she can be brought to reason."

"A whip would do it," Sir Gilbert said, red faced and angry. "On her knees, she'd not speak so loud."

Sir Brian began to agree.

"Perhaps not," Lord Raoul said, and the knife at his side swung as he moved.

"Be not too hasty," Sir Brian amended speech. "My lord of Maneth, Sir Gilbert, Lord Raoul. . ."

Raoul motioned him away. "The Lady Ann had right to speech."

Maneth raised his brows. "Such mad fantasies?" he said.

"Such lies," Gilbert broke in. When he moved, he was slow as if sinking into marshland. "I told you we were friends. How could we plan to kill them? It was so long ago, what could she remember?"

Lord Guy took his son's arm. The knuckles were white where he gripped.

"She can know nothing," he said, quick-witted where Gilbert was dense.

For me, their guilt stood around them like a pall, yet, I doubt if any other there saw it. Except Maneth himself. He was fast sensing out what I could know, could only guess at.

He said to Lord Raoul, "You should consider many things before we withdraw. For we have ridden in haste, not letting time and weather stand upon our coming. Your object to my suit this spring was well taken. I have no grievance with that; she is too young for me and our ages do not match. You who are younger see clearer, although I have not felt myself old and may look for a wife of my own still. But Gilbert is not old, not so much above your age. He would be a stout ally in these wars. As I said before, we lords of Maneth would give you support. You need vassals you can rely upon, and our help may be sought by many sides. In bad times, we need to stick together, else there will be rich picking for someone in the end."

"I do not expect to have my lands picked over," Lord Raoul said. There was an edge to his voice that made the others step back. "I think to see to my own demesne lands yet. The lords of Cambray were loyal vassals in their day. They will not be easy to replace."

Lord Guy's face flushed also at that. But with an effort he controlled himself and shrugged.

"If you think so, my lord. Ill news travels fast these days. I thought my help of use after the loss of your lands in France."

They eyed each other, the two men almost of a height, the older sturdier, solid, the younger light, more flexible.

So once, long ago, had my father and Talisin looked beside each other. I thought, Dear God, they will be at each other's throats, and that will be my fault. But there was nothing I could do.

"All the more so," Gilbert said breathlessly, thrusting his way forward again, his eyes bulging with the import of his news, "that Cambray keep is taken this month past."

We all stared at that, his father in most anger of all that Gilbert had let slip a piece of information he would have kept to his advantage. I thought he would have struck Gilbert where he stood.

"My lords, this is grave news," Sir Brian cried. "How, by whom? Lord Raoul, this comes untimely. . . ."

Lord Raoul said nothing, but held Lord Guy so in his look that the older man shifted and fell back again.

"I would have spoken of it first off," he said. He was a smooth liar when he talked. "You may judge how much I cared to push this match that despite the loss of Cambray, I would have it go ahead. It will be of small consequence if we find quick means to drive them out."

"It cannot be the Angevins," Sir Brian said. "Henry of Anjou could not have passed the coast without our knowledge. Who then?"

"The Celts, my lord, have not sat idly by. You know how long the bond has been between them and Cambray. A band came skirmishing down from the mountain passes, claiming to be bringing messages of good will."

"And the fools of Cambray let them in," Gilbert broke in viciously. "There be your loyal vassals, my lord. Fools."

"Well," said his father more lamely, for after all, Cambray was what he wanted, too, "they have got their foot inside and will not budge. Cambray was not well manned. The castle guard, such as it was, needed supplies and trusted the Celts. I do not fault them, my lord of Sedgemont. But Cambray is a strong castle to besiege. By foolishness the Celts got in."

"And as easily will be whipped out again," Lord Raoul said lazily. You would not have guessed those words had robbed him of a third of his English lands. "The Celts like not to be penned inside. They are hill people, preferring the mountain freedom. They will not adapt to castle life."

"If you have time, my lord," Lord Guy said smoothly, "or men enough to hem them round. The border is long if you must watch it as well. You should think what troops you have at command, although for courtesy I would not have mentioned it before. But if Gilbert becomes Lord of Cambray, then that frees you from a burden at once. He can use soldiers from Maneth to that siege, leaving you freer with your own men. And mine will also be at your service. . . ." He paused to let the words sink in. "And Gilbert still would be wed, even if the keep of Cambray be not free. Despite the unseemliness we have witnessed here, he would be wed."

"His anxiety becomes him as well as your solicitude for the lands and titles of Cambray," Lord Raoul drawled. "But I shall have time to put my own affairs to rights and hold the western marches for King Stephen."

"Then have it as you will," Maneth said angrily, and his hand twitched to his side. So must he have looked when he came in the spring. "Let things fall out as best they may. Think not to have me at your call when Henry of Anjou comes."

"He has not yet come," Lord Raoul said. "Much may happen before that day. After all, we have driven the Angevins out before and will do so again. Do you think of that, my lord of Maneth, lest you be forced to change your tune. As I think you did last time."

It was a remark meant to anger and provoke. Lord Guy's men were eyeing the space between them and the door, closing behind their master. Lord Raoul's squire was at his side, but none of the other older Sedgemont men were armed; Sir Brian did not even have a knife.

For seconds again, they wavered.

Then Lord Guy turned his back, his cloak flaring behind, clanking forth from the Great Hall with Gilbert braying at his heels. Yet one word more he dropped, spilled like venom before he left. "And who helped the Celts to enter so easily? Ask what traffic she has had with Cambray." Then he was gone.

Sir Brian and the older men poured after him, snatching at sword and shield from their places along the wall as they went. The younger knights came running. But there would be no brawl in the outer bailey. The moment for attack would have been here, with only Raoul and his squire armed. And now he and I were left alone in the Great Hall.

"That was done well," he said to me. "You have made a friend today, for me, for the king, for yourself." His voice was cold, withdrawn, but the pulse beat in his cheek.

"And I thank you for your defense," I said. "I expected no favors from you."

"Favors!" He whirled on me. "I stand not on such niceties. You heard him, that he should think to juggle with my affairs. Could not you keep your mouth shut to play your games elsewhere?"

So did he judge what I had said. Well, I would not enlighten him.

"By the rood," he said, "there were better ways to show your dislike than that. It is an insult no man can bear."

He wheeled about again. "It is as ill done as if you knew it all planned before. Are you sure your hand is not in this with the help of your mother's kin?"

"You need not shout," I said. "You have accused me of such dealings before, although not so openly. I know nothing of Cambray's capture, by whom or how. But we may not even now know the truth, for Lord Guy may have lied also in this. Send to find out."

"So I shall," he snarled again. "More than that, I shall go myself. I do not mean to let Cambray go begging whilst I have head and hands to get it back. But do not plot against me. . . ."

"I am no traitor," I shouted then, "although you have called me so since you first saw me."

"I never thought so," he said, "until now."

"You lie," I said, angry enough to tell a man he lied to his face. "You and Sir Brian both, while I lay as in a swoon, you talked. I heard you then, what you hoped and planned. Sly and smooth as a snake you called me."

He was silent.

"And you spoke then also of Cambray. And of your need for Maneth's support. For his help were you willing to sell Cambray and me. What is this Maneth, a man of no worth, an evil man, you heard what I said, a murderer. Rot you in hell, my lord of Sedgemont, that was not knightly done."

He strode back and forth, debating with himself.

"Calm yourself, my lady," he said at last. "Do not look at me so. I do not know what has distressed you, but sure I will believe that it has moved you greatly. Such passion, such look, cannot be counterfeit."

There was more fairness in his words than I would have given him credit for.

"What proof have you in what you accuse him of?" he asked. "Against father as against son. Gilbert would not move a foot without his father's will. And he is stupid. He let slip that news of Cambray without his father's leave."

And you would have me wed such a man, I thought.

"I have no proof," I said, "as you would hold the word."

How reasonably I spoke, whose heart was throbbing still with shock.

"Too many years ago it was," he said.

"There may be those who will talk, if you could but find them," I said. "My lord, I know it. I cannot explain it or tell you how I know."

He looked at me searchingly. But I would not answer him further.

"It is said," he said slowly, "that there be those of your race who have power to see what the rest of us cannot."

"I do not know about that," I said, "but we believe that the dead do not rest until they are avenged. With or without proof, I shall have vengeance."

"Not you alone," he said unexpectedly. "They were my friends, too. Yet never hint or thought of wrong until now."

"Or last spring," I said. "You have forgotten Gwendyth's death. He was here then."

He said suddenly, as if against his will, "But why? I believe you, Lady Ann, though it goes against the grain of common sense. But why now, after so long? Cambray is..." He stopped as if collecting thought, then went on as if to answer himself. "Cambray is important to us. Its loss is a drawback which I will admit to you, if not to him. Since you have charged me with false speaking, I will tell you straight, this sets all else amiss. For I must lead my forces out now, not waiting until Anjou comes, or catching him as he lands. The coast must watch for itself. I shall run before him to the border. Maneth is right. It will be harder without his troops to besiege Cambray, and I have not enough among my own men. We shall have to camp rough, for a start, and scrounge for what we need. The Celts can exist on air, but Norman soldiers prefer a Norman castle at their back. And Maneth will be breathing malice to the north. After this, I cannot count on his neutrality. As for you..."

He eyed me speculatively. "There will be no safety for you now, if the Lord of Maneth thinks to come a-wooing here again. And you have shown too well that Sedgemont is no place to hold you. My mother's cousin is prioress of a convent nearby. There shall you cool your heels."

I was appalled.

"I thought to come with you to Cambray," I began.

He almost laughed, but a bitter laugh.

"Think you this a pleasure jaunt? Thanks to you, my hoped-for ally is lost. Thanks to your kin, my base is lost. Anjou may linger in France until the Yuletide is past. But he is coming back to England to wage war again. Unless we are careful, he will have the whole western island on his side. And without revenues to hire more soldiers, and I have not those moneys, my losses in France will leave me that much the poorer. I cannot keep an army in the field longer than my vassals are willing to honor their feudal duty. If we cannot push him to decisive battle right away... but that may be difficult."

I was intrigued despite myself.

"And does not King Stephen give you help?" I asked. "Does he not send you troops?"

He laugh was bitter again.

"King Stephen has much on his mind," he said. "Too much to know what to do first, so he wavers back and forth and achieves nothing. He has quarreled with the Church, which first supported him. He has lost many of his barons and fears to lose the rest. His son, Prince Eustace, is ungovernable, a man of sudden fits and rages. His queen, whom all loved, is dead. She was a strength to him that he will lack. But while he sits besotted with his grief and will not move hand or foot to save himself, he puts all in jeopardy. I will get no troops or support from him. Yet I have told him that I shall hold the west. So is our life made up, Lady Ann, by oath and trust to each other, to him who is above, to him who is below. I have sworn an oath to Stephen as my king. I can do no other but abide by it."

He paused as if reflecting on what he had said.

"And even if my loyalty to him did not bid me," he said at last, "I needs must have a care for Sedgemont. I have had knowledge of these Angevins before, as I told you. When I was a child, I have an early memory of how they rode through my lands at Sieux, slashing at the crops and vines because the castle withstood them. What will they make of this country but a place to harvest loot as other men harvest grain? So even if King Stephen is sunk with indecision and grief, others must think and act for him. What if a cause be half-lost, one need not fight the less."

"You do not think Anjou will win?" I cried.

He shrugged. "You have not seen yet what desolation war can bring. Lands destroyed, people homeless, crops ruined, families torn asunder. We need a strong king to put things back in order. When there is no strong king or he forgets his duty, the land is dead, waste. Men like Maneth can yet prey upon it, bit by bit, they build up their power. Yes, Cambray will be useful to Lord Guy. It will crown all his efforts. And all over England now there are such men, taking advantage of the times to gain their own ends. We need a strong man to push them back in place again. If Stephen cannot do it, then people may turn to Anjou in the hopes he will. Yet which is worse, a king who lets all slip to anarchy, or a tyrant who will crush both good and bad beneath his heel? If Stephen will bestir himself, he can win. If not, he will not."

"But may not Anjou change?" I cried again. "Are there not laws, rules, to bind our kings?"

He laughed. "A tyrant will make his own rules," he said, "not caring for what he will find here. Besides, what customs, laws, can he find? England is not one country but three. What customs are there in common among Norman, Saxon, and Celt? See how great difference there is between your race and mine. It will not be difficult for Henry to make his own laws."

"But what of me then?" I cried, for as he spoke, an idea had come into my mind, so strange I almost fell over at its daring. "I too can be tenacious of purpose. Because two men have bid for me, one too old, one too stupid, does not mean that Cambray should not be commanded by my husband. You still could have someone."

"Devil fry us," he said, "I speak of state affairs, lady, life, death, a kingdom. . . ."

"And I am tired of such things," I said, with a coolness I felt far from. "Your affairs of state, a king, a duke, have led you to gamble with Cambray to achieve one man's crown, another's support, a third's defeat. . . . My wants are less complicated than that—home, husband, children perhaps."

"So be it," he said, controlling himself with effort. "You speak but as women do. . . ."

"I am glad you grant me that at last," I was waspishly. "And it is clear to me you have scant respect for women, although I suppose in that you are no different from most men. My father and your grandfather would not have a woman on the throne. Is not that the cause of all these wars, that you men would not have a woman, Matilda, to rule you?"

"You jest," he began. "She was imperious, overproud, thinking to drag England to her husband's rule. We'd have had the Angevins run wild, tearing at our throats before a month had passed. . . ."

"Perhaps," I said, "but she would have understood, as you seem not, that I would have my rights, too."

"Rights!" he shouted. Then, "So be it. Quick. Although the words be shaking about us, what paragon of virtue have you in mind? Or is it thought of convent life that frights you, that you'd change it for wedded bliss?"

"No convent would alarm me," I lied. "It will be quiet there away from men and their plots. But I plan to marry to my liking."

"Liking, is it now. You seek much from this married state."

"My father and mother married for love," I said roundly. "But I am not such a fool to hope for that, merely that it not be with such men as the lords of Maneth."

"Enough of them," he shouted at me, resuming his pacing back and forth. "I would not have wed you in any case. Betrothed was all I had in mind. And you need not have feared for Gilbert. They say he has little liking for maids, which should have kept you safe. As for love, look what it has done for our king that he must overmourn the queen's death. And I heard that your parents were bound to make a peace."

"Peace came after," I said, "and that is much to look for, in marriage as in affairs of state. But I have no mind to be betrothed for years, as your poor lady in France was. Men may wear such betrothal easily, for who is to overwatch their faithfulness when they are far away? Maids are more easily tamed, that they sit chastely by and let their youth slip past."

"Give no thought for my French bride," he shouted again. "If I was not so chaste nor was she either. There was no love lost between us."

"I am glad to hear it," I said primly, "for I know now it is no paragon I seek. I can be as practical as the rest. I suggest, my lord, you marry me."

He stopped mid-bellow.

"Listen now," I said, stumbling over the words in my haste before he outshouted me. "You need Cambray. Maneth will take it if he can. The Celts hold it. If I come with you, they may listen to me, and save you much effort and pain. And when we have it, why do not you keep it? Take it back as part of your own demesne. You most of anyone knows what needs to be done with it."

He sat down, as dazed, upon one of the chairs, brushing aside the spilled chess pieces.

"I have learned much these past months," I said. "From the Lady Mildred, as you bade me. I am strong, well made, quick. My father was old when he wed and my mother old when I was born, but they say children of such unions are blessed. And Celtic women are fruitful beyond their prime. My years number more than fifteen. My courses flow every month that you may know I am in truth a woman. I know I am not beautiful, but no man, I think, would call me 'skin and bone' as you did this spring. I could bear you many sons. And I can win the Celts to your cause."

It was the longest speech I think I had ever made.

He said when it was done, "By the Mass, lady, I would not call you that again. God knows you are not that." He bit back other words. "But I will echo Gilbert of Maneth. I think you bewitched."

"But you do not hate me so greatly?" I cried, suddenly anxious. For having offered him so much on an impulse, I feared his reply.

"Hate you!" he said. "One does not love or hate a gadfly that stings. God's teeth, but how you do knot up words. What of liking? I thought rather that you hated me."

I looked at him curiously. For the first time I heard a hint of laughter in his voice. And yet, I thought, remembering his warm breath and tight arms, the mocking words he had spoken, *A maid could do worse than marry him.*

"I prefer you, in truth," I said bluntly, "to those lords of Maneth."

Then he did laugh. "Dear God," he said, "it is well all maidens do not set my worth so high. Why, Ann, what would you offer if a kingdom were at stake?"

"I have nothing more," I said.

He caught his breath. "No, and no and no again," he said. "I shall have you safe to a nunnery before and there's my oath on it. Thank me not," as I struggled with words. "Let me rather thank you for your offer, the first such that I have received. But I cannot wed you. Such a marriage stands not within my intent."

"I was not thanking you," I cried. "I was about to show you where you are wrong. It would solve all."

He drew me to him so that I stood trapped within his knees.

"Little Ann," he said more gently than I had heard him speak before, "I have done you wrong that I have not taken in seriousness all that you have thought and said. I will not mistake you for a child again, if you will have it so. But I will not wed you. There are many things in this world that you know not of, and I would not be the one to teach you. Yet, beshrew me, although you run upon the spear points like that old boar, I would not have you change."

"You treat me as a child," I cried, tears forming. "I am nothing more."

"Not so," he said. "By my troth, if you were any maid and

I any man, nothing would give me greater pleasure than to have you in my bed. Have I not also shown you that a hundred times since I first saw you in my Hall? But we are not any maid, any man. You see how we are caught up, in spite of ourselves, in greater things. The lords of Sedgemont are not the highest in the land, nor yet the least either. I am not free to do all that I would like, although you may think so. As I hold oath to Stephen, so hold I it to you. I will not seduce you, although you have tried me hard enough. There is the protection you seek of me."

"I do not understand you," I cried.

"Then think of it this way," he said. "I will not have it said that Raoul of Sedgemont could not keep his own ward safe. And I will not marry to get your lands because I could not keep them otherwise. I have not kept you ward to put that slur upon my name."

"You will forget all that when you are gone from Sedgemont," I cried.

"Well," he said, "I will not swear to be a eunuch to give you joy. But I shall not forget you. Strange wild thing. I would as soon chain a bird and watch it beat its wings apart. No, do not cry," more hopelessly, "I have never thought of love to understand its meaning."

"Nor I," I said amid tears, "but I shall sorely lack you and Sedgemont if we must be parted."

He smoothed back my hair.

"Stay safely in your nunnery," he said. "I promise I shall get back Cambray. And when it is in our hands then shall I send word. Then shall you find your brother's enemies. Then, if luck be on our side, shall we find you a husband."

"I made an offer that was fair," I said. "Do not send me away."

"As fair an offer as any man could want," he said softly. "I would have bartered your lands for my own ends, but you have bartered with yourself. I have known many maids, little

Ann, but none as just as that. But by my feudal oath shall I keep you safe, and by my feudal oath I shall go. May God have each to his care."

I could only say "amen" to that.

5

ATER, THERE WOULD BE TIME ENOUGH
to think. Now all was put in readiness for imme-
diate departure. Today, in calmer seasons, great
lords are used to journeys. They move from one
part of their lands to another, just as the rest of us set out on
a short morning ride. But that is how the great of this world
live: traveling back and forth, even across the sea that divides
England from France, seeing to their estates, ministering their
rough sort of justice, overlooking the peasants who work their
fields for them, and eating up the produce that has been gathered in their barns. Then, like a swarm of locusts, they move
on again, leaving seneschal or bailiff to act for them until their
next return. I have even become used to it myself, although
it does not please me. But in less-frantic times, there is some
warning; households have a chance to pack, put all in order.
A castle called to war is another matter.

I was too young to remember the last time Lord Raoul had
called his levies out. Now I could see for myself, and admire
even as I deplored, the haste and purpose that set all in motion.
Everything moved smoothly, like some contraption whose
wheels mesh into place. You saw how all had been planned
to this end, how all the labor from smiths and armorers, the
training of squires and knights, the preparations in stables and
byres had fallen to this pattern. Since his return from France,
this work had been going forward, although I, at least, had
not marked its importance before. Now, when the need came,
the weapons were sharpened, the armor repaired, the supplies

at hand. Lord Raoul did not even wait for his vassals, those lords he had tried to entertain at the great boar hunt, although they and their men would make up a large part of his troops. For the moment he must rely on his own guard at Sedgemont, calling upon the others to follow him as best they could. Nor could he leave Sedgemont defended by a woman this time. Openly at arms against an avowed enemy for an unpredictable king, he feared for its safety, did all he could to keep it secure. Sir Brian would be in charge with a carefully chosen group of men. Supplies that could be ill spared would be left, and space made within the keep for the peasants of the surrounding villages. His own men would have to travel light; they would have to hunt for their needs as he had said. There would be no long baggage trains. Nor any womenfolk. They must remain at Sedgemont, weeping the while, Cecile in floods of tears for father and lover both, children screaming. Despite the noise and confusion, each knew his allotted place, what he must do. Except for me, who had no place left at Sedgemont and went out by another road to another destiny.

From the castle walls I watched them leave as I had watched them come. Lord Raoul rode at their head on that shifty-eyed, bad-tempered black stallion which I would not have mounted for all the gold of Araby. His helmet was on, his face hidden, his mail coat buckled; he rode armed and fast. At his heels came his flag bearer, the red standard of Sedgemont fluttering with its golden hawks. Behind them marched the men-at-arms. A great cry rose up at their leaving. Almost all were married men with families they left behind, and knew not when they would meet again. Yet they clattered over the drawbridge in good array, well armed, too, in padded jerkins fitted with plates of steel, steel caps close to the neck, their bows slung for safer keeping on their backs in oiled skins to keep the strings dry. Behind them came the knights and squires, lances up, their red coats marking them the castle guard. They rode out most gallantly of all, the young men setting their horses rearing and stamping to make a braver show. Giles rode among them, grim faced with determination.

"You shall see Cambray before I do after all," I said to him, trying to smile as with trembling fingers I set his sword belt and hooked the scabbard in place. But Giles was as excited as the others, behind the calm he pretended.

"Have no fear for me, my lady," he said. "I have become so expert at the tilt yard here that no one will knock me from **my** horse."

His boasting was to make me laugh, but I was far from laughing when I saw him gallop across the drawbridge, his gloved hand raised in salute. At least he had saluted. Lord Raoul had looked neither right nor left, had made no sign, had not spoken to me again. A last group of mounted men as rear guard, then all were gone, banners streaming, dust settling. A fast, determined group. But few. They expected others to join them. But few, to hold a border and save a kingdom.

There was time after to bid Cecile and the other women farewell. I would not have thought it such a hard parting, even from the Lady Mildred. To Cecile, her fair face stained with tears, I promised to send news when I had any, but no one knew when that would be or by what means.

"Yet I will send," I said to her with an assurance I did not feel. And with that thought we comforted each other.

Then before Sir Brian gave the order to wind down the portcullis and raise the drawbridge for the last time, I too set out on my journey. It seemed fitting that he should have the last word as he had had the first.

"A hard journey you will have," he said, standing there in the morning sun, venerable in his armor and responsibility, his shield and helmet at hand, although his task was not to ride but to wait. I think it was the first time he had been left behind. He must have felt his age that day, who had served the lords of Sedgemont all these years.

"Your escort will take you to the convent, then swing west

to join again with my lord," he said. His words implied the waste of time and energy.

"You must keep up as best you can. We cannot stand on ceremony. . . ."

Nor ever have where I have been concerned, I thought, but had the sense to keep that to myself.

"I shall not hinder Lord Raoul's men about his business," I said.

He nodded, not even having the grace to look satisfied. "The convent is old," he went on, "endowered by his grandmother, first Lady of Sedgemont, when she came here from Sieux. His mother was raised there. It is no ordinary place, but bound to his family by many ties. The lady prioress is his devoted kinswoman who will keep you safe in these troublesome times. Take comfort in that. Lord Raoul has had a care for you. . . ."

It was true, of course, all he said. Lord Raoul had treated me more gently than the others would have done. Sir Gilbert would not have been so lenient, nor Sir Brian himself either. I looked at Sir Brian again. He was an old man beneath that armored coat. He had grown old in the service of his lord and would have died on his behalf. He disliked me but he loved Lord Raoul.

"So be it, Sir Brian," I said. "We part in haste but yet I hope in peace. One day yet, I may do good to your lord."

And we rode across the bridge.

As he had warned, we rode at top speed, swords drawn, lances ready. For fear of attack, for certainly the men expected it, and were nervous, eager to see their charge bestowed so they could join with the rest of Sedgemont troops. But we heard nothing, saw nothing. Yet everywhere were signs of fear and distrust. The great meadows around the castle were empty; no horses, no cattle. Peasants with strained and anxious faces went scuttling from our path. They must have known who we were. Some of them I knew well from my early days at Sedgemont, but they would not return greetings or look at us.

Suddenly, any armed men, even those they recognized, were menacing, a warning of what worse was to come. All they could think of, and you could see it in their faces, was how to bring the remnants of their flocks and herds and their families as fast as possible within the shelter of the castle. They would stay there then until, they hoped, some better news would give them chance to scuttle out to tend the fields for the spring sowing. Or if bad news came, at least they would be safe and only their homes and plantings would be lost or destroyed. But if what Lord Raoul feared came to pass, all the land would look as deserted soon. It was a frightening thought.

I turned back once before we entered the forest. Behind us rose the towers and parapets of the castle of Sedgemont, built and enlarged so carefully by its former lords and by the earl himself. There flowed the river, deep and swift, under its walls. As we watched, we heard the ominous sound of the great gate being wound down, of the bridge swinging back into place. Thus was Sedgemont bolted up, as I remembered as a child. It seemed impossible to imagine those proud walls torn down, these meadows and fair lands destroyed by siege. But now it seemed that I should never see it again. The forest closed about us, and we rode far away.

It is not my intent to tell you all my story during the next months. For all your prodding, scribe, poet, I cannot write of despair. That is the burden of your songs, or so you tell me. But you are still young and innocent. You write of despair as your invention romanticizes, not as it is. Remembering, I should only sink into it, like a stone thrown into the waters of your mountain lakes, down to peat-black depths. Sufficient to say, I came safely to the convent. It too looked secure, set at the foot of those distant hills that used to tempt me from Sedgemont battlements. High walls surrounded it, although a determined man could have scaled them easily. Yet their massive strength and brooding quality gave them the appearance of protection, and their complexity, set one within the other like a series of boxes, made them seem impenetrable. But the place was gloomy, placed within a hollow of hills, and the swiftness with which the main gate opened a crack to let me in, then slammed, without chance to say farewell, enhanced the feeling of isolation, of gloom. Lord Raoul's men must have ridden off with a sense of relief. Yet this had once been a happy place. Both Lord Raoul and Sir Brian spoke of it as truthfully as they remembered it. And had they known the changes that had taken place, would they have acted otherwise? I think not. As Sir Brian had said, a man hard pressed stands not on niceties. How could they have known that the old prioress, the gentle soul whom Lord Raoul loved for the love she bore his mother, was dead? Had they known her place was taken by another, younger woman from France, trained in another regime and rule, with regulations already formed to beat the devil out of gentler souls, would that have concerned them? No again, for they would have reasoned that even if Sedgemont castle should fall, was not the right of sanctuary still preserved there, for the lord's ward? Who would have thought enemies would come creeping in so close on the borders of Sedgemont? But I digress. Sufficient to say that these White Nuns, as they are called, grow apace everywhere now. They double their energies yearly to show their virtue and so double their possessions. Even in the Celtic lands are they spreading, in the untilled parts, like mushroom patches in damp hollows. Aye, I shall be careful what I say. I know it is not wise these days to speak too openly. Yet I dare affirm that humans made by God in His image, in love, have no need to worship, in such bleakness and despair, Him who is the source of all life and joy. And I tell you, the cloisters where once the ladies of Sedgemont had walked and played had become a fearful place, inhabited by fearful and self-righteous ghosts who crept, white robed, into our lives.

Let me rather tell you first what became of Lord Raoul and his men, and all the great events that shook our island kingdom at that time. Long after did I hear of it, and Giles told me, in fits and starts as I drew it from him. For we met again, as you shall learn, and he showed how it was that Giles, a stable boy who scarcely knew the further side of the castle gates, rode forth with an army and saw the world. So while I sank within those convent walls, so mewed up that any life outside seemed almost unreal, Lord Raoul and his men rode swiftly toward the western border and Cambray.

"A hard ride it was," Giles admitted at last, when I pressured him. "And we have complained of living roughly before. This was nothing but rain and cold and damp so that you could not sit or lie or ride but the water dripped and fell upon you, and all your gear was wet, even the horses' reins slippery to the touch. Our Yuletide was a camp upon sodden ground, with a saddle over our head and bread that was moldy enough to sprout. I have eaten poorly at Sedgemont, but never as poor as that. And these were Norman knights too, who crave their meat and red wine, and will not make a move without a jug of ale in the morning. I will say this for them, they may grumble but they do not give in easily. They keep on moving like wheels that turn over and over.

"And so we came to Cambray. Dreary cold it was, and the sea white like frost. Not that we saw much of it either, for we circled the castle from a distance. Dark and desolate it seemed, to beg your pardon, and all the fields about it run wild. Whoever was inside answered neither greetings nor challenge, and when we brought up a battering ram to try the main gate, they still gave no word. But on the walls above they appeared a raggle bunch as ever I have seen, not a knight among them. And they carried those great long bows I have heard Dylan speak of; so strong are they, they can put an arrow through a breastplate and stick out the point at the back. Those bows drove us out, and we were too few to make a close siege round. And then news came as we had expected, that the Lord of Anjou had landed."

"Where was that?"

"They said that he came to Wareham in the south, sometime in the middle of the month of January, although we heard of it later. But he, it seems, had heard of us, for instead of heading toward the border as he had intended, he swung north toward Devizes, where he was joined by many great lords. For he dared not come too close to us, putting our numbers far higher than they were. Which was perhaps fortunate for us. The guards from Sedgemont were perhaps fifty, and we had lost some of them from the winter cold, although they recovered later to be of service when we needed them. Half that number again of squires and men-at-arms. And half again of knights and men riding with Lord Raoul's vassals, all these, with some of his lesser lords, made up our total, perhaps to one hundred and twenty. Yet all came willingly, out of feudal love, that was one thing. Henry of Anjou had perhaps one hundred and forty knights, and three hundred foot, to say nothing of those troops who rode with the greater lords. But few of those had any real love or duty for him. All was expediency."

"Those great lords, who were they? Would I know them?"

"Great earls they were, of Chester, Salisbury, and Hereford, who, they say, had already quarreled with King Stephen and were therefore forced to Anjou's side. And the earl of that land which lies even further west than Cambray, of Cornwall, where they say all men are giants. But Anjou's main troops were mercenaries, whom he had hired in Gascony. And more ruffian soldiers there have never been."

So spoke my gentle Giles, as if he had been bred a soldier for war.

"For when we caught up with him at Malmesbury, his Gascon mercenaries went wild. They seized the city first, and killed all within it, women and children too. It was my first sight of battle, Lady Ann. The city was a shambles. They had not even sorted through the piles of dead who sprawled in clusters as if taking comfort of one another. Yet they would never have seized Malmesbury castle had not the king's castellan opened it to them, treacherously."

He fell silent then, as if the memory was too strong, and it was long before I could get him to continue.

When he did, it was a sad tale he had to tell.

"We came upon Henry of Anjou's army the next day, having spent the night bivouacked in the woods beyond the river there. Our arrival was well timed. For on the selfsame day the king himself arrived, with all his lords and barons, and camped on the farther side of the stream. That day should the battle have been joined. For the Angevin troops had run amok and could not be brought to discipline. And Stephen had with him a great army. And at Henry of Anjou's back, we waited."

"So, what happened then?"

"All day we sent messages to alert the king. Four times we sent, and three times our men were taken before they forded the river, by those same Gascons who would as soon split a man as look at him. The last time, Lord Raoul would have ridden forth himself, but his other lords dissuaded him, for he was a-froth with rage, that we should sit there idle while the king deliberated. I think he would have charged alone for very shame had not finally King Stephen sent word that we too must wait."

"And then?"

"All night long the rains came back, a deluge, sent from God perhaps. The ground along the river became so deep in mud that even the horses could not keep a footing, and had the men-at-arms marched out, they could have sunk down to their waists. And the king sent word again—wait.

"'We have him in a pincer,' Lord Raoul cried. He had been in the saddle three days and the rain ran down his face like tears. 'If we let go, he will slip out. What better chance than now?'

"But the rains continued; there came warnings of more floods. The king turned back to London and ordered Lord Raoul to

follow behind Anjou where he went, to keep him from the
west and drive him farther east toward better battle sites.

"'What better than here?' Lord Raoul said again, and swore
a great oath that for weakness or fear of his own men, the king
missed his chance to rid the country of the blight that had
fallen on it."

"Then what did Lord Raoul do?"

"As the king ordered. But this was the hardest part. King
Stephen had many Flemish mercenaries among his army. They
rioted when he would not satisfy their demands for more pay.
The Gascon troops, as poorly served, took out their anger in
pillage as they went. Between both contending sides, there
was not much left that they did not destroy. I would not tell
you all, to sicken your ears with horror. But I have seen half
of the great places of the land: Coventry, Bedford, Leices-
ter. . . . They all look alike, full of dead and dying men and
broken stones."

"And Henry of Anjou?"

"Like quicksilver. You cannot pin him down. Trap him, and
he slides away. If the king had spared us some troops, if we
had had a larger force . . . if Prince Eustace could have been
persuaded to join with us instead of striking off on his
own . . . They say battles are lost for want of a horseshoe nail.
We wanted a little more than that, but not so much that Lord
Raoul should not have had it. But we kept our part of the
bargain. Anjou could not turn west and so at last we pushed
him to another confrontation with the king."

He hesitated, then blurted out, "I tell you, Lady Ann, by
then it was high summer and I am not sure which is worse:
the winter's rain or to be riding armed all day in the heat and
dust, with a stubble bed at night and vermin to make you itch
and sweat. And fever. I would have a hundred times been in
the stable at Sedgemont."

"And Lord Raoul?"

He hesitated again, not because he feared to displease me

with his new loyalties but because, in some ways, he had
already said it all. His speech was laced with Raoul. His very
words were Raoul's. But Raoul had been angry. He had always
taken risks; a waiting game was not his strategy. Finally, he
had baited the trap that brought Henry "out of nowhere" to
the River Thames, there to seize the bridge that crossed it at
Wallingford. But first Henry had to take the king's siege castle
at Crowmarsh. This was the king's chance to hem him round
again.

"And then?"

Giles shrugged, a perfect parody of Raoul's shrug if he had
but known it. "It was the same as before. The king and all his
men on one side, Henry of Anjou with his army on the other.
And they skirmished across the wretched stream, among the
water reeds, as if hunting for duck. Finally there was a meeting."

"With whom?"

"The king, Prince Eustace, and the lords of England. Lord
Raoul was summoned. I went with him. Ann, I, a stable boy,
saw the King of England!"

In his excitement of reliving that time, he called me by name
as he used to do, before awkwardness had made us formal with
each other. He chatted freely then, explaining. How he and
Geoffrey had been chosen to go with Lord Raoul, how they
had washed and shaved in haste, tipping cold river water over
their heads, how somewhere, from the remnants of their supply
train, pages had dug out three fine shirts, and new red surcoats
embroidered in gold thread by the Lady Mildred for such an
occasion. Then, mounted and armed, they had forded the
stream and ridden to the king's pavilion on the eastern bank.

"Did you stay outside?"

"No, although it would have been better if I had. My lord's
black brute kicked a fence apart and took three men to hold
him. No, Geoffrey and I stood within, with the other squires
at the door, and held our lord's cloak and sword. There were
many great lords; richly dressed they were for war, not like

us who had crammed our finery over the wear and tear of a year's campaign."

"And King Stephen?"

"A kingly man, tall, gray faced, quiet. They said that he had fallen not once but thrice from his horse as he came toward Wallingford, but even I ride better than that. Lord Raoul said aloud, although under his breath so only we heard, 'Dear God, but he has aged.' Yet they greeted each other affectionately. Not a word did Lord Raoul say then or again about the mishap at Malmesbury."

"And the meeting?"

"Quiet at first, each great lord standing to give his thoughts. Or rather, not so much thoughts as fears. I could not follow all their reasoning but it seemed to me they were reluctant to speak out what was in their hearts. The king sat apart and chewed his nails. Until Lord Raoul stepped forward."

"And his advice?"

"My lady, he spoke quietly too. I cannot explain all the arguments he used, but Geoffrey told me later. To sum up, he said to the king and his court, 'Either you must fight Henry of Anjou and destroy him. Army to army, or, if need be, man to man. Call out your champion and let there be combat between him in your name and Henry's, for the settlement of this quarrel. Or if not war, then peace.'"

"Did the others agree?"

"At first, some cried for a champion. Some said it would be Lord Raoul himself. Then all took up the same cry. Those who had shifted and shuffled most loudly of all, to make a peace. Except the king's son, Prince Eustace, a tall stout man, who shouted it was treason to persuade the king against his will. My lord outfaced him. Lady Ann, he was a greater lord in his worn clothes with the red and scarlet draped over than the prince in his furs and jewels.

"'The king's will is his own,' Lord Raoul said. 'But no man, not even a king, can rule without the help of his friends. For this reason are we summoned here. Look round, my lords of England. We have slashed stripes across this broad land like pieces of raw flesh that will never be healed while this war lingers on. What will be left for any king to rule if we do not halt it now.'

"Then the king himself stood up and said, 'My lords, barons, princes, I have heard your speech and it comforts me, that despite all these troubles I have loyal friends. If there cannot be a decisive battle, and you all fear there cannot be, then there must be peace.' So a treaty was made."

"Were you at the peace treaty then?"

"It did not happen right away. And we had already gone before the signing. But look, Lady Ann." He pulled from beneath his sleeve a gold piece sewn up in a small purse. "While we were leaving, the king came to us and thanked us for our pains, a most gracious lord he is, and gave both Geoffrey and me a gift." He turned the coin over and over, the first he had ever owned, and a king had given it to him.

"But the treaty. There was peace?"

"Not at first." Giles spoke reluctantly. "If the barons and their knights were for it, the mercenaries were not. Nor the prince either. It seems in his anger he rode off and began to sack lands in Cambridgeshire, and waste the whole region around. But it was the mercenaries who caused the most trouble. For if they could not fight, how would they get their pleasure or reward?"

"But the treaty was signed?"

"I do not know, lady. We were not there."

"Not there? But Raoul had counseled it? Saw he not the king again?"

"My lady, yes. But it was a private meeting. I was not witness to it."

I knew he was not telling me the truth of that, but nothing I said could make him reveal what else he knew. I found out about that later. All he would tell me was that the king had ordered Lord Raoul and his men back to the border, there to win a treaty with the Celts so that all the plans they made would not come undone by a surprise attack from the west. So back they trailed, and camped along the border again. But to tell how that happened, I must now return to my first arrival at the convent, Lord Raoul's "safe place" in the hills.

A wild bird cannot fit itself to captivity as can one bred in a cage. Had I lived at Cambray, my father would have sent me to such a place. He used to say that maids who were convent bred made the best wives, but that was because he thought them tractable. I came too late to such a life, with thoughts and ideas already formed. And this was not the soft and gentle rule that the ladies of Sedgemont had enjoyed. There were no other ladies there, no one to talk to, for the nuns lived by the strict rule of silence, even at mealtimes. Save for one little half-witted boy, whom they kept to tend their herds and whom I befriended with scraps of bread thrown over into the outer courtyard where he lived, I had no speech with anyone. And he was too shy or too stupid to reply. I heard no news, saw no one, was so shut off that whether Henry of Anjou had landed or not, whether Raoul lived or not, whether Sedgemont stood or not, I did not know, and had no way of knowing.

As a guest there, I should have lived apart from their rules. At first, the new prioress and her nuns seemed anxious to please, showing, if truth be told, more deference than any had at Sedgemont, speaking with honeyed words when they did speak, which made me uncomfortable. But suddenly, without warning, these obsequious ways changed. The gardens where I had been allowed to walk were closed to me. The little room where I lodged comfortably, if not in luxury, was replaced by one of their cells. The goods and possessions that I had managed to bring with me disappeared, save for Giles's little dagger, which I had had the foresight to bury in the garden. My clothes even were exchanged for the long habit of unwashed, undyed wool, which gives their order its name of "White." And rougher fabric to irritate the skin does not exist. Instead then of walking at leisure, I must work with the rest of them in their fields, must attend their constant services, must keep silence and fast as they did. . . . Well, such things I could bear. I did not mind the loss of luxury; I was not used to it as great ladies are; I could live on bread and water again. Nor did the hard work trouble me. I could almost enjoy putting plants in place and helping them to grow. Are not the herb gardens at Cambray famous still? And prayer. Have we not all need of prayers to see us through this world? If youth minds the loss of sleep, the long watches in the night, well, then was there the time I have spoken of, to think on and to pray for the souls of those I had loved, and who in shocking-wise suddenly had seemed as if new-killed. And for those who still lived, I could remember them. Comrades, friends, old companions, Giles, Dylan, Geoffrey . . . and most of all to think on Lord Raoul. But to be forced to these things—work, prayer, contemplation, poverty, obedience, chastity—the laws of these holy orders are known to us all now. And if you do not know them, praise God you do not. Peace, you bid me again, that I not anger the Holy Church. I do not concern myself with the Church, and all these quarrels between Crown and Church that have plagued this land are beyond my understanding. But to make a nun of me . . . Poor I was already, none poorer, obedient perforce to Lord Raoul's will, and chaste perhaps against my own. But I had not been sent here to be shut away forever. When next you write of despair, name it imprisonment without cause or escape.

I know now that it is against their strictest rule to force someone into religious life. I know now that first there is a long trial or apprenticeship as novice. But who is to distinguish between force and persuasion? I had no choice. By subtle means at first, then openly, was I shown the path of salvation until, with close-cropped hair, undyed robe, silence, and prayer, I could have been taken for any other there. Except I would not take the vow.

That was not easily done, to stand against them. God never had such zealous workers on His behalf as these. It is a logic

I have never understood, that to be a soldier in the holy wars you may kill your enemy to save his soul. But I am stubborn, as you know, and that may have saved mine.

Then came a day when all was made clear. At first, it seemed like all the other days that since the summer months had merged into one. Why do I remember it so well—because of what the lady prioress said, what she did? Because it was the first time that I sensed the hopelessness of my case, as one senses decay? Or because, as it happened, it was also the last time? The day had begun early, before dawn. I had been summoned to the prioress's room after the morning prayers. I was still dazed with sleep, drugged with the fume of incense and the drone of voices. Hunger gnawed. Her words beat like the flies that buzzed in the warm autumn air.

"I was sent here for safety's keeping," I said at last, as I had said often before. "Nothing more."

"Safe from what?" she said shrewdly, eyeing me askance from under her fine-arched brows. "Was it to be safe perhaps from sin? Did you not ask for a man to marry you? Who was your lover? They say it was one of Sedgemont's groomsmen. Was that the sin for which your lord sent you here?"

I would have argued with her, but she was too full of words for me, who had once used them myself as weapons.

"Or is it the Lord of Sedgemont who was the danger? Is not he young and vigorous? Did not you try to overthrow him with your body before his men?"

She had never dared say that before. I wondered almost idly who had been the talebearer. None had spoken of it in my presence until now.

"Or have you thought," she said, pressing close, "that he may intend to keep you here forever? Locked up, that no one should know where you are? But should you count yourself among the blessed, free of all wordly ties, then could you bestow your lands as you wished, freely to God's House. Naked and poor would you make a worthy bride."

Had I been quicker, I would have pondered that "naked and

poor." Ladies of rank are not expected to come empty-handed to holy orders. "Naked and poor" would have little to recommend it. But it was what she had said first that struck hardest. And she sensed that at once.

"For, Sister," she said, calling me that name although I was no kith or kin of hers, "is it not also true that having asked for a man, you refused the one who offered? And he was no stable groom, he. What makes you set yourself so high that you may pick and choose among the great lords of the land?"

She rattled off the names of women in the holy works who had defied their earthly lords to their eternal damnation. I have told you before I had little skill with books, but I have hated learning the more since she used it against me.

"I do not choose to wed at all," I said, when silence became painful.

"So. Then earthly marriage is not to your liking. And if Lord Raoul of Sedgemont will not let you go, but means to pen you here all your life, why cavil at becoming a Bride of Christ? Is it not pride puffed up to think that you, a silly maid, can know better than those who are set to rule and guide you? Did you think to defy the Lord of Sedgemont and not anger him?"

"He did not send me here to make a nun of me!" I cried at last, fear making me speak it aloud.

She looked at me again, searching, pitying.

"And if he did?" she said, pressing hard. "How would you know? Or how prevent it?"

And again, she said later, "They say your mother had converse with the devil, that she could foresee the future plain and clear. Is not that the devil's work? And did she see what would bring her joy?"

And then later again, each time upon the hour did she return. . . .

"And did not you shout out against the friends of Lord Raoul, in his own Hall, that all should think you had visions too?

Would you be held in league with the Prince of Darkness? Those who consort with him are burned for it, on earth here as in hell hereafter."

And again.

"Have you thought of the burning?" Her eyes dark and fierce, pressing on the nerve of fear. "Dare you think of it? Put your hand then upon this flame." And she held out a taper, faint and wan in her bleak room where even in the morning all seemed dark.

"See how your flesh shrinks back. But that was but a moment's pain. Imagine it for eternity."

And then again, when neither candle flame nor whip could make me speak.

"Imagine eternity. Then is every second as a year, every hour a torment without cease. But those who are among the saved, God's children, shall await the Second Coming with joy. As a Bride of Christ, would you be named among the blessed. You should be on your knees, you child of death, to give thanks to God, that thus you can at one time be saved from sin and from the Lord of Sedgemont's doom."

I turned aside, hunching my shoulders against the blows, hiding my scorched fingers in the folds of my gown. I knew she lied in many things, but there was such a mixture of truth and lie, and both so intertwined, that it would have taken a clearer head than mine to have sorted them out. But one thing she did not know. The mention of my mother, that unknown woman I knew so little of, gave me an extra kind of endurance that she herself must have had—the courage that perhaps Lord Raoul had spoken of when he had said one need not fight the less because the cause is lost—well, even if my cause was lost, I still would not give way.

Yet later that same day, when I was working in the field, my courage ran not so high. My back was stiff where the lash had fallen; and although I could have been glad for the open air and the keen cool smell and taste of autumn, yet they weighed upon me. Almost a year ago, Lord Raoul had returned to Sedgemont, and we had hunted the great boar through the forests there. A year gone by then. And what had become of him, I thought, and of his little band of men, of Giles and Geoffrey and the others who had ridden out of Sedgemont, that they should have forgotten me? And for the first time I wondered what would happen if they all should die upon some far-off battlefield, God forbid, for who then would I have to remember, and who would then remember me? But someone had not forgotten me, and then, suddenly, horribly, all the rest was made clear.

We worked on in the faint sun of that autumn day, our long gowns scratching harshly as they dragged across the earth. Like bleached figures we moved upon the brown fields. Presently the sun would sink behind the hills, the long services would begin, the long arguments. Perhaps, I thought for the first time, there is little use to stand against her, perhaps I should listen to what she says. To give up everything is to have no desire. Perhaps that is the easiest way.

The girl ahead of me, a small homely soul, younger than I but already about to take her vows, mouthed at me. It was against the strictest rule for her to speak. Yet she was calling me by name, and we were all nameless here.

"Lady Ann," her lips were saying, "Lady Ann, listen, pretend not to look."

How could she know my name? How dared she break the rule? We pulled on the autumn weeds until we were again at the far part of the field, where the others were out of earshot.

"A messenger," she said, "from the west. Go to the tree and see for yourself."

I knew at once where she meant, what tree. But why?

We bent and pulled, two rows apart, she slightly in front. I could feel the sudden hope flare in my cheeks. Out of the silence to find a friend. Out of the waiting to find news.

We turned the row along an inner wall.

"Hurry," she said aloud, so I could not miss her words, "there is danger."

My first thought, of course, had been that the message came from Lord Raoul, but that thought died upon the instant. Had it been his message, whatever it was, they could not have kept that from me. From Sedgemont, then? But that, too, seemed unlikely.

"At the hour of prayer," she said again, when we turned at the next corner. "I heard them talk. Go then."

I understood her perfectly, although she spoke in broken phrases, as if pulled from her with the effort. We worked on in silence in the afternoon's growing chill. The sound of the chapel bell was a sword thrust. The other nuns stood upright, smoothing their skirts, wiping their hems free of dirt. They began to drift slowly toward the gate that led to the chapel courtyard. She waited behind them, gathering our tools in a wicker basket, spreading her skirt to shield me as I slid into a corner. Out of the silence to find such a friend. I sought her long after, that small homely girl with the red cheeks that the wind nipped, but she was lost somewhere among those silent white-gowned women. She waited as long as she dared, lingering, so that the others would not suspect if they turned back. When the last one had disappeared, she pushed something into my hand.

"I heard them," she cried. "I heard and stole this."

But then she was gone too, in a flurry of white. The bell had stopped ringing now. The chapel doors would be shut. All the nuns and the lay workers would be inside. They would miss me, but it would be a while before they would send to search. I held the little bag she had handed me, thinking it looked familiar, although until I opened it I did not remember what it was. Cecile had given it to me before I had left Sedgemont. Inside were my mother's chaplet and my father's ring, the heavy gold ring with his seal that he had always worn. I stared at both, holding them in my hands. How had she found

them? Where? Both had been taken away with the rest of my
belongings. What had she heard that had made her dare? I
stood for a long time staring, as the last rays of the sun caught
and sparkled on the gold.

Then, gathering thoughts, I turned and ran. Let me explain.
The convent was built, as are many such places, in a square,
with an inner courtyard in the center and the main buildings
grouped about the edge. The cloisters or covered walks ran
around these central buildings that contained the ones of main
importance: the chapel, the dormitories, and the refectory,
where we slept and ate. Around that central block were open
fields, where we had been working. Beyond them, another
line of buildings that housed storerooms, granaries, stables,
and rooms for the lay workers and for visitors. The high walls
of these outer buildings helped enclose the inner block more
securely. But there was one place where, if one could climb
up high enough, one could look over the wall and see beyond
it into the small courtyard that, in turn, opened onto the main
gates. Once, perhaps all newcomers to the convent knew the
place, and had learned to climb the tree that hung over its
wall; once the younger nuns would have played in the garden
there with their lady guests. Now all was overgrown and de-
cayed, rank with reeds. But I had gone there in the early days,
scaled the tree to whistle to the dumb boy who lived on the
other side, and had hidden Giles's knife at its roots. I knew at
once where I was to go. The grasses and weeds slashed at my
ankles as I ran. In the gathering darkness, I could have been
any shadow, scratching in the earth among the roots to find
the little knife I had buried there. I freed it from its oiled
wrappings and slid it into my sleeve as I began to climb the
branches of the tree that hung over the wall. When I was high
enough, I could swing myself out so I could see what was in
the courtyard beneath. I had not run so fast or climbed so high
for a long time and my skirts hampered me, but although out
of breath, I began to whistle as I used to, to summon the boy.

He had always come willingly, like a wild thing, famished for scraps of food that I saved from my own frugal meals, but it had been months since I had seen him, had been free of my own time, and he might have forgotten. In any case, I thought, suddenly desperate, he cannot help me, for how can I explain to him what I must find out, although death and danger should mean something even to his feeble mind. And then the whistle died, half-uttered. I did not need to find out what I could see for myself—the great war horse, still saddled from its ride, tethered in the yard below. Nor did I need to see its rider to recognize it. I could still remember Giles's description in the stables at Sedgemont.

"Two bays," he had said, "that came the first time. One tall and big-boned, with a mane that falls forward and one white sock upon the off-hind foot. One that came the first time but did not return a second."

And there it stood, the bay horse from Maneth's stable. And there was the man, stepping out of the small room that must once have seen the comings and goings of many guests but now was always empty. Perhaps he had gone outside to relieve himself, for he was still fumbling with his clothes when he came to stand beside the horse. And he stared at the boy who came running toward the tree, his face lit up with smiles. It was too late to make gesture to silence or secrecy. Both boy and man had seen me at the same instant.

"And who is come to spy untimely upon men's affairs?"

The man himself I had never seen, a short squat fellow with a slash across one cheek. But the voice I knew, had heard a hundred times in nightmares echoing down those winding stairs. Paralyzed with fright, I looked down at him as he looked up at me. Then with one hand he dragged the terrified boy to his side, while with the other he reached up above his head to grab for me. I began to hurl myself backward, not caring how I went, but he was too quick and caught at the dangling folds of my gown, tugging and ripping until he could pry my

arms free and pull me down into the courtyard. It was a long
hard fall although he took some of the weight. But I landed
crookedly, with a jar that sent all things reeling. Before I could
struggle, he had dragged me into the entrance of his room and
thrust the boy before him to cower in a corner. I could feel
his hands about my face and body pushing back the clothes.
His breath was hot with sweat and wine, and with something
else that made the skin freeze where it touched.

"What white dove is it," he panted, "fluttering down?"

I closed my ears and eyes to that hissing sound I had hoped
never to hear again. He was running his fingers across my
breasts, squeezing and pulling, until he came to the velvet
purse that I had strung about my waist. He dropped me abruptly
when he felt it, and took it to the table where he could shake
out its contents, kicking the boy aside as he went. I heard his
whistle and the clink of gold. I struggled to sit upright, and
saw him standing there, a squat figure with legs apart, his
shadow dense and thick in the candlelight. In one hand he
held my father's ring, slipping it on and off his finger with a
strange, slow gesture.

"Now by all that's holy," he swore, hissing at me.

He picked up the candle and came back, holding it so close
that the hot wax dripped upon my skin as he pushed back the
coverings from my shorn hair.

"By all that's holy," he repeated, and a grin, I cannot describe
it, covered half his face and yet was not a grin at all, but was
a mask that twisted the unscarred side. I could see now, as he
spoke, how the one part of the mouth did not move, so that
the saliva sprayed forth from the other.

"Do not tell me that I have come all this way with a sack
of gold to pay for the prioress's prize and you have come
tumbling at my feet." He grinned again. "Who are you, dove?"

I pursed my lips. He caught at my neck with his thick hand,
my father's ring gleaming in the light. Had my hair been
longer, he would have torn it from its roots, but he twisted
my neck until I could scarcely breathe.

"Who, who," he hissed, "but Ann of Cambray herself, with her red scalp and her mother's eyes. Right, am I?"

A sound behind him made him swirl. The boy, who had been slowly edging toward the door, had struck his hand against a goblet of wine that stood on a stool. With a bound, the man was upon him again, dragging him to his feet. The boy opened his mouth to cry, but no sound came, although his hands beat wildly in terror.

"Two of you, eh?" he said. "Since she won't talk, you shall. Who is she, my thief here, what is her name?"

And with each word, he battered at the boy's face until it became a sheet of blood.

"Stop," I screamed, finding my own voice at last, scrabbling forward. "He cannot speak, he is dumb. Stop."

He released the boy, letting him fall like a small bundle of rags against the table.

"But you can speak," he said. "And I know you, Ann of Cambray. Back from the dead yourself, although we thought you dead."

He paused as if to flavor the strangeness of it, walking about, stepping over the boy as if he did not exist.

"What if I am?" I said at last, knowing that it made no difference whether I spoke or kept silent. He would kill us either way. I could tell that from his walk.

"My master would pay well for you," he said with his wolfish smirk. "Once it was for you dead. Now for you to be kept shut up here, but more, I think, to have you in his possession, alive. But how to get you out of here? No need for the lady prioress to have her bribe to keep you if you'll come willingly, my dove."

He stared at me thoughtfully, his eyes bright with anticipation. Then again he acted swiftly. Before I knew what he was about, he seized the boy and slapped his head against the wall, so that I heard it snap like a piece of dried stick.

"Take off those clothes," he shouted at me, "before I knock you brainless the same way."

He held the boy in his hands and began to peel off the stained shirt and jacket, throwing them at my feet.

"Fast, faster," he shouted. "They'll be about us otherwise. I've other ways to make you fast, although I won't touch your face, yet."

I stood unbelieving. I heard the bell chime out the quarter hour. A quarter hour since I had run from the field and climbed the tree and discovered what danger it was that my friend had tried to warn me of, that she must have overheard.

He threw down the boy like a used sack upon the ground. His limbs came spilling out white and heavy; so had Talisin looked that day that he had died. A quarter of an hour. And I had stood and seen murder done, without lifting a finger to help. A poor half-witted boy, broken apart like a bag of bones because he could not speak.

"Hurry," he said again, "or you will know the same. Put those things on."

I felt the tears start and run down my face. I kept my eyes on him as I tore the rest of my dress free, shaking the pieces from my shoulders. And felt the sharp edge of the little knife slide into my waiting hand, point first, as Lord Raoul had shown me months ago.

6

HE MAN STOOD TO ONE SIDE SHOUTING
orders at me while he went about his preparations,
putting his belongings into piles, setting out his
boots and spurs, placing my velvet bag alongside
one of his own that clanked, heavy with coins, as he moved
it. The feel of the well-known hilt in my hand, the wicked
point, steadied me. I almost heard Lord Raoul's voice laughing
as he said, *Remember you have but one chance to strike, so strike home.*

With that thought, breath and resolution returned. I stared
at the man, never taking my eyes from his face, while the
white robe curled about my feet and I lifted first one leg and
then the other to step free of it. He had stopped what he was
doing now and was staring, too, resolution fading from his
eyes, something dark and hot taking its place. He said nothing,
moved purposefully, unbuckling sword and knife, unbuttoning
his jerkin.

"Well, well, dove," he said, and his voice had taken a new
quality, the sound men make to themselves when they curry
a horse, half-whistle, half-purr, and his tongue flicked between
his lips, "so that is what my master was biding on. So."

I let him look at me. God forgive me, but I let him, calmly,
part of my mind registering the effect my nakedness had on
him. Lust mounted in him like a wave, cresting at his face,
which seemed to swell, bloated with desire. I stepped back,
appalled, disgust rising in my throat like vomit, new fear like
sweat across my skin. The wall jarred against my back and I
had not known I had moved.

He was unfastening his belt now, his hands clumsy, letting

it fall with a clatter. He caught at the shirt beneath the outer jacket, tearing at the fastenings until his bare skin came tumbling out, wet as if with rain, and his hair was matted.

"We'll not leave awhile yet," he said, whispering, his half-grin breaking out. "We'll lie low and let them search for you. We've time for fun."

Still not taking his eyes from me, he began to fumble with his nether hose, straining to burst the laces. Then he came toward me, hair on head and face and body raised like a dog's.

I heard Raoul's voice in my ear again: *Hold firm, hold firm.*

He stood still once, like that boar in the forest, scenting out what was before him, thrusting with his horn that swung before.

"By all that's holy," he breathed, "to have all this."

And then he came upon me in a rush, head down, shoulders squared, and all his swollen front thrust forward. Almost against my will, I felt my hand tighten and prepare. The wall was at my back, and without my trying, he ran himself full tilt against the dagger point. I felt it slide as if through butter, and for a moment all his wet pulsating flesh lay against mine, pinning me to the wall. I could not see, felt only the rank wheeze of his breath, his thick wet skin. Then breath and flesh and skin seemed to shrivel and fade. He slid sideways, stiffly, his arms still outspread, and the gush of blood that followed pooled about us on the floor.

Then nothing. No sound. Only the faint gutterings of the candle and the painful thud of my own heart. I stood as if frozen, unable to move or think, the knife held stiffly in my blood-caked hand.

The sound of the bell brought me back. Another quarter hour was done. I moved with a cry over that lifeless body and felt waves of sickness tear my chest apart, as if loathing and relief would drown me. I have seen men die since then, God forgive me, but seldom death so vile, to perish full-bellied on the swell of lust. Gwendyth had vengeance, but my soul cringed from the taking of it. But there was no time for thoughts, regrets, then. They come later, long after in the dark of night, alone.

Two bells had rung out their chimes. If I was to make a move, I must do it now. They should still be at their chanting. But they might have sent already to begin the search, or they might be waiting to the end, to hunt together, a blind man's bluff with darkness as the hood and here the game's end. If they found me with these dead bodies, what then could I do? Without thought, without hesitation, I took the poor pitiful clothes of the dead boy and slid them on. They were too short, but they would suffice for the time. I folded my own white gown to hide the stains and tears and arranged it as a shroud about him, prayers coming to my lips almost by instinct, although I did not know I was thinking of them. I was able to straighten his tumbled arms and legs although not the twisted angle of his head. But I wiped his face clean, and pillowed it on some straw that I dragged off the bed. Then, with loathing but design, I pulled the dead man beside him, throwing the rest of the straw from the pallet about, heaping his clothes over him. Stopping one last time, I wrested my father's ring from his finger, then ran to the chamber door. Luck was with me: there was no noise of search or outcry, only the pigeons cooing in the cot above the archway, the horse softly feeding.

I tiptoed to the entrance of the courtyard; again nothing, except a second empty yard and the gate of the convent with the great bar set to keep it locked. I struggled with the bar, breaking nails and skin until, with a groan, it swung back and the gates creaked half-open.

Still no noise. But now I must be quick. When they came looking, there must be something to distract them. I ran back to the room. With shaking hand, I took the candle and thrust it in the straw, so that it flared up with a wicked roar. There was nothing else of use, sword and belt too large, spurs too heavy. At the last moment I remembered the bag of gold coins and my small velvet pouch, and reached across to snatch them as the flames began to lick at the wooden furniture. Then to where the horse was tied, straining nervously now with flaring eyes at the sight and sound of fire. I scrambled onto its back as best I could, wasting time, for it would not stand still, and with my knife hacked at the rope that tied it. And then as the first cries of alarm were raised, I kicked and wrenched the horse round, sending it squealing and stamping through the archway into the second courtyard, crashing past the outer gate into that forest beyond.

How far I rode in the darkness, full tilt down one of the forest tracks, I cannot say. Even the horse began to weary. So gradually, as no sound or pursuit followed, we slackened speed and began to plod more slowly forward. Then there was time to think. Among the thoughts (and the others I keep to myself, they are private, I tell you, sad and private thoughts) were practical ones. As far as I could tell, we had followed the same direction that we had taken last year from Sedgemont. But I did not mean to return to Sedgemont. Somewhere I must find the track that turned to the west, the way the soldiers would have gone after they had left us. To the west lay Cambray. I would go westward.

At length, when I judged we could ride no more, I turned off the path, found a resting place under some trees, tied the horse with the dangling rope end, and settled for the night. The saddlebags were still in place, filled with scraps of food and meat. I ate slowly as I considered my position. First, as I might have thought of earlier, there would be no pursuit, the convent having neither horses nor men able to ride after me. Secondly, if the prioress sent for help, what would she say, to whom would she go? Not to Sedgemont, that was certain, nor to the lords of Maneth, at least not yet, if she must report my loss. Thirdly, the fire would certainly hinder her, for although she might find evidence, she would not know its meaning. She might even think that I had perished in the flames.

She might be loath to report that also, for what reward could she expect from Maneth if I were dead? So I could feel fairly safe for the moment, on all or any of these accounts. And if her lies had, at last, been made clear, well, at least she had given me back faith in my own friends and in myself.

Yet, on the other hand, what hope could I, a maid, have, to ride unescorted in these rough and dangerous times? How could I expect to get through to the western border undetected? Yet as I worried, food and rest gave me courage. Why should not I travel as a boy, a page, about his master's business? As Lady Ann, I could not go alone. And, for all I knew, Guy of Maneth would be out scouring the countryside for me, even if I had a score of knights beside me. As page, about my lord's affairs, mounted, with a sharp dagger at my side, I could be as safe as any other on the road, provided I kept at a distance from anyone else and was wary in all I said and did. But then, I thought again, there were too many inconsistencies—clothes and steed, for example, did not match with each other: a swine-herd on a knight's war horse? Besides, there might be others who later on would recognize, as I had done, a bay from Maneth's stable. Yet, I thought again, if I can exchange this horse for something more suiting my size and needs, and find clothes becoming to my new station, a warm cloak and hood, I may pass. . . .

So did I plan, and with that, slept. God grant us all such easy sleep, such dreamless rest, as I had then, still patterned with the blood of the man I had slain, still dressed in the clothes of a boy I had seen murdered. Yet patience, patience. God has His way to requite those who break His laws, even in the end. I have seen men die since; but the first death at your conscience comes the hardest, may cost more dear, although the debt be long in its repayment.

At earliest dawn I was on my way again. In daylight, I could at least see which of the many paths would put the sun behind me; without that knowledge, I would have been lost, for the forest here spilled out on all sides like a great gray sea and the dead leaves underfoot rustled like shingle. I was caught in an endless mesh of branch and thicket, alone. If I had had sling or arrows, I could have had fresh meat in plenty, for hares and rabbits bounded away in front of us almost close enough to touch. At length, about midday, I came to a village deep in a clearing, with only a few half-tilled fields set about. They were a strange race, those villagers, living far from other humans, not wresting their living from the land with crops and herds, but hewing it forth from the trees that they cut and hauled for the iron and steel makers farther north. They were a dark and dirty crew, as like to have pulled me from my horse as not, but I kept at a distance, and with voice and gesture copied from the fair-haired Geoffrey when he wished to make a good impression, promised them money from my little hoard if they would furnish my needs, pivoting my own horse about so no one could come creeping up behind me.

My story or manner convinced them. Or perhaps it was the sight of the coins. Or perhaps luck was still with me. They brought up a smaller pony, with food and clothes strapped on, stolen no doubt, at least the pony must have been, for it was a well-bred beast, better than I had right to hope for.

After letting them trot it up and down for inspection, I had them lead it to a clearing in the forest and then back off, so I could effect a change, having told them some improbable story which I now forget. They may have taken me for a thief myself with my bruised and swollen face, the bloodstains visible still. Having taken precaution to hack through reins and saddle girths to prevent pursuit, I threw myself from one mount to the other, fearing to ride on with the bay in case it should betray me, fearing to leave it behind if they would use it to swing out after me. I galloped from the clearing and did not feel safe until a half-day's hard ride had convinced me that I was free. Then I could go on, more slowly again, for the first time feeling that perhaps this improbable venture would suc-

ceed. Dressed in my new finery I scarce knew myself, and
once was startled by my own reflection when we stopped to
drink at a woodland pool. I had not realized how my face,
still marked with rough usage, the close-crisped hair, the jerkin, boots, dagger, all enhanced the role I had chosen to play.
I even began to savor the part—a young gentleman about
some important business on his father's behalf for his lord, for
so my story grew, with hint of something illicit, some minor
crime perhaps, some fault that had made the shelter of the
woods a better place for the while, some little hint of danger
that I thought might make people leery of me. One thing was
certain: in this young boy, half-defiant, half-aggressive, no
one would see the Lady Ann of Cambray.

The next days passed without incident, although the weather
worsened, changing suddenly to sleet and rain, so that I was
forced to find shelter at times, although once I was obliged to
spend the night huddled underneath a hollow tree, and worse
lodgings I have never known. But I would have had to make
contact with people in any case, my food supplies having run
out and the western reaches of the forest appearing to thin
out abruptly. Isolated farms and villages took the place of trees.
I would have avoided these places if I had had a choice, for I
was still not sure of my way, and although certain I was moving
westward, I was always fearful of coming too far north and
encroaching on Maneth lands. I had been only once on this
way, and then as a child, but the distant line of mountains,
whence came the storms weeping down—those I did remember. And the fertile valleys at their foot.

Yet the storms were a boon to me. They hid my tracks,
made pursuit difficult, so that when finally the Lord of Maneth
heard of my escape from the convent where they had thought
to lock me away forever, it was too late to throw a ring of
men around the forest edge; I had already slipped past. But I
did not know all this at the time, nor that the cold and wet
that hindered me made me safe, although, as you will hear,

at a later date, an even wilder storm helped me in similar fashion.

So now I moved on, albeit slowly, bettering my story with each retelling until no one seemed to question it or me. In this way did I, in my small fashion, repeat those greater, weightier journeys of which I was to hear later from Giles.

In one incident especially did I reflect those adventures of greater import, although to compare them would be vanity beyond foolishness. When I came to the upland plains, which you have to cross to reach the hill country proper, then did I see for myself the desolation that had haunted Giles. The villages there were not so large or important as the ones he had seen, but once they must have been prosperous, full of people busy about their affairs, rural people content to work on the land for their overlord. Now everything was unkempt, as if those who lived there no longer cared what became of them. And once, by chance, my path crossed that of the armies' although they had long moved on, where, no one seemed to know or care either. But here, equally in small-wise, did my experience repeat the feeling of our times—that nowhere was safe territory, nowhere were homes or fields or occupations or inhabitants secure from desolation.

It was a poor sort of place, this village, one of the worst I had passed through. The villagers at Sedgemont lived as princes in comparison. Caught by a new blizzard, I had lodged at what must at one time have been an inn. Now, its doors and shutters battered down, its flooring ripped apart, it might have served as a cattle pen. Yet people lived there, many of them, whose own hovels had been razed to the ground. I noticed how they burned the wooden boards that might have been used to make repairs. Even the fence pickets they burned, as if there was no need to preserve them.

Usually, too, western people are curious with strangers. Not open themselves, they nevertheless like to hear the news of the greater world. These people were listless. You could see it in the way men sat hunched around their fire with never stick or strap to keep them occupied, and women crouched against the walls without wool or thread. There were few children, no cattle, and no work in the fields. I think people were too apathetic to take heed of my tale, however well I told it. Save one man, old but still alert; you could tell that by the way his eyes still gleamed faintly and his toothless jaw jutted out when he was displeased. He took me aside the second day. I was not frightened of him. He was as thin and dry as a reed, no taller than I was, and bent about the joints like a gnarled stump. And I had Giles's knife at hand.

"Who would it be you are seeking now?" he asked in his singsong voice. I had forgotten how they spoke there, Norman-French, but with such a Celtic lilt as to make it neither one language nor another. I did not answer at first, seeing to my pony for the next day's ride, wary of a trap.

He gestured with his knotted hands at all the broken doors and walls. "Many passed through here last spring," he said, "going east, as doubtless you have heard. Then back they came again, twice within months."

He spat among the nettles that still grew through the shattered floor.

"Back and forth like hounds baiting. From France most of them came, panting to devour us."

He spat again. "I'll show you where one company camped," he said. "If you've a mind to go there. Up yonder." He nodded to the hill above the village ruins. "Only fools would stay down here to tear at what had already been stripped bare. But up there, great walls of stone they built, wondrous to behold, and set up camp in proper-wise."

Against my better judgment, I went up with him. Yet I was curious, too, to see what manner of men these raveners had been. It was still light, although the sky was studded with the wrack of clouds, scudding along behind the storm. We climbed slowly, for the ground was iced with hail and sleet. We went at his pace, but I took care that he walked in front, and kept my hand upon my knife hilt for security. It was a strange place he brought me to, yet he was right that it was better kept than the ruins below. Walled round it was with large stone blocks, and divided by stone pillars into storage areas, stalls, and barracks. It was also clear no men could have built it recently— it was too well made for that—and yet the walls had clearly fallen in places too, and although the pillars marked the different parts, the dividing walls there were quite gone. I had heard Talisin speak of such stone fortresses as these along the border. My father had used stones from one to build Cambray, having not the time or skill to quarry new ones.

I wandered through it in the cold, wrapping my cloak twice about me for warmth, noting how the most recent troops had bestowed themselves, wondering who were the original builders and what had befallen them.

The old man coughed and spat again. "No one will come up here," he said, using a local term that meant "churl" or "serf," or "peasant" perhaps, a term, in any case, of contempt. "They are afeard."

I remember how my father had talked of camping in such a place when he had first come to the borderlands, before Cambray was built. "Better to sleep with some protection," he had said, "even if the ground be haunted by godless men. Evil it may be, but those who built there knew their craft."

"But they who camped here," the old man said, "were not so bad. They were Norman French themselves, and they carried red banners with falcons of gold."

I felt myself start at his words.

"Which way went they?" I asked, pleasure making me throw caution aside.

"East, I told you," he said snappishly, "where there was a battle. Then back again towards the border where the Giant Causeway stretches between us and the Celts. Where serves your master?"

Again he must have felt my start of surprise. Intent on hearing any news about Sedgemont, I had almost forgotten what I had told him of my own purposes.

"Nay, lad," he said, "it is all one to me. But if you should serve him ot the golden birds, you'd find more favor here. Or do you serve the Lord of Maneth? I'd not boast of that, although they say he has a taste for boys."

"Are these Maneth lands then?" I said, frightened, searching for words that would not show my interests, afraid he might be a spy.

"No one's land," he said, his voice suddenly swift and bitter. "Once they were as fair as any man's, when I was young and served with their overlord, he who was the great Duke Robert of Gloucester, half-brother to the Empress Matilda, who claimed to be Queen of England. I was one of those who were spared at the Battle of Winchester, the 'Rout of Winchester' they call it, when we were captured at the battle's end at Stockbridge ford. A goodly man was the duke. Since his death, no man has claimed these lands, and all men have fought over them. So if your master," he made the word sound an obscenity, "be the Lord of Maneth, tell him from me, we are weary of being playthings for his pleasure. We have given him our share of crops and herds to fill his barns and stalls; he has taken our young men without right for his castle guard. He has taken our young women for their amusement. Look around you. Who is left to take but ancient men and sick, the ugliest of women, the ailing? We belong now to no man, so all men claim us."

His old weak voice echoed what Lord Raoul had said, what Giles had said: that people without protection, lordless men, know the worst fate of all.

"My master fights for Stephen," I said at last, "King of England."

He spat again, hacking his lungs out on the shriveled grass. "And what has that King Stephen done for us?" he said. "Had I my strength as when I was young, you'd not dare talk to me of him. There has been but one king, he who was Henry before these wars. There was a king. There was a man. He it was who first gave us fair laws. We had need of them. The Norman French took our land and language and customs. But Henry gave us justice, the 'King's Law,' he called it, to protect the rights even of our people. Where is there justice in your Stephen's time? Yet that young lord I spake of, he who camped here, was better than most. He did not let his men come down to loot and burn in the village. One might do worse than serve with him. But it's all one to me now."

Before I could prevent him, he put his hand, cold and thin, about my face. I could have pushed him over in a trice, he was so light, yet it was not to do me harm that he felt at my skin. Had not the cloak been wrapped round twice, his other arm would have been about my waist.

"And had I my strength," he said in his old voice, "you'd not trick me. I know a maid when I see one, although she hold her hand to her dagger hilt like a man. You keep your legs too close together, even when you walk, and you sit as if with gown about your knees. Well, if you run after one of those who serve the golden birds, I'd not fault you, although things were different in my day. But there were lusty men among them. My sister's girl is already big with child and that's the first begetting here since Duke Robert died. I'd say the man you seek would be as lucky."

He stretched out his hand again. This time I did not turn away.

"Darken your face," he said, suddenly angry, "toughen it with sand and water so it look not so smooth. And your fingers, look how dainty you hold them. Throw back your shoulders. God's wounds, were I a young man, you'd not fool me. And were I as I was, your traipsing abroad would end here."

"Perhaps," I said, "but leave I shall. I'll remember your words when I see Lord Raoul."

"Lord Raoul," he said, pouncing on the name. "Lord, is it.

You've mighty thoughts above your station. Better to stay here and tend for an old man. He's not the one for you."

"You may be right," I said to humor him. I could not be downhearted. Just to have some glimpse of news brightened my hopes.

"You're no whore," he said, his sharp eyes peering. "I've known them and honest women both. I can smell virginity on you like honey. What great lord would value it? Why hasn't he taken it before now, then? Great lords are no nicer than simpler men, and twice as like to take what they want whether it is offered or not. You're no camp follower yet. And that's a harsh life for a tender skin. Something sits not right here."

He shook his head to clear his thoughts.

"You see too much," I said, suddenly aware of what he might say next. He had only to shout to the village below and they would all be after me. How was I to tell if he was lying about Maneth, about Raoul, about all things?

"I'm no man's spy," he said as if guessing my thoughts. "No need to blab out to other men what I can see for myself. I've wits enough to keep secrets quiet, and what I've said to you would string me up from Maneth's walls. But what you do makes not sense. Go home, lass. You'll break your heart running after great lords. Or stay with me. Eh, my sweeting, if I were younger, had my strength, you'd not look further than here. Not that I'm so old there isn't green life somewhere."

He spat again.

"Down there, the churls are gone to ruin, rotting they are in their sloth. But not all's done for yet. It makes no sense to run after lords who can have free picking wherever they go. He'll have long ago forgotten you."

The words rankled.

"Best bide with me," he said, his smile a caricature of what once it must have been. "Stay here with me."

His sticklike hand was harder then, clawlike, clinging. An old soldier, he had kept his best tricks to the end. I thrust myself free, scraping his hand against the wall to loose its grasp, weeping for fear and all his broken strength that left him gasping for breath on the ground.

Fear made me run, fear and pity, although his panting cries came floating down afterward. Back in the village, I threw on saddle and gear, rode very fast away through the night, and slept once more out in the open. Yet long after I thought I heard his voice following me, and what he said has haunted me. And once, in dreams, I saw what he must have been. So I went on, sickened by neglect and poverty and despair that brought to waste all things which once were fair. And everywhere I rode, decay came thrusting up. That is the underside of all those marches, countermarches, skirmishes, with which Henry of Anjou, duke, and Stephen of England, king, blighted the land they both wanted... *a decisive battle or peace.* What use is peace if there be no way to implement it? I reached the borderland at last with a feeling that I had come through a sort of hell, not red-hot and blazing, but cold, despairing, and empty.

I would have known the border as soon as I saw it, without the old soldier's reminder, by the great ditch or dyke that twists along its edge, running roughly north and south. I came upon it midway, too far north toward Maneth for comfort, yet not so far that I could not know that Cambray lay somewhere beyond its most southern tip. All I must do now was ride along the eastern rim and I would come home. And that was what I planned to do; at least I told myself it was. It does not make for easy riding, that countryside, being overgrown and the dyke itself is fallen down in places so that you have to beat about to find it again. Sometimes it is easier to go on foot than ride, so we made slow progress. But sometimes when I came up upon a high ridge, I would see the great scar, twisted like a snake below, and would remember all the stories I had heard about it: how giants from the most western parts had come here to fight their enemies, bringing with them stones and boulders as weapons, and how they had scooped out the soil with their bare hands and thrown it in the distance to make the mountains, which now came much clearer into view. Others claim the Celts built the dyke in the old days when the Saxons first came, but that I doubt, as any will who walk beside it, for it was clear to me that it was made to keep the western men hemmed in, not the eastern Saxons out. But behind it, to the west, is Celtic land. And at times when the clouds lifted long enough, you could see the highest mountain peaks, dark and threatening. Under their shadow lived my mother's kin. Somewhere to the south lay Cambray; somewhere in between, Lord Raoul and his men.

I might have been wandering yet along those silent lands had not carelessness, I shall call it that, but fate, if you prefer, decided things for me. The hour was late; my little horse was tired, but I was forcing it on against a cold wind, trying to make up lost time, when I came upon a group of men. Armed they were, lances set, and their faces stern and ready. Had I seen them in time, I would have turned aside, but muffled up, head down, I blundered upon them.

They rode horses that could have outrun mine and there were four to my one. I had no choice then but to come on, praying hard. Three were men-at-arms, as I judged, escort to an older man, their lord. I noticed how they paused, regrouped, closing together. They were four to one but were taking no chances. I might look harmless but I also might have a band awaiting my call. I might be a Celtic decoy. I tried to sit my pony easily, look nonchalant, ride on with arm upheld in greeting. And that is hard, when you also see the way their leg muscles tighten against their chargers' sides, their hands twitch to their sword hilts. I was frightened as I approached, I tell you, yet as we observed each other closely, suddenly fear left me. They did not have an evil air about them. They did not weigh me as heavily as cutthroats would have done. They had a solid comfortable feel of men about their own business, not eager to interfere with mine. They looked as out-of-place on that lonely trail as no doubt I did. Relief made me thoughtless again. I should have passed them by then, without further delay, had not I begun to talk in that self-important way I had adopted of late.

"Art alone, lad?" the older man asked kindly enough. "These be dangerous parts. The Celts across the border there have a liking for lone travelers."

"I am seeking my lord," I said in Geoffrey's best manner. On impulse I added, "At Cambray."

One of the men-at-arms whistled, edging his horse closer to mine.

"You are far from the mark," he said, eyeing me curiously, "unless you serve a Celt."

"How so?" I asked boldly, although my heart sank. I knew the answer before he gave it, yet I suppose I had been hoping for some different news. And I had given myself away, which was worse.

He said, "Why, the Celts still hold it. A ruffianly crew. Since they took it a year ago, no one has edged them out, although Lord Raoul of Sedgemont tried last year."

"But it is my lord of Sedgemont I seek," I said foolishly. To this day, I cannot tell you if I said what I had always meant to say and it came out against my knowledge, or if I wanted to allay their suspicions. I do not know.

"Sedgemont," they said together in surprise.

The older man spoke afterward. "Then you should know where he is," he said curtly. "Have they kept you so short of news to let you roam at will among these hills?"

I guessed from the way he spoke and held himself that he was what I had thought—a minor lord, not wealthy enough to have great entourage, but sure of himself and his standing—a blunt, plain man who would brook no inconsistency.

"I come from Sedgemont itself," I said, as close to the truth as I could. "Sir Brian and his lady are close-mouthed about outside affairs, not eager to know anything that lies outside Sedgemont lands."

They nodded at that. It was a fact that all who knew the Lady Mildred would jest at.

"But it is not Lord Raoul himself, I mean, I seek his vassal who serves with him. . . ." I babbled on of sickness, family news, mixing it with fact about Sedgemont life that none should doubt my story. And I saw how their eyes glazed with boredom under the spate of words. Yet they would have caught me soon enough at an outright lie. And had I evil intent in mind, they would have known it. They were simple men, not stupid, not overeager to untangle my tale upon a cold wet road.

"You had best ride on with us," the older man said, cutting in upon me, giving orders so that from the moment on, I had no choice.

"You will wander too far otherwise before you reach the camp, and the guards may not let you pass. We have been there before and remember the way, or should do, if the devil does not make us lose our footing in the bogs. Go you with us."

I went along with them, cursing, as I have had reason before, my own thoughtless tongue. Yet, without them I should in truth have been lost. Their story as they told it was as simple as they were themselves. Their leader was a small lord, holding lands of Sedgemont, and perhaps he had been present at the great boar hunt, for we talked of it and he remembered it, although not so vividly as I did. After Lord Raoul's departure, he had followed him, joined him for the spring offensive, and returned to his own lands after Malmesbury, his days of feudal service then having run their course. And now was he come back again, as was his duty, to serve a second time, having had chance in between to see to his own affairs. A good man he was, loyal to his overlord and to his feudal oath. Our land knew many such men once and might have need of them again.

It was pleasure to ride on with him and hear his talk, news of Sedgemont and other places that I knew well. And in this way we came to Lord Raoul's camp, which lay at the edge of high waste grassland, or moor, stretching south for many miles.

The camp was made in a pass where one of the high plateaus cut down to the valley floor, following a woodland stream that widened into an estuary, still far from the open sea. It had the taste and flavor of the sea about it and in some ways reminded me of Cambray, especially the open moors that stretched down from the hill on all sides. Lord Raoul had set his pickets and lines within the confines of some old fortifications, partly made of stone like the one the soldier had shown me, partly older still, great mounds of dirt thrown up to form an encircling triple barricade. Within these outer dirt walls were open spaces where the outlines of former buildings could be traced, so straight and angular you could have drawn lines from each corner of the great rectangle that had enclosed them. The main gates, which had been freshly hung, faced the moorland; the opposite side faced a cliff, where a river fell into the estuary. The horse lines had been placed there, with small paths made to give access to the water below.

And in the center of it all, the red standards of Sedgemont were set before Lord Raoul's own pavilion. Whoever had first built that fort had stationed it well, for it guarded the only way south at this part. And on the moors around watchtowers had been built, or rather the remains of old stone towers still stood, linked one to the other with a series of protected paths so troops could move between them under cover even if attacked. Had I ridden on alone, sooner or later I must have fallen among those guards. And things might not have gone so easily as they now did.

We were challenged by the keepers of the tower long before we were within distance of the main fort. I say "we" because it was the older lord who gave response, singing out his name and title proudly, as was his due, and so I passed on with him as part of his company. By this time I could not have turned aside had I wanted to—all paths led toward this one gap— and had I tried to ride apart, I should have soon been spotted and hunted down. No wonder so many generations of soldiers had made their fort here, guarding their lair like wolves. The best I could do was follow as unobtrusively as I could and hope to slip into the camp unobserved. And here again, fate helped me.

The old lord had but one horse, which he cherished, it being, of course, life and death to him. Along the way it had lamed itself, and to help lighten the load I had offered to bear his shield. A great heavy old-fashioned affair it was, so that I was almost bowed beneath its weight. When we were stopped at the outer bank to prove our full identity, I had difficulties in keeping abreast of the others, my pony grown skittish at the unaccustomed sound of camp and horses, and the shield caught in my way as I tried to force the beast on.

The others had already passed through when I arrived on a rush, fretting and pivoting with the shield banging uncomfortably before me. They let me in with bawled oath for oafishness, shouting out my rank as inadequate shieldbearer to the lord who had gone ahead. He, in turn, preoccupied with clambering down from the high saddle and seeing to his horse, paid me little heed. I thrust the shield upon one of his men, muttered farewell, and wheeled past them without ceremony, down the lines of tents to where the horses stood in their stables. I tethered my poor pony there, and wrapped in my cloak with head upon my knees, waited until darkness fell. And considered what next to do.

Since then, I have met many women who have traveled with fighting men, not just the whores and camp followers but honest wives and daughters who have gone to the wars, yes, and fought in them when they had to. I have never yet met a woman who lived as a man among them. Yet, as you can see, I had not planned to do so, although rumors have said it ever since. I have planned little in my life, save only once, and that in time you shall hear. But then I had made no plans, was caught by my own unruly tongue, and did not know what next to do. The more I thought, the more advantageous my disguise seemed to me, the more sensible it appeared to continue as I was and remain here, hopefully undetected, until suitable time. To begin with, I reasoned, no one knew who I was or where I was; there was no one to betray me except myself. If any thought about me, they reckoned me shut away, safe, in the Sedgemont convent. The last thing the prioress would want was that word of her betrayal reach Lord Raoul. Then, too, I had taken pains in the last week to darken my skin with bark and leaves, and although there was little I could do about my speech or walk, or manner of sitting, at least my traveling companions had not suspected me, and that gave me heart. Then, too, if I was lucky, I might not meet many as observant as that old lecher. Provided I kept clear of former friends like Giles or Geoffrey or even Dylan, there were few who would be likely to recognize me. As for Lord Raoul— but that did not bear thinking on, so him I put out of mind.

Then, too, there was the fact that I had nowhere else to go. Cambray was still occupied. Even if I had gone there, I might not have been well received. I could not return to Sedgemont. And unless I came full-heralded, escorted as was fitting, welcomed, in short, as to my rightful place and accepted with due pomp and dignities, I meant to have no dealings with the Lord of Sedgemont at all.

When the time is ripe, I thought, not knowing when or how that would be; but feeling that it was due me at sometime, only then will I show him who I am. It did not fit my self-image to be caught skulking about his camp.

I know as well as you that it is sin for women to go abroad in men's guise, but what would you have me do else? I could not have crept among the camp women; indeed, would never have thought of that had not the old man in the village put

me in mind of it. No doubt, there were many women attached
leechlike to this camp as to all others, if not within, then close
without the walls. What army moves without them? Older
perhaps, more experienced, I might have attempted it. I believe
I could at least have spoken like them still; they would be
Celts, most of them here, although it was long since I had
talked in my own tongue. But other things were beyond my
counterfeiting at that time, not so much because I had led a
sheltered life, but because I had had no practice at any other.
And within the camp itself, there were added advantages that,
in my case, made life easier for me.

First of all, I was not unaccustomed to work about stable
and yard. Had not I lived at Sedgemont as I had, I could not
have managed it. Then, too, I was slight enough to be taken
for one of the younger pages, who were always underfoot,
doing the most menial of tasks. Then, too, most of the men
who served Lord Raoul were like my friendly companion: plain,
serviceable lords not given to flaunting rank and badges in the
Angevin style. Except for the hawks of Sedgemont, worn by
Lord Raoul's household guard in Norman fashion, his vassals
were content as my father had been with plain colors, plain
gear. Today a page who does not wear his master's device even
to the toes of his long shoes is an object of ridicule. Then I
could merge without difficulty into a group of nondescript
youths, whose ranks varied, depending how their masters came
and went. For this was a feudal host, not mercenary troops;
they served a few weeks at a time, as long as their feudal bond
ordered. Some stayed longer, some less. Some welcomed the
chance, perhaps, of life in the field as place of adventure,
although the routines, when one learned them, were not so
exciting as all that. Had my old lord spoken to anyone of me,
he would have found it hard to track me down, to say nothing
of a "father's overlord." And all this coming and going gave
me opportunity to hide myself away from too-close contact,
from scrutiny.

How did I live, then, in a camp of men? Among the boys, keeping myself to myself, running errands for the older among us, helping the younger, speaking seldom so I gained a reputation for moroseness. The weather improved, which was fortunate, mild now with sudden promise of spring, which comes earlier to the western reaches of the country. Night caused most difficulties, but I bedded near my horse, wrapped in my cloak with bundles of leaves and twigs to soften the ground. Sometimes then I would lie back beneath clear skies and try to imagine what my life would become. At times that seemed as difficult as remembering what it had been. At times, when the soughing of the wind over the moors was like waves upon a beach, a long slow sound, I would think of Cambray and wonder if, after all, like one of those Celtic women warriors of old, I would ride my horse up to its walls and storm them with my men. Or, in more thoughtful mood, I would realize again that if Lord Raoul and all his men could not take it by force then we must think of some trick, some subterfuge, and I would rack memory for some clue as to how the walls might be breached. Or, best of all, I would imagine how it might be that Lord Raoul himself would come to me and beg for help, and pledge my full right to Cambray at last. But these were all childish imaginings, the last I would have. Childhood had long gone.

It was a rough life. The Lady Mildred, I thought, might have swooned for horror of it, and yet perhaps not. She was harder than she seemed. When grief came to her, she endured with more grace and courage than I would have done. Lord Raoul kept his men occupied. He worked to form them to a coherent group, and when they were not on patrol, he tired them at drills and exercises. They were often restless with each other though, wild and angry, mainly because they saw no end to their work, more than a year of it. A thankless task is a border watch, chasing strays for the most part, like dogs, back where they belong. There were often fights among the common men, once a knifing that left two dead. The younger boys crowded avidly after such sights, partly no doubt because it satisfied their desire for action. I saw men punished for wrongs they had done, and the punishments, although just, were swift and hard. A flogging I saw, a branding of a thief. I went quickly away to stop my ears from the screams, but they echoed on. We ate roughly, but in this warmer, milder weather—better than Giles's reports would suggest—I learned to scrabble for myself at the communal kitchens, and water was to be had in plenty from a spring in a dell or niche at the cliff's edge among a scrawny stand of trees. Our greatest lack was bread, for grain was always in short supply along the border; and under pain of death, it had been forbidden to take supplies without payment of some kind. Lord Raoul's vassals dined apart from the common mass, waited on by their squires and pages, but they ate no better or worse than we did. And so the pattern of life continued.

We rose at dawn, when the mists were still thick like crusts and frost sometimes lay like shards upon the grass. We took the horses to be watered down the steep cliff paths to the river, and we groomed and saddled those that were to be ridden out. Many a cuff for some imagined flaw I had dodged myself. Yet it was easier than now. The horses' gear was plain and serviceable, like the men who rode them; neither needed cosseting, finery, or favors. The patrols rode out in the early morning and returned by late afternoon. Once I saw Lord Raoul at their head, his standard flying. Once I saw him return and watched how the Celtic women, who, as I had thought, had leave to roam into the camp, came running to cheer.

Like the womenfolk of Sedgemont, I thought, turning aside, and remembered what the old man had warned: *He will have forgotten you.* Well, when the patrols were gone out, those left behind rode at the tilt, or practiced sword play (I watched Giles at that one day; he had improved, but he did not win the bout), while the boys ran errands, cleared up the debris of the camp, and cleaned arms and tack, that everlasting cleaning of sword and shield. Yet I learned the value of it. A rust spot will catch as you seek to draw your sword free of its sheath, and that delay will kill you if your enemy is faster. A dented shield cannot deflect a blow as rapidly as a perfect one. Bowstrings that are not coiled will not tighten around the bow. A warped arrow will not fly true. So a knight relies upon his pages and squires to see that all his accoutrements are in order, as once he served his lord. Each in turn knows that if he fails, another man's life rests on his conscience. That, too, is a trust among fighting men, one bound to the next as in a chain. And in the evening, when the patrols had returned, with game, if we were lucky, caught on their way back, the great wooden gates that had been fitted to the entrance were swung into place. Then, when horses were cared for, and weary men pulled off their sweat-stained mail coats—then was there time for gossip and talk. Sometimes the older boys who waited on their lords at table would bring back some piece of news which we fastened on as eagerly as we did the scraps of food they smuggled out. Sometimes, someone would take up a lute or pipe and sing songs, bawdy, most of them, but funny for all that. Sometimes we would even creep to the main tent where Lord Raoul and his friends dined and hear him play, although I never stayed to listen myself for fear of discovery. And sometimes we would go down to the outer bank where the Celtic women would dance and sing for the men, if they did not scare us away. And if one of these, a tall red-haired woman I had noticed before, often left by herself and slipped toward Lord Raoul's tent, well then, that too had to be borne.

One day there was a surge of excitement. A group of Celtic riders had come up to the outer guards and were let pass. First came their foot soldiers, running with their spears held at a slant. Then the horsemen themselves. It was strange to see them coming down off the moors on their small ponies in their furred hooded cloaks, stranger still to have them pass without

stopping to salute as once they would have done. Had I been
in my father's keep, they would have tossed some gift at my
feet: strings of polished stones, fox skins, once, when I sat
with Talisin, a basket of woven reed with faint speckled eggs
glowing in their nest of fern. They brought no gifts to Lord
Raoul's tent, nor did they knuckle salute as they used to do to
my father, but rode their ponies swiftly, hands close to hips
near their axe shafts. I craned among the rest to catch glimpse
of them, to hear their talk perhaps, but they said nothing. And
when they left, they were still silent. Later, they sent gifts of
their own Celtic beer and wine, thick with honey, but they
never came again; and hopes that they might have been envoys
for the greater Welsh princes died away, and with it the hope
of the treaty that made this border watch meaningful.

Perhaps it was their coming that made me careless again,
or perhaps it had released some tension among us all. Or, as
is most likely, my luck ran out. I had been in the camp for
several weeks now. Looking back, I see how unlikely it was
that I had remained so long without being detected. But I
might have survived awhile longer had I been careful and kept
to my silent, unobtrusive role.

There were many rumors abroad: that once the treaty with
the Celts was made, Lord Raoul would move against the Angevins again; that he and the king would meet; that we would
all go back to Sedgemont—this last, perhaps a source of disappointment to the younger boys who had not yet fleshed
their swords. Over such military discussion was I undone. The
hour was early, yet already smoke of woodfires began to stain
the upper air. Huntsmen had been bringing in venison on large
stretchers of wood. We would eat well tonight when the patrols
returned. It was the time when weary men doffed their harness
and lolled at ease in their tents waiting for the evening feast.
There had been a flurry of activity in the women's quarters.
We had heard them laughing and shouting in their place against
the wall, and I thought, too, how they would be kept busy

that night, although that thought gave me no pleasure. Perhaps even, it was hearing them that made my mind wander. I had become so used to thinking of myself like one of my companions, thin and dirty in my rough, stained clothes. Catching glimpse of those women, among them the red-haired one I mentioned before, cavorting in her new finery, made me suddenly conscious of where I was and who I was. I sat glumly at the edge of a circle of boys, not moving away by myself, which, if I had kept to my usual habit, I would have done. And in this way I became involved in their quarrels. This was ill fortune, not contrived by malice. They were used to me, thinking, no doubt, if they thought at all, that I served some good-tempered lord who was more lenient, or that, which was part true, I served no man, was one of the flotsam that always attaches itself to a soldiers' camp. Some of them lay on their backs idly, with eyes half-closed. Others ruminated aloud about the state of our affairs. Perhaps if I had kept some work in hand, I would not have been noticed. I have yet to meet a boy who will complain or question anyone willing to help him at some task he hates. But I know, if I am to be honest, that it was my unfortunate tongue. One dark-haired youth, son of a vassal lord and therefore privy to the latest news, was telling us what he had heard at his father's table. Lord Raoul had been present.

"And he says," the boy was ending his story triumphantly, "that if the Celts could be persuaded we would keep faith with them, then they would be more willing to treat with us. But the lords of Maneth must be curbed first. They threaten all the borderlands to our north."

They laughed. "As soon as tell the north wind not to blow," one mocked. "The Lord of Maneth pays little heed to us. You cannot hope to have him by the horns until the affair of Anjou is settled."

How they weighed the country's woes, these young boys scarce in their teens, world-weary men they were, when they spoke of such things.

"And you cannot take Anjou," another said, "unless the king be with you."

"And the king will not stir up trouble..." a third chimed in.

"Unless he must," they all sang out together.

How cynical they sounded for ones so young, untried yet, still novices to war.

"But there still is Cambray...."

"Lord Raoul spoke on that, too. He said, finally, 'It is not worth the risk.'"

"Therein his thinking runs astray," I said angrily. "Cambray holds the key to all the south."

"Indeed, Sir Know-All." It was my turn to be mocked. "Lay your battle plans before him, Sir Know-All. He would welcome them, Sir Know-All."

They laughed at their joke.

"Had the old Lord of Cambray, Falk, still lived, that would have been another tale. Or his son. But they are both dead. There is no one to claim or hold Cambray."

"There is a daughter of the house," I said, a devil prompting me.

"Mark at him," they crowed again, "she's dead or gone. In a convent somewhere. You've thoughts of her perhaps?"

A bigger, older boy I had always avoided sat heavily beside me, leaning on the shield he had been polishing so that I was forced to give ground.

"For one who does so little," he said, "you have great ideas and take up great space. Go tend your master's wants. God's wounds, have you nothing better to do than babble rubbish."

"Let him be," the dark-haired boy intervened. "It is but a poor spineless thing at best. Because your Sir Richard works you to the bone, do not envy those whose tasks are lighter. No master claims him, fool, because he is not worth it."

I did not mind their jibes. I knew of what little value they held me; they had often told me so before.

"But who is his master?" said the older boy slowly. "Even if the man is dead now, he must have had a name. What was his degree, his rank? How came this worthless worm to tag along with us?"

He turned to me, nudging me with the shield edge.

"Churl," he said, "who serves you? Or who did you serve? Your name?"

I was already slipping aside, but one of my companions caught me by the leg so my tormentor could rise and grab my arm. Between them I was caught as in a vise. As they tugged and pulled, I tried to break free again, kicking at them with my other leg. That was a second mistake. I should have known better, ought to have lain still, let them abuse me to their pleasure. I should have tried to talk my way free as I had done before. Showing violence pleased them.

The elder boy swung his fist at me, knocking me to the ground. Before he could follow with a second blow, the dark-haired boy leaped at him. Within seconds, they were all scrabbling furiously together, I, as the original cause of the disturbance, forgotten in the pleasure of hitting at one another. I lay in their midst, half-dazed, but with presence of mind to drag the shield beside me for cover. When there was a lull, I planned to crawl away. But ill luck dogged me that day. As the others pushed and fought, part in anger, part in jest, as I had seen them a hundred times, a man's voice shouted at us. I heard horse's hooves thundering to a stop. The struggle ended abruptly, which should have been warning enough. Had it been someone of less importance, they would not have been so prompt to obey. Then, too, I should have stayed where I was, half-hidden, but in the protracted silence that followed, I moved the shield aside to see what was happening. The other boys had stepped back so that I still remained in the center.

Before us stood a horse, a man upon its back. He must have just returned for he was wearing full mail and was still armed. The horse was lathered with hard riding and champed and snorted as its rider held it to the bit. But the man's helmet was off, and his silver-blond hair blew freely. Ill luck that he should have passed by at this time. Ill luck that he should have chosen now to ride about his camp. Ill luck that he should catch me off guard. I tried frantically to look aside, pulled at the hood that covered my head, but it had been knocked askew in the struggle.

He cannot know me, I thought, in the dust and shadow he will not know who I am.

But I would have known him anywhere.

"You, boy," Lord Raoul said. "Come here."

7

LOWLY I BEGAN TO RISE, DUSTING MY clothes to give myself time to think. That too was a mistake. I heard the others hiss. I should have leaped to my feet when he bade me.

He spurred his horse to make it turn, bad-tempered beast, like its master.

"You," he said again, in a voice that made me cringe. "I mean you."

The other boys backed away from me then as the horse moved restlessly. They could understand my reluctance, no doubt, but then, if someone was to take the brunt of blame, better I than they. He was scowling now, high above me on his great horse. But he looked well, his face was brown, his hair tousled, the mail coat unlaced at the throat.

"You," he said again, "look at me."

Perhaps even then I could have braved him out. Perhaps, if I had not panicked, I could have satisfied his curiosity and the incident would have passed by. But as always in his presence, something cracked my resolution no matter how I tried to hold it.

Without warning, I suddenly hurled the shield that I had been holding under his horse's feet, making it rear and shy away with a great clatter of hooves, and almost unseating him, so that he had to grab at rein and bit to keep it under control. The confusion was my chance. Without clear thought except to escape, I leaped past the group of pages who had scattered in fear and plunged down the slope of the hill toward the first of the horse lines. There was a small stone wall there, more

a bank than a wall, but I went over it head first, enough to
have broken my neck had not there been a group of serfs
beneath, sitting with backs against the stones, playing some
game of chance in the dust. I landed on them, sending them
sprawling in turn. Before they could recover, I took to my
heels down the line of horses, tied head to wall, putting as
much distance as possible between us, slipping beneath the
tethers to the next row, setting them all snorting and stamping.

But, as usual, I had misjudged Lord Raoul. I should have
remembered he was quick, too. A mounted man does not
readily give up advantage, but hardly had I gone over the wall
than he had hurled himself from his saddle and followed me,
sending the groomsmen sprawling a second time. When I
looked back, he was already on his feet, seizing one by his
hair.

There are several men, I thought, sliding softly into the
third row of tethered animals. It will take him time to sort
them through. I crawled along as fast as I could, ducking in
and out of the partitions. But behind me the noise increased,
shouts, curses, running feet. I should have thought that what
I had done would have set the whole camp by the ears. Lord
Raoul would not let such defiance go unchecked.

I came at last to the end of the line. There was no way out.
The sally ports had been long closed and there was no escape
from the cliff by the small paths there. Lord Raoul would have
every piece of straw dragged out until he found me. I did not
intend to sit cowering in a stall like a cornered animal. But
there was not much choice.

Stealthily, I unfastened a horse, leading it by its halter to
the gap in the partition that led to a path to the big inner
meadow they used for exercising. There was no one there
now, even the guards had turned their heads to stare at the
commotion behind them. Using the wall as leverage, I clambered onto the horse, forcing it up and forward, as the startled
sentry whirled around. The shouts increased, an outroar. A

scattered shower of arrows whistled past. I could hear the sound of horses following, and more cries. I was coming up to the opening in the inner or second circle of wall or bank. More guards were waiting for me there. Later, I wondered why they did not shoot me down; but perhaps I was too close, or perhaps they thought I was on a runaway. Yet I must have made a clear target against the evening sky. I thrust the horse at them so that they were forced to jump away, hanging down from the farther side so that they could not get clear hold to drag me off. Then we were through the gap, had crossed the ditch beyond, and were heading for the outer bank. Once clear of that, there was the open moor.

I could hear other horses, closer now, but there was no time to look round. I could not hope to force the main gates, but must try to ride over the bank at a weak place. I veered off to the right, frantically searching for a break in the bushes and brush that crested the mound of earth. The horse was laboring now; God's teeth, I thought, savagely twisting its head round, ill luck again to have chosen the poorest beast of the lot. The mound came up slowly. I edged along it; all was thick and matted. No horse could breast its way through that tangle there. I veered aside again as a pursuing horse went hurtling by, and calmly set my poor creature directly at the bank that rose some ten feet or more above our heads. It was an impossible jump and I felt the horse tremble as I urged it on with hand and voice. Then something snatched at me, catching hold of the belt around my waist, and when that broke, at the slack of my shirt. Like a bundle, I was swung into the air, for a fraction hanging there before falling face down, heavily, across a saddle bow. The horse I had been riding, nudged off its feet by the impact, went somersaulting at the bottom of the bank; other riders on each side pulled back to avoid crowding us. I could hear their voices still shouting, hoarse with alarm and amusement both. Exhausted, battered, the air knocked out of me, I lay and fought for breath as Lord Raoul

wheeled round, one hand still holding me, riding easily back
the way we had come. I remembered the way he had laughed
and jested after the fiasco of the hunt, to set the others at
ease, to make light of what had happened then. I recognized
the same quality to his voice now, calling out to the riders
who had accompanied him, half his guard, I suppose, shouting
to the men-at-arms who came scrabbling with their weapons,
that it was nothing worth their alarm. Nothing! He circled the
camp leisurely, making a complete tour to see that all was set
in order again before returning to his pavilion in the center
field.

He swung himself out of the saddle, and someone came
running to take his horse. I felt them inspect it for damage.
Yet all this while I lay face down upon the saddle like a bundle
of clothes. But before I could get back breath to speak, he had
reached up, dragged me off still bundlelike, and slung me inside
upon the floor. I rolled over as small as possible, knees under
chin, hood pulled down over face, not thinking, not daring
to think. But I have noticed, when you *are* forced to a decisive
stand, how it is the small trivial things that catch attention,
blotting out those that are more important. I was aware of his
striding back and forth across the floor of his tent; I heard him
give orders, although what they were I could not have said. I
heard the clatter of his sword belt and spurs; pages ran with
softer tread to undo the mail coat and take the sword and
gauntlets. I saw his sword propped against a wooden chest. It
was as large as my father's and I had thought his the largest
in the world. More pages came running with water, wine. I
heard him pace again, and order the commander of the guard
to set the watch, to close the main gate for the night, to bid
his vassals dine with him to plan the next day's patrol. I watched
him pacing to and fro, and when all else was done, heard a
woman's voice speak out, not speak perhaps, but rather heard
her move, a rustle of skirts somewhere in the background, and
heard his answer, sharp and decisive. Like a rolled-up rug, I

lay and waited. And it could not have been worse to have cowered in the horses' stalls.

Yet gradually, during this time, blind panic had ceased. I became aware of the bustle and sounds outside, of the silence within. I became aware of the aches of my own body, ringed around as with fire. I heard the panting of my own breath.

Suddenly he let out a great oath that I blush to repeat.

"Come hither, boy," he said so softly that my blood froze. "Come hither."

I did not move. He said nothing, but waited like a cat with mouse, drinking his wine and waiting.

With all my strength, I forced myself upright, knees buckling with the effort, straightening my back against the entrance pole. The tent was cool and dim. Outside, the sentries paced. It was still light enough to see them and the outline of the arrogant banner whose folds fell limply in the evening air. The hum and murmur of the camp seemed a lifetime away. They would be sitting at their rations now, no doubt discussing me and my fate.

He was seated in a carved chair, legs outstretched as was his habit, goblet in one hand, shirt unfastened at neck and wrist, booted feet upon a stool. Beyond him were heaped rugs, furs, chests, a hinged table spread with parchment. A leather curtain framed an inner room, and as I watched, I thought I saw a hand stretch out to close the gap and heard steps pass from time to time, stealthily.

He waited. I moved toward him.

"Closer yet," he said, not looking at me, examining the side of the goblet as if all that interested him lay within it. "Closer again."

Step by shameful step, I came to stand within a hand's reach.

As suddenly he snarled at me, "What meant you?"

I did not reply. If I spoke, he would certainly know me.

"Speak, boy," he said, and I knew from his voice that he mocked me. "What do you here?"

"You live well, my lord Raoul," I snarled back at him then. "Better than your men in the field."

His head flew up at that. I saw his eyes at their darkest gray, the twitch in his cheek obvious.

"With wine, and soft rugs. And women."

Then his hand did come out, catching at the slack of the torn and ragged shirt, whilst with the other hand he pushed back the hood that hid my hair. Well, there too I had miscalculated. In the past weeks it had already begun to grow, and although not long, it was already wisped and flared about my cheeks. His feet came crashing to the floor. With both hands he forced my head toward the light. I would not blink or drop my gaze, yet I felt the trembling begin at his touch.

"And how long," he said, so quietly that only I could hear, "have you been in my camp?"

As near as I could reckon the days, I told him.

"And how got you away from the lady prioress?"

Part of this only I told him, the how of it being that much easier than the why.

With one of his soldier's oaths, he hurled me to one side.

"Will nothing content you?" he said.

His voice was low, so cold it frightened me. But I would not show my fear.

"I shall not go back, my lord," I said, the more loudly that he spoke low. My nether lip stuck out as it does when I am determined.

"You cannot shut me up there again. I mean to have Cambray."

"God's teeth," he roared out then. "Do you stand there as if at Sedgemont, as if no time has passed, and argue trivialities with me? We are in a war camp. Do you bear a charmed life that you set it in jeopardy? Do you think to make a mock of me before my men?"

I remembered the way he had slammed his fist before.

"Then you should know better than I it will not be possible

to send me back," I said as coolly as I could. "You cannot spare
even a few men of your guard as escort. Keep me here under
your own eyes, where I shall be safe. Let Giles watch. . . . Nay,"
as he made a movement, "he does not know I am here. No
one knows, but you."

"And how explain your sudden arrival?" he said. "God's
wounds, but your affrontery would frighten the most hardened
of men. This is no time for trickery."

"You would not have known me," I said, "had not that bully
forced me into quarrel. Say what you will. They have not seen
through my disguise and I shall not speak of it."

"Perhaps," he said, "but they have an eye for whores who
come creeping where they're not welcome."

"If you mean by that," I shouted then, "that I have lost my
virginity, put not such slanders on my name. I have had rough
lying without insult as well."

"You must bear best witness," he said.

"As to that, my lord," I retorted hotly, forgetting my appearance, my helplessness, "reputations are kept or marred
without as within convents. You keep your men too busy to
have them chasing after maids. If my reputation is safe with
them, so will yours be with me, if that most concerns you. . . ."

"Now, by God," he said, rising, "you speak too shrewishly.
Who bade you, girl, woman, what you are, meddle in men's
affairs?"

"Then kill me," I cried passionately. "Have done with your
mockery. There is your sword. All your men know that a half-
fledged boy tried to unseat you from your horse. He deserves
death for that. But I tell you, I will kill myself in getting free
again, or die shut up. I would at least die as a human being
now. Thus will your reputation be upheld."

We stared at each other. I think he almost hated me then,
and yet I did not hate him, although I would not give way
before him.

He ground out at me, "This is no place for a woman."

His echo almost of the mother prioress's arguments stung me to even more rash reply.

"But, my lord, you have women here. Is there not a red-headed wench within the inner tent?" I pointed to where I had sensed rather than seen the shadow move against the curtain, although I think it had long slipped away.

He choked with rage.

"So how is that different?" I pressed home advantage although I knew no man likes to have his arguments turned against him.

"I can be as safe as she is. If you keep her safe, why not me?"

But I had gone too far. Few men, I think, would have listened to me this long. But I fight most fiercely when I am undermost, and I had not learned restraint.

His arm shot out again, dragging me toward him, tearing the rest of the shirt off my back. I tried to duck, half-turned aside so that the blow fell with a crack against my ear, making me stagger with the shock. But I would not cringe before him. I gritted my teeth although his hand was raised to strike again. Then I heard his gasp. He pulled me toward him, turning my back toward the light.

"Who did that?" His voice was taut with fury.

I had forgotten the marks of the convent whip. The scabs had long since healed but I had not known the scars would last so long.

His grip tightened. "Who?"

Still smarting from the lash of his open hand, I muttered at him, "I had forgotten it. But it is not for that I will not return. . . ."

As he still held tight, "The lady prioress, then. She had not your scruples. . . ."

He spun me round once more to face him. "You have not told me all," he said. "What prioress would dare use you so? I have no time for slippery evasions."

So I told him all, what I would not before have said, and he heard my halting story without comment, although his fist whitened until the bones showed through when I spoke of Maneth's messenger. But, God help me, I did not speak of the manner of his death, not then, only that on seeing him I had realized my peril and had fled.

"You were not to know, my lord," I said at last when the tale was done and still he did not speak. "All who remember her talk of the old prioress with affection. This is a new regime, a new rule."

He stirred at last. "No," he said, "I was not to know."

"And so you see, my lord," I said overeagerly, "I have spoken the truth when I say only here will I be safe."

He sat back watching, a strange look on his face. I held myself upright, for all my body ached and where he had struck smarted as flame. I could feel weariness against my backbone like to cut it in two.

Suddenly he stretched out his hand again and pulled back the shreds of shirt into place.

"Before God, Ann," he said almost wonderingly, "it seems but a day ago when we last warred with each other. I know no other woman who can bring me to such a froth of rage, and then show me why I should not feel it. Well, once you thought to win me to your way, but in the end had I the best of you. Yet see how we are confounded that our enemies make a liar out of me, a fugitive of you. I do not know anymore what a man of sense would say. But since on all counts have I been proved wrong, let us try another plan."

It was my turn to stare, not believing what I heard.

"It is no trick," he said, "although you gape as if expecting tail and horns to sprout. By the Mass, you turn all to madness as you go. How could I have forgotten it. . . ." He stopped and began again. "You have lived within my camp to know what comfort I have to offer you, although better perhaps than the ground you have been lying on. We'll have no explanations of your arrival. Let them think you flew in on the wind. And as far as I know, you may have. Well, since you are here, we'll use you as bait. Wooing these Celtic kin of yours is like coaxing a fox from its den. With your permission, or without, we'll tempt them to us with news of you. How like you that?"

"Better," I said, "if I knew to what purpose."

Then he did smile at last, throwing back his shoulders as if to let a weight drop.

"There speaks the canny Celt I know," he said. "Why, lady, if you had not asked me that, I should have thought they'd beaten out your brains as well. To good purpose, Lady Ann, as you shall see. You shall be privy to all my plans. But now," and his fingers touched my cheek as if to feel that I was there, as if to repent perhaps of his blow, "as host, let me offer you courtesies. Beneath that dirt, you have a hungry look. As fellow soldier, I can guess your needs."

He began to walk about, eyeing me, no doubt, as he would a tethered pig or goat. As ever, his jesting made me nervous, ill at ease.

"When you lie on the ground, my lord," I said, "I suspect you have an unwashed air. I do not like sleeping on stones, or fending for my food, or breathing the dust of your horses. I did so because I must."

"You even complain like a trooper," he said. Then, with that sudden sense of justice that always caught me off guard, "Why, Ann, you owe me no explanations, to whom expiation is due."

At my look, he began to laugh. "And I could threaten you, beat, nay, put you to the torment," he said. "You'd spit defiance with every breath. Look not so fierce when I praise you. No man in my command would have outfaced me as you did today. Recognize you! I knew your style even before you came as slowly as you dared from beneath that shield. There are few women who would have borne so much as you with so little complaint. And if my men could ride as well, we'd rid England of its troubles within the month. Take me as a simple man who would do you honor."

He shouted for his pages, who came at a run, bringing food and wine and, at his orders, a large wooden contraption filled with hot water. When they had withdrawn, I asked, "What, my lord, is that for?"

"Washing," he said abruptly.

I was appalled. "With you here?"

"You do not expect me to skulk outside my own tent," he said reasonably. "I did not invite you within it. But I tell you plainly, you will not stay unless you rid yourself of dirt. And vermin."

I could not suppress a cry.

"Or did you think," he continued, "because you are high-born, lice and fleas will leave you alone? Be comforted. Had you stayed with us much longer, you must have been discovered. Soldiers have little regard for such things, but if the fine weather continues, I'll have us all stripped in the river for health's sake."

"I'd rather the river," I said, eyeing him dubiously, although I cannot tell how the thought of warmth and cleanliness seemed inviting.

"With a hundred men to watch?" he said.

"Rather that than one..."

"Disinterested."

"I do not know that," I said, retreating before his laughing look. "And I have nothing to wear afterward."

He made a careless gesture. "There are shirts enough," he said. "I do not carry a woman's coffer to war. Take what you will, all or nothing, it is the same to me." As he still advanced.

"Or would you rather I borrow from your women," I said. "They may not need their kirtles as much as I do."

He stopped, taken aback. "What do you know of that?" he said at length.

"Enough," I said. "I have eyes and ears. Not that it is my concern..."

"By God, it is not," he said, still staring. "You fight roughly these days, Lady Ann. But since you welcome plainness, I tell you plainly. Call her here, for any reason whatever, she'll have your eyeballs forth, and worse from me." He gave a grin. "In truth, she holds me so dear as to carve me to flesh and bone rather than let you close...."

"There is not the slightest fear of that," I said haughtily. "You need not end your wenching on my account."

Then he did begin to laugh. "Oh that you are rich," he cried. "I did not know I had missed your honeyed tongue until I heard it again. Come, I will tease you no more. Cry quits. Except one last thing."

He watched me. I should always have mistrusted him when he poised to strike. "Why ran you for safety here? There are other, nearer places as safe."

Confusion stained my cheeks. I looked at him, wordless, and felt the blush painful and slow spread across my skin. Nothing would have dragged those tangled emotions into speech. Once again, he stretched out his hand, his fingers barely brushing my chin.

I said at last, slowly, "I use you to get Cambray."

Once I would have shouted forth my wish, but now I felt that he would know it for the lie it was in part. There were other things I wanted as well.

"So be it, my..."

And he turned upon his heel.

The water was still warm, as balm to aches and bruises. I was black and blue with them and caked with dirt. But best luxury of all was the sudden realization that I no longer had to pretend. I had not known the strain was so great until, not having it, I knew the luxury of being without it. I have said that my life had taken on a pattern of its own, that within that pattern there was much I had come to admire. I felt what I had missed only when I was given my real self back again. And, ingrate that I was, I dropped the new life for the old without regret, almost without remembrance. In this, I think,

I was no different from others who have found themselves caught up in strange events, who revert to normal when they can. I think too that without the training of my early days at Sedgemont, I would never have learned such adaptability. I say this not to praise myself. For in one thing I stand completely at fault, although I was to pay for my lack of thought, a heavy price in the end.

In my complacency, I quite forgot the woman in the inner tent. She must have long before slipped away, for she was not there when I dressed myself, in one of those embroidered smocks the Lady Mildred must once have worked. Laughing to myself at the thought of her anger had she but known the use made of it, rejoicing in my return to womanhood, I forgot my rival quite; what she might feel, might do, could have heard. I was still young and arrogant in those days. I could dismiss her from my mind as easily as I dismissed my life as a common page within the camp. Since then I have told myself a thousand times that Lord Raoul spoke true although he clothed his words in jest. His lustings were not my concern. He knew best how to handle them. He might have said more, as truthfully—that as I was his ward, I had no claim to his affections; that as his vassal, I stood so far beneath him that it was presumption on my part to expect any; that as a woman, I should be used to men's ways, be hardened to their infidelities. For it is also true, as I have said before, that men are not expected to think as women do, nor have we women any right to complain, being considered incapable ourselves of thought. My pleasure at being with him again (which I did not deny, although I would have concealed it from him) was tempered by the warning given by the old soldier in the ruined fort.

Great lords do not need to wait for such as you. He will long have forgotten you.

It appeared he had. And I did not like the woman who had replaced me. I thought myself demeaned by her. I resented her very presence in the camp.

But if my thoughts were vexed and perturbed, what might

that other woman's have been? Might she not have felt as threatened, as grieved, by me? Might not jealousy have struck her as deep? It is a trait we Celts all share. Even you, my poet, bear witness to that. Those verses you scribble when you leave this room, the rhymes you mutter as you roam about the shore, do not they concern the emotions of the world: love, and hate, and all their attendant woes? Do not we sing them more loudly, suffer them more deeply, than any other race? For all my fine feelings, I was not as open-honest as she might have been. She would have no one close to him, have no one share him. I would not have her close, but was not yet ready to take her place. As later that, too, became clear.

When Lord Raoul returned, we were content enough to act as old comrades might. We exchanged stories, thoughts, adventures, over a hunk of meat and cups of wine. I had almost forgotten dainty manners and the pleasure of sitting at a meal without having to fight for scraps. I do not know what explanations he had given of my appearance, either good enough or curt enough to reduce surprise or show of curiosity, although what was said behind my back, God knows, and there has been gossip about it ever since.

He told me that on the morrow he would meet with his chiefest lords to let news of my arrival seep out among the Celtic hosts. Meanwhile, I must learn to be patient as they had. He encouraged me to eat and drink, and to tell my tales of soldier's life as I had found it. What I said both amused and angered him, I think, for he could not forget how I had tricked him, even when he most swore it was forgotten, and to crown all, I fell asleep in the midst of one of his most raucous camp yarns, which, a year ago, even I might not have understood.

I roused as he placed me gently within the inner tent. The floor there was strewn with rugs and a couch was stretched against the farther wall. As I had surmised, it was empty.

"I will not turn you forth from here," I said, as he laid me on the couch.

"There is no need," he said, his voice warm with wine, low

and husky as I had not heard in him before, although I had heard it so in other men. "There is room for both."

I came full awake at that.

"Count not on me to make the pair," I said. "You already have a bed mate."

"Now, by Saint George," he said, stopped midway in pulling off his shirt. "That is meanly said. Harp you still to the same tune. You have a shrewish mind, my lady. He who beds you must be girded about with steel that you should watch his every move."

"And why not?" I said, retreating to the far end of the bed. "It is known that a woman's virtue lies in her chastity. Perhaps a man's should, too."

"You have a way of looking at things," he said, shaking his head, "that defies all rules I have heard of. Learned you such ideas in your convent, Mistress Pert?"

He would not take me seriously. And yet, God knows, it would have tempted many a woman to have had him thus, alone to herself.

"I know," I said, "that great lords abide by their own rules. You scatter bastards as other men do corn, along the byways and highways of this world. Look at your King Henry. But marriage, I think, is worth more pains than that. I would have a husband who would keep faith with me, as I with him."

"I had forgot," he said, "these great hopes you place on wedlock. But I am not husband yet, nor as far as I know have I fathered bastards. There are other choices between those extremes."

"Lord Raoul," I said, "I have offered to wed you. But that does not give you leave to bed me first."

"Now, by the rood," he said, stopping to stare again, "spoken like a trooper. I had forgot that you could be so blunt."

"No doubt you find my words strange," I said, "coming from one who lies so far beneath you. . . ."

"Not so far beneath as I could wish," he said, his eyes

glinting. "By Jesu, it would tempt any man to stop you."

"I have not come all this way," I said, "to have you rape me at the end."

"Rape, is it," he said. "You speak of things you know little of. You have been with my men these past weeks. Did you think of rape then? There would have been none to hear your screams. If my men had caught you, they would not have been gentle.

"As I can be," he added, when I did not reply. "I have brought neither bastards nor rape to my bed, Lady Ann. If you were willing, we might yet find joy within."

"I will save that for my wedding day," I said.

"Marriage is but a game," he said contemptuously. "It is you maids who talk it out-of-place, to make its importance loom so large."

"Then is Cambray a pawn still," I said. "Not even for love must I forget that."

"What do you know of love, Lady Ann," he said, watching me carefully, his voice stern and thoughtful, "that you name love and lust so lightly?"

"As much as your Celtic harlots, at least," I said angrily.

"Nay," he said, "I do not swear to love them forever and a day, nor do they expect it. But if it be love to enjoy and pleasure one body to another, that I have known. When you have learned that much, then may you talk to me again of love."

"So speak all men," I cried, "making women your playthings, to sport with."

He looked at me and shrugged. "Perhaps," he said, "but I find few that complain. Even you might not. Think on that."

I summoned up my purpose. For he was handsome, young, and all his maleness tempted me. It would have been so easy then to have let resistance go. I had but to bend my head or move my arms, or smile, and those strong hands I had felt before would have closed tight. If he had made a move toward me that night, I know that I could not have withstood him. I think he knew it too. It says perhaps something of the man he was that he did not press advantage home, although not even he may have known why.

"But then no man will wed me," I cried. "If you use me, Lord Raoul, who then will have me? And how will I keep Cambray?"

He stared for a while, not speaking, not smiling. Then, without another word, he turned and left.

Alone in the large bed, I raged at my willfulness. Cambray had cost me dear that night.

With the morning, all seemed easier between us. Perhaps that was because, as at Sedgemont, I saw him seldom. I think he avoided me except the few times we met formally. I dined with him and his chief lords once, fewer in numbers than I had imagined, but seeming cheerful enough. My old lord, fellow companion of the journey, sat at the other end of the table. I would have spoken to him for old times' sake, but thought it wiser then to keep silent; we never talked again, he and I, and afterward it was too late. The men spoke mainly among themselves, of horses and hunting, and the elusive Celts who vanished like mist before they could track them down. Sometimes they reminisced of the war, mending their speech when they remembered I was there; but had I been one of the squires who listened so avidly, I would have gathered little news.

One story that I do remember, I think they told more to warn than to amuse . . . how the Countess of Warrick, that goodly dame, left guardian of the castle in her husband's absence, had gone against his wishes and opened the gates to Anjou's men, despite the fact that King Stephen's guard had come to help her.

"And so the shrew let in the Angevins," said one, "and out the king. There's no faith in women ever. For when her husband, the earl, heard of it, he died of shock. And she sat there with Henry, drinking her husband's wine, convinced she had done well by him, that she had made way for him to join with Anjou against the king."

"I'd keep my wife where I could see her," said another.

"Yet she guards your keep while you are here," said a third, amid a burst of laughter.

"These wars have given them power they do not need," said the first. "The more we leave them to watch and ward, the more they'll move the world about our ears. Women were more modest once."

He raised his goblet and drank, not looking at me. I do not think they liked having me there; a woman in a camp of men may be a cause of trouble, an evil sign. But Raoul was ever cheerful, sending out his messengers farther each day, using, as he had said he would, my presence as bait to lure the Celts toward us.

All the news of what had happened before I got from Giles, whom, as I have said, I persuaded to give forth his information, piece by piece, until most of it became clear as I have told you already. But what the situation now was I could not be sure. And whether war or peace or endless waiting, no man seemed willing to judge. Giles himself had learned, too, to be discreet. He asked no questions of me, although once he would have hung on every word I said. He had grown taller, thinner, quieter. Yet there was still much we could talk of, still have in common. He had seen the gray horses of Cambray running wild upon the moors, and we sometimes spoke of how we would tame them again and bring them back to the stables there as in my father's day. But never did Giles ask me what I had done all this while, or where I had been or how come here. And if he showed, in many ways, his enthusiasm for his new life and his new master, that too was as it should be.

One other thing—I mean besides giving me Giles as guard— did Lord Raoul do for my comfort. Since it was not fitting that I remain alone, he brought an old woman and her daughters to attend me. How or where he found them I cannot say, but when she spoke to me in the old tongue, the words fell like music on my ears. Almost ten years it was since I had last spoken it, yet I still remembered it. And she had known Cambray when it had been a happy place. Whether Raoul knew this also, or whether it was by chance, I could not tell, but for the first time I found someone to talk of my early home, my brother, and, most of all, my mother, whom I had never known. Much at that time was revealed to me, of my mother's love for her own Norman knight, and his for her, that her death was a loss he could not bear, so that even to look at me was to make him turn aside for grief.

"And like you are to her, my lady," the old woman said, "hair, eyes, height. Lord Falk must have seen her anew each day. If he had lived to see you grown, he would have loved and forgiven you. But there are men like that, who love deeply only once. So was it with him, so with her."

"And did she foresee the end?" I asked once, remembering the prioress's taunts.

"Who knows what she knew," the old woman said, looking at me askance with the deep, dark eyes of her race. "There be those who say it was a gift we all once had, we Celts, to foretell the future; and having lost it, we have lost all our power that made us masters of this land and others besides. If you had not gone so far away, you would have heard many rumors of your father's and Talisin's deaths. For Lord Falk was growing old; he doted on his son. He paid too little heed to dangers that were without his walls and kept all his thoughts and energies within his own keep."

She brushed my hair, restored now to its own length, twining it with ribbons in the new style.

"There is an old song," she said, "that they still sing in the hills."

She began to croon to herself, one of those Celtic lays that you, my poet, so much admire, so strive to emulate. It tells of death, betrayal, disaster; which of our songs does not? There was one part I think I must have heard Gwendyth sing, for it sounded familiar, especially the line that begins, 'Warriors all, we fall before our time, drowned in the arms of the sea. . . .'

I had forgotten words and tune, but on hearing them I marveled that they were so familiar.

When she had finished, she said, "Our strength has been destroyed, our fate controlled by these last years. When was there not a time that our young men were not betrayed, our hopes ended?"

"But if she knew of their deaths," I cried, "could not she have saved her son, saved her husband?"

"You speak as if it were a gift, this knowledge, to grant, to withhold," the old woman said. She shook her head. "I cannot answer you. To know is one thing; to change what happens, another."

She put her hand on mine; it was still strong and firm, like Gwendyth's, showing no sign of age.

"If she had had the power to alter the future, be assured she would have, although God grant us mercy from such power. She loved her children dearly, even you, whom she saw but for one short hour."

She patted my hand again, guessing perhaps at the sadness that welled forth from my heart.

"It was long ago," she said again. "Had she and Lord Falk lived, they would have held your worth as high as your brother's. But your father was Norman, lady. Why would he listen or understand such things as we have been speaking of? Why would she warn him, to break his heart before its time. It died soon enough when your noble brother died. That all men could see for themselves. But when she left him, his life stopped."

We did not always speak of such far off and melancholy things. Nor was the Cambray I knew such a sad place. But the most part of what I can tell you comes from the lips of that old dame, God rest her soul. And in strange way, she com-

forted me. Since then, whenever the future has looked dark,
I have found strength in marveling at my mother's courage,
who, knowing, had tried to shield the others from the pain of
knowledge. God grant us all such depth of love, such endurance.

So we passed time peacefully enough, in the pavilion Lord
Raoul had set for my use apart from the others. It was surrounded by guards under Giles's command, but I did not feel
confined; there was so much to talk and to think about. Sometimes I walked in the evening with my womenfolk and saw the
boys and squires about their accustomed tasks, and was tempted
to stop and speak with them, although I never did. And once
I went to the outer wall, where I used to creep in the evenings,
and heard the outcry from the women's quarters beyond the
lines. They were leaving, had been ordered to leave. I forced
myself to turn away without watching, although I would have
dearly loved to wait and see if all had gone, including the red-
haired woman. Shame prevented my asking or speaking of her.
Yet jealousy of her still burned my thoughts. Had Talisin had
such a woman, I would have shrugged, knowing it was the
way of men. But not with Raoul.

Jealousy is a deadly sin, they say, and rightly so, hot and
spiteful, turning all things sharp with malice. I told myself this,
berated myself for such pettiness. I was no simpering maid,
reared to high thoughts and flowering words; I had already
killed a man for lust. You have seen how I was dragged up at
the castle tail, scrabbling in the back corners of the peasants'
world. But there had been a time, in the golden afternoons at
Sedgemont, when I had thought, too, of love as golden, full
of promise. And Raoul was right when he taunted me with
such hopes. But whether he sent her away to please me, or
whether, as I suspect, it was good sense, not wanting to jeopardize his standing if the Celtic lords should come, I do not
know. Nor what parting, if any, they had. Those were questions better left unasked, better unanswered.

I have said I saw Lord Raoul but seldom. By day, he was often gone with his guard, riding with them from dawn to dusk across the moors through the wildest parts of the borderline. Sometimes they came dragging back, the horses deep in mud, the men too tired to roll from their backs. By such patrols he kept the southern marches firm, free of looters such as I had seen at work farther north, rid of raiding tribes like the one that had taken Cambray. There were frequent skirmishes, to keep his men in training, minor affairs without loss of life. But he drove himself and his men all the harder that the Celtic leaders still had sent no word, made no response to his messages. Until one day...

I was listening to another of those long tales of love and grief that delight our Celtic taste, when I heard the sudden clash of arms, the sound of footsteps, voices. He burst in upon me, smiling, dressed in more-noble fashion than I had yet seen, charm high upon him like a sheen.

"Bestir yourself, my lady of Cambray," he said. "Put on your geegaws and your courtesies. They are coming."

"Who, my lord?" I asked, pretending calm although my heart raced at seeing him. But he was pulling me up from the chair, where the women had been braiding my hair, so that it fell loose.

"Your mother's kin," he said, smiling down, his eyes bright, even his hair alive. "Your Celtic lords, your sly foxes lured into the open at last. God's wounds, I began to think they had no family pride, to want to greet you. Put on your mother's jewels to show them all previous rumors have lied, that you are cared for, safe. They have come to see you as your father's heir. And make treaty with his overlord, God willing. Then will our work here be done."

There was an eagerness in his voice that told me something I had not thought before, how much perhaps he too wished to be away from here, how grievously this long, unexpected exile from Stephen's court had cost him.

I sent my women scurrying.

He held me still, that hand I remembered heavy on my shoulder.

"They are not children to play at games," he said. "I will show you to them to satisfy their curiosity. I would not have you speak out of turn. Say nothing, do nothing, that I do not bid you. All that is needed is that you be there."

I could guess at the anxiety behind his words. He had been waiting for this occasion for months. It galled him, no doubt, to have to owe it to me. Yet he should not have feared that I would spoil the chance for him.

"I will say nothing to disgrace you," I told him stiffly. "I will be a model of decorum, my lord."

He put his finger across my mouth.

"Swear not so much," he said. "Tempt not your Celtic gods. But think, think, before you speak. I have set no trap for them. They come of their own accord and I will offer them a treaty such as we had in King Henry's day: to rule freely behind the boundaries they agreed to then. There is no treachery unless they will see one."

"I shall be honey sweet, my lord of Sedgemont," I said coldly. "As overlord, you can do no other than order me."

"That is what I am afraid of," he said. "Play not Countess of Warrick with me here. I shall not drop dead of shock, but you may wish it."

I wanted to say again, "Trust me." But could not.

"Well, then," he said, letting me go. "See to it. The fate of Cambray as well may rest upon it. They have already crossed the outer guards."

"I cannot be ready in time," I cried in panic, sending everyone flying before me.

"You will be," he said. And I was, in a dress they had sewn for me these past weeks, pale green it was, with the sides and underarms caught up to show the darker kirtle beneath. Giles went before me to hand me over the rough ground, and a small page, one of those I had lived among, came behind carrying my mother's gold circle, for they had told me I should not wear it as a maid unwed, a nicety I had not thought on before.

Lord Raoul was standing to greet me, still dressed in his splendid clothes. Coming toward him over the grass in the innermost part of the camp where his pavilion stood, I had the feeling of brilliancy everywhere, blue sky, green fields, burnished mail, gleaming weapons, standard blazing in the spring sun.

"The Lady of Cambray," Lord Raoul said. His voice was vibrant as I remembered, his hand steady. I took it so he could lead me forward. Beside him sat a small, dark man, overflowing one of those wooden stools soldiers use. He was half-smothered in furs despite the warmth of the day. When he stood up, he scarce came to Raoul's shoulder, yet he was broad and solid, and when he moved, his legs, bound with thongs, seemed like trees, thick and ponderous. But his gait was stately, too, his hair was long and black, and his eyes small and quick, with a brightness that reminded me of Gwendyth. I would not have known him, but there was something about him that gave me pause to think.

"So this is little Ann of Cambray, full grown," he said. "I should know you, kinswoman. I am half-brother to your mother, whom I dearly loved. She was as second mother to me years ago, before marriage took her far away."

He spoke in Norman-French as we did, slowly and coldly. Yet I sensed a warmth beneath his words.

"The Lady Ann has spoken often of her Celtic kin," Lord Raoul said at my side, "although her home has been at Sedgemont."

The Celtic lord nodded almost disdainfully, and behind him I heard his entourage cough and stamp, as nervous as horses in new quarters.

We sat down, Lord Raoul, the Celtic lord, and myself, and

wine was brought. It seemed wrong to be sitting as with strangers.

"I was young when I left the borderland," I said suddenly in our own tongue. "But I have never forgotten it."

I felt Lord Raoul's start of displeasure, but before he could restrain me, or the interpreter beside us could speak, I translated for him myself, giving my most brilliant smile. On the other side, I felt my Celtic kinsman shift and half-smile, in turn, and a flicker crossed the faces of his men.

Lord Raoul looked at me, neither smiling nor moving.

"Tell him," he said—was there warning in his look?—"that as he and his kindred were good friends to Lord Falk of Cambray, and through him to the Earl of Sedgemont, so would I stand high in their esteem."

"My lord uncle," I said, and again I saw a half-smile cross his face, "as dear as you were to my mother, so dear we would be to you and yours again."

I could hear the translator repeating the words back for Lord Raoul. He could not fault me so far.

"Times have brought us far apart. But Lord Raoul of Sedgemont would be as good a friend as his grandfather, the late earl, was."

"I knew your father, Falk, well," said my uncle—half-uncle?—but I think he liked the name. "He broke no treaty with us; we were as blood kin."

"Think of me ever so," I said. "And as my father was vassal to the lords of Sedgemont, so hold we faith of them."

Beside me, I could feel Lord Raoul shift in his turn.

"Bid him know that we would renew those treaties, ever made in friendship."

"It is what we also wish, my lord of Sedgemont," the Celtic voice broke in, speaking again in Norman-French, taking again that sterner tone. "But these past years have been hard on borderlands. Ten years almost it is since Falk died, and who has kept the border policies since then? It has not been our men who have raided and despoilt the villages and farms."

Raoul said patiently, "There have been errors on both sides, my lord."

"And we have heard many rumors, accounts of battle and rebellion," my uncle said. "Even rumor of your death, kinswoman." He turned back to me. "They said you died at Sedgemont." There was a pause. Even Raoul did not know how to answer that.

"Yet here I am," I said with my bright smile. "Come back with the spring and end of war."

They all laughed at that. The wine went round more freely. Lord Raoul let out his breath again.

"The old treaty set the boundary marks," he said. "Lord Falk and his men kept the Norman side safe, your men the other. Both parties to the treaty were content. We have not seen many Celtic patrols, although we have been here these past months."

My uncle said, "During the reign of King Henry, late of memory, the boundary was agreed upon, and on your side you built a line of castles to hold it firm. That was to our advantage as well as yours. But since these civil wars, who cares where the boundary runs? New castles have been built across the line. Year by year, our lands are eroded away by your settlements."

I could see Raoul was thinking of Cambray.

"And we have lost Cambray, my uncle," I said, leaning on his arm, forestalling Raoul. "I would go there if I could."

My uncle watched us both through his small half-shut eyes. Then he took a great pull of wine.

"Your wars have plagued us as well," he said at last. "When men fight for a throne, there are always those who take advantage. We have our malcontents as well as you. We do not like these shifts of fashion that lure the restless and misfit among our people across the border, to their loss and shame. Only Lord Falk's good sense prevented greater evil when the wars first began. If Cambray were restored to you, would you not restore the lands we have lost farther north to the lords of Maneth, the greatest offenders of the Norman treaty?"

"While we have a king over us," said Raoul, "we must hold faith to him. So would you find that your chief concern if one of your princes became overlord of all. I am empowered to make a treaty as it was made originally in King Henry's day. When the time comes to fight at Cambray or Maneth, and we shall, you have my promise, we shall put both to rights, be those at fault Norman or Celt."

He spoke grimly. My uncle watched him closely again.

"So be it," he said. "Then shall I bear back tidings to my kinsmen and great lords, that they may talk of it. For they, too, long for peace as it was in the days of Falk and the Earl Raymond, both blessed in memory. I feasted with your grandfather, my lord, near to Cambray once. It was close to the start of these wars. 'If men fight for the honor of their king,' he said, 'then will the kingdom be torn apart.'"

"He was a man of sense," Lord Raoul said. "All men of sense must deplore what civil war will bring."

"But not ambitious men," my uncle said. "They welcome it."

They looked at each other, not needing me now, speaking to each other face to face.

Suddenly Raoul smiled and stretched out his hand.

"Men of good sense are many years in the making," he said. "My lord, I am young, but I know a man of sense when I see one."

My uncle grasped his hand in his great paw. "Then hope I to know one in the making," he said, and he too smiled, showing all his ill-formed teeth. He gestured to his men, who moved forward, their cloaks swinging to their heels. Outside in the warm sunlight, they swung themselves up into the saddles of their small ponies, not in the Norman way of Raoul and his men, who had to manage shield and sword and were weighed down with a mail coat about their knees, and who rode stiff legged in their high saddles as if standing upright.

These horses were so small that if Raoul had ridden Norman style, he would have trailed his legs upon the ground. Yet my uncle did not look so misplaced, for all that.

On an impulse, I stepped forward and curtsied, holding out to him some of the flowers that had been wound into my hair.

He took them without speaking at first, the lines upon his dark skin showing deeper in the sun.

"Daughter of my sister," he said at last, "who was the light of our threshold, why stayed you away so long from us? I came to see for myself that you lived, that you were who you claim to be. For all my previous doubts, I see my sister alive before me again. What news shall I give your kinsfolk?"

"My uncle," I said, "tell them that I have been growing under wardship to the Lord of Sedgemont in his care, as was right and fitting. Now am I come to get Cambray, as also is right. Tell them that I am well, and that I await them here."

Again I heard Raoul let out his breath. My uncle nodded, saluted, wrapped his cloak and reins around his right arm, and trotted off, a small shapeless bundle followed by his men. At the main gates, his footmen, who had been crouching in the grass, leaped to their feet and ran beside him toward the open moors.

8

E WAITED UNTIL THEY HAD DISAPPEARED
over the crest of the hill. Then Lord Raoul turned
to me. Before all his men, he put his hands about
my waist, lifting me from the ground to swing me
up.

"Now, by my troth," he said, "that was well done, *ma mie.*"
And he kissed me full upon the lips.

He set me down hastily and turned to the others, drawing
his lords apart.

Before I had left them they were already discussing, explaining, assessing what had been done, what achieved. I walked
slowly away, my women a distance off, and wandered toward
the first embankment, the one I had burst through on horseback how many weeks ago now? It was already spring, and I
had scarcely noticed, one of those spring days when the sky
is so pale blue it seems to shine with a light of its own. I sat
among the grasses at the foot of the great bank, wondering,
as I always did whenever I passed by, what manner of men
had first thrown it up, and why; twined flowers that grew
there into garlands, presently, not thinking, simply sitting
and waiting. But the day had already paled, the smoke of
the campfires darkened the pale blue, the wind grown chill,
before he came.

"Come, Lady Ann," he said, "your hand. Walk awhile beside
me here."

He helped me to my feet, then paced beside me, forgetting sometimes to match his steps with mine, so that before long I was hard put to keep up with him.

"That kinsman of yours," he said abruptly, "this uncle. What do you remember of him?"

"I recall many things," I said, "simply, none clear. I would not have remembered him if you had asked me. Seeing him, I think I do."

"And his standing?" he said.

"Standing?" I asked. "He is a great lord. My mother was a princess of their race."

"Yes, yes," he said, almost impatiently, "they are all great princes. But privy to what master then? Who serves he?"

"I do not know," I said. "Whoever are highest in these parts."

He made a gesture. "And who are they?" he said. "They change from day to day."

"No different then from your Norman kings," I said.

He smiled down at me and bade me walk on. I watched him now as we went. It suddenly seemed to me that although this was the time of day when the work was done, all was still confused about us. The great gates were not yet closed. Even as I looked, I saw men gallop out. And Lord Raoul himself: I did not remember he wore his mail coat beneath his robe before, or that he had his spurs upon his heels, or fingered his dagger hilt so as he walked.

"It is good news then, my lord," I said.

"Aye," he said, not listening to me, watching in his turn.

"Those horses are too close tethered," he bawled out suddenly, leaning over the bank. The men below scurried to obey.

"You do not expect treachery, my lord?" I asked at last.

"I do not expect anything," he said. "The work today was well done. Now comes the night. One must be prepared."

"My uncle came in good faith," I said hotly. "You told me there was no trap."

"Yes," said Raoul. "For all our flattery of each other, I believe he is a man of sense. But he also spoke the truth in this: he is but one among many. He made no promises on others' behalf. What he tells them, and how they respond, is in God's hands. But he has also seen how we are deployed, our strengths, our weaknesses."

"You did not have to let him come into your camp if you feared him," I cried angrily.

"That also is true," he said, "but then he might not have come at all. One plays one chance against another, sets one thing against the opposite. That is the way of the world."

"Not mine," I said. "Does it not tire you, my lord, always outguessing your friends and foes?"

The scorn in my voice must have touched some nerve. "I have long been used to it," he said shortly.

"So you said once before," I said.

"I also told you," he said, "if you but remember, that although we may scheme and plan, events outside our control are not so nice as to wait upon our ordering."

"I remember many things," I said, "including that you have had your enemy within your grasp and let him go."

"Where heard you news such as that?" he said, coming to full stop. "Not at my table or in my camp. But if you mean that Henry of Anjou escaped from us, that I would not argue with. But I did not let him go."

It was a distinction that was fair, but I was angered.

"And at Crowmarsh," I said, "what happened after that to send you trailing back here to this makeshift camp?"

He said evenly, although I saw how he bit his lip to hide his rage, "Since you speak of what I do not care to talk, well then, the king would not fight. Would you have had us turn against him and the Angevins both? So peace was signed."

"And you signed it?"

"There were good points to it, even those that your uncle spoke of today, to tear down those unlicensed castles that have sprouted everywhere, and to send back the mercenaries, be they Flemish or Gascon, who feed on the English lands. I counseled for the truce at Wallingford."

"And you signed it."

"I did not counsel, I did not sign the treaty that followed, at Westminster."

"What treaty? I have not heard of it," I cried.

"No doubt," he said, dryly, "you were still in your priory, I think. It made the king's new heir. Henry of Anjou will be king when Stephen dies. But I, and thus my vassals, did not agree to it."

"But that cannot be," I said, facing him squarely. "King Stephen has a son, Prince Eustace. He will rule after his father. . . ."

"The prince died in August," said Lord Raoul, "as he lived, a violent man by violent means. Without him, there is no other heir."

Here then was news that Giles had breathed no word of. And yet I had already guessed he knew more than he would say. Now Lord Raoul confirmed my belief.

"But Stephen has other sons," I cried. "They should rule. . . ."

"His one other son is William," Lord Raoul said evenly, "who has had no part of these affairs, not being an 'ambitious man' as your kinsman would say. By his marriage he has acquired great wealth, and Henry of Anjou has sworn to uphold his lands in France. He has no real need or ambition for a crown. So Henry will have it."

Only then did the implication of what he was saying sink in.

"But the other nobles will not have it so," I cried.

"The treaty was signed at Westminster, lady. Eustace died last August. In November, Stephen recognized Henry of Anjou as his heir. The lords and barons of England have been summoned twice to pay homage to him as the heir."

"But you, you did not?"

When he did not reply, I suddenly remembered Giles's reluctance to speak of the second meeting with the king. A fear grew in me.

"Did you not do homage to Henry with the rest?" When again he did not reply, "That was wrongly done."

Then his anger did break out, the more because he knew better than anyone the complications of that refusal, the anger it would have caused to Stephen and Henry both.

"Rot me," he cried, "but you will teach me how to use my sword, or bestride my horse. What was the first cause of all these long and bitter wars? Think! That we nobles should pay homage to an heir before the reigning king was dead. You once were brash enough to tell me it was because we would not have a woman on the throne. Man or woman, it matters not, acceptance of an heir over a living king foments unrest, destroys the peace, breeds revolution and sedition. Whatever the Treaty of Westminster would have achieved is already lost. The old Earl of Sedgemont said as much to his king. And I have said it to mine."

"And no doubt to Henry of Anjou himself, who was overjoyed at the telling." He did not reply to that jibe.

"But Stephen is your friend," I cried. "He will surely stand between you and Anjou."

"While he lives, perhaps," he said, and I knew from his tone how little faith he put in that. "Such oaths make mockery of oath taking. Stephen has put his own life in jeopardy that now his enemies have reason to get rid of him. It has made Anjou a pawn of other men's desires. Who will use him to advance themselves."

He caught my glance and held it this time.

"Like the Lord of Maneth, who seeks to outdo all those other faithless lords who ravage in the east as he himself ravages the west. It is not only the Celts who will take advantage of our stupidity, lady. All over England are there such men. I think you should know that as well as I. Maneth began his plots against you in your convent only after he saw which way the die would fall. God's teeth," he cried, "why should they wait for Stephen's death to make Henry king? Maneth may seem less dangerous than the others, that is all, because as long as we remain here in our 'makeshift camp,' as you call it, he is not free to throw all his weight on Henry's side. And if this treaty with the Celts is made, well, that may contain him. They like him as little as I do. And I shall have fulfilled the charge Stephen, in his anger, laid upon me. He will not ask anything else of me, who has defied his wishes. But if the Celtic treaty fails..."

"Then what?"

"You are good at advice," he snarled, "so advise me what to choose. Shall we sack Cambray to rid it of the Celts and bring your kinsmen about our ear? Shall we attack Maneth and thus close against his ally, the next heir of England, Henry of Anjou? Or shall we turn against a king who has already thrown his kingdom away?"

"There must be some other choice than those," I said, refusing to let him see how his words affected me. "You paint a gloomy picture, my lord."

"Yes," he said, for once not turning aside my words with a jest. "By the Mass, were I truly a man of sense, I would show my back quick enough to them all. There are other struggles, other battles. Overseas, I could find a better war. But look not apprehensive. I have not turned coward yet, although the world looks beckoning. Forget what I have said. Let me thank you instead for your help. You spoke me fair this day, you looked fair. And you did not say we had mistreated you at Sedgemont. That, at least, was gently done."

"Did you expect that I would?" I said.

"Ah, that I cannot tell," he said, "except you are ever ready to place me in the wrong. Would it not please you, lady, to have me proved a coward, a man of no faith?"

We had come full circle now in our pacing, and he was waiting to hand me down from the path, toward my tent. The light was almost gone, yet the air was golden with reflected sun and the wind blew about his hair as he stood below me, one foot still upon the bank. Suddenly I saw the differences that had not been there a year ago: the tiredness, the frown between those wide-spaced eyes, the shadow beneath them that picked up the high cheek bones, the disdain that hid bitterness, the pride, which showed through. Beneath his robe, the mail coat curved and shimmered and his golden spurs glittered at his heels.

Many were the things I have regretted not saying, a thousand things could I have said then.

"I did not think it would matter how I judged you, my lord," I said coldly, all the gladness of the day already wasted away. "You follow your own desires without let or hindrance from me."

It was not only desires of state and governance that I spoke of.

And he knew it.

"Hold yourself in readiness, then, lady," he said as coldly, formally. "We shall see what this night brings forth."

And he strode away, already putting thoughts aside, shouting to his squire to bring his sword and belt, calling for his horse, his guard. I watched him go without kindly word. That was not well done either.

I do not know who slept well that night. I know he did not sleep at all and all the camp kept uneasy watch. I lay full clothed upon my bed, running over and over in my mind the events and words of the day until they blurred to one, and when at last I closed my eyes, my dreams were dark, uneasy, full of anxious partings and harsh words that need not have been said. Long after I have remembered that time, how pride kept me from repenting of my anger. Yet had he not set double watch, kept the gates himself, with extra guards along the outer banks, they would have overrun us as we lay. As it was, they took the outer watchtowers by stealth, one by one, but there were enough men who survived to give the warning.

They came before dawn, like shadows, drifting down from the moors on their swift-footed ponies that stole across the heather and brush. They made no sound at first, sliding toward the camp, where Raoul and his men waited for them. It was the sound of that first clash of arms, the shouts, the snarl of trumpets blaring the alert, that wakened me from the dark dreams where I had fallen. I ran to the entrance of the tent, where my womenfolk had already huddled, as sheep before a storm. Over the crest of the hill, where we had watched them leave, they came swarming back again, like dark ants, a string of running horsemen, bundled in their furs, circling and circling again. Giles was already at his post, leather coated, steel coifed, sword ready. There were more shouts, answers, the scream of horses and the sudden acrid smell of fire. With a thunder of hooves, Lord Raoul rode past, hauling at the reins to bring his horse to a stop. For all my boasting, I would not have known him then, with his battle helm on, his shield and lance set. Only by that black horse and the red banner would I have recognized who he was.

"Guard her," he cried to Giles, "away to the wagons, down yonder with the boys. Lady Ann, stay close; it is but a raiding party. Mount, mount, man, they are upon us."

Then he was gone again, thundering back toward the gates, his household guard at his heels, swords swinging. I had not chance to bid him farewell, wish him Godspeed, as he rode to take the most dangerous place before the main entrance. I watched him afar off, how he rode easier after a while, hand on hip, stopping to joke with this group, reposition that one. The other mounted men swung out behind him and he was hidden from view.

"They have overrun the outer pickets," Giles said, "even the double watch that we had set there. They must have crawled past them in the dark."

He brought up my horse, swung me on, then mounted himself.

"They must have spied upon the fortifications yesterday. Treacherous dogs!"

"Not my uncle's men," I cried. "He would not attack without cause."

Giles did not reply. He led the way down toward the spring and the hollow at the lower end of the camp, farthest from the gates. The food carts had been hurriedly drawn there last night. The pages and younger boys were already stationed there, fingering their short knives and muttering excitedly. My women cowered within the shelter of the wagons.

"Do not be afeard, my lady," Giles echoed Raoul's tone of voice, "we are out of harm."

A shout came from one of his men, "They are circling, Giles. Watch to the right here."

Then nothing, silence, a clash of conflict, screams, farther off to our left. We moved down the hollow a little toward the cliff where the stream fell softly over the escarpment, feet below. It was damp and cool in the hollow, sheltered by some wind-bent trees and bushes that grew on the cliff edge. One of the horses dipped its mouth into the water and swung up, dripping like silver. The morning mists curled across the open field above us. Silence.

Then again shouts, a cry cut off short: "Behind, behind."

We turned in our saddles, the horses shifting nervously, nostrils flaring at the smell and sounds. Before my eyes, as in my dream, I saw the inner wall and hedge close to us break apart, as if churned underfoot. I saw three men in Sedgemont red stumble and fall like dolls upon the bank as a handful of men poured over them like water. Following them, a group of horsemen rode them over, friend and foe alike, bent over their ponies' sides to shield themselves. Giles thrust my horse behind his; a bowman at his side fitted arrows to his bow and drew again. Where was Raoul? I strained to see through the shifting shadows toward the main gates, half-hidden now by the curve of the inner bank. Where were his guards? They would be taken from the rear, pinned back against the great wooden planks of their own gate. But the horsemen did not ride out toward the gates, they veered instead and came straight toward us, toward the supply wagons, the unarmed boys, the womenfolk.

With a cry, Giles and his men rode out to meet them. I sat on my horse in the cool shade while the light of the early dawn began to burn and shimmer on the glittering blades. There was a sudden violent shock as sword and shield came together. Then they were all woven into one another, a tangled mesh of steel and hooves and flesh. I could still count our men: two had fallen, another fell with a strangled cry. Giles was out in front, his short sword rising and stabbing. I thought, Oh God, he is no horseman, he is not a soldier born. Where is Raoul?

Another shout, an answering echo. I saw some of the Sedgemont men leap down from the circling banks and begin to run in our direction. But they were too far off, and the horsemen at the gates were already engaged. Giles and his little band were forced back as more Celtic horsemen flowed across the gap. The silver stream turned to mud as they flailed and slashed across the water. Beside me, the bowman fell in a gout of blood. There were other enemy archers on the banks now; I recognized their long Welsh bows before they shot down upon us. Some of their horsemen wheeled to cut off a countercharge. The rest drove headlong into the clearing, slashing at the boys and womenfolk as they came. The air was thick with noise, with clash and blare and shout, breaking like a wave of sound that deafened the ears. I thought again, Oh God, I have heard this noise before, I have seen all this before. And I watched again, as in a dream, how Giles's horse suddenly reared and stretched, and he fell sideways across its neck, one hand curled up to grasp the rein, the other arm flung wide.

"Giles, Giles," I screamed, throwing myself to the ground. I began to run toward him, running without motion across the torn and bloodied grass. He was lying sprawled at the water's edge as I had seen him those years ago in the forest. In a moment he would leap to his feet, laughing and wiping the mud from his eyes. "What ails you, Lady Ann," he would say, "I did but slip. . . ."

Around me all was noise, confusion, death. I ran without motion, without color, without sound, and knelt beside him on the blood-soaked bank. I took his shattered head within my arms, but all the smiles were gone, the eyes already closed, the last breaths faint upon his lips.

"Giles," I whispered into the silence, but he did not speak, did not move, and the silence washed over us like a cold, dark wind.

I do not know how long it was before the darkness lifted. Hours, days. . . I remember odd snatches of things disconnected, like escaped fragments between sleep and wake: being caught up somehow, the feel of fur and leather, the bite of rope about hands and feet that seemed not to belong to me. Above all, a recurrent theme, the outstretched arms, the brown hair awash in the stream, the blood-furrowed face. I think I slept, or perhaps not slept, put consciousness away, so as not to see.

We stopped once, again, we rode on, I carried before or behind some trooper like a bundle slung across a saddle. We changed mounts, bigger and faster now, prepared for us in some valley. Somewhere between consciousness and unconsciousness, between sleep and wake, I knew we were going north, across the desolate region I had traversed but a few months before—north, not west. Somehow I came to realize that although at first we had ridden Celtic ponies, these new ones were not, and that the men who rode them, although some were Celt, the others spoke Norman-French, wore Norman mail, and carried Norman weapons beneath their Celtic furs and capes.

But all these were fragments, flung splintering out of silence, making no sense until at last we came to a full halt, and all came jarring together, coherent, real. I can only explain it as if a veil had been thrust across my eyes, and suddenly now it was torn back and I could see things about me as they truly were. It must have been high noon, although of which day I could not say. We had come to a halt in one of those deserted villages that I have spoken of, in the shadow of hovels whose broken walls gleamed against fire-blackened timbers. A soldier held me upright before him, his arm slack, as if I were a burden he was familiar with, as used to as any other part of his equipment. I felt the ache of my own body, stretched and tight against the roughness of his leather coat. I felt the sweat on my skin, caked like dust, and the dried blood. Most of all, I became aware of the stares of the other men, those who had been riding with us and those who lounged in the village square, waiting, it seemed, for us to arrive.

Lord Guy of Maneth rode out from behind the cottage wall. Beside him, his son Gilbert, and behind them, the guard of Maneth, armed and ready.

"Is this the one?" he said. "No mistake this time."

"Aye, good, my lord."

"Where is the Celtic woman?"

There was a scuffle inside the ruined house. Two soldiers dragged a woman forward, kicking and scratching in the dust. They threw her down in front of Lord Maneth's horse in the dirt and she lay there until one of the men kicked her to her feet. It was the red-haired woman I had seen in Lord Raoul's tent, the one I had watched and envied in the camp.

"You," said Lord Guy of Maneth, his voice dark and ominous. "Is this the one?"

She flung a look at me sideways, tossing her long red hair.

"Yes, my lord," she said in her singsong voice. "Would I lie to you? Did I not show you where, and when, show you the way through the lines? Why would I lie about her?"

I heard a clink of metal, a fall of coins.

"This for your pains. So do I reward those who serve me well. Those who do not, or seek to cheat me, or talk too much..." There was a squeal of pain. Then she went on scratching in the dirt. I raised my head and looked upon them all—the lords of Maneth on their horses, full armed in the sun, their men-at-arms leaning forward to miss nothing, the red-haired woman hunting for the scattered coins.

"Welcome then, Lady of Cambray," said Lord Guy of Maneth. "At last we meet up with you again. You recall my son and heir, I think."

My lips were cracked with heat and dirt. It was difficult to speak and I could not yet think clearly.

Gilbert, at his side, gave a roar of laughter. "We have long awaited you," he said. "Ladies, you should know each other." And with the end of his sword he prodded at the woman on the ground so that she left off her scrabbling and for a moment looked at me straight.

We knew each other then, who we both were, why we both were here. There was no surprise. I knew her as she knew me, what she had done and why. Then she turned around quickly, fitting the scattered silver into her pocket, limping out of sight. I felt no anger, she no remorse. Had our positions been reversed, might I not have done the same? Revenge is sweet, to the lowest as to the high.

Gilbert laughed again, that braying laugh I remembered from before.

"And like to two peas in a pod," he said. "There is Celtic kinship for you. On the ground, there's no telling base-born from noble." He laughed again. "And both the castoffs from Sedgemont's bed. Which is best jest of all."

His words had not the power to wound. Yet I felt then, and feel even more, what I deserved of them. I had not cared what became of her. And she, had she betrayed Raoul for vengeance? And what, I wondered suddenly, will any of it mean to him, not knowing what has become of either of us?

Great lords feel not the lack of bedmates.

There would be plenty more for him to pick and choose.

Lord Guy urged his horse forward to stop his son's mirth. "Peace," I heard him say, "are you a fool to babble her ill fame abroad for all men to make a mockery of?"

I saw the flush on Gilbert's face as he pulled back, muttering. Lord Guy turned to me once more, triumph and caution battling for the upper hand.

"Your silence becomes you at last, Lady Ann," he said. He snapped his fingers at his men. "I would have bid you welcome to my castle myself, but failing that, have waited to see you safe on Maneth lands. My son would still have you as bride, although your reputation be not so spotless as once it was. Better to have stayed at your convent and let us fetch you from there. But be thankful for his courtesy. Other men might not show such indulgence."

Then I did find speech.

"You cannot think to hold me against my will. Lord Raoul . . ."

"Lord Raoul!" Gilbert spat out the words contemptuously. "Far away, chasing Celtic shadows across their border. He did not think how easy it was to gather up some ragtail Celts and slip our men among them. Tricked he was, as neatly by a mock Celtic host as by a Celtic whore."

He grinned at his father, his sallow face abrim with spite.

"Lord Raoul is not so lightly tricked," I cried. "He is a true and caring lord . . . which is more than you can boast of."

"You still have some spirit left," sneered Lord Guy. "Well, we have means at Maneth to break it. I regret that I shall not be there to watch."

He nudged his horse against the one that I was on, the skirt of his mail coat crushing my leg.

"Your Lord Raoul is a fool who sends his vassals to their death. A fool again that he jeopardizes the treaty he was ordered to make. You see, I know many things. We have been waiting for the Celts to make a move so we could make ours."

"And like a fool he walked into the trap," Gilbert brayed again. "True, you say. To which king? There is but one king and my father sails with him now as he leaves for France. Ask Henry of Anjou, next King of England, how he will repay the loyalty of Raoul of Sedgemont." Again his father motioned to him for silence.

I must remember what Gilbert says, I thought. He is the fool who gives too much away.

Lord Guy was pressing on against me, making the man who held me saw at his horse to keep it steady.

"Tell your Lord Raoul, if ever you see him again, that only fools set themselves up to be the better of their neighbors. These are not times to vaunt honor. Only a madman follows loyalty when the choice is life and death. Oath keeping will not save his lands or titles."

"The Celtic princes will not let you hold me prisoner," I cried. "In tricking Raoul, you trick them."

"Once we have you," Gilbert laughed, "they'll make their peace with us. As soon us than him. They'll come knocking at our gates. But first we'll let them deal with him. What price his honor that he attacks them unprovoked on their own lands? Is that not what they have feared? Short shrift they'll make of him and his treachery. Your Raoul is as a dead man already."

I thought his father might have stopped his mouth again, but even Guy of Maneth allowed himself the luxury of watching my dismay. I felt myself quail against such malice, unchecked, exultant.

"So you should thank your Raoul," Gilbert was sneering again, "for showing us your value. We can use you as bait as well as he can. When they have done with him and his men, then will they listen to our offer. Our friendship will mean as much to them then as Cambray's. And we'll take Cambray to boot."

"Cambray is still in the Lord of Sedgemont's demesne,"

I said hoarsely. "It is in his gift. You cannot have it."

"And if you have a son to inherit, eh?" said Lord Guy. "As by then you shall. A son to the house of Maneth to inherit Cambray. But come, lady, I have a long journey ahead, to France. Be sure I will speak most lovingly of Sedgemont and Cambray, so lovingly that Henry of Anjou will not have the heart to deny me any part of what I want. Think of that as you ride on to Maneth castle. And one embrace before we part, then, as your new father."

I felt my cheek flare under his lips; his mouth covered mine so I could not breathe. As he drew back contemptuously, I bit at him, feeling the blood start. He reigned back with a muffled cry, then surged forward, almost knocking horse and man over. His hand hit the side of my head so that all reeled and went black.

"That was foolishly done," I heard him say. "That, too, shall be remembered. I have not forgotten how you put shame upon me and my son. Murderers, you called us, liars, in front of my men. Nor have I forgotten the little matter of a missing messenger. Died by fire, they say. We shall find out."

"I'll bear Gilbert no sons," I said, although the words swam before me as I spoke.

He caught hold of my hair, pulling it back until my neck arched, like an animal's before you cut it.

"You will have a son," he said in my ear. "Shudder at such a thought? Mine or Gilbert's. Better our get than Sedgemont's. For I will have title to Cambray, and legally. But you should have picked more wisely when you had the chance. At least I know woman's ways. I wager that when I return you will look forward to what I can show you."

He let me go and beckoned to his son; wheeled his horse round and about as if still uneasy, as if undecided whether to leave or not.

"I must ride fast," I heard him say to Gilbert. "Anjou will not await our coming. Do not waste time but go on to Maneth.

I would she were already penned between the walls before I went."

"He is lost in the mountains ere this," Gilbert said sulkily. "Lost, or the Celts have already killed him for trespass. Who else is there to fear?"

"This crowns ten years' work," I heard him say again. "Such things need care to the very end. Then will our power stretch north and south, greater than any man's since the death of the Earl of Gloucester. I would have had all safely locked within my keep before I left."

"It has already been agreed," Gilbert said. "You to work to our purpose with the Angevins in France, I, here."

"Be careful, cautious," Lord Guy continued to exhort him, giving final instructions, clasping his arm about his son's shoulder while Gilbert sat black faced upon his horse. Had he heard his father's whispers to me? Was he being told what he must do?

"Aye, aye, my good father," he said at last, sullen like a boy. "There is no danger. Maneth castle is but a few hours' ride away. I tell you, all will go as you have planned."

Lord Guy beckoned at last to his men. I heard him order those who stayed behind to ride on as soon as he was gone; then with half-oath, half-order, he wheeled about, riding out to the east, his guard crowding after. The rest waited in the village square, expectant to begin the march to Maneth. It was hot and still. I could hear the flies buzzing about the horses, the same noise that still buzzed within my ears. I could feel the hot sun, smell the faint smell of burnt wood, hear the shiftings of the charred beams as they resettled in the heat. Giles was dead, Raoul most like was dead, and I was prisoner of my enemies.

With an oath, Gilbert thrust himself heavily out of his saddle, calling to his squires to give him aid. He beckoned to the soldier who still held me on his horse.

"Drop her," he shouted. The man slashed at the ropes that

bound me and I went sprawling to the ground. Gilbert laughed, hands on hips, legs akimbo, slowly peeling off his gauntlets, beckoning to his men to unfasten his mail coat.

On the ground, there's no telling base-born from noble. . . . I lay in the dirt with my green gown torn and stained with blood.

"Get up," he shouted next, and when I did not, he pricked at my side with his heel. "On your feet, slut."

I could not move; the ropes that had bound me so long had deadened my arms and legs so that even when he snarled at his men to haul me by the hair, I could not resist or comply.

"Into the hut," he cried. "There's time before we need to ride on. Maneth castle is not a kingdom away. Let's see what she's made of first. Drag her inside."

There was a mutter at that, either because of what he said or because his orders reversed those given by his father. I think the latter, for his voice changed then. He walked from one man to the next, fingering his dagger hilt, angry yet cajoling at the one time.

"There's wine aplenty," he said, "the day is still young. Time to ride on in the evening cool."

When they still did not respond, "Am I master here?" he sputtered. "By my oath, who thwarts me when I bid him shall pay for it. Lord Guy of Maneth is growing old. He is forever fearful of what lies ahead. Fear and caution are as meat and drink to him. We, who are younger, heh, must look to present pleasure. They say she graced the Lord of Sedgemont's bed as his page. What say we find the truth of that?"

At last he did raise a laugh among the younger, wilder-looking of his men. Two of them took me by the arms and dragged me inside the hut, leaving me there propped up against a bench. The place had already been used, clothes and food were scattered about, and there were wine flasks in plenty. The men winked at me as they went.

"A kind master we have," one said, "share and share. You'll see." He seized one of the wineskins and they went outside again. I sat against the bench, legs outstretched, hair tumbled awry, bruises beginning to ache and smart. Yet, although my head still reeled under the buffet Lord Guy had given me, my mind began to work again, as if the blow had cleared away some deeper, deadlier hurt. Outside, I heard Gilbert's snarl raised, saw his pages hurry to tug off the armor that encased his plump body, saw him struggle into gown and fur-lined cape, and slick back his hair before a mirror into a semblance of those fashionable locks that younger men wore. It was obvious he intended to stay here, even against his father's express command. Well, in that there could be hope. As long as we were not at Maneth, there was still hope. Once within the castle would be time to know that all was lost. I began to remember what people said of this man. Even his father called him fool, and his men, if they obeyed him, did so partly from fear, partly because there was some sly bond between them. "He talks too much," Lord Raoul had said. Yet his father entrusted him with his most-secret affairs. Perhaps, if I could keep him talking, I could find out what they were. But I was deathly afraid of him, even as I steadied my thoughts with these plans. The father terrified me, but the son much more. I feared him as one fears an overgrown and petulant child who smashes what he wants out of greed. . . . What else his father had hinted at, and the old man in the ruined fort, and even Lord Raoul himself, those were things that bore not thinking on. . . . Stupid and sly, and evil. . . Lord Guy of Maneth must have thought himself safe indeed if he left such a man to finish what he had begun so long ago.

Gilbert came to the door then, ungainly in his costly robes, belted with chain of gold. A gold purse hung at his side and he tottered on high-heeled shoes. The impression I had had when I saw him before at Sedgemont increased. Underneath that luxury there was something soft, white, unwholesome. His men came crowding after, pushing one another at the door.

"Outside," he said to them, not turning round, waving his hand at them. "Wait."

They laughed, moving back reluctantly like oxen driven from a water hole. And we were left together, Gilbert of Maneth and I. He eyed me furtively, lounging to the table, where he poured himself wine, spilling some in his haste. He swilled it down, wiping at his mouth with his embroidered sleeve. I felt fear and hatred rise up, yet I would not show him what I felt.

"Faugh," he said, making a gesture of disgust, "you stink of sweat and blood. Is there no way to clean you first?"

"It was a good man's blood," I said, my voice husky with pain and horror. "No shame to him. And it will be avenged, as will my brother's."

He laughed uneasily, although the words came carelessly enough.

"You speak of things long past, forgotten. Who thinks of the lords of Cambray? They moulder these ten years."

He poured more wine and drank it eagerly, running his hand over his chin where the black growth showed along the heavy jaw.

"You should remember things more recent," he said. "That I hold power of life and death, even over you."

"You would not dare kill me now," I said. "You have already found out that I am worth more alive. The time to have killed me was when Talisin died. Or that first time at Sedgemont. That was bungling indeed."

He swore then, cursing in vile terms, raising his fist to strike.

"Better you had drowned at Cambray," he said at last. "We should have taken all of you at one time. But there will be no more mistakes. We have you. We shall have Cambray. And when your Celtic kinsmen come looking for you, we'll have them. Let them kill off Raoul of Sedgemont for us first, saving us the trouble. Then we can pick our time and deal with them."

"There speaks your father's voice," I mocked. "Have you no say in these plans?"

He drank again, watching me with his narrow eyes.

"He will be far off in France," I taunted again. "Will you sit obediently until his return?"

His fist came crashing down at that.

"Enough," he shouted. "I am master here. I do what I want. I shall trick the Celts with offers of treaty in return for you, and when they come, we shall be waiting for them. As for Cambray, there are other ways to get it than waiting for your son to inherit. I can take it when I want."

"Easier said than done," I said. "You were the first to point that out to Lord Raoul."

"Raoul, Raoul," he mimicked me. "Without our help, he'd have neither force enough nor skill. But if a handful of Celts could make their way inside by trickery, then Normans can do better."

"It is too strong for that," I said, taunting. "You'll never overpower the walls by trickery."

"Who speaks of taking walls," he said with a laugh. "True, a handful of men could hold Cambray, but we'll leave them to watch their walls. When we take Cambray, there are other ways. Your father built it strong, but not wisely. He thought to make it safe as all those Norman castles where he had served in France."

He drank again. As I hoped, the wine was making him free with his talk.

"He thought to build as strong a keep as any he had known. But he should have kept his intentions close. We took an old comrade of his to Maneth the other day. He told us enough to make things clear. Or rather," and he smiled at me, showing the pointed edges of his big teeth, "or rather, we persuaded him to it, poor dog, squealing out his master's secrets for an hour's more breath. Your father had ideas above his rank. His pride will be his own undoing, now we have the key to Cambray's defense."

He poked his finger at my face. "Your precious Raoul does not know what it is. And my father does not know I plan to use it. While he's away in France. Then shall I be master of Maneth and Lord of Cambray before him."

His words made greater impact that they seemed to echo some memory.

"Then you do not need me at all," was all I said.

"Ah, yes," he said, "because we need an heir to make things legal. A son would set a seal of legitimacy."

"That has not bothered you, wherever else you have robbed and stolen," I cried.

"Perhaps not," he boasted again. "But Cambray is worth more than the rest. And how do you know what we have robbed or stolen?"

I did not reply. For a new thought had come to me.

"Why is it," I asked him wonderingly, "that you hate us so much that you would destroy us one by one?"

He suddenly shouted back, "You do me wrong. I never hated Talisin. Had we been left to ourselves, he would not have hated me, nor I him. But the lords of Maneth were nothing to you at Cambray, less than hate, of no consequence at all. One among many who fawned on your father and brother. What were they, a poor man and his son raised out of obscurity to little fame? See how the tables are now turned. I tell you I shall be lord of all. I shall take Cambray before my father's return, and when I have finished with the Celtic lords, I'll have their lands, too. The whole of the border shall be mine. And all these lands that I have already destroyed."

His gesture took in the ruined huts, the deserted village, those desolate tracts I had seen.

"Then will Gilbert of Maneth rank higher than the lords of Cambray. And when I have their sister, daughter, to do what I want with..."

He surged toward me, pale faced, the sweat standing out on his forehead. Before I knew what he was about, he had dragged me away from the bench to the floor.

"Your father and brother reckoned themselves so far above me," he shouted. "See how you fall beneath. I have waited all my life to have them grovel for mercy before me."

"I do not ask for mercy," I gasped, "not for myself or for their memory."

He put a hand across his face to wipe the rivulets of sweat that ran from his hair.

"So looked he," he said almost incoherently; then, more rationally, "but there was never proof of foul play. Why should you blame me? I warned him of the tides. They knew I hated the water. Talisin ever mocked me for it. Had he not mocked me, had he begged, even then, although I could not swim, I would have dragged him forth, rescued him at my own life's risk."

"Say rather that you would have spared him," I said, "to mock him before you thrust him under."

He let go my arms, where he had caught me to shake his words into my ears.

"So looked your father, also," he whispered, "when I brought the word. Turn your eyes aside, you devil's bitch. Pride and grief killed your father, pride and scorn your brother."

He gulped another drink, another, swaying on his small feet as he stood. Hate and desire struggled in his face, a child who, for spite, destroys what he wants. So perhaps he had stood long ago by the sea at Cambray until hate sent him lumbering forward. . . .

"How many men have you lain with?" he said suddenly. "Raoul, your groomsman, the soldiers of the camp; how many have you had, slut?"

"You will never know," I said.

"Like your mother, then," he swore. "They say she bedded every man your father brought to Cambray. Skill she had to cover everyone, that they all sang her praises. No woman else could have so besotted them."

"Do you hope so much from me?" I said through swollen

lips, and saw him pale again with sweat. "Then you will never know if the child you want is yours or someone else's. Some churl's perhaps, that one day will sit at the High Table at Maneth. If I am slut and a child of a slut, I will not change my ways."

"I'll tie you rather like a cur," he said, "a bitch in heat to be serviced on a chain. You heard my father. We've ways at Maneth to break your spirit yet."

He ran a finger under his silk collar, sweating heavily, repeating vile words beneath his breath. It was almost as if the words themselves pleasured him. Only then did it occur to me that this man would rape me with the muck of other men, as if he could not do it with his own desire. Against my will, what others had said of him flooded into my ears, what even his father had hinted at, what his own men had suggested. There would be no escape this time. The door stood open, but there were too many men outside in the sun-filled square. I could hear them laughing, moving about, a woman's voice singing. There would be no help from her either.

"Slut and whore," he was repeating, "open to all men." And hit me with his fist at each word to make me reply.

Do not speak of rape, Lord Raoul had warned me. *You know not what you say.* I had thought I did. Now I saw something else, that even rape can have some ways more foul than others. And when he had hit me enough, he threw himself across me on the ground. I let him flail at me, knowing by instinct that to give resistance would have pleased him better, and let him grope and paw the more, like a beast that tears first here, then there, too ravenous to favor any part long. I felt him fumble with himself beneath his gown, engorged, yet soft as tallow, thrusting up at me under my own. Where he thrust, there was pain, yet it came rather from his weight and the movement of his ungainly body thrashing to and fro. And the more he heaved, the more he receded away.

He pushed me aside at last, staggered to the table, downed

another flagon of wine, and stood panting and shaking.

"You lied," he hissed. "You are virgin."

He stood swaying before me, the wine dripping from his chin. I was frightened then. This was how he killed, a man twisted with his desires, distorted, like a wet cord that swings and cuts as it swings.

Again he swore a dark, cruel oath. In his hand, as if sprung there, he held his dagger, turning it first one way, then the other, as he had fingered it in the square to subdue his men.

"Before God," he cried, "you devil's bitch, to make a mock of me. Does not death and hell frighten you?"

"I go where better men await me," I whispered, "who will be avenged yet."

At that he started back. "The devil take you then," he cried, almost weeping in some recollection of self-pity, "that for ten years I should be accused by them, unbegging, unafraid. I could kill you where you lie and you would haunt me the same. God rot my father's soul to make me sport to dead men. For his ambitions do I pay, for his plans do my nights turn to torment. But you'll not unman me again. Bedeviled I said when I saw you first. Bedeviled that I should consent to my father's wish against my own. But I'll be master here. Put on that shirt, cover your nakedness with men's clothes. You've done as much before."

He flung the scattered garments at my feet and I shrugged within them, shirt and tunic, while he turned aside for rage. Then on a rush he came at me a second time. This time I did try to leap aside, thinking he would stab me as I lay. He was not as quick as I was and wine had fuddled his brain, but I saw my mistake as soon as I had turned to the door.

"Ho, there, watch, ho," he mouthed forth, loud enough for me to start back, for the cry to be heard without. I kept the bench between us, but with a kick he was able to overthrow it, and the men who came to the doorway pushed me back toward him. He bowled me over again, while they shouted and laughed, and he knelt beside me on the floor, one hand to hold my arms together, the other to still my body.

My struggles seemed to inflame him, or was it the catcalls of his men? He muttered endearments in my ear, his lips sour with wine and sweat, calling me his sweeting, and his page. And when all else failed, he took up the dagger in his hand and presented it at me hilt first. There was a rush of breath, a sudden silence then. I understood what he meant to do. But twist and fight and turn, I could not shake him off. Other hands grasped my feet. I saw his face intent as he struggled with breath to get at me and pry my legs apart. I heard my own scream thin and high.

Then there was a roaring in my ears. I thought it was death come to spare me this shame, until I heard the echoing screams outside, the thud against the open door. The mass of men crowded there whirled back, and I heard a great gasp at the lance that struck there quivering. Then they scattered, some running outside, some tugging at their swords or daggers, their mouths agape although no sound came trickling out. Those who had been holding me let go, ran here and there in the room as fish dart in the shallows. I rolled back out of their way, trying to pull my clothes about my nakedness, huddling up as small as I could. I saw a shape that seemed to tower in the sunlight there, a dark shape tall and menacing. A flash of light followed in its path, the downward sweep of a sword that danced and sang as it fell.

Gilbert of Maneth saw it too. He scrambled to his feet, tripping on his silken robe, his face turned to palsied white. He ran behind the other men, holding up the skirts of his robe as he tried to use them to cover himself. The great sword flashed again and again, each time cutting down through flesh, through bone. I saw an arm hacked through, a chest ripped wide. Gilbert tried to speak, tried to run. He held the dagger still in his hand, but he had not the will to lift it in his defense. The great blade caught him as he turned,

9

HE MEN AT THE DOORWAY HAD ALREADY
gone down, wordless, folding under, as insub-
stantial as rags. Raoul was in the room, leaning on
his bloodstained sword. His panting filled the air.
About him, the dead men's bodies sagged. He bent and scooped
up the one that lolled across my legs, dragging me upright
against the table. His hands were about my face and body,
causing more pain, for he forgot he wore mail gauntlets, but
the pain made me feel alive. I could not see his face beneath
the coif and heavy helmet, and he forgot them too, mouthing
words at me that I could not hear. His flag bearer, more
sensible, brought some of the wine, which he poured out in
a gush, most of it running freely on the floor where the boards
were already turned to red. At last, when he seemed convinced
that no real harm had come to me, although I turned aside for
shame and could not speak, he straightened himself. I heard
the quick rasp of boots and spurs as he took the floor in a
stride.

"Upon your life," he snarled at his guard who waited at the
doorway, where they had cleared away the huddle of bodies
that had been caught there. I heard him swing himself upon
his horse, heard it start and plunge foaming in the pitiless sun.

"A moi, Sedgemont," he shouted, his voice strangely harsh,
cut off short, as if breathless. A roar answered. I heard the
clash of swords again, the deadly rasp and slash of weapons.
And the worst cry of all: "No quarter."

I shall not speak of the carnage in the square. You are not the man for such a task, poet, nor am I. We see the blood and brains, but they are words on paper, not hot reality. I hope it is long before I see the dust turn red, churned underfoot, hear the thrust, the shriek, the cut-short cry for mercy. No quarter had Sir Gilbert's men, although they threw down their weapons and cried out for it. Lord Raoul was angry. His own men, bone-weary from battle and pursuit, were in no mood for restraint. This was what war is, this was what Giles had tried to describe: war, stark and cruel. Soon, too soon, the screaming stopped, and the silence was more dreadful after. When the guards led me forth, bore me forth, for I could not walk, the silence seemed to contain all those deaths that I must recall. Even Gilbert's, whose last gasp hung about the hate-drenched room. I turned my head aside to avoid their work. But they had been merciful in this, that by that time there was little to be seen, only a rear guard hastily smoothing over the churned ground, and a great pit where they tipped the bodies unceremoniously. Yet I caught a flutter of a long blue gown, until I averted my eyes again even from that. I would not have her death upon my conscience. They left Gilbert of Maneth's body where it had fallen, pulling down the frame of the house about him, fitting tomb, a place that he himself had pillaged and burned. Yet to die thus, unholy, unshriven, a knight with his sins gloating about him. Hard vengeance had my brother, Talisin of Cambray, that day. But do not look to write down all I think. Such thoughts do lie too deep, must be remembered with fasting and prayer.

Lord Raoul had brought up a horse for me to ride, but when he saw I could not mount, he bade them set me before him, crooked in the folds of his cloak that bore the weight from off my battered and bruised body. We rode slowly away. His rage had been white hot; it held him taut even now so that I could feel it under the hard case of his armor, as if nerves and sinews were bolted into place. Later, they told how he had ridden without sleep, fearing to reach us too late. Coldly and deliberately had he driven his men, then burst into white heat when he reached the village. Yet, had Gilbert of Maneth not lingered the afternoon away, tempted to exhibit his independence, Maneth castle would have shut its gates in Raoul's face.

We rode on slowly without speech through the rest of that golden afternoon. No one spoke. We were like horses who have so torn their hearts out in effort that to make one move more would destroy us. Around us, all was peaceful, a spring day when you hear sounds far off, when the air is still as a mountain lake, when even the sun seems loath to set. We were not yet safe, being overclose to Maneth, although it would be too soon for the castle watch to become alarmed when Gilbert and his men did not return. Fresh troops on our trail, fresh attacks, would have been hard to fight off. Yet the very presence of those tired, hungry men, even slumped in their saddles, they had a watchful look, made danger seem far off. It was still light when we came to the cutting in the hills where we could stop to feed the horses and rest ourselves.

I went away from the circle of men and beasts and pulled my way down through the rushes and briars to the stream's edge. Not caring if any watched, I stripped off the poor torn clothes and slid into the running water. It was a mountain-fed brook, cold and clear. My bruises stung like fire. With handfuls of sand did I scour my skin, as if all the running water in the world would not wash it clean again. And when I had done, I found a pile of female clothes that someone had left upon the bank, a cloak that, wrapped around, gave back warmth. I came up, walking as an old woman does when she is tired, yet beneath the tiredness I could feel already the life flowing into veins and heart. Lord Raoul was standing beside a boulder, too weary even to sit or to move to any comfortable place. His squires had unlaced his byrnie, drawn off his gloves, and placed sword and shield, still stained and battered, within reach. They had brought him water and trickles of it ran slowly down his hair about the linen shirt he wore beneath his mail. He was wiping his hands upon a rag, over and over, as if, like me, he hoped to wipe them clean. I saw how they still shook; so does the aftermath of battle take some men, often those of strongest heart and will.

I took the cloth from him.

"You are overreached, my lord," I said. "Rest. The evening will be long, the night mild. We are as safe here as anyplace."

At my words, he turned his head slowly, his eyes still dark, almost unfocused in their intent. Gradually I felt the tension slacken. He gave a great sigh and leaned his head back upon the stone. His men brought food, kneeling to serve him as if at some courtly feast until with a gesture half-impatient, half-amused, he waved them away. Later, they told me how he had swept through the square, an arm that rose and fell with but one purpose, a cry that ordered one thing only: vengeance. Now gradually he came back to his own self again. His men, squatting close about us, their swords laid ready beside them, talking quietly among themselves. We could hear the horses rustling through the undergrowth, the call of the outer guards; soft, farther off, the dash and rush of the stream. We could have been a thousand miles, a thousand years, away from death.

"My lord," I said at last. At the same instant, he turned to me and spoke; we were like two who try to pass in a narrow place. I smiled at that. He stretched out his hand and suddenly took mine.

"That is good," he said. "I thought never to see you smile again."

"And I, my lord," I said, "I thought you too were gone forever. These have been bad times. God willing, we shall put them behind us."

I thought I heard someone say, "Amen." Lord Raoul gestured to his squires to unfasten the wineskins they had strung about their saddles before leaving the village.

"It will not be such as we have at Sedgemont," he said, "but better stuff than we have known these past months. And what if we eat rough and forage like horses a few more days. Soon it will be time to go home."

They gave a cheer at that, drinking to it willingly, and bit into the tough scraps of food without complaint. Tired they were, weary of counting over their losses, tending their wounded, yet not downhearted. I sensed again even stronger the bond among them that let them all sit together in silence. So we stayed, some asleep, some watchful, while the moon rose. All the cruelty of that day seemed washed away at last. Later there would be time to explain, to grieve. That night I thought we lay like ones disoriented after a nightmare, waking to find all things beautiful and fair.

We were off again before dawn. Enchantment has its limits. I was still too stiff to walk or ride and my face was swollen and dark. Raoul was on edge, his voice harsh as he ordered the line of march. His men, who had fought two battles and ridden a hundred leagues or more within days, were foul-mouthed and bleary. Hunger did not improve their tempers. And we still had a long way to go before we could count ourselves free of pursuit. They had taken the horses at the village, but were loath to turn their own mounts loose for fear of their giving us away, and, if truth be told, not being willing to lose a chance at returning with two horses in the stead of one if they could. We rode more slowly than Raoul wished, burdened therefore with pack horses and lead animals, yet as the cavalcade wound its weary way through these deserted lands, we found the time, at last, to talk of all the things that must be said. In this way, sitting before him on his war horse, whose black body still seemed coiled to rage and energy, I could tell him how Guy of Maneth had boasted of the Celtic attack, how he had watched for my uncle's coming as the perfect chance to spring the trap, how he and his son had sent out their own men disguised among some Celtic scavengers whom they had wed to their service, and how they had waited for our return in the village where Raoul had found us. But of the part the red-haired woman had played, how her information about the camp had helped and how she had revealed my presence there, told Maneth where to find me, that I did not tell. It would have been an unfair charge that he must have borne.

Lord Raoul, in turn, did not speak of Giles, not then, although I learned their losses had been heavy, not only among the fighting men but also among those who had waited by the stream. Many of my former friends were gone, pages and younger boys I had known well, and the old Celtic woman and her daughters who had been cut down as they hid. As he had boasted, Maneth had planned carefully. Once I had been taken, the attackers had fallen back. Lord Raoul's men, infuriated by the unprovoked killing of the noncombatants, had taken this as proof, if proof was needed, that such cruelty, contrary to the rules of war, was the work of barbarians. Those of the attackers who were left behind they cut down without mercy. Lord Raoul's first thought then had been as Maneth had surmised, to send out a search party to follow hard upon the tribesmen over the boundary. But then, as tempers had cooled, signs appeared that all was not as it seemed. There were plenty of Celtic dead, it is true, no doubt of that, and some of the attackers had obviously returned to their mountain lairs, presumably paid in advance by Maneth. But a few bodies were found with Norman gear beneath their furs; a man cried out in Norman-French. One lived long enough to taunt them with stupidity. Raoul began to remember my uncle's words, that there were always renegades who could be coaxed across the border in return for loot. He recalled, too, what had been told him of Maneth before, that he got his men wherever he could find them. He did not have time to deliberate. If it were true what he then suspected, Maneth's forces would have already turned north, heading for the safety of their castle. He had divided his forces then, abandoning the camp altogether, sending one fast group across the border, the other under his command taking the most direct way to Maneth castle. At first, it seemed he had misjudged, there being such little evidence. But then they came upon the Celtic ponies that had been left behind. The villagers where we had made our first stop came creeping out, seeing who it was, to give what news they had, the double burden on one horse, the castoff Celtic dress, the signs they knew, only too well, of a war party from Maneth. Except the lords of Maneth this time did not lead it themselves.

In turn, I told him what I had learned of Maneth's plans, letting him piece together the scraps of news, for my brain ached at the thought. He reined up on hearing that Lord Guy had already left to join Henry of Anjou in France.

"Now, by God," he exclaimed when I repeated that Henry of Anjou intended to sail for France, "before God and Saint George, that is the best news yet."

"Best?" I repeated. I was still sitting before him, and he slid back upon the broad seat of his saddle to give me room to turn. "Best, when there he will be coiled, Maneth, coiled at your enemy's ear to win favor for himself against us. And when he hears news of his son's death?"

"He'll not get news of that awhile," Lord Raoul said more soberly. "We have buried that evidence well. And who is left to accuse us? A hundred of his enemies it could have been, even the Celts, who have as much cause to fear and dislike him. Lady Ann, you cannot know what monsters these lords have become, how many poor souls they have captured and robbed and tortured. Their license this past year runs beyond any man's reckoning. But we have witnesses who have escaped their torture racks to bring the proof. They lack not for enemies. It is only thanks to God they did not have you fast within the cursed place."

We were both silent for a while, thinking our own thoughts. Then he said, "But if Henry of Anjou has gone from England, if only briefly, well then, here comes the respite we all have been waiting for. If England is free of him, so are we. That is news worth all this hard ride."

"You mean to go back to Sedgemont?" I asked.

My face must have revealed my thoughts because suddenly he began to laugh. I had almost forgotten how attractive his laugh was, and his teasing voice, when he said next, "Why, Lady Ann, see how small a group we are. Look round about you. Here we are, the men of Sedgemont with dulled swords and week's beards. You can count us as you ride. My other vassals I have sent across the border, and if my messengers do not reach them first before the Celts attack them, they will be dead by now. If stopped in time, then they, too, will be heading home. No, no, I do but tease you. They are safe, thank God. But I have not the heart to lure them back upon a personal quarrel. Even you would see the fairness of that. And where should we go, our camp being overrun?"

"Yes," I said slow, "they have done enough. And so have you."

He laughed at me, showing his teeth white against the growth of beard. At the sound, his men seemed to sit firmer in their saddles; their horses even pricked their ears.

"By Jesu," he said aloud, "we are free then. But I did not say I would go home again, not yet."

I stared at him, not understanding.

"Why," he said again, with that flash, that lilt, that was part of his personality, "if Gilbert of Maneth was so sure to take Cambray, perhaps we can do for him that much honor to take it in his stead. What, shall we have our enemies call us fools and not give them the lie?"

There was a ripple among the men.

"Where is Dylan?" he said. "He knows Cambray better than any soldier here."

A man came pushing forward, Dylan it was indeed, to whom I had not spoken since that day in the stables at Sedgemont.

He grinned at me, a dirty cloth about his head, another, darker stained, about his forearm.

"My lady." He saluted me, his dark eyes impudent, although he did not smile.

I hid the memory of that last meeting when we three, he and I and Giles, had talked of Cambray. Now as I unwound the cloths about his wounds, he and Raoul spoke while the other men gathered round to listen. But first they made me repeat all that Gilbert had said, and his boasts that he could find a way within the castle without setting siege to it.

"Dylan," said Lord Raoul when I was through, "what think you of that?"

"We have all seen Cambray," Dylan said slowly, taking no more heed of what I was doing to his arm than if I had been a fly. "We are too few to hem it round and it is too strong to take by frontal attack. If someone would open the gates, as was done for the Celts..."

"Or by some secret, other way?"

Dylan considered. "It could be, my lord," he said at last. "Lord Falk of Cambray was clever. He had a long life living by his wits. In attack or defense, none was more skillful."

"I think that was what Maneth meant," I broke in, excited suddenly, despite the calm way they spoke. "It sticks in my memory how he seemed overjoyed as if at some secret. He boasted mindlessly, yet I think he had some knowledge that he believed in. Wrung from my father's old comrade, poor soul."

"My lord," Dylan said, grimacing at last as I pulled a rag tighter across the slash on his arm, "my lord, if I understand you right, what Gilbert of Maneth hinted at was that somehow Lord Falk had built an escape passage from Cambray. He would have thought of it as safeguard, the last route by which the defenders could flee if the castle was ever taken. I myself do not know of it, nor have I ever heard tell of it. But it is possible one of his longtime followers who came with him from France would know. In giving away that information, he would have told an enemy how to get inside the castle. Retrace the path and there you are. But that, too, I do not know. I was not there when the castle was built. And Lord Falk was close-mouthed, as you know, about his affairs."

"Cambray is made of stone," Raoul mused. "Although it is built to simple design, a square within a round, a keep within an encircling wall, it is made of stone. Few border castles are. They are mainly thrown up in haste of wood. But there are castles in Normandy, more elaborate 'tis true, which have many secrets built within their walls. If there was a passage, it must be from the keep. The keep would be the last place where they would make a stand. That, too, is made of stone."

Lord Raoul turned to me. "Lady Ann, do you know aught of this?"

I said slowly, afraid they would mock me, "Gilbert's words stuck in my mind the more they seemed to recall some memory, something that Talisin once said. But I cannot get it straight." And I thought again of how I used to dream in the camp of recapturing Cambray, how even then, elusive memories had clung to me, although never before had I put words to them.

"If anyone would have known, the young Lord Talisin would," Dylan said as slowly. "My lord, there may be something to it. It would be a family secret, perhaps entrusted also to one or two faithful retainers, but to no one else."

"How stands the castle, the keep? Refresh my memory."

Lord Raoul had turned again to Dylan. I watched them as they spoke, lord and soldier, yet man and man as well.

"Here, my lord." The two men swung off their horses, the others crowding round, although I noted how, without orders, several remained watchful on the outskirts.

Dylan squatted on the ground, drawing faint lines in the dirt with his dagger point. A circle for the outer crenellated walls, a space for the bailey, a square to indicate the keep, wavy lines to indicate the cliffs and sea.

"Here be the outer walls, my lord," Dylan explained, using his dagger as marker. "Of fitted stone, not dressed. Lord Falk, they say, took the stones from an old ruined fort nearby. I have not seen stones cut so before. The main gate here, facing east away from the shore. On the opposite side, the walls go down to the cliff face. The keep, thus. A guardroom beneath, a narrow circular stair up to the Hall, another narrow stair to the women's quarters in the solar above. I know not how they are arranged."

"Built on solid ground?"

"Nay," said Dylan almost proudly, "on rock, my lord. Rock that goes a hundred feet into the sea."

These last words too seemed to ring into my ear. "Raoul," I cried in excitement, not noticing that for the first time I had called him by his given name. "Raoul, listen."

They looked at me expectantly, those tired dirty men, their armor ripped and stained, hacked like beggars' cloaks at a fair. Yet there was a glint about them, you could feel it, almost touch it. I tried to put coherently what Dylan's words had conjured up, a sunlit day when as a small child I had played at some game with the women in the solar. The ball had rolled behind a tapestry. The tapestry was long and hung from the ceiling, covering a narrow gap between two walls that led to a window set up high at the end. Talisin had snatched the ball away from me and pushed me back from behind the tapestry, where I had crept to retrieve it.

Don't play there, he had said. *It leads a hundred feet into the sea.*

I said, concentrating, "In the solar, there is only one side that faces the sea. It is a large, squarish room with several narrow cells set into the thick walls for storage and sleeping space. On one side, I think, over the main gate to the east, there are three window openings. You can look out of them. On the opposite seawall there is but one window space, set up too high to look out, and a passage leading to it, never used, a short corridor if you will, cut into the thickness of the wall, hid by a curtain before it. And it seems to me you can hear the surging of the sea, as if the wall goes down to the sea itself. . . ."

"The western wall." Raoul and Dylan spoke as one. They turned back to the rough sketch in the earth. "On the seaward side."

Raoul pointed again to Dylan's marks, questioning this one, then that.

"And at sea level?"

I was leaning over the edge of the saddle, as intent as the rest.

"I can tell you that," I said. "Caves. There are caves—the cliffs are riddled with them."

"Tide-washed?"

"Some yes, completely. Others are large and I think above sea level, at least during the neap tides. You think a passage there, then?"

My question fell on deaf ears. They were intent about the drawings now, making new ones, measuring, arguing.

"We need time to find which one," Raoul said, "some clue. We might search a week. A portal, perhaps, set in the rock face. Or supplies stored at the exit, a boat..."

"I can tell you that, too," I said above their voices. "We keep, or always kept, a boat drawn up inside one of the caves. For fishing. Gwendyth and I used to go to it sometimes. We used to refill the water jugs from time to time. . . ." My voice trailed off as the impact of what I was saying dawned on me, too.

Lord Raoul leaned back upon his heels and smiled at me.

"Why, Lady Ann," he teased, "we've no need of thumbscrew and rack. You'd tell all you know as freely as the wind. I could have picked any brat at Cambray and asked him. They could all tell me what I need to know."

He sprang back into the saddle behind me, gathering reins and urging us forward. I could hear the other men talking among themselves as they followed us, one whistling as we went, another holding his reins between his teeth as he worked his sword back and forth in the scabbard. Still not sure what it meant, uncertain of hope, I suddenly let out one of Raoul's soldier oaths.

"What is it you are about then?" I asked, and heard that ripple of amusement run through his men again.

Raoul raised one eyebrow in protest. But all he said was, "Your father was wiser than I thought. The passage by which he planned his escape, if worst came to worst, may yet allow us entrance. We go to Cambray, Lady Ann. That is what we are about."

I had known he was going to say it, yet the words still took my breath away. I could almost smell, taste, feel, what I had so long hungered for. Then sense took over.

"Is it safe?" I asked. "Perhaps we should wait. . . ."

He let forth an oath more violent than my own, digging his spurs into his horse's sides until the animal almost reared up as if fresh from the stable, and I had to catch at him to avoid being tossed off.

"By the Mass, lady," he said, "we have been waiting enough these past months. It is not a virtue that sits easily with me. Or my men. I think it was not so long ago you chided me for it also. We have done with waiting."

There was an answering murmur from the others.

He slid forward again to speak into my ear. "You see they feel the same," he said. "It would be cruelty to deprive us now. They do not like being made to look foolish, either. And I have been but an indifferent keeper of you and your estates since you first came to Sedgemont. As you have long been telling me. I owe you this much."

"But, Raoul," I protested, speaking, because he was so close, into his hair. I could feel the warm breath on my face and the touch of his cheek as he answered me.

"But, Raoul, I have a hasty tongue, as you know. I would

not goad you and your men into further danger against your will."

He laughed softly, the sound trickling past. "I never thought to hear you say that much," he said. "All you have given us is the excuse to do what we wanted. Thanks to you for that."

He pulled the cloak up closer around my shoulders, taking advantage of the movement to put his hand beneath my chin, forcing my head to face his. I could feel the cold of his hand, the calluses upon the palm from rein and hilt, the long and surprisingly slender fingers, which traced the scars and bruises on my face.

"If for nothing else," he said, "for those. I owe you that, *ma mie*. It is already decided."

"So easily," I was about to say, for I knew my surprise showed. "Your men know what to do?"

He smiled again, and shook the rein to set us cantering. "It is not hard to decide," he said, "when hearts and minds are agreed. We know one another well by now, my men and I. I think we understand what is to be done. Doing is easier than explaining."

Behind him, the other horses also shook themselves into renewed vigor. The saddlebags slapped against the horses' sides. The flag bearer broke out the standard of Sedgemont, and the gold hawks floated behind us freely in the breeze.

His hands were tight around me now, warmer and steady under the cover of the cloak.

"Guy of Maneth will not look to harm my ward again," he said. "Had Gilbert forced you to his desire, I'd have had him gelded before he died. Since he did not succeed..."

"No, no, my lord," I protested, feeling the blushes start. "Indeed he did but try, to no avail."

"That, too, is good," he whispered in my ear again. "I had thought on saving that for myself...."

* * *

We came to Cambray four days later at dusk. That ride is one of the memories of my life. I rode with them as friend, as equal; title, sex, age put aside for the moment. As comrades we lived together. I saw what Raoul meant about his men: when hearts and minds are acting as one, all things are easy. He and his men had lived as one for a long while now. And when we reached Cambray, there was not even need to rehearse what they would do. They knew it like a second skin, where to go, when, who was to lead, how. We dismounted far back from the castle itself. I could see it dimly through the darkness, above the outcrop of trees and bushes that seemed to have crept up about it. Those bushes, which my father would have had uprooted as they grew, served us now as cover from any guards on the castle walls, although, as Giles had remarked before, there seemed no one on watch. The village was deserted and overgrown. And Cambray itself might have been abandoned, an empty pile of stone and crag, not large, but impenetrable, like a rock face. It was strange to stare at it from below as if I were a stranger here. For all that I had seen it so often in my thoughts, it could have been any place, any menacing place that stood brooding in the darkness. I felt a shiver of apprehension run through me. This was not the homecoming I had envisioned. But also, this was not the time to voice my fears aloud.

We had already divided into two groups: one, with their horses at hand, held ready as close to the castle wall as they could. When or if the others got inside, they would storm the main gates to help break them down. That would be their only chance of entrance. The other, smaller gates had already been so blocked up as to make attack there hopeless. And we could not attempt to scale the walls.

The rest of us picked our way on foot across the base of the cliff. The tide was out, a faint white line of foam and a faroff sound of waves. They fell like thunder, rolling closer, so that I was for hastening ahead, mindful of the way that we could be trapped against the rocks by the incoming tide. But Lord Raoul held me back. He had kept me with him this time, against his will, but, as he pointed out, almost as if arguing with himself, I knew the cave that they must find, and I alone knew the upper floor of the keep.

"And since no other place seems safe," he said, and I knew from his expression that he, too, was remembering Giles, "best be under my eyes where I can guard you myself." But he had given me the best protection he could, an old mail coat that had belonged to a page killed too young in some skirmish. It was too long and heavy for comfort, but at least I could move in it and it came low enough about the hips to give some protection from a glancing blow. Armed with Giles's little knife, I was as ready as Raoul could make me. But the rest of them had stripped down to leather coats and caps, their chain mail left behind with their horses. They wore soft leather boots, for fear that spurs and steel would make a sound upon the stone floors. In the darkness I fretted about that: I might be equipped, but they were not. And would I remember which cave? In the night, all looked alike. Perhaps they had changed over the years; did not the sea eat away at rocks as at sand? What if the cliff had fallen or the cave entrance been blocked, or the passage, if there was one, been covered by fallen stones? We would be trapped then, inside, like rats, unable to get back out of our hole, and in the morning light our enemies would hunt us down, catching us between the cliffs and the sea.

We passed two smaller entrances, black shadows against the grayness of the cliff. The one we wanted was the third, as I remembered. I used to sit outside sometimes while Gwendyth gathered seaweeds and shells for her potions and watch the sea otters that swam there in the spring. We splashed through the pools, now green and slippery with weed, the men cursing as they stumbled in the dark, no knightly task, this, to go a-wading in the wet and cold. The entrance was as I remembered it, narrow and black, like a slit, running

back into the steep cliffs between two high piles of rock.
You would have to go out on the open beach and crane
upward to see the castle wall above the cliff's edge there.
We waited inside the entrance until someone struck a flint
against the rock and all the wet and reeking walls flared for
an instant. I remembered then how the green weeds grew
halfway up the walls, a warning that this was no place to
be caught by the inrushing sea. We let the torchbearer move
ahead as we slid farther inside, going in single file, moving
slightly uphill until we came to the piles of broken logs and
sticks upon the shingle that marked the high-water line.
Beyond that, dry sand, still slanting uphill. If this was the
right cave, we would come now to the little skiff that sometimes, on fine days, we would drag down to the water's edge
and float off into the bay. The torch picked out its shape
sooner than I had expected, a light-frame boat more like a
coracle or round Celtic boat, still spread with the skins we
covered over it carefully after each use. Beyond it, the cave
curved to the right, out of sight. We stopped then in silence,
looking at the boat, the sound of the sea quite gone, only
the sputter of the resin and our own breathing to disturb us.
Lord Raoul pulled back the skins. They fell apart at his
touch, rotted through by ten years' exposure and damp, but
underneath, the wood had still kept its shape. The oars were
still in place, the canvas sail and the water jars set in the
prow of the boat. Seeing these things now with new intent,
I began to hope. We had used the little boat for our pleasure,
but why had it been kept there, and why else had we taken
such pains to have it sea-ready, except in case of need? We
skirted past it and began the next stage of the climb. I had
never gone beyond this part before and it had always frightened me as a child to come so far. Usually I had waited
outside for Gwendyth. Even by daylight this section of cave
would have been dark. Yet the air still smelled fresh, although
salty with the tang of the sea. The tunnel, I must call it
that, went on, slanting uphill, room for two men abreast,

the walls black about us. The last part was so steep we had
to scrabble for hand- as well as footholds among the boulders
that were thickly strewn. I could not tell if they were new
fallen or had always been there; at least they were dry. I
held back then, blocking the men who came behind me as
I stood uncertainly. Raoul, who had clambered ahead, turned
round. There seemed no end to the tunnel; the roof was
lower now in the last few yards, the footing underneath
changed to rock. We soon might be forced to crawl on hands
and knees into the darkness.

"I am not sure, my lord," I said, biting at my nether lip. "I
do not know where we are."

Raoul put his finger to his own lips, so that we all stood
still. Above us, or perhaps somewhere to our right, there was
a new sound. It struck eerily when we heard it, and at first,
none was willing to accept it for what it was: the sound of
men laughing. We listened to that half-caught noise as if it
were something we had never heard before. It was awesome
to hear men's laughter while we worked toward them like moles
underground.

"Yes, you do," Raoul whispered at last, when we had stood
for a long time listening, "we have not missed the way." He
extinguished the torch; we moved on slowly, fearful of making
a sound to betray our presence.

A hundred feet of rock, Dylan had said.

Well, so it was before we came to the narrow steps, hewn
out of the rock itself at first, then of rough-cut stone spiraling
upward. The noise and laughter, sounds of men drinking and
moving, were beneath us now. We had come to a level place
within the thickness of the stairwell with a narrow window slit
set in the wall, a high opening from which no one could see
out, but from which, at this vantage point, one could look in.
Then four or five more steps down, and a stone slab set at the
passage end beneath the window...

Raoul moved back to give me chance to look through the
window slit. There was no covering tapestry now, only the

little passage that led into the main room. As far as I could tell, it was empty, used as storage place, for it was littered with odd bundles and chests. But where would the Celts have found women, or why should they have used it for its original purpose? I could not see clearly, for it was still dark, but I could at least point out to them the corner where the staircase led to the Hall below, tell them the twists they must make and how they must cross the Hall itself to gain the next stair to the lower courtyard.

Lord Falk was clever.

My father had built a keep that the defenders could hold inch by inch, withdrawing finally to this upper room, this passage, for the last stand of all. But all his safeguards for escape made difficulties for invaders to break in. We had no idea how many were the enemy. They might feel secure enough to keep scant watch upon the walls, but they would not be so foolhardy as to go unarmed in their own guardroom. The staircases were narrow, room enough for one man to hold. That meant our men must go down one by one. If they could not break through to the second staircase in sufficient numbers, they could not hope to reach the gates in the courtyard beneath. But they knew all this, had already planned what they would do. Night after night on our ride here had they talked and planned. Beside me now, Raoul smiled and eased his sword from its sheath. I could feel confidence flowing from them as they stood.

Dylan winked at me as he passed. "No women," I heard him breathe, "a lost chance." And he slid after Raoul down the last four steps.

The men put their backs against the stone. At first it did not move; then, with a groan, it fell back. At Raoul's nod, they crept through the gap like shadows, moving swiftly out of the short passage and into the main room. I was to wait behind in the stairwell. I had agreed to that, knowing there was no time for argument. Each must serve his special place, and this time I must take my chances with the rest, since there was no one to spare for escort. But was not this what I had always wanted, to lead my men into Cambray myself? I watched as the shadows drifted noiselessly to the Hall stairway, and took their places, one behind the other, Raoul first.

"Oh God," I prayed, "that it be not a trap to catch them."

Were they still there, or were they already tiptoeing down the steps, swords held loosely, daggers in their other hands, crouched to increase impetus. The empty room above had given them all the confidence they needed. It was one less place to fight for; surprise, and surprise alone, would help them take the rest. But I prayed in that endless wait, almost mindlessly. When the first shock of the attack rang out, it was like a beacon flare against the night sky. I could not bear to stay where I was, but slid down into the empty room, stumbling and tripping to the narrow staircase. I could hear the sounds now, that mixture you must pray never to hear, the strike of weapon against weapon, the duller thud of a butcher blow, the shouts, cut short, of men taken unawares, Raoul's voice singing out his battle cry. It was the struggle in the village square again. I turned to the other openings that overlooked the main courtyard, registering surprise even then that I could see through them without having to drag a stool into place. The yard had already sprung to life, torches flared, and more lights came to make it bright as day. I could see the thin line of black figures racing for the ropes and bars that held the gates. Run and turn, hack and parry. There was a great cry as someone swarmed upon the battlement above and began to slash at the ropes. The gate fell outward with a crash that shook. Then there was a familiar drumming as mounted men appeared at the gates, horses stamping and snorting, men shouting to their friends, pouring into the stone courtyard, the hooves sending sparks. I knew how few they were, but in that confined space they seemed an army. The air was lighter now, blue gray instead of black. Men ran and slashed with less purpose. Already groups of them had huddled in a circle against the wall, their weapons dropped at their feet. The shouts and screaming dragged into silence and I heard Raoul's voice cry hold.

I was still clinging to the window frame, still listening to those last dreadful cries, when they came to fetch me, two of my comrades, handing me down the stairs into the Great Hall with such courtesy as if I had never put foot outside a ladies' solar before. How had they gone so quietly down these treacherous steps? I had forgotten how steep and narrow they were. My first thought when I saw the Great Hall of Cambray again was how small it seemed; my second, that it had been used as a stable or barn, it was so begrimed and foul. My third, which should have been first, how quickly the work had been finished. Most of the bodies had already been dragged aside. A man lay moaning under an upturned table; a few others, all Sedgemont men, nursed their wounds dazedly. Raoul himself seemed unhurt. He stood upon the dais where my father's chair used to be and beside him, grinning openly, stood Dylan. Even as I watched, a group of half-dressed, unarmed men came stumbling into the room, driven up the stairs by the Sedgemont men from the courtyard beneath. Lord Raoul turned to greet me. Well, we looked as rough and filthy as those other poor souls, our clothes stained and torn, our faces as white and tired. There was another scurry, a stamp of feet upon the stairs, another scarecrow group tumbling into light, lurching and gawking. I hardly knew what to make of them at first. Their faces were puffed and gray, overgrown with hair like that of an animal let out from some den, until they came close and hailed Dylan. Then suddenly their features came into focus: the men I remembered, or half-remembered, although they all then remembered me, this remnant of my father's guard who had been left at Cambray and lost it. They came crowding round, tears staining their wasted cheeks, dropping to their knees upon the flea-ridden rushes to call my name. It should

have done my heart good to hear "Cambray" again, yet I felt
no triumph, no pleasure, as I moved among these men, urging
them to their feet, letting them touch me like men half-blind.
I have seen prisoners since who looked worse than they did,
but none who regained their freedom with such relief, shut
away this long, still bitter at the trick that had robbed them
of liberty and dignity at the same time. I turned from them at
last to find Lord Raoul still watching me. Was not this what
I had always told him, "Bring me home, and my people will
know me." How now would he deal with them, with us?

"Well, Ann of Cambray," he said, his voice neutral, "how
will you bid us welcome?"

Despite myself, I knew I showed dismay. I knew what was
due, of course: there should have been servants to bear him
wine, spiced and hot, and fresh water for washing, clean linen
for him and his men, food on tables, serfs to take his horse
and gear, fires to burn, the plate upon the sideboards burnished.

He laughed at my expression. "Well," he said, "as you stand
amazed, we'll fend for ourselves."

"There may be stores, my lord," I said, collecting my wits,
recalling what I had learned from the Lady Mildred at Sedgemont, although her hospitality was often pinched and miserly.
"And wine, there should be wine from my father's day."

"If they've not drunk it all." He gestured to the Celtic prisoners, crouching now against the wall.

"What shall we do with them, my lord?" It was Dylan,
indicating them with his thumb. "Chuck them over the cliff?"

There was a cry of agreement at that, from Cambray men
loudest of all. I looked at them, then back at Lord Raoul, then
back to the Celts again. Their leader had been killed at the
first assault. His horn goblet still rolled underfoot where people
walked. A son who might have succeeded him barely lived.
The others were a poor and rabid lot, "scum," as my uncle had
called them, making their little bid for power, caught off guard

in their flush of success. Yet we had heard them laughing as
we had climbed up through the castle walls.

"They'd show no mercy to you," one Cambray man called
out, "as they showed none to us. Death, they deserve." Hate
made his eyes bright, yet it was his stupidity that had let these
men in so long ago. They, themselves, seemed to shrink back
against the wall, squatting like whipped curs. No cry for mercy,
not even a flicker of hope came from them.

"My lord," I said to Raoul before he could speak. "Can we
not use them? We need men to restore the damage, till the
fields, harvest. Guarded, could not they work for us?"

There was a murmur in the Hall at my words. I thought
someone called, "Death," again.

"No," I said suddenly. "No. Let there be an end. We have
had enough of death and killing."

"You make first claim to your victor's spoils," Raoul said.

"I make no such claim," I said, blushing. "The victory is
yours. I shall plead but woman's weakness, that there has been
enough killing. I want no more deaths on my conscience."

"Here is a new idea," he said. "I thought Cambray worth a
Mass or two."

"Not for the souls of my friends," I cried out, all the pent-
up sadness and anxiety bursting forth. "Not for all that has
been seen and done. Not for Giles's death."

"Nor did I ever think to hear you say that," he said, suddenly
sober. "Why, lady, this newfound delicacy does you honor.
Take these men to your liking. Certainly they are more use
alive than dead."

"Well, then," I said hesitatingly, for I was not used to giving
such orders. "Let them first help with the wounded, then clean
what they have befouled."

"To your charge then." He picked up the sword that lay
unsheathed before him.

I heard him echo my command to separate the wounded
from the whole, to bind the prisoners that they could work,

to make space for the horses, clean out the debris from the stables, and bring fodder, for the Celts had kept no mounts of their own. He, with others of his guard, would ride forth from Cambray to view the surrounding countryside, rout out the villagers if any remained in hiding nearby, and hunt again for food. I was left in the Great Hall with a few men to attend me and the wounded to care for.

Those I could help I did, cleansing and binding as best I could, for there were no herbs, no drugs; the Celts had taken everything like maggots that pick bones clean. I cared for their wounded last of all. They lay, for the most part, as if impervious to pain, even the young son who was most grievous hurt. When all of them had settled into the small antechambers that lay within the thick walls of the hall, it was broad daylight. Lord Raoul and his patrols had already ridden out, the gates had been shut tight upon them, and guards had been set on the walls. When the Sedgemont men had made their inspection and caught food enough, they would return. Now was there time for me to set things to rights to greet them.

But there was one thing first that must be done. The little niche we call a chapel has been much enlarged since then. I doubt if you would have known it for what it was, since this passion for church building has sent us all into a flurry of flaring beams and elaborate traceries and rich-covered altar. But you would recognize, as I did not, the three simple slabs that lie in the old part, three stone slabs set into a stone floor. As I did not, I say. When I had been there last, there was but one, with my mother's Celtic name engraved upon it, nothing more, as if that said all. When I had been there last, my father sat where now I stood, his sword drawn across his knees and his eyes blank and unseeing. Talisin lay wrapped in his cloak, his own sword stretched above it. And I had crept in unwillingly, to tug at my father's arms and bid him speak to me. I, who had, by living, destroyed what he loved most; who, in begging, reminded him of what he next had lost. I knelt now on the floor and smoothed the stones, delicately at first, then more passionately, to clear away the dirt and leaves that covered them, until I could see for myself the names and titles engraved on the two newer ones. How could they be as gray, look as worn, as that first one? How could ten years have aged them all the same? I knelt and smoothed the stones as if I could smooth away the years, as if time had never been, as if in a moment I would hear them striding up the stairway from the lower court, taking the steps as they used at a bound, their hounds leaping before them, their voices making the servants run to do their will. Talisin of Cambray, Falk of Cambray, your castle is free again, your deaths avenged. Where are you gone that you share not in the triumph? Where are your spirits flown that I cannot find you? I knelt and smoothed the stones, touching the names again and again until, for weariness, I fell asleep on my knees.

When I awoke, stiff and numb, the light had already faded. For a moment, forgetting where I was, I thought myself a child.

Then time came running back and I remembered. There was no noise, only the murmur of the wounded men, the soft shuffle of the prisoners about their tasks, the clank of the guard outside. Soon, then, the patrols would return. I had thought to have all ready on their return. That thought jarred me out of melancholy. Yet I tell you, poet, those whom we have loved live on in our prayers and thoughts. The love that I, an unwanted child, poured out upon those dead gray stones will keep them timeless... and in the quietness that surrounds us now, I have but to close my eyes and those who lie there come toward me, alive and whole.

When I went back to the Hall, I was startled to see how fast the day had gone. While I had slept, the work of Cambray had progressed. Dylan was sitting on the dais steps, overseeing things there. He looked tired and the wound in his arm had bled again. I retied the bandages while he grumbled at the disrepair he found on all sides: stables like a midden piled high with refuse, storerooms stripped bare and used as prisons, not fit for entering in, his old comrades reduced to shakes and agues by entombment there.

"Cheer yourself, old friend," I said. "You have done well as it is."

For he had found somewhere the great carved table and chair to set there in place, although the rest of the hall was bare, as if the Celts had burned all the other furnishings or hacked them up for pleasure.

He shook his head. "They are but wild beasts," he said, eyeing the prisoners who, with chains about their legs, came shuffling to and fro, sweeping the debris out of the Hall and bringing fresh logs to light the fires. "They have no care of those things a man should need." Yet he was partly Celt and so was I.

"Patience," I said. "We shall teach them our ways in time."

Giving orders that water should be readied, I went up the stairs to the women's quarters. Here, too, the rubbish had been swept away, and the great frame of the bed dragged clear, although, in truth, no one had ever slept there to my knowledge. Gwendyth had used it for a storage space, setting our own small trestle beds beneath. My mother's loom had also been put together, although the work it had always held had vanished, and two small wooden chests, which I had previously noticed, had been put in place against the wall. The stone door that led to the rock tunnel had been closed and a great beam set across it to prevent its being reopened from without. And there was an equally strong beam placed across the new-hung door that blocked the stairway to the Hall. I rummaged in the chests, which seemed filled with loot of various sorts, and came upon clean linen and shirts that I thought might do for Lord Raoul and his men. At the bottom, stuck under rags and shards, was a folded dress that looked familiar, and when I shook it out, the dried herbs and flowers fell to the ground, giving off their faint fragrance that I remembered. This gown had been my mother's. Cut in the old style, threaded with ribbons that had lost their luster, it fitted me and was not too moth-ravished to wear.

By then two pages had come sweating and grumbling up the narrow stairs with a bucket of water. I closed the new door and bathed, drying myself afterward with some shreds of linen. On impulse, I took my father's ring from the little bag where I had carried it since that evening in the convent fields, and although it was too big, I slipped it on my finger. I had to grasp my hand tight so it would not slide off. Yet my mother's dress, saved all these years in some place that perhaps Gwendyth alone had known, fitted as if made for me. Made ready then as best I could, I sat upon the edge of the great bed and waited until I heard the sounds of arrival, cheerful sounds of men and horses and hounds, sounds that must have been sadly lacking here these past years. Then I rose and went down the stairs.

Except for lack of furnishings, even of the most rudimentary kind, the Hall looked more as I remembered it. A fire was burning in the central hearth. Pages were running with flagons of wine—those, at least, Dylan had rescued—the wine being, I suppose, too sharp for Celtic taste. I could smell the meat roasting on the spits. Lord Raoul had his back to me, but I could tell from the expression of the man he was speaking to that he was warned of my approach. I stopped one of the pages and took a goblet from him.

In my father's time there were heavy cups of pewter and a great one of silver that he had won at a tourney in his youth and kept all these years as security for his old age. He had redeemed it from France when he came here, and used it with pride for all honored guests. He would have served his overlord with it himself.

I picked a flagon from the table, pouring the wine with hands that trembled for all my care, and offered it to Lord

Raoul. He was dressed as I had seen him earlier in the day, but there was no disgrace in that. I could see the faint marks where his mail coat had chafed at neck and wrist. At least, he had ridden out fully armed and had returned, as was proper, to his own keep.

It swept over me like a wave how much I owed to him that we were here. Slowly, almost without thought, I found myself on my knees before him, on my outstretched hand my father's ring.

"My lord of Sedgemont," I said, loud enough for all to hear, his men, my own, the Celts in the rear. "I, Ann of Cambray, do now, in turn, recognize you as liege lord, having over us at Cambray command of title and lands within your gift as in my father's time. I acknowledge your help in restoring what had been lost. I acknowledge your wardship over me, as is fitting. In return for these favors, I do you homage, swearing to keep faith and loyalty to you as your loyal vassal, commending myself and those who serve me to your protection and defense."

There was silence at first, followed by a murmur, I think, of agreement.

Lord Raoul took the ring I offered him and turned it slowly about. When he spoke, it was as formally as I had done, but better phrased, no doubt, I having but the feelings of my own heart to guide me.

"I, Raoul, liege lord of the lands and honor of Cambray, Lord of Sedgemont, Count of Sieux, of Auterre"—how long the list of titles and names, of places he no longer controlled, yet still in truth were his—"I, Raoul, acknowledge Ann of Cambray as sole heir of her father, loyal and loving vassal to me, holding this keep and lands for me in return for watch and ward upon the marcher lands beyond. For which service, as her father, Falk of Cambray, rendered unto me, to her I give Cambray in equal friendship and trust."

There was a ragged cheer at that, from my own men loudest of all.

He put the ring upon his finger then—how strange to see it worn again—and helped me to my feet. And as he had done once before, he kissed me full upon the lips, the kiss of peace.

"Now, Ann of Cambray," he said, and smiled at me, "is your liege lord made welcome to Cambray."

10

WE DINED WELL THAT NIGHT, ALL OF us seated about the fire as if still on the march. The cooks brought steaming platters—the huntsmen reported that the woods about teemed with game as all the borderlands are reputed to—and each new course roused a cheer. We ate and drank and talked of past adventures, old friends. And when it was grown late and the men were settled to their drinking, he took me by the hand and led me up the narrow stair to the upper chamber.

Since I had been there earlier in the evening, someone had come to make improvements, I suppose you would call them, although they were simple enough: a covering strung across the little passage to hide the stone doorway; a fire lit, although I had never known the fireplace used before, and it had smoked mightily; the bed, which, too, I have said was never used, spread with fresh cloaks and furs for comfort. The page who walked before us to light the way threw more logs upon the fire so that it sputtered and flared. But even as I took note of all these things, the page was bringing Lord Raoul his wine, his cloak, handing him, unsheathed, his sword to set in its place beside the bed. The door closed softly behind and we were left alone.

I said, half-foolish, half-worried, "My father slept below with my brother and his men."

"Indeed. And where slept you?"

I told him of the trestle bed, of Gwendyth, stumbling over explanation, as if it were of interest to him. But once my parents must have lived and loved here. That, too, I had never thought on before.

I eyed him warily. "And you, my lord?"

"Why, here," he said, as if it were the most natural thing. I knew his calm would anger me eventually. I strove for my own.

"Your men lodge below."

"I should hope so," he said. I knew he mocked me, although his voice was even, and he went about the preparations for the night, setting his belt in its place, his cloak, sitting on a stool before the fire to unstrap his boots.

"But then," he added when I did not rise to his bait, "we have lived in each other's pockets long enough. I weary of them as bedfellows."

He cocked his eyebrow at me. "You seem nervous, Lady Ann. Look how safe we are. If you peer out of yonder windows, you will see the watch is already set. And I have put guards on the strand so no one can pass that way again." He drew aside the hanging to show me the thick beam of wood that barred the stone door as I had noticed earlier in the day.

"And another here." He thrust home the one across the stairway. "And all my men to fight through in the Hall below. No one can get in."

"Nor yet get out," I said sourly.

"Who wishes to?" He was openly smiling now.

"I," I said, "or rather you."

"I shall be comfortable here."

I began again, "My lord Raoul, your men and mine are not so drunk or confused with sleep they will not notice what you do. . . ."

He said slowly, wrestling with a buckle, "They drink because they deserve it. They sleep because they are weary. They think highly of you. They take you as fellow comrade, have you not seen it? It is a compliment they pay you. Why should they care what we do?"

He was standing by the fire, drinking the wine, my father's wine, my father's gold ring gleaming on his hand.

I said, not angry yet, reasonably, "Say rather, it is that they care not what *you* do. You are all men together. No doubt, they think it a compliment you show me. But I will not play a whore to please you."

He said, "The choice of words, as usual, is yours, not mine."

My control snapped. I screamed at him, loud enough for all to hear, as no doubt they did, for afterward the very walls seemed to hold their breath, "I will not be another woman for your desire. I am no Celtic harlot for you to use as chattel."

He said softly, "What has made you think I value women so low?"

I could have told him then what I had heard of him: Two-Handed Raoul, who charmed women to his beck and call. I could have told him what I had guessed from the first, when, unknowing, he had put that charm on me. I could have accused him then of his Celtic mistress who had betrayed him and me for love, and died for it. But I did not.

He said, "If indeed, as you have cause, you have come to hate all men, I would not fault you. You have had scant luck of them."

He smiled at me. I felt my defenses weaken when he smiled like that; a wide generous mouth he had, meant for smiling.

"When you were still young," he said, "you offered me strange things. But I think then I was innocent as well. I still believed the world could be saved by high thoughts, high deeds. We have both seen ugliness and cruelty since then. Where is honor or law now? I did wrong, I think, to refuse you."

"I offered marriage," I said.

"I remember all you offered," he said. "Marriage for Cambray, I think you told me." He made a gesture. "Here is Cambray. What will you give me for it?"

"Nothing."

"That is ungenerous," he teased.

I said, shouting at him again, "You laughed at me once. Why should I give you anything? It has not stopped you sleeping with half the world when I was not at hand. . . ."

"But I have never forgotten you," he said softly. "I have not forgotten what you said. I have waited until now to claim it."

"But it is sin," I said.

"And where is church," he said, "or monk, or priest to tell us what be sin, or shrive us of it if we do wrong? I have come to believe something else, Lady Ann, while the world is tumbling about us. Out of all reason have we been given some respite, a breathing space here. We should use it to good purpose while we may; it would be sin indeed to turn our backs on it."

"It is not marriage," I whispered.

I had put out my hand to fend him off, but he took it instead in both of his. I could feel the strength of them although he held me lightly. His nearness, his arguments, flustered me. He spoke to charm my thoughts away from sense. I slipped my hand free and backed again, ending up against the frame of the great bed that blocked the center wall. While he did not touch me, I could resist his arguments.

"What is marriage," he said, "but legal oath, church oath, to bind two people, perhaps against their will, that their offspring should inherit what lands and names and wealth they combine together. . . . I cannot marry you, my little Ann. But I thought after all this, we did not need the sanctity of the Church to tell us what we should mean each to each."

"My lord," I said, "you woo with sweetened words. It is true I owe you much."

"I unsay that," he said. "I will not put such discourtesy before you."

"It is true," I continued, "that you are a great lord, far above me, your vassal. You might woo and wed any woman in the land. But I am not so low, my lord . . ."

"Speak my name," he interrupted me again. "You were freer with it before. And high, low, what meaning have these words for us here? Who counts among the highest of Sedgemont men? He who leads the way? He who falls at the first charge? He who opens the gate to let his comrades through? Far are we from the great world, and I, for one, am grateful for it at last. I have longed too much for those courts of kings and princes. Here is neither high nor low; we are comrades all, not made for passing judgment on each other. Here is there neither high nor low, nor bargaining for power and prestige. We are all simple creatures of God here, left to the justice of our own desires."

I knew he lied; he twisted words to his own ends, but the lies were sweet.

"Desire," I cried. "It is all you men think of."

His smile grew wider. "Perhaps," he said, "when all else is lost, it is the only thing worth thinking on. Perhaps it goes before us even without our knowledge."

His voice grew quiet. "Perhaps love and loving are all that will be left us in the end."

I should have been on guard. He was most dangerous when he was quiet, and his spring toward me took me by surprise. I turned to flee across the bed. There was a creaking as he thrust his weight upon it, a resounding crash. The old slats and withies that had bound the frame gave way beneath the covers newly spread upon them. We fell together in a tangle of broken lathes and slivered wood.

When he could catch breath, "Judas," he shouted, "where have you trapped us now?"

He struggled to his knees, caught fast by one arm where his greater weight had borne him to the floor. With his free arm, he tried to haul me up, smashing through the broken edges with his fist. I came up slowly, feet first, bundled in the clothes that I had caught up to protect myself.

He swore again. "Strapped down like..." He struggled for the words.

"Like a rutting boar, my lord," I said demurely when I, too, could speak.

He turned to shout again at me, although we were separated by inches, his hair on end, great red marks scored across his arms and forehead. We faced each other across a network of shattered wood that shifted ominously as we moved.

"God's wounds," he said through gritted teeth. "When I get loose of this..."

He struggled with the slats but could not shift them.

"Easier said than done," I said as demurely as before. "And as you have just been pointing out, who is to get inside the room to free us?".

He opened his mouth to speak, but I reached up my hand and stopped him.

"If you swear by God's wounds again," I said, "I shall scream. Think up some other oath. My cuts are smarting as it is. I was as weary as you, fellow comrade. These are my wounds that bleed."

We eyed each other, almost face to face, scowling, until the tears of laughter eased their way down our cheeks. We laughed until our sore ribs ached of it and the whole bed shook.

"By the Mass," he said at last, "if that oath pleases you better, what should we do?"

"If you can stretch out your left hand," I said, "I can try to push your sword within your grasp."

"Take care," he said. "You are so handy with weapons these days, you may take my head off instead of yours."

I paid him no heed, strained to reach the sword hilt, and finally pushed it where he could take it up himself. He began to saw at the jagged ends, no easy task, for the blade had not been honed for such homely work, and if it slipped it might indeed take arm or leg. Two-Handed Raoul—the skill that gave him that name came in useful that night. But at last he had made room to break his shoulders free. Then, with foot and knee, he could widen the gap to let us both pass through. But we were weak with mirth by then, so spent with laughter that he had to pick me up and sling me forth across his shoulder, still bundled up in furs and wraps. He dropped me unceremoniously upon the hearth, both still festooned with shreds of linen, the mass of scratches dried by now, except one long one across his forearm that still ran red.

"Well, lady," he said, "who would have her lover pull down dragons from the sky to show his devotion, see what a rescue I have performed. Have not I done greater work than handing you your enemy's head on a platter?"

"You have already given me that," I said.

"Forgive me, love," he said, contrite. His arms were about me to unwind sheet and coverlet until there was nothing between us save the fabric of my gown, and that, too, he was stripping off, "forgive me, that I should have you remember that. Had Gilbert done you harm that day, then had the world lost half its light. Then would there be but little left for us to hope for in this desolation. See how the gods have smiled upon us even in this. Little Ann, look not so frightened. Not for all the kingdom would I have you frightened. Since first I saw you, defiant and alone in my Hall, I have longed to comfort you."

His hand was on my back, gentling along the skin. Beneath the cloth, his fingers stroked like fire.

"Shall not we please each other at last," he said. "Have not we earned that right?

"Now shall you know what desire is, *ma mie*," he whispered at my throat, breast, and his hand was lower, cupped upon the center cleft of desire. Beneath him there, I felt myself run molten, dissolve the more that in him, hope and delight hardened into resolve. And I felt my body spread and open wide to let him in.

Thus did Raoul of Sedgemont have knowledge of me that night; thus did I pleasure with him first at Cambray.

Afterward he held me. I had not known the lack of tenderness until tenderness came about me then. I had not known

delight until he showed it me. Wordless, he lay with me and
held me, and at last I knew I was safely home. . . .

Thus came we to time of respite at Cambray. I do not mean
we lazed the days away. We all had to work hard, masters
and men, if we were to survive. Even the wounded, when they
could, were set to labor, to repair the damage and make all
secure for the winter ahead. But it seemed so easy to me then,
not work, to restore fields left untilled, clear thickets and brush
that encroached upon the castle walls, to unblock the ditches
and dykes that drained the fertile land. . . .

All this by day. And by night, when we went up the stair
and barred the door, it was as he had promised, more and
more of pleasure, more of joy. Sometimes, looking at him
there, I felt a surge of happiness that I cannot pretend now to
explain. I had seen men's bodies before; I knew no sheltered
childhood. But his shone golden like those golden days that
surrounded us. Its sleek strength fascinated me. I felt sometimes
that if I could bury within it, I would be safe, that if we barred
the door long enough, the rest of the world would go away.
Even in my old age do I unwind the memory of those days; I
shall die happy in them. Sin it was, and yet no sin. And I have
already told you, God in his own time will requite it. Once,
years ago, I had mistaken Raoul for what I had then loved
most in the world. Now was it given back to me, as if it had
never been stolen away.

We all worked hard, although the work was strange to men
trained to fight. Even the Celtic prisoners became good at
husbandry, although in general they are less skilled than most,
being breeders of cattle, not farmers, in their high hills.

Toward the end of the first month, a group rode in from
Sedgemont, among them Geoffrey of the yellow hair and silver
tongue, all smiles, full of himself and his news. After the attack
upon the camp, he had been one of the squires to ride across
the border. Fortunately, as it now appeared, my uncle and his
men had vanished, swallowed up by mist or bogs; and having

escaped a similar fate themselves, Geoffrey's party had turned back toward Sedgemont as bidden by Raoul's messenger when he caught up with them. Whether the Celts would, in their turn, consider this invasion of their territory a hostile threat could not be judged, but despite the hardships he had suffered there, Geoffrey remained fascinated by all that he had seen. Contrary to what one might have thought, his experiences seemed to have roused his curiosity. He, more than anyone else at Cambray, interested himself in the Celtic prisoners, talked to them in a strange mixture of languages, which he regarded with pride as fluency, and made friends with the young son who survived despite his wounds.

From Geoffrey we learned the news also from Sedgemont, that all there were well, although they lacked Raoul's presence, awaited his return. Twice had the castle been attacked, more by bands of disorganized mercenaries than regular troops, and twice had the attackers gone away without hurt to the castle and its folk. It was pleasant to have Geoffrey in our midst again. His good humor was undiminished, and, unlike some of the younger men, he was not above grubbing in the soil when he had to.

"But then," I heard him say one day when the grumbling had been especially loud, "a landless man cannot be proud. The first Norman French who came here were not all great lords. They had to sweat for the land that they took from the Saxons."

But, in truth, the grumbling was mostly in jest. Without food, we all would starve. A castle, even one built of stone, well manned, is only as safe as it is well supplied. The Lady Mildred should have been proud of me that I hoarded our small resources and replenished them as best I could. While the new crops ripened—and we were lucky, too, with the planting: cool, damp weather for the sowing, then days of brilliant sun to swell the grain—Dylan and I set the men to gathering berries and plants, having the Celts show us which to pluck, they being used to such foods and healthier for them, seldom being prone to diseases we castle folk fall prey to: bleeding of the gums and loss of teeth and hair the most common. And when the shoals of fish came running into the bay, we persuaded men who had never seen the sea before to go up to their necks in water with long string nets to pull the catch ashore. Smoked and dried fish makes good winter eating, although the Sedgemont men would have turned their noses up, salt fish being considered siege rations at best. Our greatest need was wooden barrels and bins to hold these stores, the Celts having burned or used for vile purpose all that had been here at Cambray, but even in this we found men willing to turn their hand to such work. . . . And on a day when I was free to ride with them abroad, we came up to the high moors behind the castle and saw the gray horses of Cambray, just as Giles had described them, running wild in their own valley.

"They seem too beautiful to tame," I said watching them. How often as a child had I seen my father stand in his meadow down below and count them over as a miser does his gold. Some of them had been so well trained that they would come at his call, and Talisin could make his stallions stop or run or swerve as he willed from far off.

"I wish Giles were here," I said, almost without thinking, for it was still difficult to speak of him or reconcile his death.

"Aye," Raoul said, leaning forward in the saddle, narrowing his eyes against the sun. "He said as much, wishing for you when we caught glimpse of them last spring. I'll bid the men come here and take several, to fill the stables again. They have run free too long, like other things at Cambray."

And he smiled at me, that lazy smile that made my heart leap.

For it was not I who wished for freedom. One memory will I unfold for you. Remember it, poet. True misery only shows itself in contrast with joy. Such as we found there needs must be followed by worse. It was late summer now. One of Raoul's men had found and tamed a hawk, perhaps strayed from some noble household, for it soon was retrained and answered to the lure. We went hunting one day, Raoul on one of the new-caught gray horses, I on another. This was not a hunting party from Sedgemont; gone were the beaters, the baying hounds, the huntsmen to steer the game in proper style, and Raoul and I soon outdistanced all the others who rode with us. Raoul let the hawk fly and we watched it soar and wheel, a speck against the sky, until we set our spurs and traced it as best we could. It came to rest high in the branches of an old dead tree that stuck up white and gnarled out of a tangle of gorse. I lay upon the soft grass, content with sun and wind, while Raoul fought his way in to get at her. There was no one nearby. The sky was as a bowl above, pale blue, infinite. You could hear the rustle of the dry gorse, the heather, smell the honey in the flowers. At last Raoul came back, clothes torn, face bleeding from the thorns, cursing.

"I cannot get in close," he swore. "Judas, but such briars make for better walls than stones."

"Then you must wait," I said, eyes closed against the sun, "until the others find you and help you break the thickets down."

I heard him move and opened my eyes slowly. What I saw made me sit up, for he had already removed his jerkin and was struggling with shirt and boots.

"What are you about?" I said. "This is high noon. Think you in your chamber?"

He laughed at me. "In truth," he teased, "I was but so full of thorns, I took off my shirt to rid me of them. But now you have put me in mind of other things. . . ."

He limped toward me, one boot off. When I would have slipped from his grasp, he fell with me to the ground. The soft air breathed of mint and clover, the soft grass bent like down.

"They will see us," I cried. But I did not really care. Is that not what desire is, blotting out all senses save that one? Is that not what love is, protection against the cold and dread to come? We lay together in that open place with only sky and sun, and at night we barred the door and were alone.

There be those who love but once and cannot let it go.

The old woman who had first told me that had warned that it was both blessing and curse. I think I must have known long ago, even when Giles and I were in the forest together, how it would be for me.

Yet, beneath, there was still darkness, fear, despite my effort to keep it at bay. We held the world at a distance, but it has habit of crowding in when least expected. When he spoke of freedom, it was not only the loss of mine, but his, too. I sometimes thought I had only myself to blame to think that I might tame him, win him to content here. For it was not love, nor its surfeit, that made him restless, so that sometimes in the night I would hear him pacing in our room, soft footed, in the way he had when something troubled him. Remember, he was trained from youth to administer large estates, command men. It was not easy for him to sit down as a country knight amid our rural pursuits. I do not mean either that he shirked what must be done. He worked as hard as anyone. I have seen him knee-deep in mud, straining with thongs to shift the fallen stumps that blocked a sluice; there was nothing that the men did that he would not try himself. It was only that it seemed less fitting somehow, as if by strapping on one of those new horse collars they use these days, one could be expected to make a war-horse pull a plow. Raoul never complained, like Geoffrey, he was at heart optimistic, and Geoffrey, I have always held, the most sweet of men. But at times I sensed a weariness in Raoul, a dark side that I did not understand. He had told me that first night at Cambray that he felt a respite, and that I think was true. He also said that we were far from the great world, but that I think he really did not believe. Reserve and caution had become part of his nature;

he would not even know how he used them against those with whom he should be most open. We all have secrets, it is true. As you now know, some of mine have lain silent these many years. Well, I did not know all his secrets either. And in the end it was they, not another woman, that drove him from my side.

We had slept well that night after the hawking expedition, to the low surging of the sea, which I remembered from childhood. No wonder salt winds are so much a part of me: they have woven themselves into all my childhood dreams, culled up from the deep sea caves into the windings of the castle walls. During the night there had been rain, drumming through the darkness, but it ceased just before the dawn. I awoke to silence, as if released from some loud sound. Or was it the drumming of my own heart? My first thought, as always now, was that someone had crept up through the passageway, but that was already well blocked with fallen stone and we kept a guard posted. My second thought was for the castle walls, but when I ran to the triple window I could see the watch pacing back and forth, could even hear the snap of the Sedgemont pennon as it beat against the staff. The air was thick with mist, warm and soft, having within it promise of more rain. As my eyes adjusted to the light, I saw Raoul, leaning against the battlements, staring off into the distance. He had wound a cloak around himself for warmth, and the wind blew at his hair; he might have been one of those statues carved from stone they use now to decorate church towers.

I hurried into my clothes, not staying to braid my hair or tie my shoes. In the Hall beneath, men were still abed, lying in rows against the walls. I crossed among their sleeping bodies, hushing the dogs that rose up from the hearth and moaned when they saw me. I drew the bar upon the lower door and went down into the clean-smelling air. Cocks were already crowing in the yard. The men who had taken an earlier watch were stretching themselves by the well, laughing loudly at

some sly jest. Within the guardroom, tapers were still lit, and
I could hear voices laughing and talking, reminding me of the
time we had heard men laugh as we stole toward them.

The Celts themselves were stirring. We kept them chained
by the leg to an outer wall. I frowned at that as I went by.
There must be better way to keep them than tied like beasts.
The young boy watched as I passed, and when I gave him
greeting in his own tongue, his scared face broken into a smile.

There is no treachery here, I thought, and felt my sense of
panic ebb. I ran up the steps to the battlements above. Raoul
was still where I had seen him and did not turn at my approach.
I leaned against him, feeling the beating of my heart steady
itself, feeling the warmth, the nearness of him.

The gray mist was lifting. Away to the west, the great rack
of clouds that had brought the rain had settled over the mountains; behind us, the blue line of sea faded away. And before
us spread the open fields, divided into strips as is the custom
although there were no peasants left to take their share and
the village lay desolate, in ruins. Each strip ran a different
shade of green, washed clear and bright by the storm. Beyond
them, as far as the eye could see, the open moors stretched
to the world's rim, softly purple in the early sun. Nothing
stirred in field or moor. Down below in the castle yard, the
leisured morning rituals began, a thin blue streak of smoke
curled upward, we heard a muffled cry and response. All was
as peaceful as a jeweled picture book.

Raoul felt it too, although when he spoke it was not of
Cambray but of Sieux.

"It was a place like this," he said, "although the castle was
old and large. A gem set among the woods and flowering
meadows, *les beaux prés de France*. Someday should I sing for you
the lays of Normandy to show you all its beauty. Or ask Sir
Brian, who has ever loved both songs and place. The hunting
there is so rich that you can stand and watch the wild fowl fly
overhead. In ranks they fly until the air is dark with them, and

they cry mournfully to each other among the riverbeds. And on such a day as this the Angevins took and burned my castle there."

He was silent, thinking of far-off things. His next words surprised me. "Lord Falk," he said, and as he spoke he played with my father's ring, "Lord Falk was once a simple knight, was he not, without demesne, taking service among the lords of Normandy as he could find it, until he came to my grandfather at Sieux, a landless knight who came to fortune late?"

"Aye," I said, "he never sought to hide it. Fate had nothing worse, he used to say, than to be a landless knight, for when old age had dulled your skill, then were you thrown at the world's mercy. A landless knight has but two roads: to follow his lord in battle or to make a round of the tourneys in peace. In either case he hires out his skills at other men's commands, and when those skills are gone, he too is ended."

"Or goes perhaps to the holy wars, where God will reward you if this world does not."

"You do not think of Outremer, across the distant seas," I said, suddenly anxious, for he had spoken of it before. He did not answer me but spoke again of Cambray.

"And the lands he held here of my grandfather were dear to him?"

"My lord," I said patiently, for he must have known it, "before your grandfather brought him to England as one of his household knights, he was already old as men are reckoned. He did not expect such graciousness even from the Earl of Sedgemont."

"And he was an honest man, a keeper of oaths?"

"You have said so yourself," I said, puzzled. "All my men say so. I do not boast of it."

"You should," he cried, startling me. "A man without such honor is an empty husk. What if that loyalty, which brought my grandfather fame and made your father's fortune, brings to me no fortune? I have wasted my patrimony in King Stephen's wars, but I do not seek to break my oath to him. Nor do I complain or doubt. I speak but to give myself purpose."

"Purpose?" I repeated stupidly.

"Ann," he said, "I have not told you all the nature of this king. I have not fairly set him before you that you may know him better. I have not even told you how we first met. All men will testify to his charm, his grace then. He wore it as some men don costly chain about their necks. He had no false sense of position, he was not too proud to mix with his fellow men. We met in the mud, and he pulled me from it with his own hand."

He mused awhile, remembering, no doubt. Then he roused himself to tell the story.

"The battle was not my first; even in France, there was war enough, and I have told you how the Angevins had raided Sieux before. But I was raw then, untried, overeager. He saw how my horse was broached and I like to be pricked by a half-dozen spears. It was the second battle of Lincoln where he sought perhaps to make amends for the humiliation of the first, when he had been captured by the Empress Matilda. He and his squire, they straddled my body on foot, and when he had beaten the enemy back with his great war ax, he raised me and stanched the blood himself."

He stretched out his arm. My father's ring gleamed dully, but he was not looking at that. I saw the thick red scar that I had first noticed long ago, a scar that ran across his right wrist.

That all but cost me my life.

So that was the story of his wounding that gave him his nickname; that was how his life had been saved. That scar was as a band of steel then, a chain, to bind him to the man who had rescued him.

Blood oath he swore, Dylan had said. It would not let him go.

He said, "Upon the battlefield, when I could speak again, I swore oath, blood oath to Stephen for my life. He was as young as a god then, Ann. Joyous he walked. Men ran to follow him, a man of honor who made that sour-faced Empress Matilda seem a harpy, intent to rend and harry the country she coveted. Did you know that when he, in turn, had the empress in his power, at Oxford, he let her go for courtesy? And when her son, this Henry, a half-wild boy, came back to England without consent it was Stephen who sent him gold to buy a passage back to France, as to a son? That was the sort of man I served. . . ."

He mused awhile again. "Yet there was another side of him," he said abruptly. "His father, who was Count of Blois before him, led his men to the Holy Land. In a beleaguered castle there he left them, abandoned them to perish whilst he escaped, letting himself down from the walls in a basket. Stephen of Blois has lived with knowledge of his father's shame, although the old count returned to the wars, driven there, they say, by his wife, that he might wipe out the disgrace by his death. The thought of it has haunted Stephen all his life; given him title of most chivalrous knight in its despite. And cursed him with the same weakness of will. . ."

He turned to me at last. "And now," he said, "he has summoned me back, although I angered him so when last we met. I thought we should not meet again."

I could not hide how my bright thoughts dulled, joy spilling from my bones at his words.

"Why?" was all I said, but the how and wherefore rang like thunder in my head.

He said, as if to justify himself, "You have long known that I am Stephen's man. My grandfather had the same knack I seem to have inherited: to quarrel with those we most admire, or rather, to tell them when they do not act as they should. But that does not change our loyalties. After the signing of the Treaty of Westminster, which I would not sign, I came back to the border because Stephen, in his rage, told me to waste my life away there. I would have achieved what even he thought impossible, obtained a treaty from the Celts, with your help, had not Maneth attacked."

I said, "Stephen has not treated you well. Long is the list

of grievances against him. Twice did he betray you in the wars that you fought on his behalf."

"I do not complain," he said moodily. "If others speak of these things they speak out of turn."

"Giles told no tales," I said, "but I know as well as you, you would not have stayed so long here had there been hope of mending your cause with the king."

"I will not deny it," he said. He smiled. "Come, it is not so grave. Perhaps he has called me to make me earl at last."

"Earldom is a title he has bestowed on many men," I broke in. "It is an empty honor at best."

"I did but jest," he said quietly. "That is not the honor I speak of. Come, love, do not quarrel with me this last day. The king's messenger came last night. Did not you hear him, hammering at the gates as if to wake the dead? We must prepare to leave as soon as he is ready, this noontide, if we can. . . ."

"So soon," I said, but my thoughts ran ahead, frightening me with their clarity. "You will leave me, Raoul, after all, although you know that Stephen has not been just or faithful to you. For such faithlessness will you abandon me and Cambray. And then what will become of us?"

How easily he slipped home the blade that ended hope, and how meekly I accepted its wound. The Lady Mildred herself could not have been more humble, more self-effacing, as I followed him down the steps to the courtyard where I could already see the horses being bridled, the saddlebags prepared. Then to the Hall, where we must sit and hear the messenger's complaints until, overcome by his efforts, he fell into a doze over his flagon of ale. Then, whilst he slept, to ride out for one last look at Cambray. How shall I describe so bittersweet, so golden-gray a day? The long damp wheat shimmered at our passage; the tassels of oats and rye dropped under their own weight; Cambray shone rich with harvest about us. And all I saw was desolation, as he gave instructions for the care of this, the care of that.

He knew me well enough to sense what I was thinking, the more because I did not speak of it. And if I had, would not he have said, "It is the lot of women to have their men ride out to danger. It is the lot of men to be lured away from safety to war, else are they not men."

Dispute that argument, if you can, poet. I cannot. Yet then I was still young, still hopeful. I knew he showed his concern by cheerfulness, refusing to turn to tragedy what time was left. I thought perhaps I could change his purpose if I made one last attempt, one other way. In that, too, I was mistaken. I should have kept quiet. Yet, if I had, how much else would have been changed.

The sun was already high when we returned. Then had I to go first to see about domestic affairs, for pride's sake, we set a good table that day, although such feasting taxed our resources. But a king's messenger must be honored. And when I had seen all prepared to my liking, I slipped out from the castle and made my way down to the sands. The squires were waiting where they always used to wait, at the back of the dunes, so the horses could crop among the rough grasses growing there. They knuckled salute as I went by and turned back to their dicing. Even the guard who spun round on hearing me smiled and pointed with his sword blade which way I should go. I might have been a child again, so little did my presence concern them. But I had no childlike purpose in mind.

The sands were wide and empty at low tide, smooth except for footprints that went down to the sea beyond the rocks where the tide turns. Across the bay, the water shimmered and the breakers came creaming in. I could see Raoul far out among the waves. How long since I had sat like this, gathering piles of clothes at my feet, waiting for him to return? He came presently, running and stumbling through the shallows to stand before me.

I sat up with my cloak around my shoulders.

"Take me with you," I said.

"I cannot," he said. "It will not be for long." But I knew he lied.

"Then stay here."

"Ann," he pleaded with me, "you have not understood what I must do. If your Celtic gifts had power to see ahead, you could foretell me all the future. If you cannot, I must not wait it here, like some caged bear."

"I see nothing," I said, "that does not include us both. What should I be or do after this, if you are not there as well?"

He said at last, "You have Cambray. Since I first knew you, that was what you yearned for. It is worth the keeping."

How could I tell him that it was as nothing after all; thus do the gods make sport of us to turn our dearest wishes to dust.

"Then go and be damned," I cried. "Find some highborn lady at your court. Forget us here."

"Ann," he said through gritted teeth, "I have had high women and low, and have had enough of both. And of courts and courtiers as well. If I could stay, I would. . . ."

"I do not believe you," I cried. "Men are ever so, dishonest at the end."

"Dishonest," he said, angry now. "By all the saints, where is this honesty of women to be found? Was my betrothed in France so honest that when I first visited her, I surprised her with her lover? Bound I was to her as a boy, and yet would have kept my vows. But even thoughts of my land and wealth could not keep her lust still. And the Celtic woman of my camp, who betrayed us to the lords of Maneth. . . Ah, you knew of that?"

"I knew."

"You never spoke of her."

"Nor you, my lord," I said. "But I do not hold her blameworthy. So shall I do if you forsake me. I count that honesty."

He shook me hard so that my cloak fell off and all my nakedness was revealed cold to the wind that blew the fine sand in stinging gusts.

"So you have come, like the rest," he said almost bitterly, "to use your charms. A siren to tempt me... I thought for something more than that from you."

"Then am I no more than any other of your women," I said, "that you have loved and left. Lord Raoul has had his sport of me, too: is that what I should think?"

He looked at me hard. Well, we have but one life and may pay for it through eternity, but it seemed to me that what life is and all its vigor, its essence, shone in him then. He was alive, from the salt-crusted curls to the long, lean body where the wind had turned old wounds blue against the brown flesh.

"Do not forsake me, Raoul," I said, wiping my eyes where the wind stung.

"I would not forsake you. . . ."

"Oh, God," he said, and there was misery in his voice. "Do not tempt me. Think instead that free of me, you can keep Cambray safe at least."

"What do you mean by that?"

He had turned aside again, staring out to sea with his sea-gray eyes.

"Think," he said. "You can still hold Cambray of the next Lord of Sedgemont."

As I tried to interrupt, he said, "What did you expect? We have had a little respite here, that is all. When Henry returns, he will have that vengeance you once warned me of. Think. If I can influence Stephen, I shall. But I live on borrowed time. Free of me, you keep your lands, avoid my fate."

"Say it is not so, Raoul, say it will not be so."

I clung to him then, trying to stop his mouth against such bleakness. I had goaded him into the truth; I wished that he had never spoken it. I should have kept quiet myself. What could I say except encompass him that he might drown in me, find there an end to whatever search for honor, hope, drove him on.

"Or is it," he said, his mouth at my neck bone, "that you truly seek me out for passion's sake, that you burn for it? I cry you pardon. I thought you wooed my lands and name. . . ."

"Do not jest now," I whispered. "We have such little time."

He said, his mouth lower still, "Nice ladies at court are not so generous with their favors. Did once I call you skin and bone? You are flesh and heart and cunt and all that men could desire. Remember that I, Raoul of Sedgemont, say that. Ann, I am not Talisin. I cannot recreate the past for you. And all the future looks dark. But this present, this now, I have given you, as you have given it to me. Remember it."

We fell upon the sands, we struggled with each other, part in love, part fear. Except once, before passion was spent, he raised himself upon his arms, forcing me to look at him, that I might take in his naked flesh and my own.

"Now, now," he cried, every word a thrust, a plunge, that his self might burrow into mine, "this is now. Remember me so."

I clung to him that his force might be passed on to me, an empty well that he would replenish, that there beside the sea, some spark of what we had been might live on, even when we were done. This was our parting, our farewell.

Afterward we helped each other dress, wordless, brushed off the sand, wiped away stains of love. Then, separate, apart, we walked back up the beach, the wind already freshening. The sentry saluted, squires sprang to their feet, horses snorted and stamped. From the courtyard, I watched the bustle of departure as if it happened far away, in another time that concerned not me. Raoul waved off his pages impatiently as they fussed with the setting of the last straps. He strode across the yard, his mail swinging to his knees, his face framed by the steel coif that he wore beneath his helmet, already remote, gone a long way off.

"I shall send word," he said. "Look for my seal that you know me."

He dipped his head that they might set his helmet in place, a mask that hid all I must remember.

They brought up the black stallion, but he bade them let

it go, gathered the reins, and vaulted into the saddle without touching stirrup. His flag bearer swung up on his own horse; the king's messenger, well fed but still white faced for weariness, still mud splattered, climbed upon his own. He wore full armor, too, carried the king's crest as proof of his mission, but his face was drawn, and faint-hearted was his smile, as if he doubted his ability even to find the king's court again.

The other men were already waiting. They knew Raoul never stayed about his parting. He raised his arm; they thundered across the bridge. I ran to the walk around the battlements where this morning we had stood and talked, and watched them move across the faint purple moors until they dipped from sight and were gone. But long after, I followed them in my mind's eye that I should understand all that he had said, should remember rightly.

I live on borrowed time.

What good is life or youth or love that cannot withstand another man's revenge? What means honor to a man dead? Who shall remember anything when time and death have faded it?

I have tried to explain before how Raoul did not reveal all his thoughts at once, although I think that day I had shaken him enough for him to show more than he meant. I do not speak now of plans, of strategy, but of his own self, his own identity. I had not known before, for example, that he had felt betrayed by women, that he came as slowly as I toward the idea of love. And although I have long known what honor was—a man's oath is as a promise to God, not lightly made, not lightly broken, and death is better than dishonor—I had not known how he would choose when faced with a decision between honor and—what? Deep, harsh things lay beneath the abrupt words I had forced from him. I have thought them over many times since then; by shifts and starts have some of them become clear at last, part from what other men said later, part from what I could guess at myself. Let me put them in order for you here, although to do so I must take you to the world of the court and its high affairs, that world we had both, for a moment, thought to escape. But we were as trapped by it as anyone; no one escapes its hold.

Anything that the great do has some effect on everyone. Now saw I what he meant. Now fell it with full force upon us.

As I look back from a long life, I see more clearly than he could then, although he guessed at it, how much the nature of our world has altered since. We live in an age of change. One day people will reflect on it and give it names of their own to explain and justify. You have but to look around you to see the changes for yourself: in church, in village, in castle keep. The way we think, the prayers we say, the rules we abide by, all these were new and strange to me, who has seen the changes harden into custom, law. Yet then I would not have thought them possible. . . . And danger, you who live in settled times have forgotten what death and danger are, what civil war can destroy, that even when the war is over, private quarrels still rage on. Consider for a moment a traitor's death. They hang you first, choking and gasping for breath, and cut you down alive and rip the bowels from you, geld you, burn your genitals before your living eyes before they hack you limb by limb. I have seen a man die thus. It is no death for any man, but, for a young one, vibrant with life, perhaps knowing himself beloved, knowing love for the first time . . .

Raoul kept his thoughts to himself but he must have guessed what name Henry would brand him with. He had not wished to speak of it, but sometime I would have to know. . . .

Free of me, you keep your lands, avoid my fate.

I cannot marry you.

A traitor drags with him all his kin. Wife, children, family, all must share the consequence, if not the manner, of his death, to be burned out root and stem, cut off from lands and titles evermore.

What if a cause be half-lost, one need not fight the less.

He had half-guessed his fate perhaps since his return from France; certainly he knew it when he rode out from Sedgemont to await the landing of Henry of Anjou, when he saw how Stephen had lost heart and will. But if he anticipated what his loyalty would cost, he would not swerve from it. What man of honor could?

Would it please you to have me proved a coward, a man of no faith?

Long have I regretted my silence when he hurled that question at me.

Raoul knew he had been a marked man long before Wallingford, when those who would have avoided open battle nevertheless would have accepted him as the king's champion to fight against Anjou, long before the Treaty of Westminster, which followed; long perhaps before Raoul had come back to England to inherit Sedgemont.

I have known these Angevins before.

Well, what he knew of them, they, too, would know of him. The struggle between the counts of Sieux, the counts of Anjou stretch back into an earlier history when, as descendants of those Norse bands who had invaded northern France, both had fought over the same territory there. Was it wise then to antagonize the heir of a family that had now grown so strong as to control almost all of those northern lands? Why had Raoul put himself in the forefront of the opposition to Henry of Anjou? And would Henry kill him when he came to power in England?

The first two questions I cannot answer. Judge the last for yourself. Number in your mind, if you dare not aloud, the names, in France and England both, whom Henry has destroyed. Remember, again if you dare, that archbishop slain at his own high altar at Canterbury, by that same Henry's command. And once Becket and Henry had been friends. . . .

Yet no man is all bad, and in Henry, as in others, good struggled sometimes to overcome evil as the sea may fret away at a black unyielding rock. But let Raoul speak to these last points in his own words, as afterward I heard them, to tell you what befell when he left Cambray and came again to King Stephen's court.

I have said I am no chronicler. I piece together what I can, as things were told to me, perhaps years later. The story of how he left and we met once more may seem strange to you, as improbable as the events themselves that followed hard upon that meeting. . . . Yet, had not Stephen died and Henry become king, none of them would have happened, my tale would end here. I wish it had. But as one ripple moves, it sets the next to moving.

Anything that the great do has effect on everyone.

Now were we caught full center in that widening circle. Nor can I tell you everyday occurrences, who said what, did which, to make a pattern that will please you. There are gaps in my knowledge when I was not there to see for myself. For facts you must rely upon those monkish texts which swear to the truth of all they write. But do not be surprised if some of the things I tell you never find the way into their accounts. Their idea of truth is as one-sided as mine. Except they never will admit it. Raoul's journey east, for example. It is mentioned in several of those texts, since travelers about the king's business could command royal entertainment along the way, and monasteries, bishops' palaces, are noted for their hospitality. You can read for yourself where they stayed, how long, but why they were there, what they said, what they intended, no one will tell you that.

One chronicler records even what they ate, all sixteen courses, washed down with so many drafts of mead, cider, claret, and mulberry wine. A plenteous feast for men used to soldier's fare. As the pious complaint which ends the description points out, little was left when they were done. . . .

"As locusts in the land of Egypt did they devour our sustenance. . . ."

Another passage from this same source speaks only of the

king's messenger "reeling beneath the burden of disdain, where-soever he passed people spat at him for hate. . . ."

The poor man reeled, no doubt, for weariness. As for hate and anger, Raoul saw no one who spat at them, except the monks themselves, discreetly behind their long sleeves. Yet neither were people open faced, joyful, glad to see them pass as in former days. Cautious, watchful, weary: those were the words he would have used to describe what he saw, and they were enough to trouble him, as if he journeyed through an exhausted land, too tired to concern itself about its fate.

They found the king at Dover. He had already abandoned his castle at London to his mercenaries, and had come to this small flea-infested town of hovels, dominated by its unkempt castle above the white cliffs. It in no way resembled the castle that later was to be built there, and why Stephen had chosen to go there was never explained, if he had a plan to await word of Anjou's doings in France or to travel there himself, or merely to inspect this chiefest of his Channel defenses (although, in truth, it was but a sorry imitation of defense). But as Raoul and his men clattered up the narrow cobbled streets and under the portcullis at the gate, they could see again the evidence of disinterest all about them, the neglect. Raoul restrained himself that night from clouting the stable boys when they came at last reluctantly to take the horses, for, as he said, "I remembered your complaints, that all men vent their spleen upon their grooms. Yet they deserved worse, for the stables were filthy, saddles and gear rotting on the ground, not one horse there sound for riding, not one kept in training. I was not so restrained the next day. And everywhere we went, even passing through the guards, we noted sign of slackness: ill-kept weapons, ill-kept men, passwords ignored. The king's own personal guard did not salute as they should, but slouched at their post. Great courts are not always so grand as you would think. And this was worse than most, although there may have been reason."

He laughed. "It was the coldest place I have ever known, not built like Cambray, but made to let in every sea wind, with a smell of fish that tainted even the most luxurious of feasts. We went straight to the king's chambers. They were at least heated, so much so that those who attended upon him there either broiled within or froze without. King Stephen was sitting propped on cushions, wrapped in furs and robes, before a blazing fire. Yet even so he complained of the cold, and the hand he gave me was as cold as ice. Jesu, did I think him aged the year before? He was but fifty-and-eight, but his years sat heavily upon him so that he suddenly seemed shrunk beneath them, withered, that I had to hunt for the man whom I had known. He knew me at once. There was even ghost of his former smile as he greeted me almost in his usual courteous fashion. Yet the contrast between this tired old man and the young Henry who would replace him had never seemed so obvious, not even a year ago.

"'Nay, lad,' Stephen said, in his easy way—I told you he was noted for his charm, 'never kneel to me. These stones were made for horses. So, Raoul, we meet again as friends.'

"'My lord King,' I said, moved by his words, 'we parted never as enemies, I trust.'

"'God willing,' he said. 'Good friends may have their outs but never come to enmity. Speak no more of that. And put the cares of border life behind you. Tell us more-cheerful news.'

"The gesture he made was a parody of his former self. I noticed how his accent had thickened as if, as concentration lessened, he had reverted to the speech of his childhood at Chartres. And there was something in his expression of his mother, that stern Adela, who had sent her husband to his death to atone for cowardice. I had not noticed the likeness before, and did so now perhaps because his eyes had sunk and stared out as hers used to beneath her heavy brows. Others noted the resemblance, who knew her well, a fiery woman, a daughter of that first duke, William of Normandy. They say

of her that had she been a man, she would have been as great
a warrior as her father and brother both. But perhaps it was
only that Stephen suddenly spoke so much of her, how she
had nurtured up her sons to make them famous, had trained
Stephen for court life, his younger brother for the Church,
that he seemed to take on her looks. They say that dying men
turn to the past for comfort, ignoring the present. But although
he spoke so much of former times—of her, of his brothers,
his wife, his sons—and moved restlessly as with pain, his mind
was clear. That first night he was content to have me by his
side as if to relive for us both what had been better days. He
spoke of old battles he had fought as a young man newly come
to the English court, after the death of the king's son in the
White Ship disaster. And then he spoke of all those battles of
the early years of his reign, of the great battle of the Standard
against the Scots in the earliest days when the Celts were
routed within two hours; of the first battle of Lincoln three
years later, a cold February day in 1141, when he had fought
as a man possessed, on foot, laying about him like some Viking
with his double-headed ax. But it was the other nobles who
finished the tale, reminding him that, despite his heroic stand,
he had been captured at the end, laid low by a coward's stone
thrown out of the crowd of men who ringed him round. That
day had been the lowest ebb of his life. Yet the Empress Matilda
had shown her true colors after, refusing to show any mercy
to him, her defeated cousin, ignoring the rights of his lords
and barons, refusing even to stand to greet her ally, the King
of Scotland, because of self-pride, flaunting her victory to her
own disgrace.

"Out of that defeat, Stephen had risen higher than before.
'For see, my lord King,' they soothed him, when these details
seemed to distress him, although I do not think they told him
for malice, rather because they thought he would be pleased
that they remembered, too, 'although that treacherous stone
cost you your freedom, the imprisonment did not last long.
The citizens of London rose on your behalf, and drove the

empress and her crew out of the city just as they were about to sit down to a victory feast. And at Winchester next, your own queen and wife besieged them round with so strong a hold that when they tried to make a dash for freedom, the empress's half-brother, Earl Robert of Gloucester, was captured himself and the army cut to pieces.'

"'True, true,' Stephen said, mollified, 'and so was I exchanged for Robert of Gloucester, his life for mine. It was a slight setback only, my men remained loyal to me when I was a prisoner of that bitch. And she escaped with scarcely her life then and only one man followed her. But she kept me in chains while she had me.'

"And so the long list of battles continued: Wareham, Oxford, Lincoln again, where he rescued me and where he held triumphant court at the Yuletide, although I remember little of it myself, being still ill of my wounds. So many battles then, to be refought, so many parts of England to be recalled in blood. But never word of Malmesbury, or Wallingford. Never word of Henry of Anjou.

"It drove me wild," Raoul went on, "that the king could not keep his mind upon the present. Even then, you see, I hoped that something could be saved from this morass. He could have made some provision for the future, not left us all adrift. There were the mercenaries, to give an instance. They could have been disbanded if he would have given the word. He could have tried to bring order to the council, reassessed the position of the exchequer, whose records had fallen all to pieces—where were the revenues of this once-rich land gone, but into the pocket of greedy men? He could have given orders to the law courts. What use of laws if no man enforces them? He could, at the very least, have moved against the worst offenders like the Lord of Maneth, whose name has become a curse word in the land. He could have comforted those who have suffered most from this anarchy. He could have redeemed his name.

"But the other lords who had humored him with their attention when he talked of old times were not so sanguine as I was, nor were they patient in their judgment of him when we were alone. I thought if we could force the king to listen to us, we could at least set up a council to advise him, but they were not even willing to try that. They named him shallow, inconstant, blind to unpleasantness, withdrawing from it as his father had done. I had thought as much myself. Yet I could not give up hope so easily.

"One man of consequence who was there, Richard de Luci his name, justiciar of London and the eastern counties, a patient, forceful man, yet sensible, took me aside one day upon the outer walls. The wind was keen and had driven everyone indoors except the guard, and they kept but fitful watch.

"'A storm is brewing,' de Luci said, leaning against the wall, head bent to keep it from the wind that blew like some harbinger of winter although we were still only halfway into October. He is a short man, old and shrewd. He nodded at the specks of white that flecked the air, perhaps sea spray, perhaps flurries of snow. 'From the north. There will be no crossing of the Channel yet.'

"When I did not reply, 'Do you expect another crossing?' he asked me bluntly. I did not pretend to misunderstand him.

"'The king has been sick before,' I said carelessly, hiding my concern, for it pained me to have to speak of him as if in secret. 'So close was he to death before that all were prepared to hail his son, Eustace, as king. But he recovered then, and drove his enemies from the country. He will do the same again.'

"'What a man can do at forty he may not at fifty,' de Luci said. 'Even you, Lord Raoul, may find that out one day. What will you do if he does not recover?'

"I told him I was not willing to talk of it.

"'Come, come,' he said impatiently at that, 'you need not be uneasy with me. Here we are at last safe from spies, Henry's spies. Look not so amazed. He has them planted everywhere.'

"'I am not afraid to speak what I think,' I told him, 'but

grieved to think of it. Not only for myself, my lord, although you know what peril we sit in. But we have had one sort of rule here in England since the time of William the Conqueror. A Norman-French rule it has been, based on Norman ways, spread over that Anglo-Saxon, Celtic underlayer. I know not the law as you do, my lord, but I do know that without the Norman nobles, William would never have won England at all. With their help, he gained a kingdom, as did his son, Henry, first of that name, as did this King Stephen. All three kings have acknowledged their debt to us Norman lords. They accepted that they were first among equals, bound to us as we were to them.'

"'I do not deny that you are right, Lord Raoul,' de Luci said. 'I have heard it said before that kings need advice from their lords since they are partners together. But since the study of law is my delight, I have wondered, in my turn, what will happen when the new king's laws run not in harmony with what we want. This Treaty of Westminster disturbs me, too, although for different reasons. For I have begun to be troubled by this thought—how the new king will interpret it. Does not the treaty state that those lands that have been unlawfully seized by some "intruder" are to be restored—*quae direptae erant ab invasoribus?* Now who, by God, is to say which man is an "intruder" on a piece of land, who to say our own castles are legal or not legal, or our powers that we think justly given under another king have not been usurped? You see my point, Raoul. Henry can use that treaty as he wishes, against us as for us if he chooses. I have come to believe as you do, that we were fools to agree to it. We may have signed our own lives away.'

"He did not speak for a while, staring out at the gray-flecked sea, as if to will it into order.

"'A king who picks and chooses his laws,' he said at last, putting our fears clearly as a lawyer may do, 'a king who interprets law as best suits him is a danger to that realm. For who else will advise him if we do not. And who will take our place when our power is gone.'

"What he said was what all men must think on. Yet, in some way, it gave me comfort, that I was not alone.

"De Luci is a stout-hearted man, honest, true. He stayed with Stephen almost to the end. He had administered Stephen's decrees as best he could during the worst parts of the wars. His fears were thought out, well argued. But he had no solution to them either.

"A cry came from a room beneath, making us spin round, hands on sword hilts. It was a false alarm, a soldier cursing at some underling, but it made us both frown. You see how uneasy was the time, how ripe for disorder. In former days such carelessness in the king's guard would have merited death.

"'Best part now,' de Luci said, reluctantly letting go my arm, which he had clutched as if to brace himself against the gale. 'We shall be noticed. But there will be chance for talk hereafter. Watch yourself, Raoul. You are a marked man.'"

11

HE NEXT WEEK MUST HAVE BEEN HARD and strained for the men left at Stephen's court. Although the news of the king's illness was kept secret, his flushed face and disjointed speech were marked by many. Some who had vowed to remain with him found their resolution slipping and made uneasy excuses to return to the safety of their own keeps. Others, standing less on ceremony, went quietly in the night, hoping their absence would not be noticed. Those who were left tried desperately to hold the king to business in hand, to keep the affairs of government alive. But without his cooperation, little was possible.

His mercenaries in London ran riot again. News of that did not spread to Cambray, but did certainly among the heir's men, slouching openly now about the court, scratching and cursing themselves as they waited insolently in the town below. Their speech alone, with its much more French pronunciation, should have distinguished them, but the younger ones wore the short cloaks that Henry of Anjou had made fashionable and pinned sprigs of broom in their caps in honor of the Angevins, openly proclaiming themselves, although none dared yet affect the Angevin crest. But the king would not, or could not, assert himself. Yet one day, while speaking of his brother, the Bishop of Winchester, whom he had refused to make archbishop, he began to talk wildly. It was a betrayal, Stephen had cried, a slight the brother had never forgiven. Yet, without his aid, Stephen would never have been made king.

"And I have put a slight on you, Lord Raoul," Stephen said at last, turning painfully on his side. His hair was thin and straggled about his wasted cheeks, all luster gone. Once he too had set the style among his younger knights; once they had cut their hair long as he did, worn his clothes, affected his style of speech. "I have not repaid your love as I should. Those titles which were your grandfather's should have been your father's had he lived. I gave no such honor to you, although I have made earls aplenty who have not stood by me. Raoul, at Malmesbury, at Wallingford, you would have fought Henry alone had I not prevented you. And together, lad, we could have beaten him as we did once before, is that not so? Yet I never honored you. The lack must be remedied."

He drank deeply, calling often for more wine, which he downed with a gulp, as if parched, although his physicians had forbidden it. Yet what he said was not wine induced, nor was his mind befuddled. Out of the doubts and fears that had gnawed at him, he spoke.

"But how could you have defied me at the last?" he cried painfully. "Raoul, that was ill done to deny what I could not avoid."

"My lord King," Raoul knelt beside the dying man, giving him his shoulder to lean upon that he might breathe more easily, "should I lie to you for comfort?"

"They all lie," the tormented voice ground out. "Physicians, friends, children, all. You never did. And you were right. It was an evil day when I signed the Treaty of Westminster. Yet I do not want to hear your truths. They are too great a weight. This Henry has been a weight about my shoulders all these years. Cursed have I been with him since his birth. And cursed with my own son who could do nothing right. And cursed with my own ambition that drove me to seek the crown. I could have made a good king, boy, had they not hounded me with their wars and jealousies."

"My lord King," Raoul said, "you will be remembered for

your generous spirit." He could have said more, but his grief overtook him.

Stephen's face softened. "You always thought well of me," he said. "I should have been more worthy of it. And I should honor you as you deserve."

All about them held their breath, were shocked or relieved at Raoul's noncommittal reply. It was the last time they spoke. Soon afterward, the king sank into a swoon from which he never woke again.

It was de Luci who spoke of this, later, telling how he had berated Raoul for his diffidence, as they walked again along the windswept walls.

"For such titles are not easily come by," he had said, speaking kindly to avoid offense. "You are too modest, my friend. Or too proud. It is an unfortunate combination."

Raoul did not answer at once, staring moodily over the gray, heaving sea.

"Come, it was not weakness that made the king speak as he did, but truth. And all know it."

"I had my French lands to content me once," Raoul replied at last.

De Luci smiled, his prim, almost hesitant smile that he wears when he makes a telling point. "That has been perhaps half the trouble," he said. "You see, Raoul, how I cling to my little piece of English land. But for the most part, we nobles veer from one country to the other like weather vanes. You were reared in France, as was Stephen. Henry, that most French of men, was partly brought up here, in western England. Perhaps he will understand its worth at last. As I think you do, my lord, although you pretend otherwise. My lord." He turned to him abruptly. "What is the enmity between you and Henry? Has it foundation?"

Raoul brooded again before he spoke. "It is of long standing," he said, as once he had said at Cambray. "I hold it not in my keeping as it seemed to have lodged in his. A children's en-

counter, that was all. I was older. He overbearing. I tossed
him in a bush. Since then, we have never met as friends. It
was years ago."

De Luci, in turn, brooded. "You are not wed, my lord?" he
asked then, abruptly. "Childless? That is as well. I shall send
my own wife and children away, bestow them with my vassals
who can be trusted to hide them. I advise all those with kinfolk
to do the same. Send word now to that end lest we be caught
before there is time." He turned then to others who had come
out to join them.

"My lords all," he said, his voice carrying even in the wind,
a small man with an air of authority, "I advise you all to
prepare."

"What shall we do?" said one. "Go back to our own lands?
Resist? Await him here?"

All knew who the "he" was.

De Luci slapped Raoul on the back.

"It is in God's hands," he said. "As in a battle, none knows
why or who will be saved. I cannot advise you to the right
course. But if you shut yourself up, be assured he will pull your
walls down about you. I myself will go back to my keep, throw
open the gates, and await him there. We have shed enough
blood as it is. He cannot murder us all."

There was a mutter at that. What else could they do, that
small group who remained with their dying king, that he should
not die alone, unfriended? They were all resolute men. Yet
many parted there who would not see each other again.

De Luci clapped his arm about Raoul once more.

"If we do not meet," he said, "I will tell you freely I have
been proud to be your friend. If Stephen had been more like
you, we would not be here like this today. May God have you
in His keeping, my lord."

They parted hurriedly then. Some rode to their castles
through the storm. Much good it did them; Henry came after
them. Raoul remained to the last, although finally de Luci took

his own advice and departed also, but he had dependents he must care for. Raoul stayed to bury his king. And so the end came for Stephen, King of England, whose reign is remembered also for grief.

Raoul kept his own counsel, but two things he did take advice in. The letter he wrote me was simple, but he himself had penned it in his own hand, and wrapped and double-sealed it with his own and with the Cambray crest that I might truly know it was from him. He had promised to send word, and he did, although it was bleak enough. I have the piece of parchment still, cracked and stained from so much handling.

> I recommend me to you, that you should
> hear of me. I have seen the king who lies
> grievous sick. After, I shall return to my
> own demesne within the month to put all
> things to order there. Here there be storms
> and high winds that you should escape in
> the west. If the weather does not improve,
> we shall look for worse from the south.

> Sedgemont

No word of endearment then, nothing to suggest any bond between us; yet something crossed through that could not be read. But even from the seclusion of Cambray, I could fill in the gaps. Especially of the warning of what was to come from the south, from France. The messenger could add a little more. I plied him with questions as with food and drink, and between mouthfuls, he told me that Raoul was well, and when he had left, that the king still lived. But all men were fearful of the end, and the court itself was half-empty. All was distraught, grief-stricken. Raoul had dismissed many of his guard. He himself was bidden to seek service with me here at Cambray. Nothing more, except the date and time of his leaving: October, the twenty-third day of the month, at seven in the

morning, had Raoul brought him the message and bidden him
ride out. Ten days had he been already on the road. Over a
month, then, since Raoul had left Cambray, and no likelihood
of his returning. While the messenger had battled through the
storms to reach us here, and while we at Cambray had hurried
to have the harvest done, Stephen, King of England, had died.
And, as de Luci and the others had decided, Raoul had returned
to Sedgemont to throw open his gates and await the new king,
who on the twenty-fifth of the same month obtained his heart's
desire.

Later again, much later, we understood that these same
storms that had blown up the Channel all the month had kept
Henry from crossing it to claim his throne. No king before
had waited so long to be crowned. News reached him soon
enough, but he was in no hurry. He was at Torrigny, where,
in typical fashion, he was engaged in siege against one of his
local lords. He lingered to tear down the castle before pro-
ceeding leisurely to Barfleur to join his queen and infant son.
Having no wish to risk a second White Ship disaster, which
had drowned his grandfather's hopes, drowned the boy who
should have inherited to spare us so much woe, he waited
again. Already his spies had their instructions, his envoys knew
what had to be done. So Raoul had time to see to King Stephen's burial, had seen the king laid in state with all due respect
before being entombed beside his wife and son at Faversham
Abbey. Having done that, he, in turn, had left for Sedgemont.
It was the end of the world as we had known it—the beginning
of a new age.

What brought Raoul back to Sedgemont? De Luci had
phrased it well with his precise mind. Pride, I think, and
loyalty, that same stern sense of loyalty that would not have
him bound to me, that would release his own men from their
bond to him. Instinct would have told him to bar the gates,
defy the new king. But then there would be no escape for him,
or, worse, for those who held the keep with him.

There has been enough bloodshed.

He had said it himself. I had said it; all men I think felt it. Or perhaps it was none of these thoughts, but simply the weight of responsibility for other men's lives, which, as you have seen, he could take in white-heat anger, yet felt the waste of afterward. Or perhaps it was the sight of all those honest old friends who came to greet him as he rode back across the drawbridge that December day. Sir Brian, the Lady Mildred, all the women of the castle, the castle guard, how was he best to keep them free from harm?

I told you before that the Earl of Sedgemont had built his keep so it would last, that Sedgemont would not fall by siege. I am glad I was not there that day to see how joy turned to grief on hearing what his grandson intended to do. Having decided, he worked with calm efficiency, relying on Sir Brian's obedience, if not his agreement. Did he explain himself to them? I doubt it. But they may have known. Certainly the men would, as he steadily set serf and peasant free, disbanded his squires and men-at-arms, distributing them among his vassals, who, like me, would in this way be unaffected by his fate. What moneys he had, the jewels and plate of Sedgemont, he also gave away or pawned as security for those who were old or could not find a place elsewhere. He had no heir; I was far away and safe. With clear conscience and proud mind then could he wait out Henry's men. And fast behind him they came, outrunning their king, already at work to gather in the malcontents.

But in two things did they and he miscalculate. One, that from the nearest southern port, braving the storm for fear and greed, the new claimant to the lands of Sedgemont, Lord Guy of Maneth, was already gathering his men to press toward his new estates.

And from the west, I, Ann of Cambray, was also riding east to join him, with his son and heir already conceived.

So would in due course, by God's will, we all meet there.

God had us in His keeping, I think, that we met at such a time and such a place, against all expectation.

But to return you now to Cambray with the arrival of Raoul's messenger and his harsh letter that hid many of the things he could not bring himself to say—we did not know, of course, that Stephen by then was dead, nor that already all these new forces had been set in motion. But the very brevity of Raoul's message gave chance for other interpretation. I had kept myself busy whilst he was gone, not allowing myself time to sit and think. All that we had set out to do at Cambray was now accomplished. The harvest had been gathered in and the field plowed for the winter sowing. So when we closed the gate at night, those dreams as a child I had locked in my heart had come true. I moved as mistress of my own lands, my own men guarded my keep, the keys of command hung at my waist. The Lady Mildred would have been proud of me that her teaching now stood me in such good stead that I might do all these things that were needful. But I was not content. The man I loved was in mortal peril and far away. And I already knew that beneath my waist there grew the fruit of sin, of love, that my love should not die.

It was this knowledge then—not unexpected, for I had taken no precautions that month, none of those herbs that Gwendyth had taught me how to use; I willed this child forth—that gave me courage to do what must be done. Within three days of Raoul's message was I ready to call my men out. This was no sudden whim. Like any lord, I had thought of my lands before I left, meaning to take with me only those who could be spared. For, in the long watches of the night, when there had been time to think, I, for my part, had come to accept many ideas that before had been strange to me.

Once long ago, as a child, I had maintained that I wanted no part of the greater world.

"What is this Henry to me?" I had cried. What would he be to me now, the murderer of lord, of lover, of father of my child? I came to know what Raoul had hoped to spare me. But I also believed that no man, not even this Henry, would kill for spite. Like de Luci, although for other causes, I argued that no king would wish to start his rule branded with the name of murderer. I also reasoned, knowing little of the ways of the world, as you are aware, that even if Raoul was taken, there must be friends, companions, who, wishing him well, would speak on his behalf. I judged the great, you see, by those old-fashioned rules of my own life. But I did not mean to let my man be killed because I had not tried to save him.

Such were the things I would have explained to Dylan when I revealed my decision. Dylan was beside himself. I think it was fortunate that only his inborn sense kept his right hand from twitching too close to blows, but he minced no words. And I stood out against his wrath with that same determination that once had persuaded Giles to my way of thinking.

"I go as free vassal," I said patiently. "Cambray stands in no danger. Nor do I. I shall seek to hold it of the king, since Lord Raoul's hold seems so precarious."

For I thought then that it would be an easy matter to ask audience of a king and cry my wrongs that all should hear them.

He muttered oaths against Henry of Anjou, who did not know an honest man from a villain, against me, against Lord Raoul. I let him rage, that small, squat soldier with the tenacity of a bull.

"Lady," he said at last, "I have served your father well, and Lord Raoul in his wars. I am an old man. But I tell you to your face, you meddle where no man may dare."

"And you are the best to hold Cambray whilst I am gone," I said.

"They would never have lost it in the first place," he muttered, "had I been here as I ought. And I would have been here had not Lord Raoul hauled me off about his affairs. What were those wars to us? I see no reason to traipse across the

kingdom to hold what is ours and can be best defended here.
Lady, you do wrong. And you will not save Lord Raoul. God
have him in His keeping, but if he is marked, no man can save
him. I do not say that to grieve you," he added, seeing how
my face paled at his words.

"Lady Ann, I have known you since you were a child, and
as a slip of girl when Giles first brought me to you." He sighed
suddenly. "How long ago that seems. And now you will throw
all we have won away."

"You promised me then," I said quickly, "that you would
gladly serve me. Or the man whom I would wed."

I held his gaze with my own that he should know what I
meant, until he looked away, rubbing his head for perplexity.
I almost felt sorry for him then, that I should so knot him up.

"Well then," he said slowly, reluctantly, "if that is the way
it is..."

He lapsed back to his dour, unyielding self, refusing to be
further moved by pity or fear, but his advice was invaluable
to me. It was he who suggested what men, what horses to
take—I had not thought that so complicated a choice—suggested that I have Geoffrey as highest-ranking squire to lead
them, and who, before we left, led out four of the half-broken
grays that Raoul had brought back to Cambray. Even half-
trained, their value in barter was high. And despite his original
belief, it was he who came to a solution about the Celtic
prisoners, whom we could not keep chained up much longer.

"Let them go," was his advice. "Or those who wish it can
stay and settle in the village. There be cottages empty enough
if they will work to make them whole." He suddenly gave me
one of his sly grins. "Such a one was I once," he said. "Are we
not all half-breeds, Lady Ann, along these border parts? Let
those go who wish, those stay who will work for it, to make
something of their lives. Like me again, who never thought
to wear the title of seneschal." And he grinned at the thought,
like a boy.

Before we left, I gave him formally the keys and named him guardian of Cambray in my stead. It is a title he has worn ever since. In this way was one of the bravest men rewarded for his courage and faith.

Well equipped, then, well led, almost as if Raoul himself rode before us, Geoffrey brought us out from Cambray toward Sedgemont. It was a journey he knew well by now, and had there been no cause for haste, I could have enjoyed the ride that had caused me so much pain when I made it before. But we had to force ourselves that we should not arrive too late. Had not the weather worsened—whenever had we heat or cold in proper season in those days, Nature herself seemed disordered, out-of-joint with the times—we would have missed Raoul at Sedgemont after all, and with him the French envoys who, as he had expected, had followed him soon thereafter. And always following at our heels came Maneth, panting with his new-culled men to savor his revenge.

The French envoys were not so many after all, and not so uncouth as to hack a man to pieces in his own Hall. Nor did they refuse his hospitality; it gave Raoul grim amusement that they should be so willing to dine at his expense before they took him away. Nor did they cavil that his keep seemed unwatched, his guardroom empty, his Hall scarce waited on. If they took note of those things, as they did, for I heard them speak of them myself, they gave no outward sign. Their orders had been plain: to find Raoul of Sedgemont and deal with him; the whys and wherefores of the case lay not within the scope of their concern.

All over England were the new king's envoys dealing with such matters under guise of settling the Treaty of Westminster. Even I remember the wording of the treaty now, it has been quoted at me so many times. Even I see the sense of de Luci's fears that it would be turned against the nobles to Henry's great advantage. Raoul did not try to argue with his captors; he did not even take offense that they were at such pains to

deny him his titles and lands. Sir Brian and the few men who
were left did so doubly to make up for such discourtesy. Like
one of those ancient Stoics of olden times who faced danger
without flinching, Raoul had put his affairs in order as best he
could and awaited what came next with patience and endurance. Not I. I would have screamed and fought them as I
stood.

I have said, had not the weather worsened, we should not
have met. They would have left and I would never have known
what had become of Raoul.

> In behint yon auld fail dyke
> I wot there lies a new-slain knight.
> And naebody kens that he lies there...

It is a familiar story, that. But had not some fear made us
ride on through the storms, we should have taken shelter by
the way and arrived too late. As it was, we picked the last
miles through fogs and mist so thick they seemed to choke
the air we breathed. But what was hindrance to us was hindrance to them, so that when we came to Sedgemont, they
were still there. For caution then, Geoffrey bade us hold.

The day was still not yet done, but despite the weather,
the uneasy times, the winter twilight, the gates of Sedgemont
stood wide open, the walls were unmanned, and however hard
we craned, we could not see the red pennon flying at the
battlements. Fear grew on us heavy as lead, while we waited
at the edge of the great meadows, so shrouded now in mist
that they stretched like gray, flat wastes toward the forest
behind. For caution, then, we divided our small group, ten to
come with us, ten to wait in the shelter of the trees.

The rest of us rode slowly forward, Geoffrey in the lead
with drawn sword. We picked our way toward the drawbridge,
crossed it with hollow clatter, and came again into the great
courtyard of Sedgemont.

It was not the coming that I had anticipated, nor yet the
one I could have wished for. But there came Sir Brian down

the steps, dressed in his long robe. Heavily he walked, feeling
the wall for support, and beside him a page carried his sword
and shield. There stood the groomsmen nervously holding the
saddled horses that were at least familiar. Against a farther
wall, the Lady Mildred and her women with their wraps and
bundles waited silently. They were the first to notice us, yet
gave no sign or nod, not even Cecile, who would have darted
out on seeing Geoffrey, had not someone—it must have been
the Lady Mildred—hauled her back and closed her mouth.
Not one word of welcome from Sir Brian, who paused, horror-
struck, as looking at the dead. Nor from Raoul, who waited
to one side, bare-headed, unarmed, dressed for riding forth.
But the other men who stood about him, in their short-cut
cloaks and close-cropped hair, their armor worked with a strange
device although all know it now, they made clamor enough.

"We are only travelers," Geoffrey was saying in his young-
old voice that sounded sometimes so much like Raoul's own.
"We seek shelter and safety with the Lord of Sedgemont."

"Be welcome in his name," Sir Brian said ponderously, slowly,
so that one heard the displeasure in his voice. "And what the
devil do you here?" his expression said as he glared at me.

As one man, the French envoys advanced, all three of them.
"Be welcome in the name of the King of England," they cried,
"Henry, second of that name."

But Raoul still said nothing, raked me with his gaze, never
taking his eyes from my face as if what he saw was both delight
and pain. Then he was at my side, hand outstretched to lift
me from the saddle. I jerked the beast round so that it half-
reared, like to jar me from the saddle, and made no sign by
word or look that I had ever seen him before.

"We are at the start of our ride, sirs," Geoffrey was continuing, soul of courtesy, ignoring, with all the resolution he
could summon up, his friends, his mistress, his sworn lord,
knuckling salute instead to these interlopers who seemed masters here. They, for their part, lingered by the castle steps,
part curious, part impatient at our unexpected intrusion.

"We go to London, my lords," I said, as softly as I knew, kicking the snorting horse forward so that my cloak and scarves went falling wide and my hair came tumbling free. I heard a man in the courtyard gasp and Raoul ground his teeth for rage.

"And as you seem set to depart, we would seek your company." And I gave my sweetest smile, having noted how they, too, were ready for riding forth. But they all would ride armed.

"By my troth," one of the French said then, in his strange, half-lisping way, pushing past his fellows to come to my side, "you would be right welcome. In my king's name, I, a lover of all maidens fair, welcome you."

It was the last offer he ever made; who knows what the compliment was. His elegant speech remained unfinished, whatever else he might have said. An arrow took him in the throat so that all the rest was gabbled forth on air and blood. Had he not moved when he did, it would have struck me. And had not Sir Brian moved, as agile as a young man, the second shaft would have struck Raoul. Instead, it took Sir Brian full in the back. We stared at him as he fell, the black feathers starting from his shoulders like wings. And all about us, with a hiss and clatter, the deadly rain fell a second time. We all stood as if struck ourselves, and at the castle gate, running up the walls where, as we noted, no guard was placed, a score of black-clad figures went scrabbling for position, covering us with their long bows as they went. Before them, drumming on the bridge as they rode through, another troop of armed men, and behind them from the woods, shouts and cries, my men, no doubt surprised as they waited at the forest edge.

The leader reined his horse to a jarring stop, setting the rest in the yard there starting with fear. The French envoys had drawn their men around their fallen comrade, swords out, shields locked against the flight of arrows overhead. Geoffrey was already at my side, Raoul at the other, his only weapon a dagger he had snatched from Geoffrey as he came. And in the center of the courtyard Sir Brian lay in his own blood.

The leader, a knight, heavily armed, his helmet low, sword

swinging, cried out his challenge as he came on. It echoed eerily through the empty yards and stalls, for he had not yet understood that all of Sedgemont was gathered here. And the cry he used sounded even more strange: "The Lord of Sedgemont, the Lord of Sedgemont. Behold him here."

With that he slipped off his helmet and we saw him clear: Lord Guy of Maneth, back from France to make good his claim.

"By God," Raoul said, "how came this weasel slinking back? Ann, get you behind me."

"In the king's name, the king's name," the French knights shouted, making a shield wall to cover their man although he was as dead already, his throat torn half-apart that would have uttered such sweet words.

"I come at right time, then," cried Guy of Maneth, his quick glance taking in all before him, three separate tableaux that revolved around three separate groups: the French knights ready to ride forth; Sir Brian and his womenfolk; Raoul and I and Geoffrey at one side, alone. I bit my knuckle through that I had been so thoughtless not to have considered him. But no one had. Even the French were bewildered by his presence. And Raoul's main concern was to protect me.

"Bind me that man," Maneth shouted, "nay, that one," as they lunged first at Geoffrey, who beat them back with his sword.

"My lord, my lord," Geoffrey cried in turn, throwing it hilt first to Raoul. But it was too late. There were too many of Maneth's scum and some had already run round behind them both, so that they were drawn together back-to-back and overpowered. I tried to force my horse upon them, but was afraid of trampling Raoul underneath, and before I could wheel free, Lord Guy himself had cut off my escape and his men had no difficulty in pulling me from the saddle. The French envoys still stood in their solid mass, but they were outnumbered and they knew it, although they continued to shout out defiance, threats, outrage. And by Sir Brian's body, there in the center courtyard, without protection at all, the Lady Mildred knelt, dry eyed with her women, and prayed.

"So," said Lord Guy above the cries—I heard the smirk of satisfaction in his voice, "I, too, come in the name of the king. See you here his seal."

He waved a parchment roll that he had pulled from his belt and thrust it toward the French envoys. "Henry of Anjou is king. I left him but a week ago at the French coast. Already will he have come to England for his coronation. And to me, his loyal ally, has he given deeds and rights to Sedgemont. Lord am I of Sedgemont and its castle and all its lands. Gag me that man here." He motioned toward Geoffrey, who was mouthing obscenities. "Or better yet, string him alongside his master there."

"Then are we all King Henry's men," said one of the French envoys, as he detached himself from the group; a brave man he was to step outside their shield wall. Yet I think had not one of those first arrows taken their fellow by accident, they would not have moved at all. They had no part in these petty disputes. You saw it writ upon their faces, how they moved and talked among themselves. No doubt, they would as soon a stranger killed Raoul as they themselves, provided they saw the job done cleanly. But then, my men and I were also unknown to them. Innocent bystanders we may have seemed, caught up in some other quarrel. They had no wish to be held responsible for us.

The Frenchman was stout and broad-shouldered, yes, brave in truth, to shout defiance at this mounted knight and all his men.

"In the king's name, I bid you hold. This outrage must be accounted for. Two men slain without cause, and one a spokesman for the king himself. How answer you that?"

"Sir Gautier," Lord Guy said—how well I remembered that voice—"I did not recognize you at first, nor your companions, so far from home. Nor you me, I think. But you know me in France these past months. I have been much at the king's court there, am newly come from Maneth, where I have called out my men along the border posts that have been my charge to keep the peace." How smoothly he lied, how glibly talked. "This is an ill day's work. Come we together, now, at our leisure to discuss it. These Celtic bowmen are too quick-fingered. My quarrel is not with you."

"Some English scum," the other French knight said softly, coming slowly forward himself now, "about some dirty business of his own, feathering his own nest before time no doubt. The devil shall pay for this."

"In time, in time," Sir Gautier said, hardly moving his lips. But it was clear to me, he meant in time that was safe for them.

"I have long been searching for this Raoul of Sedgemont," Guy said, twisting his mouth at the name as if to disdain the speaking of it. "Pretender to these lands, traitor to the king, in France, as here, murderer of my own son."

He leaned down from his horse, beckoning his men to drag Raoul closer.

"Murderer and traitor both," he snarled, and with his mailed fist he smote him on the face, laying open the flesh to the bone in a long red slash.

He will kill him where he stands, I thought in agony. And not one of them here will raise a hand to help him, although he is their prisoner.

There was a muttering at the blow, Geoffrey straining at the gag that bound him; even the French stared, still standing in their circle, apart from the rest of us.

"Murderer yourself," I cried, shaking off the grip of the men who held me, standing out so that all could see me. "Craven coward who dares not fight openly with armed men, only by stealth, in secret."

"Ann of Cambray," he said, "I told you, you would rue my return."

"And you thought to see us dead before it," I taunted. "We have lived this long in your despite."

"He will be dead before nightfall," he said, gesturing to

Raoul. "This time you can be sure of it. You shall watch it yourself."

"You know this woman then?" the French knight, Sir Gautier, asked. "How comes she here by chance at this time?"

"By chance as the devil gives her leave to roam," he said again. "Or to save her paramour, shield him behind her skirts. Never raise your voice at me."

He reined back as Raoul, too, shook off his captors and, bound as he was, made a leap across the cobbled stones. As Maneth's men knocked him to the ground, he still had strength to shout at me, "Say nothing." But I paid him no heed either, except to watch they did not beat him to a pulp before our eyes.

"So with your leave, my lords," Lord Guy continued as if we had not interrupted him, "I will take this Raoul from off your hands, since I hold the same commission as you. As Lord of Sedgemont, none, I think, will doubt my right to justice on my own lands, against my own enemies. He has merited death of me a thousandfold."

"That was not our order, my lord," Sir Gautier said hesitatingly. I caught the hesitation, as it struggled with caution. "We hold the king's writ. By the Treaty of Westminster is the castle of Sedgemont declared illegally built, its former master deposed of all his titles and lands, a prisoner of the king's pleasure."

On his big square face with its clipped beard and mustache, indecision sat almost comically. Yet grief struggled there, too.

"So are you saved a chore, my lords," Lord Guy began, "that I have taken him for just punishment. . . ."

"Not as just as you deserve," I cried again. "Note him well, lords, who killed my father and my brother both, who would have had me killed here in this castle, who sent the same cur to snatch me from a convent, with money yet to buy me from a holy place. Who boasted of this all when he took me in a secret raid. Whose son would have raped me before his men, had not Lord Raoul slain him justly. Where is the justice to right me all these wrongs? Will the king grant me that?"

I saw they were all watching me: the French, Raoul, with the blood still trickling on his bruised face; even Guy of Maneth paled beneath my accusations. And as the torrent of words fell, I felt prayers rising as I spoke, yet I never knew that I was praying. And never had God so put it into my mind words to say.

"This is the man," I said, "who would have married me to his son and yet have bred me himself that he might have an heir of my house to inherit my lands at Cambray." I heard Raoul groan. I had never spoken of that to him. "Claimant to Sedgemont, my lords! Look to his letters there, that he be not lying again, or has not changed vague promises into deeds. What king would support a man like this, who has ravaged all the lands about his own that he must now prey on other men's. I do not fear death, my lords. I have told him to his face. But death does not have to come in such shameful guise, wrought by the malice of liars and cowards both."

There was another murmur at that.

"She lies," Lord Guy muttered, white with rage or fear. "Who talks of murder? Ask her how my messenger was struck down. Ask how my son was killed if not within her arms."

There was an uneasy stir. The French were already whispering among themselves. They would make a break for the safety of the keep and leave us to our own disputes. Whatever quarrels were here were no concern of theirs; whatever fate Lord Guy could think up for us would be our misfortune. I must hold their attention still. Although they did not know it, they were the best hope we had for the moment. Raoul saw it too. I saw him nod at me, although the blood splattered as he moved.

"Ask what your son would have done to me," I cried, although I never thought to speak of it. "To dishonor me like a beast. Death came easy for such shame."

"Then shall it not come easy for you both," Lord Guy cried. "A rope and a long fall to make you twist and wish for death. And you shall toss dice which one will watch the other first."

"God help us all," I heard a woman moan. Was it the Lady Mildred who cried out at last?

"Yes," I said, standing stiff, feeling Raoul's cuts as if scored upon my own flesh, "God help us all if the king's law will not. Here is the avowed enemy of my house. If this new king, who loves maidens so, will not befriend me, what man will answer for me here?"

"Let God decide." Raoul's voice rang out as clear, although the blood ran from his mouth as he spoke. "I claim a Judgment of God."

There was a cry at that, even Lord Guy of Maneth cried aloud and dropped his shield arm. And all about, confusion swelled as man turned to man, to whisper and repeat.

Well, we live in an age of faith, and Raoul had evoked the oldest privilege there is, known throughout Christendom. Greater than any lord's justice it is, yea, greater than any king's. It reaches up to Heaven, beyond the scope of men. It is an awesome choice—God speaking through blood and death— to reveal the innocent, punish the guilty. By victory or defeat in battle to the death between these two men would our lives be decided. As champion, Raoul would live or die on my behalf as well. Yet, God, I know, had put it into his mind to claim it.

I shut my eyes to avoid the thought that God had also power to use it for our own defeat. Not yet, Oh God, do not use it to punish us yet, I prayed.

I could not have closed my eyes a second's space. Yet, when I opened them, all was changed. While I stood brooding on the awesome choice, there had been others who were quick to take advantage of the confusion. Even before the words had finished their echoing, before the Celtic bowmen on the walls had time to train their long bows, men had leapt to Raoul's side, cutting him and Geoffrey free. Some had driven the womenfolk like cattle before them to the safety of the keep.

Raoul, in turn, had snatched at a weapon, and raced before me so I, too, could back with him, whilst the French phalanx, still in order with their shield wall high, in turn, came behind us. Within seconds then the situation was reversed. We were still outnumbered, but lined up on the steps, with the Lady Mildred and her women already scuttling inside, we had a wall at our backs, a refuge beyond. And if we were divided, it still not being clear on whose side the French would fight, yet they were less in number than we, and we still had more men without the walls if we could get to them.

Lord Guy knew he had lost the advantage that chance before had given him. He was too busy explaining and cajoling his own followers to try to recover it.

"We could attack now and have him at our mercy," I said, speaking my thoughts aloud.

"Perhaps," Raoul said as quietly at my side, and I felt his hand in mine, alive and warm, "but we still cannot count on the French to help us. Patience. His own men will do it for us."

We stood waiting whilst the argument flared about us in the courtyard. Maneth's men, I think, at least the mounted knights who rode with him, would have ignored the import of the challenge, but the bowmen on the walls were another matter. I knew what they would be saying. We borderfolk think alike; and a Judgment of God is strange to us, strange yet binding, for we are more superstitious than the Normans, although it is their law, not ours. Maneth's Welsh bowmen, whom he needed to control the central court, would no more fight now than argue with a priest on matters of faith.

"Ann," Raoul said, his words like a breath of air, "shall I unsay what I have said? It is your life as well as mine."

"No," I whispered back, and felt the strength from him flow into me as my determination flowed back to him. "They will not dare speak against it. It is the only chance you have for a fair fight."

"They will know that we are linked together," he said. "They will suspect you."

"I know that, too," I said, suddenly turning and smiling, "so first I must convince you that that is what I wish. If God has brought us together again, perhaps he will keep us yet awhile."

"I wanted no more deaths upon my hands," he said, nodding to the courtyard, his face still taut, streaked with blood and dirt, and I knew he thought of Sir Brian lying there alone.

"You fight to avenge one more," I said. "My lord, you cannot be rid so easily of us yet awhile. We need you." And I smiled at him.

He gave a sound, half-groan, half-laugh, sleeving the blood from his cut mouth. "My God," he said, "you cling like one of your western burrs. Go you within and comfort the other womenfolk. I will come to you when I can."

I would have cried again to take care, but dared not. For I saw how the light had come back into his eyes, although his face was still strained with pain and grief. And I saw how the men I had brought from Cambray turned and closed behind him as he went toward the Frenchmen on the stairs. Someone had given him both sword and shield. He was Lord of Sedgemont again. I had no need to fear for him yet awhile.

When it was clear to me what must happen next—either that Lord Guy must retreat without the castle walls, being unable to control his men, half of whom I now saw must have come with him from France and were as contemptuous of his border people as the Celts were of them, or, as seemed most likely, he must abide by the judgment he had called upon his own head—I, too, retreated up the stairs.

Sedgemont is not built like Cambray, and these stairs are too wide to be guarded easily. But the Great Hall is designed for defense, with massive doors and window slits that give down upon the stairwell. And, in the morning, not standing on ceremony as happens now, would the two men fight each other. To the death. But now we had the night, which an hour ago we had not thought to see.

And the French, not so much bemused as relieved, were willing to let the process take place, having no way in their power now to turn it aside. They hammered their moral advantage home. All arms were to be laid down. There was to be no fighting without the gates. Except for the French, only the combatants were to carry weapons. The soft French lisped about my ears, yet I noted how the more they spoke, the more pompous rolled the words, the more precise the instructions, all in the name of the king.

Well, king he is in name and deed by now, I thought as I went up the last steps, more tired than I knew, but he may be surprised what has been done in his name today.

The other women were already setting the hall to rights as best they could, giving orders to the frightened servants who had remained to prepare something for us to eat, trying to bring order to the confusion. Like Cambray, Sedgemont looked as if it had suffered a siege, and men presently came to drag out the heavy tables and benches to form a barricade along the doors. We all worked feverishly, leaving nothing to chance, and, at the last, when the dead bodies of the French knight and Sir Brian had been brought up and set in a corner chamber, wrapped in their cloaks, I went to where the Lady Mildred sat and knelt beside her to keep watch with her.

She said nothing to me, gave me no word or look, but when the other men finally came up and barred the doors, she rose from her place, brought warm water and cloths to wash Lord Raoul's wounds, and bade the men to table although the fare was scanty at best.

Lord Raoul sat in his usual place in the great carved chair, and I sat at his right and the French envoys, silent now, to our left. We spoke but little, it still being to our advantage to keep up some semblance of unfamiliarity as I noticed Geoffrey and his men did, as if they did not know Lord Raoul, but when we drank from the common cup, I noted how Lord Raoul raised it to toast me and placed his lips for courtesy over the rim where I had pressed mine. And when the food was done, he called for a lute,. which I had never heard him play before, and sang himself, such songs from France that made our hearts both sad and gay at once. They were songs, I think, that once Sir Brian, in his youth, had loved, and he played to do his old henchman honor, that like a Norseman of the olden times he might be remembered and honored in the Hall that he had guarded so well.

No one dared to sleep that night. I joined the Lady Mildred and the other women at the death watch, and when there was time to whisper, drew such comfort as I could from Cecile, who watched with us. In the young hours of the morning, Lord Raoul came himself, bringing a taper that he bent to light from mine. His face was expressionless as he stood there looking down at the body of a man who had been as father, adviser, friend to him all his life, whose last thought perhaps, as he had moved into the arrow's path, was to protect Raoul. I knew that look now, beneath it he hid all those thoughts he did not dare reveal. And yet it seemed to me that to a man like Sir Brian, there could be no more-fitting end. It was one he would have wished for himself.

"Yet I hoped to avoid this," Lord Raoul's voice, when he spoke, reflected strangely my own thoughts, "another senseless death that most of all I would prevent. He begged me, Ann, to close the gates and fight. 'Better death than dishonor,' he said. I would not answer him, reminded him of his age, of his wife. You see how even our best intentions trap us." He sighed, his face half-hidden in the shadows. "And now once more, despite all my efforts, our lives are bound as one. If I fall, Ann, your life will be forfeit as well."

"And as you live," I said, "so shall I."

"Yes," he said, not boastingly, "I shall kill him for you. But

I would have you leave before. Tomorrow at dawn, before we can begin, we shall send word to your men outside. Geoffrey will know what to do."

"Raoul," I said, "have I not told you clearly or often enough? Without you, I care little what happens to me. Come with me then."

He said nothing in reply. His silence gave me heart to continue.

"Westward," I said, "there are ships that could bear us far away. Beyond France even, where people know nothing of these Angevins, these civil wars. I heard you speak before of Outremer. We could go there together."

After a while he moved beside me, flexing his hand along the wall so that the shadow of his fingers spread against the rough surface.

"It would only be a dream," he said. "Your father knew what is the lot of a landless man. Remember, you told me of your old soldier in the ruined fort, how you could have wept for his broken strength. And a woman at any army's tail, her fate is far, far worse. You could not come with me. And I will not run away."

"Then let me go to the king," I said. "That is what I hoped to do."

"I will not beg for my life," he said. That stubborn, bitter pride. He said abruptly, "Was it true, then, what they planned? Was Maneth a monster so vile?"

I felt the tension in him as he spoke. I did not want to speak or remember it.

"And the messenger who was killed, was that true also?"

I said, "I never spoke of it for shame, for guilt. He would have possessed me and so ran upon the knife point. I would not have spoken of it even now. But you know yourself that I was virtuous when I came to Cambray."

"Yes," he said. He did not move. "And is that all? Are there any secrets else? I would not have lies, half-lies, concealed between us. We bear the weight of too many things, too many misunderstandings. . . ."

I should have told him then the secret that most concerned him. Why kept I quiet? Because I feared I might yet be mistaken? Because it seemed unfair burden on him when he was so much under stress? Or because he, most of all men, would have a son to be proud of?

"Then," he said, "Maneth doubly deserves to die. Else will he spread those stories of your ill fame to the world to do you harm. After, shall you leave, go to where we can keep you safe. Do not fret for me. Now think. How many men have we to command?"

He numbered them aloud as I named them to prevent my speaking of these other matters, forming his plan. Geoffrey and his men made ten, but they would be unarmed. There were ten more outside, however, who would have weapons to spare, would know how to help at the right time. Ten French under their two captains, armed. Maneth's men three times as many, and bowmen on the walls, but all disorganized, perhaps unarmed if they came into the courtyard.

"Ann," he said, "we whisper here in a holy place beside the dead. God knows, I have not been a believing man, but something of your faith has come to give me hope. How often have we parted never to meet again? Perhaps there is a way out of this maze if only we know the secret. Stand watch for me beside the Lady Mildred, pray for me." He suddenly smiled. "Look not so worried, *ma mie*. This Maneth is a fighter, too. Like a cautious soldier, I go to find out how he fights, to see what my men know of him and his ways. Do not be afraid. He will not escape us this time. You shall see him fall. I fight for you, and Sir Brian and all our wrongs."

I stayed beside the bier, felt his fingers brush lightly against my hair, heard his soft footsteps retreat. Beneath the shelter of my hands, I saw how he stopped, as if by chance, to speak casually with this man and that. Perhaps he was planning his battle strategy, but I knew as well as if I listened with them that he was also arranging for my escape. Whether I would or not, he would have me gone the next day. Alone. He would not come with me. He would fight Maneth and then go to his own death with the French. Nothing I could do would change him. He would not run away himself.

I knelt and tried to pray, but I almost did not know for what I prayed. Thoughts swirled through my head like those western mists that had surrounded us all day. What would happen with the morning? What would become of Raoul? How could I save him, despite himself? It seemed to me then that we were so bound up that nothing could untangle us from the frets of our own actions, our own desires. We had become so much a part of those greater events that I had thought to avoid, that only when they were resolved would we be free of them and able to make a real peace with each other.

I knelt and prayed. But it was not for the death of that one man whose hatred had so bedeviled us all these years. Rather, I prayed that God, in His mercy, would spare Raoul, find some way to rescue him. Otherwise, it mattered not if he died at Maneth's hands tomorrow in his own courtyard, or if the French killed him in the forest quietly without witness. I, too, must die with him. But it was not our lives only. One other life was bound up with his and mine—our child's. If Raoul should not live, then tomorrow we all should die, too, or thereafter. Not all the sins in the wide world can demand the death of innocence. . . . Yet our child was the fruit of sin, of lust, and who knows what payment that requires.

"Spare Raoul," I found my lips repeating as I watched by Sir Brian's corpse. "Spare him and so spare us. I will not ask anything else."

God listens to prayers, judges us. I tell you, He requites what is required of Him. Now shall you hear how Raoul paid for his sins and mine.

12

HE MORNING CAME. TIME, WHICH AT Sedgemont had once dragged, now raced toward me. I felt as gray as the day that unfolded about us, without light, overshadowed with mist and sleet. There had been flurries of snow throughout the night, and the great courtyard was covered with a thin layer of ice. Guy of Maneth, who had camped with his men in the yard, must have rested hard, too.

Before dawn, the Sedgemont servants were dragging out benches to make a barricade and places for the spectators to watch. The French carefully supervised this; their men stood guard, heavily armed, although there were not many of them, and watched the piles of swords and knives grow at their feet. No one passed in or out of the great courtyard unless he laid his weapons by, but the gates still stood open, for Maneth's men controlled the outer walls. Along one wall facing the keep, an extra row of seats was built for the French envoys and for the ladies of Sedgemont. Today, such trials-by-combat are more elaborate, the time and place are carefully chosen, the combatants are kept apart and closely watched, but the spectators still come as to enjoy a circus. This was more rough-and-ready, but although the French were concerned about the lack of ceremony, Raoul, as challenger, had the right to set their rules aside. And, in truth, it used to be more a French custom, known but seldom practiced amongst us here. As for the Celts, I have told you we hold it in the utmost veneration and fear, thinking only a strong man, firm in his belief, would dare invoke it.

Raoul of Sedgemont, they called him thus, those arrogant French lords, without title or rank, Raoul of Sedgemont had the right to choose the weapon, the mode of battle. Never looked he more a lord than that day when he trod the arena they had built in his courtyard, tall, and lithe, only the bruises on his face and arms, the long slash on his cheek, to show what had happened the day before. I was appalled when I heard his choice: with sword and shield, on foot. I had thought he would ride his great black horse, come sweeping down from his upright stance to knock his enemy from his saddle with one swift blow. But Geoffrey comforted me. The ground was too short, he explained, the turning space too limited for that kind of maneuvering, and the ice had made the stones too slippery to manage horse and shield and lance. But on foot, neither man would have the advantage, or rather, since Raoul was young and fast, he would not tire so easily.

This comforted me until I thought of the disadvantages. "For Maneth is older, experienced," I cried aloud, "I remember how my father said he was a strong man in a fight. . . ."

"Nay, lady," Geoffrey comforted me, and even in my distress, I noticed how he stood always at my side, no doubt as Raoul had bidden him, "my lord is as an eel, you will see for yourself. Maneth will not get close to him."

There was no more time to brood. Now was the hour when we must all go forth to watch. Yet, before we went, the Lady Mildred came to me herself and took me by the arm to the women's room. There, with her ladies, she helped me prepare myself, combing and braiding my hair and changing my gown for another.

"It is one of mine," Cecile said, tears of mirth and anguish mingling. "Ever before you have returned them in shreds. Pray God it keep you safe."

I embraced her without words, standing there among them

as it seemed to me I had done years ago. But this time death himself waited for us outside.

"Hasten," Lady Mildred said, as if this were an everyday affair. "There are times one must show all men what we are made of. If the Lord of Sedgemont goes forth, then honor is due to him through us. So shall we all dress, ladies, although we perish of the cold, that no man need say we do not know what is fitting." True to the end, did she exhort us in courtly ways. But before we went out to the courtyard, she drew me aside and flung a long, furred robe about my shoulders. Of great value it was and old.

"The day is cold," she said, her eyes fierce with unshed tears. "I would not have you tremble with the cold, Lady Ann." And she curtsied.

For the first time ever had she acknowledged me, who had been part instrument in her husband's death, who might yet kill her liege lord and mine. At that moment, I longed for words to tell her how, despite all the griefs I had caused her, I, too, knew how to value her and all her services. But the moment passed too long in silence; I made her a curtsy, the first I think I had ever given her.

"Come then, Lady Ann of Cambray," she said, and her dry hand was firm upon mine like withered parchment, like steel. "In God's name go we forth and see justice done for all your wrongs."

It was perhaps already two hours from noon and yet the day was dark as if new risen. The men had swept most of the snow away and scattered straw about. At one end, a fire had been lit to give heat and light. Most of the men stood behind the barricades that had been raised along the sides. I noted quickly, as I took my place on the bench, how the Cambray men seemed to have scattered through the crowd, how some lingered at the open gate. I glanced upon the battlements, but to my surprise they were empty, the Celtic bowmen having left their post to come into the yard. Maneth, I thought, could no better control his men than he could his son. It must have been against his orders that they left the gate and courtyard unguarded. Yet, except for the French envoys and their guard, only the two combatants were armed. I watched as Raoul came forward, saw how his men had polished his shield until the hawks of Sedgemont flared upon it, how his mail shone about him.

Yet it was the Lady Mildred herself who buckled his sword belt in place, her thin fingers so nimble with silk and thread now fumbling with the heavy straps. Raoul stood by patiently until she was through, settled belt and sword against his thigh, and led her gently back to her seat. Then he waited, below us, his sword flashing once as he drew it on command. Lord Guy was dressed in his long mail coat, no device upon his shield, no color to him at all, a death figure as he loomed out of the mist. I remembered, in that way we have of thinking of little things, how once they had measured against each other here in the Hall of Sedgemont, the older man, an oak tree, seamed and powerful, the younger pliant, a sapling, yet both of a height, both strong.

The French envoy was on his feet. When he spoke fast, as he did now, the cold whipping beneath his short cloak to make him shiver, I could not follow all his speech, but it sounded well enough. The older man, Sir Gautier, gave the signal. And in the silence that followed the first clash of sword blades was a lightning flash, almost blinding, almost unlooked for.

I could not take my eyes from the two men below. They stood a sword thrust apart and hammered at each other, stroke upon stroke, until you felt their arms must falter from it, stroke upon shield until the echo ran back. I sat there wrapped in the cloak of some lady of Sedgemont, and felt the heir of Sedgemont safe beneath my folded arms, and watched its lord batter and heave and strike until the sweat ran down my cheeks and my hands were wet with it.

Stroke upon stroke, parry and thrust. Neither man yielded

ground, neither bent under the blow. Yet, gradually, almost imperceptibly at first, I saw how Raoul had changed the beat, altering his attack, no two strikes alike now, each falling from a different angle, an unexpected slant. His body swayed and dipped with each movement that he made, and his feet turned and pivoted upon the slippery stones. How could he move and bend as if the pull of that heavy mail coat, reaching to his knees, had no weight?

Guy of Maneth had to retreat now. Step by step, he was forced back out of the central court into a corner where the light was dim, where he would have his back to the fire outside the barricade. Now all of us could sense the changing rhythm, faster, both men not striking as one but one striking, the other parrying. There was a hiss, a long breath held too long, as Raoul missed a low slash, stooped to avoid the return, drove on as before. There was another cry, even Cambray men cried out, for Maneth had slipped upon a loose paving stone, or was it where the ice had formed again, and for a moment tottered off balance.

"Strike, strike," I heard Geoffrey whisper at my back. But Raoul did not strike then; he waited until the older man had recovered his balance before the restless beat began again.

Maneth was tiring. You could see his uneasiness. From time to time he shook his head as a bull does when it is baited, and his small eyes cast their restless look from side to side, the furtive look I remembered so well, so that he might estimate where he was and escape from the corner where Raoul was penning him. He had come close now to the barricade at the farthest side from the gate. His black shield rang dully, in places hammered so out of shape that the blows were not deflected but slid at angles toward him. You could hear the panting, too, both men were panting, but Maneth's was louder, almost sobbing for air. You sensed that the end of his endurance was near.

Then, although I was watching with the rest, I know not

how it happened, then he seemed to brush across the barricade. Someone gave cry of warning. Guessing what Maneth was about to do, Raoul tried to duck. Bits and pieces of debris left by the firemakers came flying through the air, for a moment blinding Raoul. It was a second's distraction only, but it was enough. Maneth lunged at him, thrusting at him viciously, his sword falling straight down. Again there was a cry; even the French knights stood up and cried aloud and so did I. For with that thrust, Maneth had driven through Raoul's guard, slashed down across him so that, for a moment, he seemed to fold in upon himself, cutting through shoulder to the bone, rending sword arm useless.

It had been a massive stroke and Maneth had put all his energy into it so that he, too, had to lean a space to catch his breath. For only Raoul's quickness had prevented him from being torn apart. As it was, his right arm hung limply, the sword tip almost touching the ground. You could see the torn gap in the mail coat where the blade had caught and ripped the woven rings of steel across his shoulder and side, and pierced the leather undercoat, so that flesh and linen shirt flared white to scarlet, and even as he stood, the ground at his feet splashed red. I willed my eyes to shut, willed that I not see the rest, and felt my nails dig into the hands that caught at me on either side to hold me upright on my feet. I willed myself not to see and I did not see.

It was Geoffrey's roar of pleasure, disbelief, that gave me sight back. Somehow, as they had watched, that drooping figure had changed his sword and shield. How had he done it, with one easy practiced motion, throwing heavy shield to the right, catching sword hilt in his uninjured left hand. The shouts came to a crescendo then, each man turning to his neighbor, the French shouting out as loud as any.

Two-Handed Raoul. Was not that what his men called him?

"Strike, my lord, strike now," Geoffrey was shouting, not whispering, and the other men cried out aloud as once more

Raoul's sword beat out its heavy sound, faster than ever upon Maneth's shield. But the rhythm had to be fast. With every step, the blood flowed. You could see the stain of it on the ground like red hawks falling. He kept his shield arm tight against his wounded side, so that it must have acted as a pad to stem the first heavy flow, but that would not serve him long.

"Faster, faster," Geoffrey cried again, for that was Raoul's only chance, to strike whilst he had the strength before loss of blood stopped him. Maneth dropped backward, was trying to keep his shield in place to fend off the blows that fell again from unexpected quarter, being driven once more in a corner where he could not swing his sword, where he could not move. But he had only to stay hunched beneath his shield and he was safe.

Then suddenly, so quickly that the eye could not remember what it saw, Raoul leaped in that beautiful, controlled way he had. Somehow his shield swung up, knocking Maneth's from his grasp so that both clattered away to the side.

For a moment, both men were latched together, then Raoul stepped back. His left arm straightened, sliced through and out. As he drew the blade forth, the black hulk of Maneth seemed to hover above him. Then it toppled slowly forward, falling as it seems all dead men fall, like empty clothes, like rags. There was only one man on his feet, and on the ground, a black thing clawed and writhed to silence. And a vast humming filled the air as if all the watchers at once had drawn breath. Raoul half-turned. Even from this distance I could see the sweat on his forehead, the matted curls, the red cut that glistened against his white face as he pushed back his helmet with his uninjured arm. He held up his sword hilt so that it glittered in the firelight, tried to say something, sank upon one knee. The blood spilled out and he, too, fell upon the ground, face forward.

I stood as stone, still clutching at the Lady Mildred and

Cecile's hands as to safety. My voice when I spoke was as stone. I did not know the words I said, not thinking, not knowing.

"Geoffrey," I said, "what Lord Raoul bade you do for me, do you now for him. At my command."

It is to Geoffrey's credit that he did not hesitate. Before I had finished speaking, he had vaulted from the bench where we sat and crossed the courtyard. A strange cry floated out— I had heard it before—and at the gate, mounted men appeared, thundering in upon us, striking back the French, who tried to head them off.

Among the crowd, each of our men turned as at a signal. Some stood and chatted with arms thrown across the shoulders of their neighbors. Some argued with them violently to distract them. Two others came running with a makeshift stretcher, while a third, having snatched a sword as his comrades rode by, stood guard above Lord Raoul.

As numb as stone, I turned to the French envoys on their feet before us.

"By God," Sir Gautier said, shaken from his usual aplomb. "I did not know he had men without. I did not think that he could win."

"My lord," I said, leaning toward him, smiling, that men afterward should say I laughed and smiled while my dear lord lay wounded before my eyes. "You did not think they would leave without him."

On the other side, Cecile had thrown her arms about the second knight so that he could not break free.

"What happens next, my lord?" she cried. "I am so afraid. Is he dead?" And she made him look to where the body of Maneth lay with some of his men about it, but it was clear he would never move again.

The Cambray men had made their turn of the courtyard. Where they could, their companions in the crowd had jumped behind them, both men striking on either side to keep the rest

back from Lord Raoul. Geoffrey and two others had stripped
off his armor, had put some clamp about the wounds, were
bearing him at a run toward the gate. As we watched, they
hoisted him in front of a horseman who waited there, the
others thundered out again. Using Lord Raoul's bloodstained
sword, Geoffrey single-handed beat back the French guard,
snatched at the last bridle as the horsemen went by, and swung
himself up and away. The French gave a great shout of anger,
thrusting us from their side. Before they could give the word
to mount and follow, the Lady Mildred herself stood before
them.

"It is God's will," she said, her voice carrying like flint through
the noise.

Sir Gautier bit his lip for rage.

"Aye, madame, in this case. Both he and this lady here are
safe. He was not dead when he fell. And he was alive when
they put him on that horse. But he is still our prisoner. . . ."

"Praise God for mercy," I said, and swooned across them,
so that they were forced to catch me when all their energies
should rather have been to raise the pursuit after. Men have
eyed me askance for that ever since, thinking it but pretense.

I regained consciousness to have the Lady Mildred patting
my hands, and Cecile bathing my face, whilst the French men
raged and swore at the delay. Sir Gautier himself still stood
beside me, looking down with an expression hard to understand. He said something that I could not follow, then turned
sharply away, leaving me to the ministrations of my ladies,
who, half in tears, half-overjoyed, did not know whether to
follow my example or take to their heels and run. Struggling
to my feet, I helped the Lady Mildred steady them and draw
them back into the shelter of the Hall, leaving Cecile to keep
watch to report all that happened next.

We did not have long to wait. Presently, the men came
straggling in, a few of ours, some with cuts and slight wounds
that had hampered them, some of Maneth's men, the rest of

the French driven back from a fruitless search by the lack of trails to follow, the failing light, and the worsening weather, which had coated them and their tired horses with a thick layer of snow. Once more the weary servants dragged themselves to prepare food for this strange group of men, no one knowing who was friend, who foe. I moved among them, binding cuts and stanching blood as best I could, gleaning the last details of news. It was clear at least that Raoul and his men had gained the shelter and safety of the forest before the French had been able to catch up with them. And that he lived, praise God, he lived. For even when the envoys had been free to shout their orders, those of our men left behind had so rushed to obey, knocking others over in their mock eagerness, that the disturbance they caused wasted even more time, making pursuit that much the slower.

Our men were part jubilant, part apprehensive, over the rescue. The plan had been simple and they had used it before. During the night it had not been difficult to send word to the men outside, and, as Raoul had once said, they all knew what to do. The lack of Maneth's bowmen on the walls had certainly been an unexpected benefit. (And they, knowing what they had done, terrified by the result of the combat, had for the most part already slipped outside the castle gates and were, no doubt, heading for the border as fast as they could go.)

But Raoul's injuries were severe. That, too, had not been expected, and although it was sure he was still alive when he left Sedgemont, I could guess their fears that he would not survive the buffeting of the ride, the cold and storm. To each of them I said what I prayed was true: "Have heart. He is young and has survived as bad wounds before. And had he not been wounded, we never would have got him away."

Cecile, when she came, half-blue from cold, could add but little more. The gates had been closed again and bolted up. Some guards had been set to watch the walls. Most of Maneth's men had gone. One or two older ones sat about the dead body of their lord and refused to move until he was given burial, which, as a tainted man, Church law would not admit. They alone showed him any honor. Cecile, too, reported how the Celtic bowmen had run off through the snow. As for those of Maneth's men who now came into the Hall, it was soon apparent that they were French, a scurvy lot who, no doubt, had joined Maneth in France in hope of loot and gain in England. They had no loyalty to him any more than to anyone, and would as soon serve with their fellow Frenchmen here.

"Have heart, Lady Ann," she said to me, echoing my own words, "no one knows what's to do. If we can but be rid of these French, who, we think, will be as glad as we to see themselves safely out of Sedgemont, we can put all to rights again, summon back the serfs who have not gone far, call back the Sedgemont guard. They are a match for any man." She smiled even as she worked to think how Geoffrey had shown such valor.

Last of all, the French envoys returned, bad-tempered, snarling with cold and rage. In one thing Cecile was correct. No Angevin has willingly set foot again in Sedgemont castle, and these were as anxious to be gone as she had said, had not the storm, which had been both hindrance and help to us, now closed about us in earnest. For two days longer it raged, fierce blizzards as I had never seen before, nor had these Frenchmen from more-southern parts, crossing themselves hourly against such devil's work.

And so another Yuletide came and went. All round so thick a blanket of snow lay that no man or horse could venture forth for fear of being sunk beneath the drifts. Even the beasts in the forest, wolves and bears, such as we have in the wildest parts, came starving out from the depths, and slunk about the frozen river's edge. At night, the howling of the wolves under the walls was as mournful as any souls lost to Paradise, and each evening, large flocks of dark-winged birds flew overhead, circling and circling with raucous note, omens of ill fortune.

So a Yuletide passed, and a New Year. In London, already Henry and his wife, Eleanor, had been crowned new king and queen. And we knew neither where Raoul of Sedgemont was nor if he lived or died.

During all this time I came to learn much of the French envoys; perforce, they were all the company we had. Their men were like any men-at-arms I have known, fond of good wine, good food, and merry and ribald songs, which, despite the presence of the unburied dead, we could not prevent.

Of the two remaining envoys, Sir Gautier was the ranking member; his younger friend was from the south, a slight man whose affected ways no doubt hid more resolution than he cared to show. This Sir Renier shivered the hours away, but Sir Gautier was hardheaded, cautious, alert, a man from Anjou. He was the first Angevin I had met and I tested him with as much caution. For already I was trying to plan ahead. I could not believe that Raoul would die, but even if he was alive, such wounds would take long to heal. What if in the meantime I tried to approach the king on his behalf? So these Frenchmen and I circled each other as dogs do, sizing each other up, although I am not sure how well I hid my intent, being new at the game.

The Lady Mildred kept the castle as before, although in a state of siege, as indeed we were, by the snow, if not by an enemy. But while we ate siege rations, she had them well served, courteously presented, as best she could, and insisted on decorous behavior in the Hall during our presence there. Since that was the only time I had chance to speak to either man, I was hard put to win their confidence enough to find out what I needed to know. But if the Lady Mildred held it sin to laugh and flirt with one's avowed enemy, she never said so to me.

It was Sir Gautier who told me most about the Angevins, how their earliest ancestor, Count Fulk the Black, had cast about on all sides to enlarge his estates a hundred years before, to give the Angevins their first taste of power. While still young, this count had had his wife burned before him as a witch. I noted the relish with which Sir Gautier rehearsed this tale—no doubt, he wished the same for me—but nodded and simpered as I ought. As an old man, this same Fulk had fought a bitter war against his son, whom, after defeat, he had forced to crawl before him, harnessed like a beast of burden. And so, he hinted, would their present king treat all his enemies.

"For thus are these Angevins," Sir Gautier said, "whom you would come to know. Wild men, Norsemen from the iceflows of their northern lands, who came with their long ships to burn and loot the French coast and, liking it enough, never left it again."

"But they were heathens, then, I think," I said, venturing softly forward, "and we are Christians now, not given to plundering and loot. Or murder."

Sir Renier gave a hoot of laughter. "She has you there," he said. "Lady, for culture and grace come you to the southern parts, to Aquitaine for example."

Sir Gautier sat in Raoul's chair and thoughtfully sipped his wine. I noticed that he did not drink as much as the younger men I have known, but nursed one cup the whole night through. Yet he was not so old for all that, his sleek hair showed no sign of gray, his beard was not yet grizzled, and his sharp eyes retained and hid all that he saw.

One night, desperate for news, torn between baring my fears to them, yet knowing that it might be death to Raoul if I did, I turned the conversation back again to what most concerned me. It was a conversation that both terrified and enticed me on. I think Sir Gautier guessed it, too, for much of what he said could be construed as warning, indirect, if not direct. Yet he did not know that this, too, cleared my thoughts, made me more certain of what I should do.

We were speaking of the French kingdom, divided, as we were not yet here in England, into many great feudal estates, with the king controlling little land of his own.

"What is this King of France," I asked, "that he should let his queen marry another man and become herself by now Queen of England?"

Both men looked at each other before they spoke.

"I will tell you one thing," Sir Renier said. "I know Paris well, having been there with Queen Eleanor, she who is now queen again. Angevins, such as our friend here, are feared at the French court. As for the French king, ask her who was his queen what to think."

"Are not the counts of Sieux as powerful?" I asked, greatly daring, but Sir Gautier replied easily enough. "It is not as great a fief as Anjou, but it is as old."

"Yet you would have taken prisoner the man who should be lord there," I said. Their silence again told me much.

"Lady Ann," Sir Gautier said. "We find ourselves trapped here with you, against our will, although I count it not so bad a fate." He smiled. "Remember I serve a master, and I have been given a commission that all those lands that have fallen into unlawful hands should be restored, their armies disbanded, their castles torn down."

"Restored to whom?" I cried. "Lord Raoul holds Sedgemont from his father and grandfather who was made earl by the first King Henry. He received no help from mercenaries. His men-at-arms were his own feudal levies. And as for the keep at Sedgemont, it is well known that his grandfather enlarged it at his king's command."

Both men shrugged. "And who claimed it before the Earl of Sedgemont?" Sir Renier asked, his lazy manner slipping for a second so that I caught a glimpse of the shrewdness he hid beneath.

"And Cambray," said Sir Gautier, his words denying his pretended ignorance, "do not many people dispute it? Are there not many lands along the border claimed by many people?"

"You should have asked Guy of Maneth that whilst you had

the chance," I said angrily. "I do not know details of this treaty you speak of, but I tell you, ask along the border who has plundered most, who seized most, who spread fear and desolation. It will not be Lord Raoul of Sedgemont. The name of Maneth is cursed among the border peoples. And God has struck him down."

"Well, Lady Ann," Sir Renier said at the end of my outburst, "I am not versed in English law as you can tell, but Lord Guy told a different story when he was with us in Anjou. Yet for all he said, I tell you I wish that Raoul of Sedgemont, or Sieux or how you wish to call him, were still here to show us how he managed that trick of his. I have seen men do it at practice, never in open fight."

"Look round you," I cried again, sensing how they would change the talk, being more willing to chat of war and arms, "is this the castle of a tyrant? Where be the torture rooms, the prison cells, the whips that Maneth's people have delighted in? Would men who hated their lord risk their lives to rescue him? I think you know more of the affairs of Sedgemont than you care to admit, my lords."

"And you more about this Raoul of Sedgemont than you would have me believe." Sir Gautier's voice was sharp. "Lady Ann, if I may, I will give you advice. It is not always wise to tell all you know, any more than it is seemly to guess at things that are managed far above us. I have not made any great inquiries into the reasons for your presence here. You should show us like courtesy since we seem to be fated to remain here together for a while."

"You would have killed him," I cried again. "Would you deny it? On what grounds?"

Their silence answered me. Yet when he spoke again, Sir Gautier was calm, seeking neither to explain nor to deny.

"It is not my place to comment on that," he said. "I am an envoy of a king. But I will tell you that there was much in that Raoul to admire. Had we met at any other time, I would have known him."

"And, by Jesu," Sir Renier said, showing more enthusiasm than I had seen before, "he had courage. I would have learned much from him. But his name was writ, my lady. We do but carry out the orders of our king."

"Then are you both murderers," I said, "like him who lies unmourned, unburied, in the courtyard below. No king's law can give you license to kill. No king is king who murders as he takes the crown."

Sir Gautier's face changed color; I think beneath his dark beard he might even have blushed. Yet he did not lose his temper as Raoul would have done.

"Those are harsh words, lady," was all he said.

"Then heed them," I said, "lest all of England cry as much. Come, ladies," I stood up and called to the other women, taking precedence for the first time over the Lady Mildred, who followed me without word, "this is no place for us." We swept from the room, leaving them sitting there.

Yet all this while it was Cecile who gave me hope, taking my hands between her own as we sat packing and repacking the things that we prepared to carry to the men in hiding, if they should send word to us.

"For look, my lady," she said, in her simple artless way, "if you shame them, then they will begin to doubt the rightness of their work. Time is what you need to bend the ear of other great lords to save Sedgemont. Then will even these French speak on our behalf."

"No," I said, miserable with cold and anxiety, and a sickliness that I had never known before that welled up in me from time to time. "I cannot force them to what their office will not allow. I must woo them to it, and I am too rough. I wish I had the Lady Mildred's courtesies. They are worth more than my harsh truths."

"Perhaps not," she said unexpectedly, taking the things I had folded and refolded, sorting out those most needful, putting in the herbs and potions a wounded man would require. "God helps those who help themselves. Have patience. Geoffrey will send word. Then can you plan where to go on from here."

A scratching at my door that night brought me wide awake. I heard Cecile run across the floor and whisper at the crack. A castle servant slipping in with wood brought news. If during the darkness we could send food and supplies, a serf waited at the forest edge to guide the way to where Raoul lived, hidden but in great want. I threw on my clothes, Cecile beside me in tears that I should not go alone.

"I shall be back at dawn, you silly child," I said, for so her hysterics made her seem, although when held to the work, as I had seen happen in need, she could be as steady as any.

"I must confer with him, with Geoffrey, decide what we must do. There is no danger. No one will see me slip out. I have done so a hundred times. I am only frightened that the thaw will give our guests thoughts of leaving. Listen." We could hear the dripping of the snow as it began to melt. "You must watch for me, and if they are up betimes, prepare to leave with them."

"Leave?" She gasped. "Where are we going? I cannot. . . ."

"Yes, you can," I said. "You knew what to do after Maneth's death. You can find the way, the courage. Choose the best horses, the fastest, strongest. Choose three men from those left, the best recovered, most stouthearted. Prepare food, warm clothing. And yourself."

"I cannot," she said. "Before, it was to save Geoffrey. That seemed easy."

If there had been time, I would have smiled at her ingeniousness.

"Then think you do it for him again," I said. "Would you have him live an outlaw all his youth?"

"But why me?" She ran behind me as I hurried to the little staircase where once I had hidden and listened to Gwendyth's killers as they passed by. I had never gone there since. Now I ran past the steps as stealthily, laden with a basket of food, wine, and warm clothes for the men.

"Because I need a woman attendant," I said, as we paused at the small sally port, unlocked it as I used, tiptoed through. She stood to close it tight behind me. "Watch for me before dawn. Have all prepared. I think they may leave today and we must be ready to go with them."

"But where are we going?" Her voice floated soft and mournful after me as I ran over the frozen grass under the shelter of the wall until I came to where the stream was shallower and I could cross. Time to tell her that when I had seen Raoul and talked to him.

Crossing the frozen river was difficult. I ducked and dodged among the boulders, hoping no one would mark me from the castle walls, although I guessed not. There were too few men to keep close watch, and the storm had made us feel safe from further attack at least. But I could not help thinking of the wild animals we had seen, and in my thoughts ever I heard the wolves' howling coming closer. But I crossed to safety. A man standing in the shadows drew me to shore and began himself to run toward the safety of the trees. I could not hurry faster because of the drifts, but at the forest's edge he had left a wood hurdle of some kind used for hauling wood, and where the snow was deep and hard he could pull me, having tied fur skins about his own boots to make the walking easier. Without him I could not have managed at all, and the effort that we made so sapped our energy that we had no time for speech. We must have plodded on for at least two hours before he left the pathway and began to cut through the trees, turning this way and that as if through a maze. At last we stopped in a small clearing. He shrugged the heavy ropes from his shoulders, standing upright for the first time, and nodded silently toward the hut, half-hidden in the undergrowth. It must have been used by woodsmen, set in a stand of trees I did not remember, and would not have recognized it anyhow; the snow had changed all things so, turning the forest into something wild, older than men themselves. But I recognized Geoffrey at the hut door, and the other men standing guard in the circle of trees. Yet he, too, had changed. I had not remembered him so thin, so white, or his face so lined with weariness and concern.

We dragged the supplies over the frozen ground. Here in the forest it was still ice cold, but yet I sensed the thaw would come here, too, with the daylight. That would ease their plight somewhat.

"We did not look for you, Lady Ann," he said, trying to smile. "We feared that others might come behind and follow where you went."

"No one has seen me," I said. "Nor would I have risked it if I had thought it possible. And I must see Lord Raoul to talk with him."

He did not respond.

"Lord Raoul is . . ."

"Alive, lady," he said abruptly, "but sick unto death. He lost much blood before we could get him here. He does not mend as he ought."

"Who tends him?"

"I do," said Geoffrey, "and his squires; we take turns. Lady, you must not go in." He tried to bar the door. "He must not be disturbed."

But I had already pushed past him, ducking under the low lintel into the hut. It was bitterly cold within, as cold as outside, and there was a smell of sickness, neglect. There was no light but I could see dimly the faint outlines of other men, the low pallet or bed stretched in a corner. The men did not move, but stood staring at me with eyes that gleamed in the dark. I beckoned to Geoffrey behind me, fumbling among my bundles until I found a tinder, which he struck. Even its pale light seemed too bright in that room. I looked at them and scarce suppressed my gasp of dismay. They looked like scarecrows, bearded, dirty, half-starved. The charcoal burners I had disturbed in the forest when I fled through it could not have looked more wild, more neglected.

I took the torch that someone silently handed me, and,

almost against my will, approached the corner. My heart contracted upon itself as I looked down. Was that Raoul? I am not sure I would have known him, his hair grown long and matted, his face unshaved, his skin waxen. His eyes were closed, but whether he slept or lay between consciousness and unconsciousness I could not tell. They had covered him with their cloaks, yet the sweat that stood out on his forehead came not from heat, and the unstrapped arm that lay outside the covers plucked at them with nerveless fingers. Thus did Raoul of Sedgemont pay for our love. Thus was God requited of him, for our sin. . . .

And I thought, Dear God, he will die here.

His men stood round me, their faces mirroring my own fears, as if I had shouted them aloud. Yet, what more could they have done? Despite myself, the thoughts that once I had had about him rose up to haunt me.

When he is alone and out of favor, let him look for loyalty. Without heat, food, without real care, was Raoul of Sedgemont now as poorly lodged as any serf in any hovel. Yet, without their loyalty, without the love of his men, he would already have been dead.

I thrust them back, tearing at the bundles I had brought. They stood aside and watched me, uncertain what to do or say, as hopeful as children. Again I felt pity overwhelm me, the household guard of Sedgemont reduced to this pitiful group. Yet their swords were unsheathed by their sides, they wore their mail coats day and night, kept watch, and would sell their lives bitterly if anyone trespassed here. What could they do? No men could have done more. First I brought out the wine to give them heart, then bread, meat, all the goods that the Lady Mildred had hoarded for their use.

"Light up the fire," I told them. "Warm this broth. It will put heart in you else you perish of the cold."

"We dare not, lady," Geoffrey said, "for fear of discovery where we have hidden here."

"No," I said, more firmly than I dared, speaking curtly to

hide my feelings. "I'll wager those French tomorrow will be gone, sick of our winter welcome. Even if they stay, the Lady Mildred will seek means to send you more supplies. No one will find you here. The worst is over."

They threw logs on the fire until it burst into flame and I could see them clearly, thin and pale, shivering in their shirts beneath the mail, without cloaks.

"Drink, all of you," I scolded. "What have you eaten? A sick man would starve in your care. Take off those covers. Lord Raoul needs warm air, not weight."

So I chided them to make them bestir themselves. Little by little, I set them tasks to keep their spirits up, giving them to eat and drink, for in truth they had been living off scraps, the best of what they had caught going to Lord Raoul, who could not swallow their rough soldier's fare, half-raw, half-cold. I showed them how to prepare the broth, and whilst it was heating had them unwind the rags that bound him, forcing myself close to look, cursing that strange sickness that made all things sway before my eyes. It was a hideous wound. The sword edge had sliced down upon the shoulder bone, breaking it and laying back the skin, then had slid down his side to his hip. This second wound was not so deep, for the blow had lost some of its force, and you could see where the leather undercoat had deflected part of it, yet it too would have felled most men. They had stitched the cuts, clumsy soldier work, as tightly as they dared, setting the shoulder bone with a rough splint. But the stitches had been pulled too tight, making the whole arm swell with anguish, so that, unknowing, he groaned when we tried to move it.

"We did the best we could," Geoffrey said. Well, we both knew why, not only to cobble the torn flesh together but to give hope that the tendons and muscles might heal as well. A man without full use of his right arm is as a cripple. They had taken that risk on his behalf, or perhaps he had urged them to it, if he had been able to make a conscious choice. But the arm could not mend if left like that.

"It is the fever that is worse," Geoffrey said, looking at me for hope as I stood thinking. "When he tosses, he dislodges the dressings, breaks all open again. It takes our strength to hold him down. . . ."

I took Geoffrey to one side, his laughing face drawn and pale, gathering my wits about me, trying to remember what Gwendyth would have done in such a case, a man she had tended once with such a slash across his arm.

I said, "The shoulder must be restitched. It will mortify as it is now. I must resew the underpart, in layers so that it has a chance to heal."

"He cannot bear it," Geoffrey said hoarsely. "It will kill him."

"Then he will die in any case," I said brutally. "The wound as yet is clean. If we wait longer, it will be too late. It is the only chance he has. And I need your help. I cannot do it alone. Geoffrey, you must help me."

I willed him to agree, although perhaps he, more than I, knew what the agony would be. Then we had to hasten, first getting Raoul to drink warm wine in which I steeped herbs that I remembered Gwendyth used in such instances to cloud the mind and nerves. He drank eagerly as if parched with thirst, not knowing what he drank, for although his eyes opened once, they were glazed with pain and there was no sense in them. We laid him back upon the dirty bed and I put my hand upon his chest. The skin was still brown from Cambray sun, but dry and hot to the touch, and beneath I felt the laboring of his heart. I forced back my own sickness, and willed my hand not to tremble as I turned to empty out the bundles that we had prepared so carefully.

"He will feel nothing," I said, my voice even, as if I spoke of everyday affairs. "I would not attempt it if he moved, so you must hold him still. First, there must be hot water to clean the wound and fresh wrappings. These old rags must be burned for fear of infection. And see, I have brought all things needful, thread, scissors. I need light and steady hands to help."

I spoke in a monotone to give myself courage as much as

them, and with Geoffrey to help, I began the work. With the small gilt scissors that so often the Lady Mildred had used, I plucked at the swollen flesh and then, with smaller careful thrusts, retied each stitch separately, restitched each layer of muscle and flesh. He did not move. He lay so still I almost would have thought him gone, except that his breathing sounded slower than normal yet constant, so that each time he breathed, I felt my own lungs contract in sympathy. I do not remember how long we labored to do all that was needed, packing the whole with wadding smeared with unguents that stop bleeding, showing Geoffrey how to wrap him in ice if the fever should return, as I was sure it would.

But when it was done, I could say with certainty, "He will sleep on for hours yet. When he wakes, give him broth to drink, warm wine, and more of these herbs that will let him sleep undisturbed again. Then when the flesh has healed, you must cut the outer stitches loose." And I showed them how to lift the thin thread and pluck it out.

"The ones beneath will loose themselves," I warned, "but if the flesh again begins to swell or discolor, you must start afresh with hot cloths and herbs to draw the poisons forth."

As brisk as Gwendyth was I then, explaining, correcting, whilst they listened like sheep, admiring, God, I thought, those small painful stitches I had taken, who could not seam a fold of cloth straight.

"And if we leave soon, as I think, then will the castle send you word. But hold him here until my message comes. He is safest here."

By then we had already stepped outside, and with a pail of ice water I was trying to cleanse my hands of their work, letting them tremble now that it was done.

"Lady Ann," Geoffrey said, a shadow by my side. "Will you go with them?"

"I must," I said. "I had hoped before I came to have word with Raoul. But since that is impossible, I shall go to London myself. I came from Cambray with that thought in mind. So shall I achieve it."

"How?" he said, worried. "What will you hope to do in London?"

I said, "They would have killed him, you know that as well as I. Had he remained at Sedgemont after the fight, they would have taken him away. You must stay and hide him here. Strange chance has saved him once, chance or God. He may be saved again, by that same chance. Without his knowledge or agreement was he rescued from Sedgemont. Without his knowledge while he lies here will you keep him safe from harm."

"I do not know," he said. "I should come with you, but I cannot be spared here."

"Dear friend," I said, and took his hands in both of mine, "without you, he would be dead already. Long is the debt we owe you. Since those happy days in the forest has it been promised. Guard him. Do not let him move an inch without you, although I do not see that he will be able to move for months ahead. By then, I may have found the means to present our suit, plead for his life, which he would not do himself."

"I fear for you," he said simply. "Is there no one to ride with you?"

"Cecile," I said. "I will twist her until she will follow. And do not think of me. I have a tongue as sharp as those lords of Maneth, spilling out their poison to the Angevin court. If there is to be justice in this land, I shall claim it."

"Who will go as escort?"

"There are a few left at Sedgemont," I said, "those who are most fit."

"Then God speed you, my lady," Geoffrey said. With silent, almost awkward gesture, he knelt before me, and the other men did likewise. "God have it that we all be free men again."

I looked down upon their bowed heads, their thin bodies, their calloused hands. Until I sent them good news, they must live as outcasts, outlawed from their lands, their friends. And for no real cause. Yet, in panic, remembering Raoul's closed eyes with the dark shadows under them, the red scar still etched across his face, his hands peaceful, no longer fumbling for the sword hilt above his bed, I thought, too, I should be rather on my knees to you, praying you to protect him, to save the father of my child.

So is our life made up by trust to Him who is above, to him who is below. We must each rely on each and pray God to have us to His care.

"Amen," I whispered, feeling as a mother might with her children before her.

Two of them came with the serf to help him drag the sled, for we had to hurry. The night was already ending when they left us as close to the forest edge as they dared. The man and I went on alone. He helped me cross the frozen river and came with me to the side gate where Cecile waited inside for my sign. What made that old man, that serf, risk his life for us?

"Lady," he said in his rough speech when I bade him farewell, "we wait in the forest, too, women and children, since the Lord of Sedgemont ordered us to hide. We are fifty people there. It is the second time in as many years we have left our homes and fields." He did not look at me as he spoke but kept his eyes fixed on the castle walls for fear of being sighted there.

"My race was Saxon," he said. "In a hundred years, we have known nothing but war and famine and destruction. Under these lords of Sedgemont we have been safe until now. But we cannot fend for the women and children long in winter, without shelter."

Again I felt the weight of what he said. Once, the peasants of Sedgemont seemed to live as princes compared with the lordless border people. Now, without Raoul, they were sunk as low.

"I will do all I can," I promised, as I slipped inside the half-opened door. "Do you the same for us."

But what was to stop him or someone like him from selling the secrets of the forest to Raoul's enemies? I leaned my head against the inside of the gate as Cecile wrestled with the bolts to draw them home, and fought down sickness and despair.

"My lady," Cecile panted behind me as we ran quietly back, past the stairs where I had hidden long ago, through the deserted kitchens, the empty rooms echoing like vaults, "they are preparing to go. I heard them talk of it. Three of our men are fit to ride. The others have helped them arm, saddled the horses. The Lady Mildred has made all ready for you. But hurry, hurry."

She had had no sleep, had watched the night through by the gate to let me in. I looked at her tired face. Like Geoffrey's, all the light of youth seemed gone, and in its place, fear and determination. I realized she was dressed for riding herself, her skirts knitted up so she could ride astride like a trooper. The Lady Mildred had warm clothes, cloaks, in readiness. She helped me change my bloodstained dress, throwing it upon the fire, and placed food and drink in front of me, although I could scarce force myself to swallow. She listened to my hasty instructions, how flimsy they sounded, depending on the goodwill of a woodcutter, a peasant, a handful of men. But we had no other help; we must cling to them. And until Raoul was fit to move, there was nowhere else he could go.

It was not quite dawn when we came into the courtyard. The French envoys were already there, mounted, waiting for the first light. Most of their men rode with them, but they left a token handful behind. Some of Maneth's men went with them, the French ones. A few stayed, along with a half-dozen of our wounded, and a couple or so of men who had served Sir Brian at Sedgemont.

Our three men were already mounted. One still had a stained bandage about his head, but he was alert, resolute, although he slouched in his saddle as I had seen them all ride once before. I knew enough now not to mistake that for discourage. Behind him, the four grays of Cambray had been loaded as pack horses.

The Lady Mildred saw my glance. "Once," she said, "when

Earl Raymond was given his title, he brought four such horses as gift, part of his feudal dues. I take it as omen, Lady Ann, that you have them with you now." She had not asked where I was going, had not sought to question me, yet her will was indomitable. And in her hands she carried, wrapped up in a sacking case that it be not noticed, a flag of Sedgemont with his crest fresh embroidered upon it. I took it without words. What words were there to answer such trust?

The French lords came up to me, riding bare headed, their faces reddened by the wind. It was not so cold; the warmth that had started the thaw would come faster now that day approached.

Sir Gautier spoke. "We go east," he said, without courtesy. "Which way ride you?"

"East, too," I said, swinging myself up with the help of my men. He eyed me sourly. On horseback, I was of a height with him. I could manage my horse as well, if, God willing, I did not heave my food before him as I already had done once this morning in secret.

"Not with me," he snapped. "We ride hard. You make no party with us."

"The roads are free for all," I said, tight lipped. "And you may find we ride as fast as you."

"Not with us," he said again. "We have no responsibility for you."

"I do not need that," I said, gesturing to my three men who had closed behind Cecile and me. "We have no need to run like dogs in the shadow of your protection. Look for us if you wish. We shall be there."

He eyed me, wheeled his horse round without word, and made signal. His escort jangled across the drawbridge, the blue banners laced with golden lions waving in the breeze. Beside me, one of our men spat. I gave the French five minutes' start before we left, standing there in the melting snows, the horses shivering at our impatience.

The Lady Mildred waited at the steps at her usual place, no emotion showing, no tears. Yet below her, wrapped in his military cloak, the body of her husband lay still unburied until the ground unfroze, and nearby lay the bodies of the other men. I looked about me in the morning air. It was light now. There was a good smell of fresh things growing through the ice. The remaining men were standing in their separate groups around the wall, some leaning despondently, some expectant, all wondering. The great walls of Sedgemont rose dark above us, unguarded. The bailey was littered still with straw, with dirt, all unkempt, unwatched.

I said suddenly, addressing the three groups of them whose three separate dead lay waiting, "We be strange companions here, but I commend you to the Lady Mildred, who will order this castle in our name until I return."

There was a murmur. One man cried out, "No one holds Sedgemont."

"Yes," I said evenly, "you do, until my return. Keep all in order lest your watch be found wanting. I seek justice for the rights and wrongs of us all. Else will we be like devil's curs, snarling over bones of wood. Without a master here, Sedgemont is as dead. Honor the Lady Mildred until our return. She acts as master and mistress both."

We turned on our heels, clattered out ourselves, a small silent group, without flag, without honor. But as my men rode by, they saluted the little figure at her place, the sharp salute of the Sedgemont guard. Then we, too, left the castle gates, went spurring after the dark shapes we could see against the white ground, already far ahead.

13

HEY RODE HARD BUT NOT SO FAST THAT we could not keep them in sight. And in some ways they made things easier for us, their larger numbers and heavier weights cutting a wide swath through the snow. At other times, the best we could do was to plod along in their wake. And when night fell and they sought shelter at some inn, we went there, too. Then did I see for myself the ease with which space was made for the king's messengers, food readied, beds made available. Not that there were many other travelers at the time, and I doubt if any were displaced to make room for us. But, at least, we were not ill treated, and the French envoys were not so petty as to forbid us the same shelter that they enjoyed. And when the morning came, we were always there and mounted and ready in good time, waiting for them to ride out before we followed. It was a hard ride. Nothing to Raoul's men, who wrapped their cloaks around their chins, and lowered their heads against the elements, solid as rocks.

Not for Cecile, who set her head high, white and determined she rode without complaint. Strangely enough, I think it was I who suffered most, and who had thought least about the difficulties, having endured them all before. But, for some reason, my body now seemed determined to betray me when I wished it most unsexed, to behave as any man would. My back ached, my very bones seemed to stretch with weariness, and the dizziness and sickness that had begun to plague me

threatened at times to overwhelm me before them all. I forced
those things aside as resolutely as Cecile did her discomforts.
No weakness of mine would make us lose place. And if it was
the effect of pregnancy, well, I was not unlearned about that
either, although so ignorant of its effects upon myself. There
would be time to think of that, hold it to its true account,
when Raoul was free again.

Unaided by our three men, we would have foundered for
certain. Without complaint, without fuss, they did all that I
should have ordered them to do but had not the wits or strength
to think of at the day's end. I often remember them, dark and
somber in their unembroidered cloaks, who once had proudly
worn the red and gold of Sedgemont. And twice did they save
our lives; loyalty again, although through what strange means,
what purpose, God knows and will set down to their credit.
Once, as we crossed a rivulet the frozen ice gave way beneath
us. We would all have been swept downstream, forced under,
had not they sat their horses in the midst of the current to
their waists in ice and mud and held the line by which the
other horses could be led across. I managed to ford it by myself,
my thick woolen skirts so wet and clinging that they made
more weight than all my body did together. Cecile they finally
bore before them, patiently taking yet another wetting in the
icy water. On the farther side, we all stripped in silence, and
warmed ourselves about a fire until we were thawed enough
to go on. That night it was so late before we found the lodging
place that we all stumbled into bed without thought of food,
every muscle crying out for rest. But the next morning, the
horses were saddled and we were waiting before the French
rode out.

The second time was more dangerous. Yet, without it, I
think much that happened afterward would not have been
possible. I have said there were few travelers abroad, the weather
being in part to blame, but also the uncertainty, that people
were unwilling to stir from their homes. By now we had come

far enough from the forest of Sedgemont to have left most of
the snow behind, although the sea of mud that replaced it was
no more agreeable. I had taken little heed of where we rode,
concentrating more on survival than curiosity, but I had noted
how, for the last few hours, we had been picking our way
through a new stretch of woodland, made up of scantily spaced
trees and wide stretches of brush and shrub. Later I recognized
it was one of those great game preserves that the Norman kings
have set aside for their own hunting grounds, then I knew only
that it made easier riding than we had known before. Suddenly,
the man who rode in front pulled back his horse so that it sank
upon its haunches and stretched his arm out behind him to
bid us hold back. We waited silently, the great horses pulling
at their lead reins to crop the grass that grew there, the first
we had seen in many days.

"Ahead of us," he said softly, "men are waiting. In that clump
of trees."

"Friends?" The other two spoke as one.

"I doubt it. I caught the glimpse of weapons. No friend hides
thus."

"How many?"

"They let the French go past. Less than they. More than
we."

They had already turned their horses round, heading to a
more open place.

"Should we not spur right through?" I asked, not yet certain
what we fled from.

"Nay." Raoul's men looked grim. By now their swords were
out, their shields unhooked from the saddles, their eyes scan-
ning on either side.

"They are waiting for us," one explained, the youngest, a
cheery fellow, his wounded knee that had kept him at Sedgemont after Raoul's escape still unknitted, yet he smiled at
the thought of danger again. "Ride through with surprise, stand
firm with attack. Do not be afeard, Lady Ann. It is only a

group of ruffians thinking to have an easy game of us."

We circled at the first convenient place, where the trees were set far enough apart not to give cover. I loosened the little knife at my belt. For a moment, panic took me as I saw the figures slipping behind us, on foot, with a horseman or two at their back. I felt my vision sway and blur as I remembered that morning by the stream when Giles and his men had awaited such an attack. Our men tightened their girths and stirrups straps, watching closely while we put Cecile and the gray horses on the inside, I with my knife to guard them. When the first men came sliding into the open, I heard their rally cry like a bird's call, and the answering echo from the farther side where others had come round to trap us. Our own knights stood up in their saddles, as Raoul had taught them, straight legged, stiff, although it must have been agony to lean on a wound scarce healed, and waited until the filthy, bearded group had advanced from the trees and came loping toward us. Then did they swing out toward them, two of them moving on together neck and neck, their arms outstretched above their heads to sweep down on either side like a storm, slashing through to the bone with all the weight they had, while the third, a length behind, cut back obliquely to turn the attack from the rear. They surged on, their sword tips crimson now, their faces beaded with sweat, and I heard the shout they gave, "Sedgemont, Cambray," echo through the forest like a trumpet blast. Three more times did they sweep out and cut our attackers down as they came. Three times they wheeled back without hurt to themselves, although had there been bowmen in the group, we would all have been dead long since. Before we could launch a fourth charge, I heard another cry, the thunder of hooves, and swinging round to right and left of us through the trees came the blue trappings of the Angevins. Then were our men relieved, although they gave no outward sign, except to shout once again, as now all three rode out, knee to knee as one man, charging through the underbrush into the midst of the outlaw gang. These, in panic, had started to throw down their weapons and begun to run for the shelter of the deeper trees, whilst their leaders, seeing that there was no hope, had already turned and galloped away. I watched as a head spun off in a gush of blood, like a bird's wing against the gray trees, and, sick and shivering, turned my face aside to vomit away all the fear and relief. When it was done, I tottered to the side of the clearing and sat upon the muddy grass turfs and waited for the men to rejoin us. They came back, as joyful as from a hunt, the youngest one whistling through his teeth, for all that his bandaged leg ran red, and his eyes were rimmed with dirt and fatigue.

"You do not think to sell yourself easily?" Sir Gautier's voice broke in upon my reverie. He and Sir Renier had come spurring up, and leaned now upon their saddles while their horses heaved and pawed, foam spraying from their bits. He pointed with his sword to my hand where I still held Giles's knife.

When I could speak, "And what would you do with that?" I said, pointing in turn to his sword. "Do not tell me that it was used on our behalf?"

"*Dieu*, I did but course after hares," he said.

"What waste of effort," I replied, scarce caring what I said as long as the sickness kept its distance whilst they were there, "to turn you back so far from your path."

My men had drawn up behind me now as I sat, Raoul's men, I should say. I had seen them exercise that formation a hundred times across the great meadows of Sedgemont and in the camp on the border.

"Who trained them to that?" Sir Renier asked. "Who serve you?"

They looked at him disinterestedly, cleaning their swords upon their cloaks, resettling their shields, their straps, without word.

Fighting the return of faintness, I said breathlessly, "While they ride with me, they serve me."

"No woman..." Sir Renier began. Then Sir Gautier, who had been observing me narrowly, broke in, "Then were you better served, my lady, to ride slower with your men. Have them bear you in a litter. Hire more men. Ride slower."

"I can keep up," I said stubbornly. "I have no choice."

"Why not?" he said, still watching me. "I do not understand your haste."

"So that the people whom I know and trust," I said slowly, forcing myself upright against the tree, "will not be reduced to living like these poor wretches, so that they are free to hunt among their own lands."

"It will kill you, lady," he said again, pulling at his beard, his round face suddenly drawn with worry.

"Should that concern you," I said bitterly, beckoning them to bring my horse so I could mount, "what will one more death be to you?"

He bit his lip, his color darkening as I had seen before, and turned away. It was Sir Renier who dismounted, helped me to the saddle, escorted Cecile, who had clung to her own horse this while, half-dead with fear, and brought us to the lodgings for the night. That night again I sank away to sleep before I could take food or drink, and dreamed that I was back at Cambray, running through the sand dunes toward the beach. The sea was out, and the breakers fell with a far-off murmur on the shore. And at the water's edge a black-hooded figure waited for the tide to turn to drag Raoul, to drag Talisin, against the rocks.

The next morning was clearer, warmer still. We did not shiver as we usually did as we awaited the Frenchmen's departure. My guard were not talkative, but even they looked more cheerful than before, as if a taste of victory had heartened them. But when the French appeared, they looked straight ahead as they always did, as if they saw no one.

Sir Gautier came over to me. "Ride you beside me," he said abruptly. "We pass through a lonely place today, where there be more vagabonds. Keep your men close behind."

"I would thank you," I said, suddenly smiling at him, "if I knew why your change of heart. . . ."

"I have not time," he said, smiling at me in return, the first smile he had given since that night at Sedgemont, "to pant back and forth upon your trail. Although I do not think you wise to keep up this pace." And there was a question in his shrewd look that suddenly made me want to turn away as if he might have guessed a secret that I thought hidden from everyone. I made pretense at gathering up the reins, putting on my gloves, settling my dagger at my side.

When his refusal to move forced me to reply, "Let me be the judge of that," I said at last, lamely, "If Cecile can, so can I."

"Yes," he said, not looking at her. "I would not have thought her capable."

"If we cannot, then shall you leave us again," I said. And with that he had to be content.

Sir Gautier was a good companion on the road. What he had guessed at, hinted at, never for decency did he mention again, at least not then, and it may have been my own guilt that suspected he knew more than I wished any man to know. He did not make concessions to Cecile and me; but by now she could manage as well as anyone, and I, well, I would, too. You come to know men when they are doing what they are best at. Sir Gautier was a good leader. Less open than Raoul with his men, less on easy terms, he was efficient and sparce. And shrewd. Both he and Renier were more shrewd and cynical than I had reckoned them, both of them having had long practice at the courts of Anjou and Aquitaine.

On the other hand, neither man was cautious about his life at court, speaking more openly of it than ever Raoul had done. It was from Renier, a Frenchman, that I learned most of London and the pleasures that awaited us there, the feasts, the fairs, the shops, which made it more large, more prosperous than any place I had ever imagined. And from Sir Gautier, all the further detail I could glean of Henry and his queen. And then again from Renier, descriptions of that hot sultry land in the south, which I never thought to see, dust-dry and hot, so unlike these muddy wet trails we rode across in this wintry landscape here, that Aquitaine, which he despaired of returning to once more.

One night we lodged at a monastery, well entertained by the abbot and his monks, far removed from those frugal silent meals I remembered. Anything less like my experience within cloistered walls cannot be described; those good men turned up their noses at Cistercian piety, sneering at the hypocrisy that made pretense that starvation and silence were sources of holiness. They munched upon the pastries and pies and haunches of venison, caught, no doubt, in the king's forest, while the abbot explained his ideas to us, waving his pudgy fingers with enthusiasm. "For things will be different," he said, "now that Henry is king. We shall have no more interference as we had under Stephen. We have had too many people poking their fingers into English Church affairs. This Henry will have learned his lesson not to meddle with us."

"I am not sure," Sir Gautier answered, smoothing his beard as he did when thoughtful. "I have known Henry a long time. He makes us all grow old with his energy. He will not be like his French king, squatting on his throne complaining of his wrongs. You may find, my lord Abbot, he puts his finger deeper in than anyone you have known. And he may outargue you to boot. He is skilled in many languages including priestly Latin."

"He will find me ever generous." The lordly abbot waved his hand again. "I will offer him the hospitality of his own hunting grounds, which I have made good use of whilst he was away in France."

"Do not suggest that to him," Sir Gautier said almost dryly. "He is generous in many things, but not his hunting privileges.

Jesu, I have known him work the whole night through, trailing from one room to the next, with his scribes running behind him, and when he had worn them out, kicking us awake to send us hawking before dawn. Nor does he welcome easy living, good food, as the rest of us do. I think he delights in bedding down upon the open fields just to watch his retinue bicker with drawn swords over the privilege of a straw pillow. I have slept so myself many times with only a cloak to cover me." He sighed. "But he is young, you see, my lord Abbot. We who are older need enjoy our creature comforts more. If he grant us them."

The abbot, who was older by thirty years, had paled at the hint, the threat implicit in those words. "Then will he find London a paradise, after these harsh customs," he said, attempting to jest.

"I doubt that." Sir Gautier's tone was brisk. "I doubt if London has held him long. Once crowned, he will not have wasted time before riding about his new kingdom to see to things himself. Look for him here, my lord. He will turn up one day without warning."

"The king is not in London?" It was my turn to stammer forth. Here was unexpected news. "How then shall I see him?"

"Unless you mean to quest across the length and breadth of England," Sir Gautier said, "you must wait like the rest of us."

I slowly pushed aside my platter, the rich food cloying in my mouth as I spoke. All about me, the red, flushed faces laughed and ate and drank, enough food to fill a town, whilst in a hovel, a woodcutter's hut, Lord Raoul and his men lay half-starved and hoped for help from me.

"I cannot," I said. "Where shall I find him? Do you not go to meet him?"

"Yes, lady," he said, "but for you, that would be impossible. I shall have to cast and cast about as in the hunting field. Where he is today, God knows; where tomorrow, when I have caught up with today?"

I stood up slowly, feeling for the back of my chair. The others eyed me, curious for a moment, as I forced my legs to carry me away. I had thought London would be the end of my search. To hear now that it must go on and on near broke my resolve. And I did not have time to waste. Time was my enemy. I must find the king and plead for Raoul before the king's messengers should hunt him out again, or he try to resist them... or before all men would know I pleaded in a special case, for the father of my bastard child....

"But I thought you sought London, Lady Ann." Sir Gautier's voice was almost perplexed. He had followed me to where I leaned against an outer wall. "You are unwell, you look unwell. Allow me to call your woman to tend you."

I could sense the concern in his tone. His dark eyes were fixed upon mine. He tugged at his beard.

"I must see the king," I said, not caring now what I revealed to him. "It is a matter of life and death. Time to me is all. Take me with you, my lord. Have I not shown I can keep up as a man?"

He did not answer me at first, tried instead to lead me to a bench that stood within the columned walks, and when I did not move, stood looking out across the dim-lit garden, all shrouded now in January grays and browns. In the spring it would be pleasant here, a garden within these monastic walls, as rich and lush as the food they ate, the life they knew.

"Lady," he said at length, and I saw how he kept his gaze fixed on the far side of the court, as if he did not wish to note what was happening underfoot. "Lady, I told you I do not need to know your affairs. What you seek, who and why, are not for me to know. I have scant knowledge of women, a bachelor knight am I. My life has been wrapped up in court. I stand close to the king, as close, that is, as any man. I tell you this not to boast, but to show you something of what I am. I am older than you by some twenty years. Before you were born was I with Count Geoffrey of Anjou, King Henry's father. I knew his heart like my right hand. The court and its ways are no secret to me. They are to you. What hope will you have, unknown, young, poor, without friends, to trail your suit before the great lords of this land?"

"Someone will help me," I said. "I am not so unbefriended. There will be someone who will speak for us."

"Do not count on it," he said dourly, as dourly as Dylan had warned me before. "You dare to thrust where other men will hold back."

"God has spoken on our behalf already," I said. "Forget not that when you tell your tales."

"I tell no tales," he said, flushing again. "I can only report what I saw happen at Sedgemont: no more, no less. Do not ask too much of me."

"It was little enough I asked," I said proudly, "an audience, that is all, to state the truth. As God has already proved it."

"They all think that they state the truth," he said, still staring away from me. "Who is there who does not think he is in the right?"

"Between right and wrong you can judge," I said. "Court life has not ruined that for you."

At that he did turn round, and beat his fist against the wall as once Raoul had beat his for rage. I saw the indecision in his gesture, that I should put pressure on him, that he should jeopardize his standing with his king.

"Yes," he said. "I know the court. Nor am I so unworldly that I do not know the facts of life. Speak not to me of right and wrong. You, I think, are with child...."

I gaped at him, stopping my hand that instinctively would have moved to cover my belly. Then I faced him.

"Then what wrong is there," I cried, "that my child's father should live? Were you in such distress, my lord, would not you wish your mistress to speak for you? Who else is there who has greater right?"

He made a gesture as if to stop his ears. "I do not want to know the whys and hows," he cried. "They are not my concern. But they will mock you for a wanton in the streets."

"I daresay Guy of Maneth has already branded me," I said.
"His son would have had all his men take turns to make me
whore. I am used to slander. Well, what if it is true I know
no great lords, as you taunt me with. But I have friends, unknown, lowly, you would call them, who have given their lives
for me. I owe them much."

I looked at him dry eyed, emotion spent.

"I thought you, too, might be my friend," I said.

"What would you have me do?" he said. "I know you have
cause. There, I have said it. But I tell you, if you speak what
I think you will to King Henry, he will not listen. Even if God
himself speaks for you! Henry," he paused a moment, "Henry
of Anjou is not as other men. He will not listen. Or he will
listen and promise and not do. Or, since you would have me
speak openly, as you are young and fair, look not so surprised,
he will listen and promise and demand payment for his services.
And that is worse."

"Then is there no hope at all?" I asked, half-whispering.

He said abruptly, "Go with Sir Renier. Tomorrow our ways
part. He will go south to the queen, I north to track down
the king. The queen has settled with her court and her young
child at Bermondsey, south of London, close to the river there.
Sir Renier will get you audience of her."

"But will he help me?" I said, stretching out my hand to
detain him.

His look told me what I needed to know. "He will do it,"
I said, "because I order so." But what he said was quite different.
"If you smile at him, Lady Ann," he said, "or look at him as
you look now, he will do anything you ask. But for good
measure, I tell you this." He smiled at me. "I am not versed
in women's ways, but I know the queen will soon give birth
again. A second son will win the king back to London fastest
of all things. She will have his ear as I have not. And your
secrets will be safe with me."

I watched him as he stood, a short man, not much taller

than I, with almost forty years of service at a great lord's court. I knew he lied about his ignorance of women, about his knowledge of me. But I did not think he lied when he said my secrets would be safe.

"Then shall I wish you Godspeed, my lord," I said, holding out my hand to him. "Do you as much for me."

He took my hand and bowed over it. I thought he said, "I wish that your errand was any other than this." But he did not repeat it and that was the last time we spoke together before our ways parted.

I slept better that night, without dreams for the first time since we began. The next day, our road ran through more-crowded parts, villages, larger and more prosperous than I had ever seen, well kept, trim, no signs here of desolation. I do not recall their names except that they were softer-sounding than our western ones, suggesting meadows and country lanes.

For the first time we saw other travelers on the road, and as we came to the river ford, their numbers seemed to grow so that our men were forced to beat a passage through, shouting the king's name as they flailed about them with the flats of their swords. And so we came at last to the bank of the great river Thames, and had our first glimpse of the city of London spread before us.

I had heard of the river only in context of war, one army stationed on one side, one on the other; had imagined it some wide and terrible flood. It looked now more gentle than the river at Sedgemont or those mountain streams along the border, flowing sluggishly between banks lined with rush and reed, in places overflowed across the placid pasturelands that lay all about. There was no snow or ice here, only gray mist along the river's edge, the same mist that concealed part of the view ahead. But I have never seen the outline of the city against its expanse of gray sky without an uplifting of heart, almost a dazzling of the eyes, at the stretch of its walls, its distant spires and towers. Three walls it had around it, seven gates, no less than one hundred and fifty church steeples. And every year, they say, it stretches out its fingers to enclose more of those gentle villages and placid meadows. It looked like a picture hung upon a curtain. I sat motionless upon my horse until it must have believed I slept, and thought I was come to my destination at last. Here was where our hopes would win or fail.

We parted company at the ford. Sir Gautier with half of the men rode north; Sir Renier turned southward with us. Sir Gautier and I had no speech again, yet he bade me farewell as courtiers do, prettily, meaning much or little. I could not tell what he thought. But we had to trust him, Raoul and I, although Raoul's name had not been mentioned by him again; it had only hung there, silently. I could not tell if his silence would include Raoul, and if he spoke, what would he say?

We passed the ford without difficulty although the current underneath was stronger than it seemed. On the other side we found the reason for the crush, a fair of some sort, with booths and stalls set up, with gingerbread and sweetmeats and spiced goods hung on display.

"Dear God," Cecile said, her eyes round with delight, "I have not seen such things in a hundred years."

And even the Sedgemont men who had come this way before were not too proud to put off their haughty looks and stare as longingly.

Reluctantly we pushed our way past; starved had we been for such a show of luxury, and even Sir Renier and his men were silent, as if unable for once to make comparisons between what we saw and what they had known in Aquitaine.

Within the city gates, they cheered up, and Sir Renier took his duty as guide seriously. He showed us the massive Norman tower, called the White Tower, which the first Norman king had built along the riverbank to hold the conquered city, a cruel huge block of stone it looked, ominous in the gray light. I shuddered as we passed. Perhaps that was where they would have taken Raoul after all, and killed him within those thick walls that never let even screams out. He showed us the ca-

thedral of the city, built even earlier, where that same Norman
king was first crowned, where Henry and his queen had been
crowned less than a month ago. And he took us past the
winding streets, the crowded wharves, the docks and ware-
houses, to yet another wooden bridge that spanned the river
and led to the south bank.

I had never heard such noise, such scurry, the sound of
hundreds of people bustling to and fro on business of their
own, all with the air of people who know where they are and
what they are about. The colors and profusion of their clothes
alone bewildered us. Bright greens, scarlet reds, russet browns,
we swirled amid a gaudy patchwork, yet underfoot all was
sodden and crushed and knee deep in rubbish. No wonder
court people affect high-heeled shoes, I thought, to keep them
above the dirt of their roads. No wonder they wear bright
colors and scent themselves with unguents to hide the filth
beneath. At Cambray we have middens or dung heaps to take
the slops. Here, all is hurled from doors and windows into the
gutters, blocked at this season into a foul and stinking mess.
In summer the smell must be atrocious, I thought. And felt
my stomach heave again at the idea.

Sir Renier chatted as we rode along. Then, for the first time,
I heard explanation of those forts which line our western lands,
for he told us that those same people, great soldiers, had also
built London, and when you dig among the city streets, beneath the cobbles, you find similar-hewn stones that they had
cut to make their fortifications there as elsewhere. And Aquitaine and Provence, he told us, were filled with mighty works
made by these same men: towers, bridges, roads, and temples
of great height and beauty. So, with his cheerful gossip lured
he us along, until by nightfall we came to Bermondsey.

It was not the king's usual residence. That was in that dreaded
White Tower itself, where Raoul's men whispered to me they
had been before. But it had been stripped bare by Stephen's
mercenaries while he lay dying at Dover, and was not fit for

living in. Nor did we go to Bermondsey ourselves, but lodged that first night in a small, dark place close to the river's edge, with Sir Renier's men on guard below, and three Sedgemont guards without our door. Now that we had finally arrived, I felt the tension of the journey greater than ever, although Cecile enjoyed the attentions paid us as important visitors. We had clean rooms, hot water, and time to rest and think, which we had not seemed to have done since I had left Cambray. But all my worries rose before me like solid walls of stone, as if I had to tear them down piecemeal. Perhaps I should have waited at Sedgemont until Raoul was well. Then could we both have fled away together, forgetting this England, all our claims here. But would he have let me go? Where would we have gone? And what would he have said knowing I was carrying a bastard child?

No bastard have I brought to my bed.

Then was he lucky perhaps in his women, more than he deserved.

An heir must have something to inherit.

What would our son have if we lost Cambray and Sedgemont?

What if I won him back his inheritance? Would some sense of duty make his child legitimate? Would he resent the blow to his pride?

"My lady," Cecile said at last, as I sat in the window ledge of our room, staring with unseeing eyes across the river where even now, in the small hours of the first watch, the bonfires still burned bright and the shouts of merrymakers echoed clear, "you must rest now if you are to meet the queen tomorrow."

I shook my head. "I am too tired to sleep," I confessed, "too eaten up with doubt."

She took my hand as she had held it at the trial at Sedgemont.

"I will worry for you," she promised. "Lie down for a while. I will stitch your dress. It seemed to have tightened about the waist, although you look more thin than before...."

We looked at each other, friend to friend.

"What shall I do?" I said.

There was no condemnation in her, only concern.

"I think," she said, "that if you bind yourself as I have known maids do before, it will not show yet, perhaps not at all, until we have accomplished what we came here to do. Now rest. Then shall you put things before the queen so she, in turn, will tell the king and we can go back home. I do not like it here, Lady Ann. For all its luxury and riches, it seems strange to me. I shall fall silent or forget my place, or weep that I am not back at Sedgemont. Do you remember that autumn day in the woods, how you first talked of Cambray and how one day we should all go there? How you would help us, Geoffrey and me, so one day we should be wed and have children of our own? We never thought we would come this far."

I lay with my eyes shut, listening to her voice as she worked. One day she and Geoffrey would marry, would people the world with smiling golden-haired children full of their good humor and calm.

Great lords do not have to seek out maids or wait for them.

When Raoul was restored to Sedgemont, far from my world at Cambray, would he still remember me?

"And do you recall the great boar hunt," she was saying, "how we all wore our best clothes and rode the best horses? Do you remember how Geoffrey leapt the oak tree three times to make his horse show its paces? Even Lord Raoul cheered him on. And how Sir Brian's cloak caught on a thorn and tore in two?"

I wanted to tell her that I had seen none of these things, had ridden apart from them on my own. I let her talk, her lighthearted chatter rising and falling with my own breath until at last I slept.

In the morning, Sir Renier came early for us. We watched him pick his way in his dainty shoes across the piles of rubbish that lay outside the doorway. His clothes were a startling red—

gone the more sober garments of our journey—he shone like a peacock in short cloak edged with squirrel fur and high-jeweled collar. It was not becoming against his sallow skin, yet he seemed proud of himself and preened before us. He made no comment upon the way we were dressed. I had fidgeted about that, for the first time having no wish to seem countrified, but I could tell from the way men's heads turned, and they looked at us as we trailed through the streets, that our appearance did us credit. Or rather Cecile, who must have labored the night through. Behind us strode my guard, still clad in their common workday clothes, but people made way for them nevertheless.

Bermondsey was not as large as I had expected, having been a monastery before being used by the royal court as a winter palace. In many ways it seemed little different from the household at Sedgemont. At all the gates and doors there were guards who stiffened to salute as we went by; but except that they wore blue, not red, they were little different from the Sedgemont guard. There was the same air of bustle and expectancy, the same messengers riding to and fro. And the same strong sense of vitality.

"The queen is expecting you, Lady Ann," Sir Renier said. "I spoke with her ladies-in-waiting last night and again today. She will hold an audience at noon, so your chance to meet her comes then."

"What is she like?" Cecile asked, chirping up behind me, where she helped hold up the train of my skirt. I would not have dared ask myself, but listened to his answer eagerly. He was not helpful.

"You will know her, mistress," he said severely. "Although she is like all other women, with eyes and tongue, no doubt."

With that, we had to bide in patience as we took our place in a large, drafty room, crammed with a score of other petitioners, all rehearsing their grievances they hoped would be set to rights before the day was done.

"Pooh," said Cecile, in the tone of voice she used whilst at

Sedgemont when Lady Mildred had said or done something to provoke us. "Geoffrey says all French women are ugly as sin. And the queen is already old. Yet the king must respect her wishes. . . ."

But she took pains to whisper so she could not be heard. I watched the other men and women, who pushed and argued around us. They were not pleasant to be with, strident and heated they became, reacting to their woes. I should never raise my voice to compete with theirs. The room itself was sumptuously hung with rich tapestries upon the walls, and rugs upon the floors instead of rushes. But it had a cold uncared-for look, and when the wind blew, the tapestries flapped. Nor was it clean. And although the courtiers wore the same rich embroidered clothes as Sir Renier, I had the feeling that underneath, they were dirty, too.

Much has been written about Eleanor, Duchess of Aquitaine, once Queen of France, now Queen of England. It might seem impertinent for me to add what I thought, who was to become her dear friend and companion. Yet I will tell you truly. It was not her beauty, or her stature, nor her fine delicate features, which all comment upon, that made impression on me then. Nor yet her speech, that danced with impatience when she was bored, which happened readily. Nor yet her logic, which could argue law and divinity with scholars of the Church or universities. Nor even her arrogance, which sits well on one who has, since childhood, been a queen, accustomed to obedience and respect. Nor her love of show and display, which, although a sin, is natural in one coming from the richest fief in France. None of these things that anyone will tell you about her and that I came, bit by bit, to know. It was simply this: she was great with child. Sir Gautier had told me of it, but I am not sure his words had sunk in then. But it came to me later how strange are the ways of the world, that I should have come to her to argue for a man's life and honor, in affairs of men, and that she should have appeared to me, not in the guise of a ruler, sovereign, queen, but as a woman, like me, weary and near her term. It was the paleness of her face and the bone-aching weariness that I noticed and felt as if they were my own.

We had waited until almost the end. That was a mistake. I could tell from Sir Renier's look. I should not have hung back until she was worn out with so much blather from the others.

"So you are Ann of Cambray," she said at last. "I have heard talk of you." I would not have understood her had I not had practice with the French envoys on the way. She slurred her vowels and rolled her r's much as they did.

"My lady Queen," I said, from a deep curtsy that the Lady Mildred would have approved. "And I of you."

She had gone to sit now in a high-backed chair, her feet propped up upon a stool while her ladies massaged her swollen ankles.

"God's wounds," she swore, "it is tiring, these everlasting requests for this and that. I think no one has had anything in England these past twenty years. And does the sun never shine?"

"Sometimes," I said. She had not spoken directly to me, but I alone seemed willing to answer. "We sometimes have a full day of sun in spring and autumn. But you must search for it."

She turned her look back to me. "You can live with that?" she said. "But you are English yourself, of course."

"Nay, my lady Queen," I said, ignoring Sir Renier's look, his gestures to me to rise, who ever contradicts royalty, who ever curtsies so she cannot stand up, "from the west, we claim an older kinship."

"Ah, yes," she said, losing interest again. "You speak differently from the others."

"As you do, Lady Queen," I said, "because we have a language of our own. I have been listening to Sir Renier talk. The language of the south must be beautiful. So is mine when we speak it among ourselves."

She shot me a quick look, opening her eyes suddenly although she had kept them closed before.

"Why are you sitting on your heels?" she asked.

I strove again to rise, but could not. They all were looking at me now, whispering. I felt my blushes begin. At last I said, vexed at myself, "I cannot. My skirts are caught at the back somewhere."

She laughed out loud then, a hoarse deep laugh at contrast with her soft whispering speech, and waved her hand at the courtiers.

"Help the Lady Ann to her feet," she said, "before she freezes to the stones."

They rushed to obey her, Sir Renier among them, tightening his grip upon my arm to give me warning. Warning of what? I had not yet said a word that would help or hinder my cause at all. As they set me on my feet, there was a tearing sound.

Forgetting myself, I let slip one of Raoul's soldier oaths, which set the ladies whispering again.

The Queen Eleanor sat upright and laughed.

"By the rood," she said, "both Sir Renier and Sir Gautier promised I should find you amusing. Come closer, child, never mind your torn skirts. Let me look at you."

I walked forward, trembling, abashed at my clumsiness, frightened.

"Or is it merely you are more used to men's wear?"

At my blush, she laughed again. "Nay, blush not for that either. I have ridden with an army myself. They called me Lady of the Golden Boots when we came to Constantinople, because I dressed in Amazon fashion. But I have never worn mail coat or sword."

"Nor I, but once," I said. "And only at Cambray. But that was a small war, not a great one as you speak of. Although I would have my castle back, and was willing to fight for it."

"Those wars were not so small," she said shrewdly, "that they did not almost cost my husband, the king, his throne."

I did not flinch at her words. "I will not deny," I said, "that as loyal vassal to my overlord, I let my men fight for him on the side of his king. We served that king, Stephen, loyally. As now, in turn, we will serve the new king, Henry, God willing."

She grunted at that, closing her eyes again, waving her hand as if to dismiss me. But I lingered. The expression on her face shocked me with its lack of color, its sag of pain.

Disregarding the looks of disdain, I knelt beside her and took her hands in mine, surprised by their cold, clammy feel. She let me chafe the cold flesh, while her courtiers nudged and murmured at this disregard of convention.

"Cold, cold and sick," she said so low I had to strain to hear her. "This child will be the death of me. I am too old for bearing children."

Her ladies gave a moan, but I spoke briskly above their cries.

"Not so, my lady. You have had a baby son before." For I had already spied the nursemaid carrying him in the background. "You shall bear one again."

"Yes," she said, "two children within three years for King Henry. Will not that be well done? Except this time, I fear it may be a daughter, like those brats I gave to Louis."

"A daughter will also be a joy, a gift," I said, "as were you once."

Her eyes flew open at those words, deep blue they were, thick lashed, bright. "Now before God, you speak to my own heart," she said. "Except that I would please my lord, I would as lief have a daughter as sons. Men are born to rend and tear you. I would have a girl close to my heart." She winced at another stab of pain. "But although I have had three children," she panted out, "none before has bedeviled me like this, like to kick his way from the living flesh."

I kept her hand in mine, rubbing it to restore the circulation as Cecile had taught me.

"You are too cold, madame," I said. "You should lie abed with down quilts to keep you warm. We should light fires, put charcoal burners by your side. This is a northern winter. Not as in France..."

"It is no worse here than Paris," she said. "*Dieu*, as you remember, Renier, *mon amour*." There was a laugh, he loudest of all. "But then," she said, "I had a priest-king as husband, who spent more time on his knees than in bed." There was another laugh.

"But pains and agues seem of less account when the sun shines," she said again, although I could see the effort it took to speak. "I wish your King Stephen had died at another time. Then would this child have been safely born. Then perhaps that one summer day would come to England. I would have taken that as courtesy."

"My lady," I said, still by her side. "I have little knowledge of childbearing, in truth, but I have some knowledge of herbs. It is a gift we of the west have. If you will permit, I will make you a warming drink to ease your pains. Let me but send my people to fetch what I need."

"Send, send," she said, "but do not leave me yourself."

"This is madness," Sir Renier hissed at my other ear as I turned to give my orders to Cecile. She stumbled away, her round face fixed with fright.

"What if it goes amiss?" Sir Renier insisted. "What then?"

I paid him no heed. What if the queen should die for lack of comfort?

"I had an old nurse," I said aloud, partly to give him confidence, partly to amuse the queen, "who had more skill with plants and roots than anyone I have ever known. I used to watch her as a child. I have not her skill, alas, but what I learned from her I have not forgotten."

"Do not the Celts have other strange skills?" she asked. "Cannot they foretell what the future will be? I have heard they can."

"Then was her death not foretold," I said almost bitterly. "That skill could not save her. Nor any of my kin."

She made no comment to that. Alarmed by her pallor, I bade her servants bring a litter and bear her out to her own chambers, which were richly decorated but as cold and damp as a church. I had them bring hot coals to slide under the bedcovers, and buckets of hot ashes to heat the air, and more and more tapestries to cover the stone walls against the drafts.

When Cecile came panting back with all I needed, it did not take me long to mix the draft as I had done for Raoul, but in lesser quantity that she would be soothed, rather than lose consciousness. I tried the mixture myself and can avow to its pleasant taste and smell.

This was the way I came to meet Eleanor the Queen, and helped her, as any woman would another in distress. And as God is my witness, I did not think of myself, or Raoul—only of her and of her unborn child and the pale little princeling who slept in his nurse's arms.

Later, Sir Renier came to me, perspiring now in his red finery, his face warm and relieved.

"Rooms are prepared for you, my lady," he said. "You will lodge here. I shall make place for your men in the guardroom, and they can stable your horses within the courtyard below. I congratulate you. The queen will not let you go now, will have you among her ladies-in-waiting."

He watched to see the effect of his words.

"That is a great honor," he said. "They are highborn ladies. You have done well for yourself."

I straightened my back painfully, wishing, if truth be told, for some of the potion myself. "I hope," I said, "you do not think I have done this to advance myself."

"Nay," he said, startled into honesty, "you have not the guile, Lady Ann. Sir Gautier sent a letter by me to the queen. I do not know, nor do I wish to know, its contents, but I know she has read it over many times. You will not need my services again. She will not forget anyone who has done her a favor."

"Nor must I," I said, dimpling at him despite my weariness.

"I shall need you, Sir Renier. There are so many things I do not understand."

"Yes," he said, "but I think it better not to try to change you." He hesitated until I smiled again. "I am at your command, my lady," he said, then kissed my hand. I remembered Sir Gautier's words and so learned another lesson in this southern diplomacy.

I stayed with the queen for the next weeks until her child was born. What did we do, what did we talk of during those times? Many things except perhaps those closest to my own heart. Often I sang to her as she kept to her bed, those long Welsh poems that I had learned in Raoul's border camp. I told her of my childhood in Sedgemont. Sometimes, too, we talked of woman's things, of babies and their care. In my growing up there had been no young women of childbearing age, nor at Cambray either. Serfs have children, but they seem to grow like weeds. Perhaps it was knowledge that this soon must be my lot that made me thoughtful. Serfs have children that grow like weeds, yet they die as easily, too. Princes should live and thrive. Yet it was clear to me that the little firstborn son was weak, could scarce sit or stand by himself, was always ailing. A second son would be double surety for this new kingdom. But sometimes, as I held the listless body of that firstborn, I felt pity sweep over me, that already he seemed displaced, set aside. An unloved child, I thought as I cradled him, is more exposed to death and want than any peasant brat who lacks all comforts, even food and warmth. And an even sharper pang filled me that my son should be such a one, unwanted, unloved, a bastard, displaced before all men.

So that was how I stayed with the queen, and saw another Henry born in England, a second son, amid all the rejoicing and public ceremony of a royal birth, and marveled that, even at such a time, she should remain so great a lady. And when it was all over, and the queen slept without need of drugs at last, and the new prince lay mewing in his basket by the fire with forty nurses to attend him, I felt the lack of my own hopes, the waiting, like a weariness stifle me. I turned to Cecile, who hovered near, fascinated and appalled by all she saw.

"Will it be like that for you?" She gasped. "Will all the men stand round and stare when the heir to Sedgemont is born?"

I know she gave no thought on what she said. It was my answer that shocked her back.

"He will be lucky to find the shelter of a serf's hut, like his father."

"Say not so," she said, her hand against her mouth. "Lady Ann, my tongue has run away with me. I have overstepped my place. I would not have offended you. God knows, your son has right to be born as high as any noble in the land, whoever is the father. It is not my place to seek his name."

Her distress comforted me. I put my arms around her.

"I am not offended," I said. "Dear friend, if I do not speak of it, it is because confidences are dangerous. It is news of small import, yet ill used could undo our plans. Secrecy we need to save Lord Raoul."

"I shall not speak of it," she said, "nor has anyone said anything to me, not Geoffrey, nor the other men, no one."

"It is not for myself," I said, "but for the child. He is a child of sin. What should he hope for?"

"Say not so," she repeated. "He also is a child of love. I saw that long ago before you did. At Sedgemont, remember, I warned you. But . . ." She broke off. I knew what the rest of the sentence must be: "But I thought to warn you against Lord Raoul."

After a while she went on, "Lady Ann, when you have spoken to the queen and she to the king, then all will come right again. I know it. Do not be downhearted."

No word then of blame or reproach she made, only the constant repetition of hope.

"You have not lain with Geoffrey," I said almost angrily.

"You have not broken any holy laws, offended God and man, and paid for it as Raoul has."

She flushed scarlet as she spoke. "I have not had the chance," she said, suddenly defiant as she spoke. "We are separated, he and I. We see each other but fleetingly. Except for the vagrancies of war, or fate, which are all men's lot, he is safe. Great men, Lady Ann, have greater privilege, but also greater danger. We are safe so we can wait. Great men have not such certainty. Why should I judge what lies not within my experience? I have come to help, not judge you."

She began to speak of other things, of how the Archbishop of Canterbury, Thibault, in his red robes, had picked up the newborn infant and blessed it, solemnly handing it then to the new chancellor. This man, tall and thin, with a pale, interesting face, had held the child up close as if peering at it with short-sighted eyes. But it may have been a scholar's look, deliberating over some page of text. All the womenfolk had remarked upon it, giggling to themselves at his curious expression. And all the other courtiers, even those who seemed most vapid and disinterested, had crowded round as if fascinated by this miracle of policy that would create new source of power and influence.

And all because a child, a little prince, was born.

So we comforted each other. I thought, as we talked, how far we had both come since that autumn day at Sedgemont when I had felt she mocked me for my poverty and ignorance. Strong is the bond that binds us each to each, stronger than any feudal tie, for it is made of friendship.

Perhaps it was reflecting on these things, thinking as I did over and over upon the fate of my own unborn babe, that what happened next occurred. I had not thought to remember it. Yet I have sworn to be truthful. I do not explain or condone. But because the queen was there when it happened, so was the chance made for me to tell her all that was in my heart. I did not seek that day any more or less than I had before.

Some paralysis of will had prevented me from baring my hopes. Afterward though numb from the effect of shock, I could talk freely at last.

I had been guarding the new prince. Fighting angry he was, red faced, struggling against the swaddling clothes that confined him. Such energy in that scrap of masculinity frightened me. One day he would stretch and grow to become a man like his father, who had terrorized half of Europe since I could remember. One day he might be King of England. I suddenly saw the fascination he had for those courtiers. Here, then, for them was where their future might lie. And my son would not even have a name.

Yet as I looked and mused, it seemed to me I heard a high wind blow as twice before it has blown around me, through my thoughts to blind me to the real world. Dry and hot it was, of a kind I had not then known, made up of dust and sand. Across a hot and arid plain, two men were riding side by side, far off, under a pale blue sky.

One of those men was my son. I knew him although I could not see his face. He rode beside his master there, a tall, huge man, red bearded, upon whose white surcoat were stamped the lions of England. That second man was king. You could see it in the way he rode and turned his head and spoke. But it was not the little Henry who lay at my feet. So, although I felt a gush of joy at the way my son rode side by side with his king in the desert of Outremer, there was pain, too, and pity. And grief, that he rode there to war, death perhaps, and I could not see his face. But he rode beside a king who smiled at him. The hot wind blew across Bermondsey, and I saw them both disappear over the sand dunes until only the trace of their horses' hoofprints was left behind. And those the wind scattered away.

Three times had it been given to me to see things caught out of sequence, out of place. Unsought, unwelcome have they been. This was the third. I did not want to see my son

ride far away. I did not want to know the fate of this baby
prince at my feet. But it was my son, he who lay beneath the
knotted girdle at my waist, who, if I could achieve it, would
grow to be acknowledged by all men as his father's heir, who,
if his father would have it so, should be loved by him among
the lords of the land.

14

OR HAVE I EVER BEFORE TOLD ANYONE what I saw. How could I? It gave no joy, no pain, it merely showed what was to be.

"Lady Ann," the queen's voice brought me back to the present there, "what ails you? You sit as pale as the layer of fog upon the Thames." She mispronounced it in her usual careless fashion. "You look to have seen a ghost."

"No ghost," I said—unless it be the ghost of dreams, other men's dreams for their children. . . .

She continued to stare at me curiously. She had made a quick recovery from childbirth, had regained all her vivacity and spirits, showed all her dislike of sickness and ill health that made her impatient with those who had not her same resilience. Already I could tell she rebelled against the restrictions of Bermondsey, longed for excitement, waited for the king's return.

"Or is it," she said, "your own child who stirs within you? Come, come, I have had enough children of my own to recognize the look. If you are with child, you had best bring forth the father first." When again I was silent, "Ah, then those tales were true."

"What tales?" I said.

"Oh tush," she said, "none of your men would speak a word against you. They are as tight mouthed as monks. Nor Cecile, like a shadow creeping beside you. But there have been rumors about you, even before I came to England. Lord Guy of Maneth had more than his share to tell." She made a face. "I could not abide him," she said, "a thing that mouths and grabs its way to favors. Henry liked him little better. Yet he felt his obligation. Maneth was, after all, vassal to his uncle the Earl of Gloucester and was loyal to him along the border. Is it true that Raoul of Sedgemont has tortured all his peasants, torn out their tongues that they cannot speak?"

At my look, "Well, so Maneth claimed. A second Geoffrey of Mandeville he called him, and, as you know, at Sir Mandeville's death, the walls of the churches he had looted wept blood. Is Raoul of Sedgemont such a monster as that?"

"For torture," I said unsteadily, forcing myself to think straight, "Guy of Maneth could have told you all you need to know."

"I am but joking," she said, "to bring the color to your cheeks. I do not believe the stories Maneth told. And I believe he deserved his end as Sir Gautier described it to me in the letter he sent. And I do believe Raoul is the father of your child, and that is crime enough, to have seduced you against your will. And I am sure he lives, else you would not be pleading for him." When I was silent again, "Or, beshrew me, is it that you have seduced him?"

How could I explain the right and wrongs of it? You know what happened. Judge you for yourself.

"My lady," I said, falling to my knees almost without knowing, "he is a just and honorable man. Spare his life is all I beg."

"Get up, you fool," she said, not unkindly. "I would hear more of this Raoul of yours. Silent as the grave have you been all these weeks, and I half-wild with curiosity. I have heard such stories about him, I know not which to think."

"He is tall, lady," I said, and at the words he flashed upon my thoughts, as if I saw him alive and well as once he had come toward me, "tall and quick, long, fair hair he has, brown skin, and eyes that change like the sea from blue green to gray. And a temper, unruly to match. But with a ready jest to laugh at you when he has angered you. Sweet tempered would he be if things would let him. And strong as hammered steel, he will not bend. . . ."

"Stubborn then," she said. "Enough of his physical charms or you will have us all on our knees praying for this god. What rank is he, what standing? Are you his equal? And what is it that has roused my husband's enmity?"

Thus asked, I poured out the story of Raoul of Sedgemont, of his grandfather Earl Raymond, Count of Sieux, and of the bond that united our two families. And I tried to tell her of the bond that bound Raoul to his king, and his pride, his stubbornness—that was her word—that would not let it go.

"Ah, yes," she sighed when I was done, "I have heard it all before: these noble men who think to win the world at the sword's point and will not for honor budge one inch from their course. I tell you such men cannot long endure. I do not say we shall lack their high honor, their loyalty, but the age of fealty as we have known it is passing, and they will end with it unless they can bend to fit the times, and many of them cannot, will not. And you are in love with him, Lady Ann. I can see that. And no doubt you fear he will feel you have tricked him to be with child, to have come here without his knowledge. I do not say he will. But others will say so. For his rank, albeit your family lies deep in his affection, is far above yours; his grandfather was an earl, his ancestors counts of Sieux."

"I know it," I said miserably. How explain that once it had seemed different when we had been two people, alone, far from thoughts of rank or position, stretching out for a little while to find warmth and content with each other.

She sighed at my stumbling words. "Long ago," she said, "I thought as you did. When I was young, I, too, loved a man. Oh, all the world has heard rumors of it, even in your castle at Sedgemont. But no one knows the truth and I do not try to explain it either. The scandal of it rocked Christendom, yet

I survived. I was Queen of France on Holy Crusade, and fell in love with a man who was my kinsman. Kinsman! Are we not all kin, being descended from one common father, Adam? And was not my marriage to Louis of France annulled because of closeness of blood? That word *consanguinity* is used by the monks to make us fear their power. And was not he kinsman, uncle, by such marriage lines that only churchmen would find the time to trace them to their end? But I say openly, without shame, I would have given crown and holy war and reputation, all, to have stayed there in Antioch with him. We were not queen, not prince, but woman and man together."

She sat a long while staring into the fire, seeing perhaps, as I had done, the hot desert, the sand, time jolted out of place.

"Louis of France would not allow that," she said suddenly, her voice cold, "either because he would not have another man want me, or because he would not have my lands slip through his grasp. Or because he was eaten with envy that I could be happy."

She sighed again. "It was a long time ago. I have changed much from that girl who would have dared anything to stay with her love. They dragged me off in the night, so we could not even say farewell. I was queen, but he was my equal in every way, a prince as Louis was not. I tell you, Ann, it is not easy to go against the world's ways. But not to try is also death. Death, such as that is, I have never forgotten. I do not fear real death itself, having lived its counterpart. But you see how I speak, as if it were in another life, had happened to someone other than myself. I am no longer wed with that Louis I despise. I have found Henry of Anjou to make me queen again. Things do not always turn out so badly as you think. I am not the one to talk of love and how to hold it from the world's fury. But I must warn you. When word came at last to Maneth of his son Gilbert's death, then was he like a man possessed. Then claimed he that you were a witch to have caused so many good men's deaths, that you saw sights and portents, had knowledge of things no one could know. There will be those who say that you have put your spells on Raoul of Sedgemont."

I did not answer her. There were other arguments more meaningful. She saw my despair.

"But these are lesser affairs and you must settle them yourselves. The main thing is to have Raoul restored, resurrected from the dead where Sir Gautier has consigned him, having considered the nature of his wounds beyond hope. Although that may be a sop to serve the king and keep him satisfied. Restored then to Henry's favor. Henry is strong-willed too. Where he loves, he will forgive much. But his hatred is implacable. Maneth's influence we shall discount. Your stories about him will outweigh any he told of you. And as I said, Henry did not like him. Henry is the difficulty. He will not be swayed by what we say, only by what he thinks. Yet I am not so sure that he has always hated Lord Raoul. At times he has spoken of him not as an enemy, but strangely, rather as some kind of rival he felt he must outdo. And you have someone else working to your ends." When I looked at her, "Sir Gautier spoke highly of you. He is a discreet and powerful friend, long in the king's inner circle. He thinks much of you, Lady Ann. He is a stout-hearted gentleman with a future that is enviable. One day he will wish to take a wife himself."

When I did not respond, "Then we must leave it at that. Let me think." She stretched herself like a cat. "When Henry returns will be the time. He will surely come back now."

All knew the king would come, but when? Sometimes I felt relief that he did not. Each day gave me chance to strengthen my case with the queen, to tell her something of my story, to set the record against Maneth's lies. But then, if we waited too long, the queen might tire of such complications, and all those other factors that worked against me, which I had painfully acknowledged when we came to the court, would still be there. One thing was certain—not my wishing, nor the queen's, would bring Henry back before he himself saw fit.

He came with the morning, unheralded, unexpected. We ladies were gathered in the queen's chambers, the babies were fed and sleeping, and the room, at least, was warm and comfortable. Queen Eleanor lay on her wide bed while her women arranged and curled her hair. Cecile and I stood to one side folding linens. Upon this simple scene, the King of England burst like a wolf into a sheep's pen.

There was a commotion outside the door where the guards were stationed. You could hear their clatter to attention as a wave of noise crested down the corridors toward us. We heard the snap of command, the clash of blades drawn in salute; the arras that framed the doorway was swept back and the iron-studded door itself was thrown open.

A group of men burst into the room. In their midst, the only calm one there, strode a young man with close-cropped red hair. He was not tall, burly rather, with thick, wide shoulders and powerful arms and a thickset head that seemed to thrust a way clear before him. He came toward the foot of the bed, his mud-caked boots clanking over the floor, two hounds fawning at his heels, yapping at the crumbs that fell from the bread he was eating. In his hand he held a large hambone, with which he pointed to give gesture to his words. As he did now.

"So still abed, madame," he said, his eyes snapping. The queen, who alone of all of us in the room seemed unstartled by the noise, the sudden outburst, looked up almost calmly, beckoning to the terrified maids to continue with their work.

"As you see, my lord," she said, observing herself in her mirror, "as it pleases you."

She laid the glass aside and smiled at him.

He laughed at that, a loud, hearty laugh that filled the room with sound and set the hounds baying.

I thought, Dear God, is that the Henry of Anjou we have all feared so much? I stared at his dirty clothes, his mud-caked boots. It was almost a boy who stood there, a loud, red-haired boy whose red cloak became him as poorly as Sir Renier's had. Behind him in the mass of men crowding into the doorway, I caught sight of Sir Gautier's solid frame. That alone convinced me, I think. This was Henry, King of England, who stood there, letting the remains of his breakfast fall to the floor. Yet the way he suddenly flicked his fingers, sending pages scurrying for towels and water to wash, for wine to drink, squires to unbuckle his sword belt and spurs, there was something royal in that bearing, something in the way he was served that gave lie to his youth and awkwardness. This was not a boy but a man who would not be trifled with.

"We hear you have a gift for us."

The queen gestured toward the cradles by the fire. He went toward them, picking unerringly the newer one, where a nurse quickly folded back the coverlets to let him look. He stood and stared for a moment or two, then bent and with one abrupt motion scooped up infant, bedclothes and all. It began to squall as he held it high in the air, turning toward the men who waited. The ladies all made sounds of dismay and alarm, instinctively moving forward, as he held the screaming baby in his hands, its head lolling dangerously.

"See, my lords of England and France," he said, "how he fights already. How he bats out with his hands. Harry of England, will you fight your father for the crown so soon?"

"Henry, my lord," Eleanor the Queen spoke still calmly, although more loudly than was her custom, "take care. He is but flesh and blood, being a month old. And fragile at that."

At her command, the nurse came back timidly and took the child into her care, easing it into safety with a sigh. Henry paced up and down, talking at first of the child, its size, its strength, his pleasure in his son. He made no mention of that older child, the little William, still asleep in his cradle. Nor did Eleanor remind him. Perhaps they both knew him of little concern now that there was a healthy second son. But a coldness troubled me, that they could be so resolved, so sure.

Presently the king began to speak of his journey through the north of his new kingdom, of his attacks against two of his northern enemies. I did not know that both men had been with Raoul at Dover before King Stephen's death, and their names were new to me: the Earl of Norfolk was one, William of Aumale the other. The earl's title he had reconfirmed to win his loyalty; William of Aumale's castle at Scarborough he had seized after a siege. I listened to these details avidly, almost stepping forward in my eagerness at the tortuous account of attack and counterattack. It sounded much as I had thought: the king would not let troublemakers rest undisturbed. But he had not killed them out-of-hand, either. In that there was hope.

He was speaking now of some battle plan before the walls of Scarborough castle in Yorkshire, a strong-built castle it was, hard to take, and he picked up a wooden casket that held the queen's toiletries to serve as model of the keep, opening and shutting its hinged cover as he talked.

The queen's maids had finished dressing her hair and she needed the combs the casket held. "My lord," she said, still in the same placid voice, "be kind enough to give me the box before you shatter the clasp full off."

He dropped it with a crash upon the table as if it stung him. At a movement from the queen, I came forward to take it from him, but he kept his hand upon the lid and stared at me. He had clear gray eyes, set in a face that was mottled with cold and freckled even in the winter. But there was fixation about his gaze that made my legs turn weak as water. "Lionlike," they call him; there was something far off and predatory about his look, something untamed and fierce that lay behind the clear gray eyes.

"Well," he said, "present us, madame."

She named me, Ann, of the honor of Cambray; although I heard my name, I could not have stirred had not Cecile jammed her fingers in my spine to make me curtsy, slow and careful, keeping one hand on the bed rail for support.

"Well," he said again, softly, talking to me now, "I have heard that name I think. Where is this Cambray of yours, *demoiselle*, that I should remember it?"

I felt my voice huskier than usual, as if the words came strangely to my tongue, like words I did not know.

"Well," he said for the third time, "I thought as much. I can tell it in the way you speak. You have that Celtic way of singing. We were once neighbors along these western marches."

"Indeed, my lord King," I said, startled.

"I spent much of my childhood with my uncle there," he said, "under his tutelage at Bristol. I remember Falk of Cambray. A thorn he was in our sides and to Celts as well."

I said proudly, "Falk of Cambray was my father, sire. It was his office to hold the border firm."

"Maybe," the king said impatiently. "I do not question that. Speak on, that I may hear your voice again. It is a long time since I heard that western lilt. Many of my uncle's men talked in that way. Little men they were, with their clothes cobbled to their backs, and stank like a stable midden. But their voices would charm you from the grave. Now how did it go?" He hummed to himself. (Strange, I thought, watching him, he looks and smells little better.) Yet at last he summoned up memory to mutter some lines in the old tongue, so ill spoken and distorted that I could scarce stop myself from smiling. I think he meant to pay a compliment, but since he had used the word for *harlot* when I suspected he meant something more polite, the effect was quite the reverse of courtly gallantry.

"How goes it, then?" he said, seeing my expression change. I repeated the phrase as I thought he must have intended.

"You see," he said, turning to the queen, "how well I have remembered it? I have not been there since my uncle died."

The queen was laughing also. "It is something, no doubt, that no honest maid should hear. My lord, here is a challenge.

If you can master that strange speech, I do not give up hope for you. You yet shall speak the language of the south with me. Langue d'oc should not come so hard."

Her words had a strange impact. They were still calm, and she gave no sign of knowing how he looked, how he had spoken to me. Yet she must have known. And what she said must have had some effect on him, seeming to recall him to where he was, what he had been about to say.

He slapped the casket down upon the table so I could rescue it, turned on his heel, and began his pacing back and forth, *prowled* would be more apt term, so much again like Raoul that I was startled by it.

Suddenly he spoke to me. "Those gray horses in our court-yard eating their weight in gold. Whose are they?"

I had forgotten them, but meanwhile, they had been cared for in the royal stables whilst we had been here at Bermondsey.

"Mine, my lord."

"Of course," he said, slapping his thigh, "the grays of Cambray. They were well known, too. I thought as much. . . ." His voice trailed off.

"They came as gift," I said hesitatingly. He spun round at me on hearing that.

"Gift," he said. "For whom? And on whose. . ."

"You speak overmuch of gift and gift giving, my lord." Eleanor spoke smoothly. She had risen herself after this last exchange, had allowed her maids to wrap her in her furred cloak, had let her long hair hang in soft folds down her back. "I have given you a gift, my lord. It seems to please you. What have you brought me in return?"

Henry wheeled to face her; the rest of his sentence died unuttered. His face lit up, and like a boy he tugged at the inside of his dirty tunic, scattering handfuls of paper scraps and straws upon the floor. When he pulled forth his hand, it was weighted with a heavy object that clattered as he swung it to and fro.

"Jesu, that I should forget," he said. "Lady Queen, pardon me. You see how remiss I am, and yet this hunk of metal has been so heavy that I scarce can walk with it. Lord Aumale was so grieved to have missed our crowning, he sends you this to make amends."

Eleanor came over to where he stood and he handed her— a fortune. It was a heavy gold collar, worked with precious stones of old and curious design, no doubt a family heirloom that the king had "persuaded" Aumale to give him.

Looted would be a better word, I thought, fascinated by it as all the court was. Eleanor held it up high, setting the lights dancing from the stones. Suddenly that glittering bauble made his words, which before had seemed so harmless, take on another meaning, as if the weight he spoke of could be measured in death and blood. And what would have been the ending of that sentence Eleanor had cut short, "A gift on whose behalf?"

I felt the impossibility of what I wanted like a dark burden that I could not shift, could not put down, but that would end in burying me, too.

The king and queen were close together now, side by side, she examining the intricate tracery with care, he watching her half-anxious, half-pleased. Presently she turned to him and laughed, her hoarse laugh, and thanked him for his thoughtfulness.

"Come, Hal," she said, "put it on yourself."

He took it from her and with clumsy fingers lifted her hair to close the clasp about her white neck. His breath came quicker then, and his eyes took on the predatory look I had sensed in them before. She held her hair steady with one hand while with the other she made that regal gesture of dismissal.

One by one, we curtsied and left the chamber, even the courtiers drawing back. The guards slammed the heavy doors closed, and stood with their backs to them, gazing outward

with their usual stern look. Behind the doors, we heard the
queen laugh again. A random thought crossed my mind, that
having watched a royal birthing, we were about to witness a
royal mating, too. For there was no doubt what Henry had in
mind. You could sense it in the way he breathed and looked,
like a stallion closing upon a mare. Yet who could tell what
the queen thought.

As I went out into the hallway, still bemused by all that
had happened in so short a time, conflicting thoughts aroused
in me, a hand caught at my long sleeve. It was Sir Gautier,
standing apart from the crush by a small window. He looked
tired and, like his king, dirty, with half the mud of England
plastered on his clothes. But he had not lost his alert, shrewd
look.

"Well, Lady Ann," he said cheerfully, "I see you are well
bestowed here. And you look well, blooming like the English
spring they keep promising us."

His knowing eyes that took in everything passed their
searching look across my face, moved openly up and down
my gown until I felt half-naked.

"And you have grown bold yourself," I said, almost crossly,
disturbed by these openly amorous looks that seemed to be
the Angevin custom. "I trust your mission was successful. How
many men have you murdered this time?"

He put his hand across his face. "Lady Ann, has not a two
months' stay at court taught you to hold your tongue? You
have heard what the king had to say. What you hint at is
treason. I merely say how fair you look, that you seem to have
won high favor, and you rend me as with your nails. Take
compliments more graciously."

"How shall I take anything when I am fretted to death," I
cried.

He stroked his beard in the way I remembered.

"I hoped," he said, "that having found a place here with the
queen, you would have had the chance to forget all your past

troubles. Both your enemies are dead. The king will declare you his royal ward."

"And who will befriend my bastard child?" I hissed. "Who know me in my unwed state? You said yourself they will mock me in the streets. . . ."

He passed a hand over his face again, as if for weariness. He was more tired than I had thought at first. He swayed upon his feet. I remembered, against my will, how he had said that to ride after Henry was an endless hunt, each day another cast, another chase, to trap him down.

"I think you should rest yourself, my lord," I said, feeling my antagonism toward him wane. "The last time we spoke, you showed concern for me. Now feel I equal concern for you."

He said ruefully, "I could sleep a week. I am not as resilient as a twenty-one-year-old. But there will be time for that here-after. Ann, without sparking all your rage anew, let me tell you I find you well and happy here at court. You look, if I may say so, beautiful, more beautiful than I had thought. Renier says the courtiers would be falling over themselves to woo you, if you but gave them leave. But it is as if you see them not, think not of them."

I said, "I have no time to waste on them. There is still too much to be done."

He watched the other men, milling and wheeling farther off, swirling still around the queen's closed door.

He said abruptly, almost as if not speaking to me, "I have done what I could. The king thinks Raoul of Sedgemont dead. I think him so myself."

"He lives, he lives," I cried, panic sweeping all dark before my eyes.

"What man could survive those wounds?" he said. "I do not say that to grieve you. It would be better that he were dead. Then would the past be buried with him."

"You wish him dead," I cried.

He said, "I have no wish of my own in the case. But you should ponder this. I knew how you left Sedgemont to seek him out the night before our departure. Ask me not why I have not acted on this knowledge. Know rather that I kept a promise I made you. I told Henry all I saw at Sedgemont, not what I guess at, and he thinks Raoul may not have lived." He turned his gaze full upon me. "I let him think that. Thus are his orders fulfilled. Thus, if Raoul lives, he is safe for the moment."

He suddenly rested his head upon his arm as if to wipe away the sweat. "And now have you secret knowledge of me," he said softly, "that would kill me too if Henry knew it. This have I done for you. I have kept your secrets safe. I have not told Henry all I know about you, Ann of Cambray. That, too, means I betray the king. Why stare you at me so?" he said angrily. "Are you so used to men that you can twist their thoughts from their duty so easily? I have long served these Angevins, will serve them still. Yet your accusations at Sedgemont touched me deeper than I thought. Else I would not be standing here, to put my life in your hands. I have told you I have kept clear of womenfolk. Yet, even to the queen have I sent word to make things easy for you. Stay here with her, with me. I would be willing to take you as you are."

"With another man's son?" I whispered, shaken by the intensity of his words.

"It is not what a man would want," he said. He almost groaned. "Lady Ann, I would wed you even so, to give you and your child a name. It is an honorable one. I hold lands of the king in Anjou. I have come to care for you. Forget what is past. There is no future for you in that, no hope."

It was strange admission, wrung from this cautious, close-mouthed man. I honored him for it. I might even have pitied him.

"I wish I could," I said. "I have promised to help Lord Raoul of Sedgemont, to restore his lands and title, so that he may give his name to his son."

He managed a smile at that. "Diplomatic to the end," he said, "not even a courtly lie to give me room for hope. I deplore your manners as I admire your tenacity. Lady Ann, be warned, be warned. You cannot come between King Henry and his will. Only time will blunt the force of his anger so that he will live to regret it. There, that too I have said against my loyalty to him. But for all your wishing, for all that you have made me help you, we cannot turn Henry from his course. That is his right as king. That is his nature as Angevin. Send word to Raoul of Sedgemont: his best hope is flight. Stay you here at court with me. As my lady wife, I can protect you."

"I cannot," I said. "I am tied to Raoul of Sedgemont. Whether he wants me is another matter. But I have given my word to him."

He ran his hand across his weary face again, making his hair stand on end, even his trim beard was overgrown and rough. "Then know this." His voice was stern as I remembered it at Sedgemont. "Be warned by what I say. The hawk has left the woods and flown eastward. If you would live, avoid him. Know, see, do nothing."

"How can that be?" I cried, when his words sank in. "He could not have dragged himself upright. Geoffrey would not let him come."

He pulled me back farther against the wall, the first real anger that I had ever seen in him flashing. "Now, God be damned," he cried. "Shout those words aloud for all men to hear and we are all dead. I give you fair warning that my men left at Sedgemont have sent me news. Work that knowledge to your best advantage. I care not if he lives to thrust his head into the noose. Save only this: as what befalls him will affect you. And that he drag not me with him for a woman's sake. Ever have I kept myself clear of female entanglements. You make me see how right I was to judge them harshly."

He paused, took breath. "Yet, God forgive me, I will still help you if I can. And if you need help afterward, it is there for the asking. I cannot turn my thoughts off and on, any more than you. But look for no more signs from me, unless you come to seek them yourself."

He turned and walked away, stiffly, upright, as one who had ridden hard and long. A good man he was, I thought. Once I might have warmed to such a one, who needed me. But not now. I turned myself, gathering up my skirts to slip between the crowds of men who stared and commented.

In the quiet of our chamber, I summoned in the three of Raoul's guard and, with Cecile, held council what next to do. For if Raoul arrived before my task was done, then might all be lost at one throw. And Sir Gautier, like me, must bear his love in silence.

The next days are as a blur. I had set each man to watch a different gate, but there were seven gates to watch. I had Cecile loiter in the entrance halls to stop him if he reached this far. I could not believe he would come unarmed, alone. I could not believe he would come openly, and how were we then to recognize him in disguise? I still attended on the queen, sat with her in her rooms, rode with her on fair days in the woodlands to the south, feasted at night in the Great Hall. I saw Sir Gautier in the distance, but never a look did he give me, never sign or word.

The queen seemed preoccupied. Yet once she bade me have patience, which might mean all or nothing. And at night, when we sat eating the food that was either too cold because the king came home late, or uncooked because he would dine early, I watched in vain for any friendly face, listened for any name that Raoul might have mentioned. The king lived to his reputation of restlessness. He was up before daybreak, hunting if it was fine, riding even on foul days, until sometimes he had saddle sores upon his legs as a horse does when it is overworked. At table he was equally distracted, sometimes spending the whole meal with his justiciars, letting the food congeal upon his golden plate. Sometimes he would get caught up in some point of custom or law with his new chancellor, Thomas

Becket, the young man with the shock of black hair whom Cecile had first noted at the queen's lying-in, and they would argue back and forth, while all of us sat silent listening to them.

Once the whole court was in an uproar at some jest the king had played, having torn off the chancellor's cloak and thrown it to a beggar in the streets. Sometimes the king would rise without ceremony, half the court pouring out with him like water from a jug. At others, he would sit as under duress, playing with those new two-pronged forks the queen had brought from France, spearing his meat with them as if practicing with a lance.

The queen seemed to pay no heed to these manners of his. She surrounded herself, at mealtimes especially, with people from her own country, like Sir Renier, with whom she would talk in their own language. What they said among themselves I cannot tell, but never by look or word did she show anger at the king. And when he returned, sometimes nonchalant, sometimes petulant like a schoolboy, she still showed him no emotion at all. Perhaps that was her secret. Or perhaps it was that he often seemed so much younger than she was, at times even younger than I, that kept him in some kind of check. A boy then, about boy's tricks, until some gesture, some expression on his face, would reveal the full-grown lion lurking underneath.

As for the queen herself, in calm moments I trusted her; at other times I could not be sure. My foolishness it was, to think that I could have persuaded either of them to my will. For both were impatient with fools, disliked obvious flattery, were quick to grasp a point, and seemed to hold each other in some kind of contest beyond my comprehension. My only hope, however, was the queen: as long as she had the king in her control, all was not over.

One night, therefore, we sat at feast. For once, the king had neither left too early nor arrived too late. He had listened

indulgently while some of the queen's young poets sang their
southern songs to please her. I, too, had come to enjoy them,
soft mouthed and lisping as if bathed in sun and flowers. The
queen had been enchanted, clapping her hands like a child
and singing with them in a low, hoarse voice. I saw for the
first time how perhaps these northern colds had pinched her
spirit as well as her flesh so that, like a spring flower set in
warm water, she suddenly broke into bloom; and I think all
men's blood quickened because of her. I know the king was
entranced. He had no eyes for anyone else that evening; there
were no wandering impatient looks that I, for one, had come
to dread when he fastened them upon me. But tonight he was
softer, mild, and the more the queen flowered before him, the
more he seemed receptive to her mood.

Afterward, I wondered. Had she known? Had she planned
it so? That, too, is something we never shall speak of. I can
only guess at it. All I do know is that Henry was well fed,
well rested, well content, as much as it is in his nature to be
so, when there was a scuffle at the door. A guard was bawling
out a name, and then a man came striding to the table where
we sat, Geoffrey hard behind him, his face still bloody where
someone had beaten him.

And Raoul of Sedgemont came into the king's hall, into the
lion's den.

Was I the only one who stood as he came up? Did I say
anything to him before Cecile pulled me down? I only knew
that he was on his feet, thin and pale, with the scar of Maneth's
fist still scored across one cheek bone. He wore rough clothes:
a leather padded shirt, no mail; he could not wear it yet. He
had given up his sword at the gate, but his sword belt hung
at his side. He could not use his right arm then, and I saw
how he rested it upon the belt. And his look was fixed upon
the king.

Henry, Count of Anjou, Duke of Normandy, King of England, leaned forward in his chair, both hands outspread

upon the table, and looked at Raoul of Sedgemont.

Perhaps I would have gone to him then, but another hand grasped mine. It was the queen's. "Leave them alone," she said. "We can do no more."

"So, Raoul of Sedgemont," the king said at last. "You come late to my crowning, sir."

"I am come late," Raoul said, "but I have come."

"For courtesy, you should have been sooner. What has kept you so long?" When Raoul did not reply, "Ravaging the western borders, meddling with the Celts against my will, killing my companion."

In the silence that followed, "It was fair fight," Geoffrey shouted out. "All who saw it will claim it was a fair fight, a Judgment of God. Save Maneth's trick to blind my lord."

I saw Sir Gautier start at his words, recognize him. But it was Geoffrey's loyalty that betrayed him.

"Peace with the Celts, my lord King," Raoul said, "lies within your command as with Stephen's. If you wish it."

He spoke carefully, choosing his words. I thought at first it was to avoid offense, but then realized it was weariness that made him slow. He swayed upon his feet as he talked, and his face was pale with fatigue. How long had he been on the journey here? When had he forced himself to leave the forest shelter? And why? Like Henry, he could ride nonstop—with broken shoulder scarcely knit, with wounds half-healed.

"We thought you dead," Henry said. He reached out and drank a goblet of wine, a long, choking drink, he who drank but seldom and then always abstemiously, having no taste for feasting.

"No," said Raoul, with a flicker of a smile, "it is not so easy to bury old acquaintances. They rise when you least expect them."

Henry drank again. For some reason, I was suddenly reminded of a time when I had burst into the Hall at Sedgemont to seek revenge. And here was Raoul, unarmed, in the midst

of his enemies. I looked round for help, not knowing then de
Luci, who was already whispering to the chancellor, not seeing
Sir Gautier move purposefully behind the servants round the
table's edge.

"There is the matter of Gilbert of Maneth," Henry said.
"Murdered. Who judges that? And the taking of Cambray castle
by force? And the seduction of the Lady of Cambray." A cruel
thrust, that last.

I jumped to my feet again, Geoffrey with me. Together,
we shouted, "Gilbert died in battle." Then I alone, "I asked
that Cambray be taken. I accuse my liege lord of nothing. All
I have comes from him."

"Now, there is loyalty," Henry sneered. "Whence comes
such loyalty as that, my lord, that even in Sieux your men
ever plot your return?"

"Here, my lord King."

The three men of Sedgemont stood forth from the back of
the Hall. Weary they were with their fruitless vigil, still dressed
in their worn clothes, still sharp and taciturn.

"And how many more do you bring against me?" Henry
sneered again.

Raoul spread open his hands, moving his right arm painfully.
At that simple, open gesture, the king's temper overflowed.
He pushed back his chair with a crash and stalked to the edge
of the dais where we sat. His face was mottled with rage, so
that the freckles stood out like dark spots and his cropped
hairs bristled like a dog's. With short neck thrust forward, his
wide shoulders, he resembled a bull that would charge everything in its way.

"When will you show such loyalty to us, Raoul of Sedgemont," he cried. "How often have you refused to submit to
me?"

"Since we first met," Raoul said calmly. "I think I can count
the times as well as you."

"And if I force you to your knees," said Henry, "here before them all, that you should hail me rightful King of England, lord of all this land?"

"Then you will force me to my knees," Raoul said as calmly as before.

They stood close to each other, of a height now that the king still kept to the platform, both breathing heavily, both panting.

"And if I kill you for it," Henry said, the veins swelling on his face, "if I order my guards to run you through for a treacherous dog?"

I think he felt he spoke to Raoul alone, as if the rest of us did not exist.

"Then you run me through," said Raoul.

"I can have you cut down," Henry's rage was frightful to behold; no man I had ever seen writhed so, rocked with anger as with pain, "a traitor, your head will rot above London gates."

Mother of God, I prayed, he will kill him where he is before us all. I made as if to go to Raoul's side, to throw myself before him and share the blow. It was the queen who caught me back again, with a grip like iron.

"Make no move," she mouthed at me. "Say nothing. Do nothing."

"He will kill Raoul." I must have said it aloud. By her side, Sir Gautier stared past me, neither hope nor condemnation in his eyes.

"Or Raoul will slay him," she suddenly cried at me. "Fool. You cannot interfere. They must battle it out between themselves. I have done what I can. But they must battle between themselves, with all the lords of England to watch and condemn what Henry will do. Oh God," she cried, and I had never seen her show fear before, "that I should be bound to such a man. Whether he kill Raoul or not, it will kill him. King he would be, must be, if he acts as a king. If he does not, he will be nothing, a madman, scorned by everyone. Oh, God," she whispered again, "it is himself he fights."

I felt her fear, her involvement, her complicity, it could not be called love, for Henry, as strong and helpless as mine for Raoul. Here then was that thing which Sir Gautier had warned me of, that he and Raoul himself, that they all knew. The king was gnawing at his wrist as if to stop his hand from twitching to his sword.

"He is no traitor, my lord King," four other voices rang out. They came from Geoffrey and the Sedgemont guard, who stood a solid phalanx to one side of the dais. Did their voices break the king's concentration? Did he use them to vent his anger? With a howl, he shouted at his own guard, who leaped upon them, thrusting them back against the wall, sword points at their throats. They thrashed and kicked, the mass of men swirling back and forth until they all four were pinioned with spear shafts across their chests, their hands shackled.

King Henry turned his back upon them, clasped his hands behind him, tightly, and began to pace up and down. Below him on the floor, Raoul kept step, as I had seen him many times, both men prowling, watchful of each other, taut like string.

"At Wallingford you bade Stephen refuse me as heir. You would not sign the Treaty of Westminster that followed. You came not to swear allegiance to me after it was signed." The long list of accusations gushed out. "What of Cambray, a border fortress thrown up without leave? What of my envoy slain? What of your raids across the Welsh border?"

"And what of Sieux," said Raoul at the end, "taken and burned without cause? Your men hold it now without right. What of my men killed or imprisoned there?"

"Casualties of war," Henry said.

"Such as I would have avoided at Sedgemont," Raoul said. "It was unguarded. Your messengers had free entry. It was not I who struck against them. Your own friends did that."

"By whose right hold you Sedgemont?" Henry said. He turned upon Raoul like a snake. "In whose name hold you those lands?"

"They were gift of your grandfather to mine," Raoul said. "And he held them of no man save the king."

"You have not those titles that once he held. . . ."

"My lord King, my lord King." A small dapper man was on his feet. I would know him later, not then.

"Stephen would have granted Lord Raoul all the rights and titles of Sedgemont. On his deathbed did he offer them. . . ."

Raoul made no sign of recognition toward the man who spoke, de Luci it was, earnest to uphold what he knew to be true. Just as he had made no movement to acknowledge Geoffrey or his men, or me.

"Refused them, why?"

"Because," Raoul said as simply as before, "it was a deathbed gift. I would not use it to protect myself."

They faced each other again, at the far end of the dais, away from the four prisoners at the other. Henry's face had smoothed, the high color faded, but the skin was still mottled as if with heat or cold.

"What should you accept from anyone," he said, almost softly, almost wondering, "that you would accept freely as gift?"

"My lord," Raoul said, standing still, "you have seen for yourself what needs to be done in this land. You have gone north and east already. What you have seen there is repeated south and west. You knew the western marches when you were a boy. Go there again and see what war has done to them. You will need Sedgemont and Cambray, even Maneth castle, if you are to bring order to the western lands at last."

"A strong rule will do it," Henry cried. "No man will move against me then."

"The king is but one man," said Raoul, "he cannot be everywhere at once. He needs strong men to help him."

The two pairs of eyes looked at each other, both dark and stormy, both stubborn, like two oaks wedged against each other, neither able to shift.

Henry began his pacing again, up and down. His voice was lower now, under control. They seemed to be speaking of military matters; I could see how Henry jabbed with his finger as he questioned, how Raoul gestured with his left hand as he replied, up and down, until gradually the tension in the Hall began to slacken. I felt, rather than heard, someone draw breath.

So this also was Henry of Anjou, this heir to the Angevin hate and temper. King or not, I thought suddenly, I would not be bound to such a man.

Behind me, Eleanor took deep, quick gasps, as if she would faint for lack of air.

"Marriage," I heard her say, "you think perhaps it solves everything. I tell you, Lady Ann, it is only the beginning for us. Without marriage, we cannot survive, not you in your little honor of Cambray, not I in my great duchy of Aquitaine. Men will come hounding us for what we have. Long will it be before they accept us for what we are, not only as images of their power, and lust. But since marriage is all we have, we are fortunate to value it for some things. I think you may be more fortunate than most. Is that your choice?" When I was able to nod. "Then," she said, "that is a thing I can help with."

She raised her voice, using the tone she had spoken to the king when she bade him not play with the forks or break the hinges of her box.

"My lord King," she said, "the Lord of Sedgemont," she stressed the words slightly, "is new recovered of his wounds. You risk his well-being to keep him on his feet and march him up and down as on parade." And indeed, it was clear to me that Raoul kept himself upright by effort of will alone.

"By the Mass," Henry cried, "I had near forgot. A fight to the death, was it not, a Judgment of God. Who are we, as God's anointed, to stand against His choice? But, Raoul, you have had other friends, less heavenly, crowing your praises here at court. Less heavenly I say, although that depends upon the point of view. Your ward, the Lady Ann, I think is from the castle of Cambray?"

Raoul made no reply but I noted how the pulse in his cheek beat at the mention of my name. It was a warning, and my heart sank.

"Cosseted with my lady wife," Henry said, "a beauty, if I be a judge of that. No doubt you come to claim her back."

"No doubt."

"So would I if she were my ward," Henry said. "But I hope you bring a strap. I know these border wenches, having cut my teeth," except he used a coarser phrase, "upon them. A well-set-up wench, I think, and fit for breeding, they tell us . . ."

He slapped Raoul upon the shoulder, seeming not to notice the stab of pain it caused. "Well, if you would have her that would be a gift from me. Suppose, my lord, I grant you your title as earl as once your grandfather held, as Stephen would have given it. . . . I have noticed, my lord, that the local soldiery fight better than hired mercenaries, and command sits better with local lords than those hired from afar. Suppose you take the old command back as Stephen gave it you. . . ."

"Then I should be your man," Raoul said slowly.

"Ah," Henry said, "we hold you to that." He laughed. "Why," he said, "I too can count the times since first I asked you to submit to me."

"You were a child," Raoul said slowly, holding to each word as to a support. "It is forgotten quite."

"But I remember," Henry said, a smile with no mirth to it on his face. It was as if he rent his own flesh as he spoke. "You tossed me to a thorn bush that time, was it not so? And then again at Rouen before my retinue . . . I watched how you leapt upon your horse after: full armed, you vaulted into the saddle. I learned that trick of you. At my knighting two years later in Scotland, I vaulted as far. I still can leap astride," he boasted with all the youth of his twenty-one years. "And you, Raoul, can you?"

Beneath the weight of his twenty-six, his wounds, Raoul said, "I could, my lord King. I may again."

"Ah, yes, if your arm heals straight." He slapped Raoul upon his shoulder again, a bluff hearty blow, one comrade to another, but the blow fell on the right side. "Come, man, you fight as well left-handed. Even with one arm disabled, you will guard that frontier still for me. So have we then resolved our mutual affairs. I shall give you title to Sedgemont and Cambray as before. And Maneth to boot. Take your ward back. Except. . ." And here a malicious glint crept back, the sliver of the claw that kept us all, his queenly wife most of all, on edge. "Except that in return for her and all these other gifts, you shall wed her to bind the estates together. How's that, my lords," he shouted, "Raoul the Double-Handed to wed." And he guffawed, a large laugh that made him seem older than his years, and slapped Raoul again upon the right shoulder. "How then, with wife and lands and titles, yea, even those in France you once had, shall you kneel to me as king?"

Raoul's face was as dark as before it had been pale.

"I shall. . ." he said, then folded like a tree cut at the bole and crashed to the floor at Henry's feet.

There was a scream; all the women stood and cried about. Men came running. Geoffrey pushed past the startled guards, shuffling forward to kneel beside Lord Raoul, bellowing at them for clumsy oafs.

"By the Holy Mass," Henry swore, a forgotten hulk in the clamor, "I did but lean upon him in jest. What ails him then?"

His queen had come to stand beside him, soothing him as one might a child.

"You smote him thrice upon an open wound," she said. "You are too strong. You forget other men are made to suffer and bleed, although you feel nought."

"I have never seen Raoul laid low before," he said, suddenly chastened. "As God is my witness, you did not think I wished to harm him here in my own Hall before my queen?"

"Still less in his own, or anywhere else without due process," she said smoothly. "I am as sure of that, my lord King, as I am of your goodness toward us all. Call him surgeons. Have them carry him forth. Come, Henry, sit and share of the warmth of Provence with me again. I will sing you new songs, and if you will not drink my southern wine, then I will fill you with its pleasures in other ways."

She turned back as if to take her place, as if all that had passed had never been. I felt a coldness strike me at the indifference, shall I call it, the disinterest in her voice. But when she turned her head to me as she passed, I could see the lines of strain beneath her eyes and bright smile. She looked older than I had ever guessed.

"Why do you linger?" she snapped at me. "What are you about, wench, to linger here? See to your lord."

I had stood as if numbed while they carried him off, while they freed the Sedgemont guard, while a mass of people drifted back and forth, overstimulated, excited by what had occurred. The king still waited at one side, with his courtiers; the queen stood with hers. I noted suddenly how Henry had surrounded himself with short men. Not tall himself, he was a head above those who stood by him: Sir Gautier, de Luci. Only his new chancellor was taller than he was. And he one day would be killed by the king he served. . . .

"Lady," said Henry softly to me as I would have slipped past. "You owe me a favor. I have done you one."

I felt the full force of his personality blaze at me. I saw Sir Gautier turn aside. What had he warned me?

He will listen and promise and have you repay him.

I said quickly, "But I have already repaid you, my lord King."

"How so?" he said, his prominent eyes narrowing, undressing me as I stood.

"There are four gray horses in your stables," I said. "Remember, you spoke of them before."

He was taken aback by my answer. At last reluctantly, "Yes, I remember." He stared at me. Well, he had put shame on me before his court, assessing me in terms of the coarsest kind, making me a sport for their laughter, to strike at Raoul.

"Then are you a witch," he said as softly, as if to me alone, "to foretell the rise of the Earl of Sedgemont. It is an earl's gift." I heard beneath his jest the glint of threat, saw the malicious grin that made one wonder if he enacted all this; but played, to keep us in suspense, to bat us back and forth to his fancy.

"Then shall I ride one of my new gifts," he said, "when I go hunting in the morning."

"They are but half-broken, my lord King," I said, suddenly worried that he might come to grief through negligence of mine.

"So much the better," he said. "I straddle half-broken fillies better than most."

And again he gave his coarse, older laugh, that made the words take on their most lewd meaning.

I gave him a sketchy curtsy, and addressed my words between him and the queen, who gave no sign that she had heard what he said.

"My lord King," I said, "my lady Queen, by your great mercy have you restored Lord Raoul. But I beg of you, put not the burden of marriage upon me. He may not requite it."

"The more fool he," the king said. "It is your duty to persuade him to our command."

"I am no man's plaything, my lord," I said, and sensed a ripple of dismay, shock, that stirred those waiting courtiers. But Henry kept his claws sheathed.

"Yea," he said, "you and he should be fit mates for each other."

"You wanted as much." The queen's voice had grown hoarse. I should heed her warning. But spoke she to me or to him?

"It is too late now to turn back on what you have," she said. "The choice is made!"

"You see?" It was the young Henry who was speaking now, the boy king. "The queen has bidden us and she knows more of love's tricks than I shall care to remember. Her word is law in the courts of love."

He put out his hand, gallant as any noble there, to lead her forward. She laid hers upon his, a handsome royal couple, such as England or the world has not seen since, as good a match for each other as any. But the smile he gave me in passing was older, wiser, threatening. "And one day," it said, "I shall be first there, as in all things else. . . ."

They went on together, their courtiers falling in behind them. Even Sir Gautier and Sir Renier passed without comment. I shrugged my way into the cloak that Cecile held, and took to my heels out of the Great Hall at Bermondsey, running to find Raoul.

15

E FOUND WHERE HE WAS SOON
enough. Geoffrey and the others stood at the
door. While Cecile and I wiped the dirt and
blood from Geoffrey's face, he told us all he
could, croaked it out, for the spear shafts that had scored
marks across his chest and throat made talking painful at first.
Lord Raoul had been as a madman, he said, when he found
that his plan for my escape from Sedgemont had not been
carried through, had been used instead for him. They had tried
to keep this knowledge from him as long as they could until
at least he had recovered enough to be fully conscious where
he was. By then, we had been long away from Sedgemont.
Twice before had he tried to leave the forest; the first time
he had reached the entrance of the hut before collapsing; the
second, he had turned back himself, seeing that he could not
manage his horse. Then had he lain back upon his bed silently,
sternly nursing his strength, willing it to return, raging in-
wardly at his weakness as at a secret humiliation. The third
time, he had not told anyone where he was going, although
it was clear to them all what his destination would be. On
pain of death had he forbidden any to follow him. The others
waited still at the forest edge. Geoffrey, braving his anger,
had ridden behind him, not so close as to be seen, not so far
away as to be out of reach. Realizing that Raoul meant to ride
into the city openly, Geoffrey had spurred forward in one last
attempt to turn Raoul back.

"But he rode me over," he whispered. "I would have argued
with him but he gave me such a buffet as to knock me from

my saddle. With his left arm no less. So I must stagger behind him and come too late to Bermondsey, not knowing then that the court had removed itself here. But not so late after all." He tried to smile. "By the Mass, Lady Ann, I think we are successful in the end, although how the thing was done is past my understanding. But this is a great day for Sedgemont. To have an earl at last. Hey, you louts." He turned to the other three men. "We shall ride out in red and gold again. Then let those French scum look to their laurels. The Sedgemont guard will outshine them. And outride them too."

They grinned, slapping each other on the back, drinking mightily as the household pages brought them wine and beer, nothing too good now for an earl's followers. I left them with Cecile crooning over Geoffrey's bruises. My part began here.

They had brought Raoul to a room off one of the many long corridors that confuse Bermondsey. Already the idle and curious had gathered around to stare and point at the place, looking for advancement, no doubt, or hoping for some tidbit of gossip; a newcomer at court is always fair game. I paid them no heed. Geoffrey and the other men would keep them back. But I had to venture within and meet this new earl face to face.

The room itself, like all the others at Bermondsey, was rich and dirty and cold. They had stripped Raoul of his jerkin and shirt and new bandaged his shoulder, and flung a furred cloak about him, but the fire was out, and the place smelled of dogs and fleas. He was sitting, as it seemed to me I so often found him, in a chair before the hearth, but this time he did not get up, did not turn his head when I scratched at the door and lifted the latch. This time he would not make any move toward me. I did not even know how to address him with his new titles around him. I could not even begin to think what I should say. Without sound, then, I went toward him, almost tiptoeing across the wooden floor.

His back was toward me but I knew his expression well, how he would be moodily staring out, eyes dark and brooding, his face showing no color except for that red scar across his cheek bone. And that, I thought, he would wear now all his life. It might fade, but it would always remain to remind us of the past. I found myself praying as once I had prayed for his safety. And I was trembling.

He said, without turning round, "There is no need to duck and bob. Step forth where I can see you."

The tone of his voice, controlled, formal, made me cringe and stiffened my resolve. I walked around to stand in front of him and felt the full force of his stare which raked me much as the king's had done. It took in, no doubt, the fashionable gown I wore with its tight-drawn laces to show the figure beneath, the waistline that cost me so much pain, the rounded breasts, which, for all Cecile's bindings, I could not hide.

"Sleek," he said, "like a cat new fed. Court life agrees with you, lady."

I dropped him curtsy, not trusting myself to speak.

"And airs to match," he said, anger showing beneath the coldness. "I have told you I like not mock servility. Or do you show but added respect for these fresh titles I now bear?"

Do not reply to him, I warned myself. It is but pain and shock that trouble him.

"Why came you here?" he blazed at me. "To make a mock of us before all men? To set your woman's touch where no woman has right to interfere? You are not countess yet to ape the Lady of Warrick, selling her husband's keep to his enemies because she thought he might win some benefit. Am I tied to your petticoats? Who bade you order my men do this, do that? Who bade you interfere in men's affairs?"

This was worse than I had thought. Was this how he would repay the fears, the hopes, the waiting?

"Or perhaps you thought to barter for me as for a slave?"

Then you are no worse treated than any woman, I thought waspishly, for we endure as much every day. But I said nothing aloud.

"Or to flaunt your independence before the world, a ward

whom no man controls, a harlot flirting with the court?"

I said calmly, "You are cold, my lord Earl of Sedgemont. Let me make up the fire." He watched me as I knelt to push the logs together, struck the tinder, blew to make the damp wood smolder back to life. And I thought, Are all those golden days, those lovely days, turned like this, to ash, to bitterness? And I felt the acrid smoke sting my eyes.

When I could turn round, "My lord," I said, "your men await your will outside. Shall I bid them enter?"

"Yes," he said. Then, "No. God's wounds, that even Geoffrey should defy me. I'll strip his hide. . . ."

"You already have done as much," I said, coldly in my turn, "small payment for his devotion."

When he did not answer, "Or have you forgotten, my lord, when you speak so mightily of loyalty and duty, that one day even you, the Earl of Sedgemont," I stressed the words, "might also stand in need of help; that those whom you have so often rushed to defend might one day be called upon to help you? That was not well done, to be so anxious to give but not receive. It shows a lack of Christmas spirit."

"And you, Madame Preacher," he said, "have grown pious faced, that once again you lecture me on duty. Ever have you done so. I'll not have a shrew to grace my hall."

"You may not have anyone to grace anything," I replied. "Count me not too much on that."

"Your king has ordered it," he said. "Heard you not what he said?"

I think then that I saw how deep the resentment lay behind his words, how deep the anger beneath that even, contemptuous voice. *I have never seen Raoul laid low before.* If Henry felt it, should not Raoul himself, should not I?

I said, "And I have told the king I might not consent."

"You did, by God," he said, almost starting up until a fresh spasm of pain caught him back. "By the Mass, and what did he say to that?"

"He will not let us slip free so easily," I said. "He wished us joy, thinking no doubt we shall rend each other as well as ever he could. But I am still afraid. I do not know what he is about."

"I told you as much before," he said, "but you would not listen. Now has he us both in his grasp. Why came you here in the first place?"

"And I have told you that, to save your life."

He said slowly, distinctly, "Think you I want it saved on such terms?"

I said, as distinctly, back, "Pride, pride, you will choke on it. What use is pride or honor to a ghost? Where are all your fine words gone if your head is stuck above the White Tower with only dead lips to mouth them?"

And I thought what the queen had said, had warned: *Such men cannot endure unless they will change their ways.*

I said, "At Sedgemont, you would not wed because you would not have your friends, your peers, think that the only way you could win back Cambray. At Cambray, you said you would not wed because you feared to have me dragged down with you. High words, fine thoughts. I accepted them. But is it not also true, you would not wed because you trust no women? Am I to blame for that? Must I bear the weight of your suspicions upon my back? What makes you think I am so faithless myself? Was it to trap you that I made my way to your border camp, that I came to Sedgemont to see you fight Maneth, that I crept out through the storm into the forest to bring you succor? If you would not wed because you would not wed, well then, that too I can accept."

"I did not know you came into the forest," he said slowly, "but I . . ."

"There are many things you do not know, will never know," I said, breaking in upon him, too angry myself now to stop. "Did Giles die, and Sir Brian, and all those other valiant men, to make a fool of you? Did Geoffrey and Cecile, and those three Sedgemont guards here outside the door, risk their lives to ruin your honor? You will not wed because you will not

wed. That I can accept. But not that you refuse to live because
I loved you. I wanted to save your titles and lands, not for
myself, why should I care for myself? Once you mocked my
parents that they were wed to make a peace. It seems to me
as good a reason as any to wed to give a son a name."

His sound arm shot out, grasped me by the sleeve, dragged
me toward him on my knees. The delicate fabric ripped and
tore. My hands were black with the fire, my face smudged
with smoke.

"Son," he said.

I would not look at him. I had not meant to spit it out, this
last secret between us. But I could not unsay it.

"You lie," he said, the pulse beating in his cheek. "You
cannot be with child, at least not mine. Whose then, if not
mine?"

"Count the months, my lord," I said, "since you were at
Cambray. It is now close to the end of March. Do you not
remember that last day before you left for Stephen's court?"

I knew he remembered. "Since that day have I wanted a
child of yours," I said, "to hold when you were no more. What
time have I had for other men? Be not so churlish, my lord. I
make no claim for myself. Only for the child."

"You cannot be with child," he repeated stubbornly. "I could
still span your waist, had I use of both hands."

I knew what he must be thinking; Cecile had shown me
many tricks I would not have thought of, would not have
known her capable of. Yet very soon, despite all our efforts,
I would not be able to hide the fact. True, sickness and constant
anxiety had taken their toll, but even I, after all these months,
must at last show some visible sign of pregnancy.

I shrugged much as he might have done when argument
was no longer worthwhile. "Then your son will be born a
bastard," I said. "But since he must be born, then will time
prove which of us is correct. Once, my lord, you told me at
Sedgemont you would not have children unless there was some-

thing for them to inherit. At least your child can have that if
you will acknowledge him. Is that not something to live for?"

He said slowly, unwillingly, "God's wounds, but how you
have changed, so stern, so fierce have you become. Yet still
proud yourself. I begin to think what you say is right after all.
So do wild cats fight for their young. But why did you not
tell me before? Had I not right to know?"

"Yes," I said. "At Sedgemont, I could have told you. But
you were fighting for your life and that seemed more than
enough. And afterward, what chance was there?"

"I would not have guessed it," he said. "I have had little
experience in such matters."

Strangely, I did not take his statement so amiss. It made
him seem younger, more vulnerable.

"If you had not let slip the fact," he said, "would you still
have told me? Most women would have blared it forth from
the start to fit their own ends."

"I have used it," I said sharply, "although not as many women
would have done, to trap you. Since Cambray have I prayed
for your son, to remember you, remember what we were."

"Who else knows?" he asked again. "Cecile, she must have
helped you."

"The queen," I said, "she guessed. And one of the French
envoys at Sedgemont," which was stretching the truth a little,
"but not, I think, the king."

"No," he said, almost absentmindedly, "else he would not
have offered us to each other, in spite of his vulgar jests. Had
he known, he would have found greater delight in keeping us
apart."

He turned his head at last, slowly. I still could not guess
what he was thinking, what he would say or do.

He said abruptly, "These new honors sit uneasily. I feel I
shall have little pleasure in this new court. There may not be
place for me here. Perhaps I should go back to Sedgemont.
Or should I give it to Geoffrey to hold for me?"

I did not know what to say, so much could not have been hoped for.

"I need someone," he was saying, almost to himself, "to take Sir Brian's place, someone who will still cherish the Lady Mildred for her full honor. We'll have him there. And Cecile to keep him in control. He has grown too full of himself these days, to be seneschal may scarce contain him. I'll have him knighted and wed and live happily thereafter. Shall that content you, lady?"

I was still uncomfortably caught between his knees, and his hand still grasped my arm so that the pressure of his fingers left marks along the skin.

He said again abruptly, the words jerked out of him by shame, "I may yet be crippled. I do not know if this arm of mine will heal. . . ."

"Of course it will," I said stoutly, pity contending with love. "You will need to use it along the western marches."

"Aye, that too," he said. He almost sighed. "I had come to enjoy life there more than I ever thought possible. When Stephen sent me back there after Wallingford, I was intended to be an exile. Angry I was with him and with myself, hating the wet and cold and loneliness. But after a while I came to enjoy even that; at Cambray, I knew what your father and brother felt. And I have come to lack the mists and bogs now that they are left behind. Perhaps I should go back there after all, and win a truce from your kinsfolk before the new king takes it upon himself to wrestle it from them by force. Although do not tell him I said so."

"I am no confidante to him," I said, "but if you take care, rest as you should, not jar your shoulder abroad as you have been doing, it will heal as straight as ever it was. You can leap astride your horse at Geoffrey's knighting as King Henry did at his. I stitched the wound for you myself. . . ."

"Now by all the saints," he said, "do I fear the worst. What, the Lady Ann who scarce could sew a seam straight, whom they mocked at Sedgemont to hem our shirts?"

In the semidarkness that surrounded us, I caught a gleam, was it of a smile?

"Do not scowl," he said, although my head was bent, so he could not know. "I thought it was a dream, an illusion, but when I lay in the forest, it seemed you came one time; the memory was comforting like coolness after fever. But that was so unlike what I had always thought of you, I could not believe it then. God's death, that is another reason to owe my life to you."

"And I to you, as equal a number," I said. "We do not play at games, my lord, to match each point with point."

"Judas," he said, "how fierce you have become. This is more like I remember you. I should not wish court life to have spoiled you."

"No, it has not," I said, trying to break his grasp.

"But you have become used to it. I wonder that it has trapped you to its comforts."

"No," I said again. "Too many times already have you hinted what you dare not say aloud, that I have accepted this new king. I am first your loyal vassal, my lord Earl of Sedgemont. As your loyalties are made, so will mine follow you. I have but waited at the court for the king to tell him what I could, to plead for our cause, yours and mine. And never had the chance even to do that."

"You said enough," he said dryly, and again I felt the ripple of, laughter, was it? that undercurrent that I had first sensed in him so long ago. "You and Geoffrey both, babbling like jesters. I thought he would string you up before us. Well, so you have outfaced him in his own Hall, as once you did me. He may not forget that, although he may not hold it against you. He admires courage of sorts."

It was the first admission I had ever heard him make, albeit grudging, that Henry was capable of any good.

"Raoul," I said, the name slipping out too easily before I

could choke it back. "Raoul, what did you do at Rouen that Henry should remember it?"

He said, "I kicked him down the cathedral steps. Well, it was a Mass held by the Angevins to celebrate his father's latest victory. Against my will was I bidden to attend by the then Duke of Normandy. Henry, as his father's son, would walk first before me in the procession. So I helped him to it with my boot."

I had a sudden image, clear as day, of the crowd of watching nobles with their retinues, the fluttering priests, the stout, red-faced boy sent sprawling headlong. And of Raoul leaping upon his horse, making it pivot close to the bottom step where Henry lay and howled. Panic welled up in me. I struggled within his grasp, catching at him at the same time as if to shield him.

"He will not only never forget that," I cried. "He will not forgive it either."

Raoul smiled again. "Perhaps not. I might find it difficult myself. But I do not expect much more. We have only found another temporary respite, an interlude, God knows how or why. This has been the first of many struggles in this new reign. It will not be forgotten either."

"But he will send someone to hunt you down," I cried, "to track you wherever you go, as he did before." And as I spoke, it seemed to me the room became dark, full of shadows, danger.

Raoul said reasonably, simply, "I think not yet. He may already be regretting the impulse that bade him move against so many at one time." He might have been speaking of something far off, impersonal, not of his life, his death. "De Luci, whom you shall meet again, said once that to contest Henry as king even in peace would be as in any battle, none knowing who would be spared or why. It seems that despite all my efforts to the contrary, I am to be spared awhile yet. But do not look for a lasting truce, although you came here to plead for it."

"As to that," I said suddenly, "why came *you* here? Sense alone should have bidden you stay far away if your own men's warnings would not persuade you. Henry would have done more than string you up."

"Aye," he said. "Ann," he said, "I sometimes have thought, have feared, you saw in me something that was not there, someone else. I have said before, I am not Talisin. I am not your brother come back to life, although you wished it, thought it, when I first met you as a child. I am not what you have ever yearned for come back to you. . . ."

"No," I said. I drew breath. "No, Talisin is dead. That, too, I have come to accept, perhaps never more so than in saying it. But doubly have you avenged his spirit. My quarrel has become yours. What more could you do?" I drew another breath. "I would not hold you to an unwelcome match for any favor you have done me, or I done you. . . ."

He went on, almost as if I had not spoken, "Once at Cambray I felt that God had forsaken us. Forget that day? Ask me rather to forget myself, my name, my honor. But since then, it seems to me, He has found a way to show His favor again, although by what means, to what ends, is beyond my comprehension. Perhaps it may be that even now, far off, we can escape the envy of the world. I came here, Ann, to find you."

"Then you have found me," I said, "and shall know where I go."

"Where will that be?"

"To Cambray," I said.

"Why there?"

"It is my home."

He said softly, so softly I almost could not hear him, "Pride, pride, you will choke of it. I would have my son born at Sieux.

"Let me take you back to Sieux, my fierce little Ann, and show you the long meadows full of flowers, the gentle river, the vineyards in the sun. I shall take back my castle there, hold it safely. I shall have wife and child, children, to content me."

He had drawn me full upon his knees, was tracing with his sound hand through my hair, ruining the curls and braids. Once, I thought, he would never have wanted such simple things, would have laughed at me because I did. The queen's words flashed through my mind again.

Such men cannot endure unless they will change their ways.

Was he admitting that he could, that he would be content to live away from court and intrigue and war? And even if he said he would, could he keep his promise? Would the world come crowding about us as it had before? Would Henry seek us out another time? I felt a shiver run along my spine.

"Cold, my love," he said, and drew the cloak around us both. The fire sputtered and smoked. There was no sound outside the room, none other than that within.

He said, as if echoing my thoughts, "What can I offer you, little Ann, a dubious future where before was none, a hope where before was none. But there is no security in anything. We can but try for it. And to have a son. A man does not think of it," he said almost shyly, "but that, too, would be something."

"Then let us be wed and off at once," I cried.

At that he did laugh, almost that lighthearted laughter I remembered, although his torn muscles cut it off short.

"Now beshrew me," he said, "how she does lust after me. Why, Ann," he teased, "I thought it was affairs of state that interested you. Or hopes of being countess after all. Well, love, there should be time for such things hereafter. Now let us seek to enjoy each other."

He mocked me, although the words he said were true, although once it was not he who would have said them.

I lay in his embrace and felt the smoothness of his skin beneath the cloak, contrasted with the puckered scar along his side, the bandages that strapped his shoulder. I could not bear to think that golden body marred, his strength impaired.

A sudden sputter from the fire lit up the room. His eyes shone for a moment as I remembered them, blue-gray; his hair was crisped, his mouth smiling. I lay in his embrace and felt his left hand smooth along my spine.

"I would not break open your wounds," I said, whispered against his ear, yet could not keep my hand still either.

He said, "*Ma mie*, there are many ways to pleasure each other. We should let the rest of the world go by while we savor them all. I cannot swear to anything else, only that."

His hand was on my face again, feeling, as a blind man who does not trust what he touches, eyes, mouth, throat.

Great men are not as other men, their pleasures greater, their danger greater.

To wed and live happily belonged to Cecile, to Geoffrey, not perhaps to us.

But, "It is enough," I said.

EPILOGUE

HE MARRIAGE OF THE EARL OF SEDGE-
mont and the Lady Ann of Cambray took place
immediately thereafter. Arranged at the king's express command and under such strange circum-
stances, it is not surprising that the world took note, although
it was also observed that the king seemed not so pleased as
might have been expected. For there is a sense of uneasiness,
mystery perhaps, that runs through those old memories, as if
even in recalling them, people are still not sure what was
gained, what expected. Yet people in general remembered, so
that many years later, when I, Urien, the Welsh bard who
writes this epilogue, questioned them, as I love to do, being
always curious about human nature, they spoke of an event
that had happened years before I was born as if it had happened
yesterday. No one could say openly what disturbed them most;
some hinted at one thing, some another, but none, I think,
not even the king, as Lord Raoul had shrewdly surmised, knew
the real reason for the haste, that the child might be born in
wedlock.

But there were so many other strange things surrounding
this wedding that the haste with which it was solemnized,
though scandalous, was not the worst. First was the matter of
the new earl's investiture. It will be remembered, for example,
that Lord Raoul had divested himself of all his assets, his plate,
his jewels, all that he could raise upon his estates before Henry's
envoys had reached him at Sedgemont. The few moneys that
the Lady Mildred had given the Lady Ann had long been spent.

Lord Raoul had arrived in London as poorly equipped as any fugitive, with a horse, lame and half-starved, a leather jacket, a sword... the relief or tax levied upon him now by the king for the new earldom was heavy, heavier than was rightly due since the lands were not new, only the title itself.

For despite Henry's having acquired the four gray horses from Cambray, he now demanded eight more, four of these to be saddled and richly bridled, and hung with breastplate, helmet, shield, and lance, all the accoutrements of war. (And in this way did he lay the foundations of his stable, which, in time, came to rival that of Cambray itself.) And other payments were also demanded: wools and hides and grain that would have strained the natural resources of the land even had there been no war, again an unjust levy since full payments had been made already to the crown when the late earl had died and Lord Raoul had first come into his inheritance. It was not surprising that the bridegroom came to the wedding feast in borrowed finery, or that all bridal gifts were lacking.

As for the bride's own dowry, that was lacking, too, since all she owned was her husband's, by virtue of his overlordship. Then, too, the oath taking left much to be desired, both king and earl speaking their part with dignity, to be sure, but rapidly, with little display of cordiality, more shame-faced than otherwise. Few would have doubted Lord Raoul's bond, once it was made, although many might have wondered why he permitted himself to give it under such constraint. As for the king—but there was no judging what the king wished, for he looked so sour and spoke so fast. Yet, when the marriage Mass was celebrated the following day, he was present as chief guest, and fidgeted his hour away while the archbishop droned slowly along. The only sign of interest he gave was to stare at the bride. Yet all stared at her, for she, at least, was fittingly arrayed in brocade and pearls, although her smile would have been dazzling enough without the rest. (And where such riches came from can only be guessed at, the queen's records for that month being more outrageous than ever—I know, I looked at them. She had a reputation for extravagance, but in this case, the purchase of silks and furs, and such miscellaneous items as bedcovers, linens, carpets, and excessive feminine trinkets of gold, may reflect her generosity rather than her own desires.)

Imagine then the young bride, decked out in the newest fashion, beautiful enough to make the court, usually immune to these events, remember. Fifty years later, they would remember.

As for the groom, he was tall and handsome, with pallor to render his looks interesting to the ladies, and pride to make his cobbled clothes, a trifle too short for him, of no importance.

The king was restless, as I have said, petulant, having the air of one who would rather be off coursing hares, biting his nails in the front pew and falling asleep at the slower parts of the service.

But the queen sat serene and detached, secretly triumphant perhaps, giving her favor to the newlywed couple despite the king's impatience.

Such was the wedding itself. But worse was to follow. For if the ceremony itself had been hastened forward, for reasons that no one seemed to have understood, the most obvious one, for some strange cause being totally ignored, the subsequent festivities were meager to the point of scandal. A marriage of this high degree, even if an unequal match by social standing, expected, yea, demanded feasting of lavish proportions, jousting, masques, entertainments. None was offered at all. For thrift? For haste again? Not even the semipublic bedding of man and wife, a ritual, it was well known, which the king, with his still-youthful enjoyment of earthy pranks, especially delighted in. It was dispensed with entirely, much to the disappointment and chagrin of the courtiers who would willingly have seen the charms of the bride displayed. But no, the weakened state of the new earl and his recent wounding must serve as excuse, that and the queen's own express request that there should be no rough games, which she said she found distasteful and crude... so no, again, not even the display of the wedding sheets the next morning, which any cynic knows can easily be arranged.

So disappointment there was then, and a sense of anticlimax, of something lacking. After all, men marry; women breed; kings must be pleased or they will sulk. There was general feeling that a more-fitting climax to the story should have been expected. The next morning provided it.

At first dawning, the king was off, in great rage, it was claimed, although accounts of the reasons are confused. But he stamped and swore in usual style, setting the confusion of a royal hunt aswirl about him. Footmen, hounds, horses, all the clatter and noise of Bermondsey, reaching up to the bridal room itself, where, perhaps for all his wanting, he could not find excuse to enter in. But as he mounted, the half-broken gray horse pivoting with fear and rage at the raking of his spurs, an equally loud, disorganized hubbub came swelling toward them along the cobbled street outside Bermondsey. Within seconds, rumors were flying as high as a falcon swung from huntsman's wrist—an army, it was said, advancing to take the king, a band of rebels, fearful of nothing. The king was seen to draw his sword and his face to brighten at the thought. Those who were mounted turned and seized what weapons were at hand. No one expected the small group of ragged men who came riding up to the gates. Lady Ann had well described them, miserable as curs driven to fend for themselves, homeless as peasants in the fields, the remnants of Lord Raoul's men whom he had left in hiding at the forest edge.

What had happened was this. When news of all that had befallen at the court was sent to the Lady Mildred at Sedgemont, as was fitting, that those who waited restlessly there could know the outcome (and some stayed to give loyal service; some left upon the hour), the messenger found opportunity to

detour from his path to find his old comrades and tell them
of their good fortune. They, in turn, had ridden hard toward
London to be at hand upon such a joyous occasion. On reaching the city, a day, or rather a night, too late, they had milled
outside until, with the dawn, they could pass within the gates.
Thus, they came at this hour to Bermondsey, bursting in upon
the king. The confrontation was short; the effects long-lasting.
The Sedgemont guard, as villainous a crew as ever roamed the
London streets, for looks, I mean, as one man swung themselves off their horses, dropped amid the filthy puddles, and,
having recognized the king in their midst, with one voice
hailed him as Henry, protector of rights, arbitrator of wrongs,
source of law and forgiveness. For seconds, Henry eyed them,
his sword blade lifted, glinting in the first sunlight, the words
of command trembling on his lips. But he hesitated too long.
The hoarse but hearty voices reverberated among the narrow
streets and overhanging roofs. Already, honest citizens had
thrown back shutters, come running to their doors to see what
was amiss. To attack undefended men who had thrown themselves at his feet would have been a coward's act. He rammed
the sword back into its sheath, muttered his replies to their
greetings, allowed his name to be shouted over and over again,
coupled with the name of Raoul and his lady wife, and finally
proclaimed their general pardon back from outlawry to the
command of their rightful lord. With how ill a grace he uttered
these words cannot be said. They were greeted with even
louder rejoicing, cheers that echoed to the chimney tops and
sent the scavenging birds wheeling along the riverbanks.

Henry sat stiff necked and acknowledged the cheers with
his usual gesture of goodwill, although his gray eyes had turned
black with rage. He knew he had no choice except to do as
he had done, but he marked them all as dangerous men and
envied, more than ever, Lord Raoul's hold upon them. But
when it was seen how they had cherished their Sedgemont
colors throughout their long ordeal, making the womenfolk

weep for pity of them, he turned aside and, it is said, muttered as to the air, "I could give half my kingdom for such ragged loyalty. I may yet give half away to subdue it." At least he had the sense not to fight against the tide, which he had no more chance of stopping than if it had been the current in the Channel. So he turned back with the Sedgemont men and saw them reunited with the earl and watched their departure after all.

In this way then the Earl of Sedgemont and the Lady Ann rode out from London escorted in fashion becoming to their rank and station, and the red-and-gold standard of Sedgemont was seen to fly once more and outshine the Angevin colors. And if rumor of hard drinking and prodigious appetite be believed, the Sedgemont men outdrank, outate, and yes, outwhored the Angevins, too, as many a London landlord found to his cost. But they left London without regret and went swiftly back to Sedgemont, there to establish Geoffrey, newly knighted and newly wed. And after welcoming back those other, humbler fugitives who had been living in the hopes of such a return, without further ceremony the earl and his wife took ship for France, the mild spring weather helping them to this purpose.

So at last they came to Sieux, and *les beaux prés de France*. There, while the king was held in England by the cares and toil of his kingdom, they rebuilt the castle, established themselves peacefully, and awaited the birth of their son, my lord, my master, my friend.

In these ways then were all things knit up, the great with the lesser, with the least; Cambray with Sedgemont; Celt with Norman.

I asked the Lady Ann once what she remembered of that time, but she would answer little.

"I was too happy," was all she would say. "I remember nothing."

You see how it is only grief that sharpens our memories,

woe that makes us think of anything at all. But we flourish such a short while in the fullness of the sun. Let it rest upon them for a moment, let its warmth capture you. We are but ripples upon an endless tide. *Ora pro nobis*.

Urien Cambrensis, the Welsh poet, writes this.